8 SANDPIPER WAY

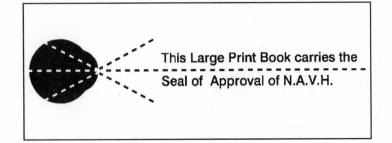
This Large Print Book carries the
Seal of Approval of N.A.V.H.

8 SANDPIPER WAY

DEBBIE MACOMBER

WHEELER PUBLISHING
A part of Gale, Cengage Learning

GALE
CENGAGE Learning™

Detroit • New York • San Francisco • New Haven, Conn • Waterville, Maine • London

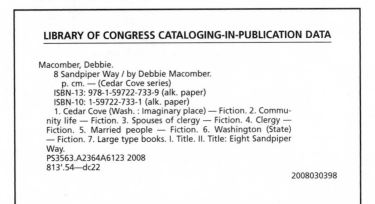

LIBRARY OF CONGRESS CATALOGING-IN-PUBLICATION DATA

Macomber, Debbie.
   8 Sandpiper Way / by Debbie Macomber.
      p. cm. — (Cedar Cove series)
      ISBN-13: 978-1-59722-733-9 (alk. paper)
      ISBN-10: 1-59722-733-1 (alk. paper)
      1. Cedar Cove (Wash. : Imaginary place) — Fiction. 2. Community life — Fiction. 3. Spouses of clergy — Fiction. 4. Clergy — Fiction. 5. Married people — Fiction. 6. Washington (State) — Fiction. 7. Large type books. I. Title. II. Title: Eight Sandpiper Way.
   PS3563.A2364A6123 2008
   813'.54—dc22

2008030398

Published in 2008 in arrangement with Harlequin Books S.A.

To Minda Butler,
Karen Sweeney
and
Hyacinthe Eykelhof-Mitchell
For their courage, strength
and
inspiration

and special thanks to my friend
Emily Myles, the fabric artist
who inspired Shirley's dragon

9/08

September 2008

Dear Friends,

Welcome to Cedar Cove! If you're a regular visitor, you'll be happy to know that Olivia, Jack, Grace and all the rest are waiting to tell you about the current events in their lives. And if you're new to town, you can expect to make a whole group of new and interesting friends.

For the readers who've complained that the Cedar Cove books come out only once a year — good news! Next month the town's story will continue with *A Cedar Cove Christmas.*

As many of you already know, Cedar Cove is loosely based on my own hometown of Port Orchard, Washington. The streets and businesses are disguised but easily recognizable. As an unexpected result of the Cedar Cove stories, our little town has become something of a tourist destination. Because of this, a group of wonderful volunteers headed by Jerry Childs and Cindy Lucarelli are planning Cedar Cove Days, which will take place in August 2009. Check my Web site at www.DebbieMacomber.com for upcoming information.

If you're interested in viewing the "lay of the land," you can download a Cedar Cove map from my Web site — or you can receive a glossy collector's edition free by sending a SASE to my office at P.O. Box 1458, Port Orchard, WA 98366.

Although I rarely mention it, take a look at the dedication page. I'm dedicating this book to three phenomenal women who've been coping with breast cancer. Minda Butler lives in our condo building in Florida. Karen Sweeney, my cousin from Omaha, is now in remission. Hyacinthe Eykelhof-Mitchell is my editor's younger sister. All three women are dear to my heart and an inspiration to everyone.

I hope you enjoy *8 Sandpiper Way*. Your Cedar Cove friends are looking forward to your visit — and I'm looking forward to hearing your thoughts.

Warmest regards,
Debbie Macomber

Some of the Residents of Cedar Cove, Washington

Olivia Lockhart Griffin: Family Court judge in Cedar Cove. Mother of Justine and James. Married to **Jack Griffin,** editor of the *Cedar Cove Chronicle.* They live at 16 Lighthouse Road.

Charlotte Jefferson Rhodes: Mother of **Olivia** and of **Will Jefferson.** Now married to widower **Ben Rhodes,** who has sons **David** and **Steven,** neither of whom lives in Cedar Cove.

Justine (Lockhart) Gunderson: Daughter of Olivia. Mother of Leif. Married to **Seth Gunderson.** The Gundersons owned The Lighthouse restaurant, recently destroyed by fire. They live at 6 Rainier Drive.

James Lockhart: Olivia's son and Justine's

younger brother. In the Navy. Lives in San Diego with his wife, Selina, daughter, Isabella, and son, Ada.

Will Jefferson: Olivia's brother, Charlotte's son. Formerly of Atlanta. Divorced, retired and back in Cedar Cove, where he has recently bought the local gallery.

Grace Sherman Harding: Olivia's best friend. Librarian. Widow of **Dan Sherman.** Mother of **Maryellen Bowman** and **Kelly Jordan.** Married to **Cliff Harding,** a retired engineer who is now a horse breeder living in Olalla, near Cedar Cove. Grace's previous address: 204 Rosewood Lane (now a rental property).

Maryellen Bowman: Oldest daughter of Grace and Dan Sherman. Mother of **Katie** and **Drake.** Married to **Jon Bowman,** photographer.

Zachary Cox: Accountant, married to Rosie. Father of **Allison** and **Eddie Cox.** The family lives at 311 Pelican Court. **Allison** is attending university in Seattle, while her boyfriend, **Anson Butler,** has joined the military.

Rachel Pendergast: Works at the Get Nailed salon. Engaged to widower **Bruce**

Peyton, who has a daughter, **Jolene.**

Bob and Peggy Beldon: Retired. Own the Thyme and Tide B and B at 44 Cranberry Point.

Roy McAfee: Private investigator, retired from Seattle police force. Two adult children, **Mack** and **Linnette.** Married to **Corrie,** who works as his office manager. The McAfees live at 50 Harbor Street.

Linnette McAfee: Daughter of Roy and Corrie. Lived in Cedar Cove and worked as a physician's assistant in the new medical clinic. Now living in North Dakota. Her brother, **Mack,** a fireman in training, is moving to Cedar Cove.

Gloria Ashton: Police officer on Bremerton force. Natural child of Roy and Corrie McAfee.

Troy Davis: Cedar Cove sheriff. Married to **Sandy,** now deceased. Father of **Megan.**

Faith Beckwith: High school girlfriend of Troy Davis, now a widow. Moving back to Cedar Cove.

Bobby Polgar and Teri Miller Polgar: He is an international chess champion; she's a hairstylist at Get Nailed. Their home is at 74 Seaside Avenue.

Christie Levitt: Sister of Teri Polgar, living in Cedar Cove.

James Wilbur: Bobby Polgar's driver.

Pastor Dave Flemming: Local Methodist minister. He and his wife, **Emily,** are the parents of Matthew and Mark.

Shirley Bliss: Widow and fabric artist, mother of Tannith (Tanni) Bliss.

Shaw Wilson: Friend of Anson Butler, Allison Cox and Tanni Bliss.

ONE

They say the wife is always the last to know.

Except that Emily Flemming did know and she'd known for more than a week. Dave, her husband, was involved with someone else. Only Dave wasn't just Dave Flemming. He was *Pastor* Dave Flemming. The thought that her husband loved another woman was intolerable, unthinkable, unbearable. Dave's betrayal was bad enough, but disregarding his moral obligations to his congregation and his God — she could hardly believe it. This shocking secret was completely inconsistent with everything she knew about her husband.

Ever since the night of their anniversary dinner, Emily had carefully guarded what she'd learned. She'd been in the church office, waiting for Dave, and had reached for his suit jacket, which hung on the back of his door. When she draped it over her arm, a diamond earring had fallen out of the pocket.

Later she'd discovered the second one in the other pocket. Emily had certainly never owned anything as extravagant as this pair of large, diamond-studded pendant earrings.

In the beginning Emily had assumed the earrings were an anniversary present; however, she quickly realized they couldn't be. For one thing, they weren't in a jeweler's box. But even if they had been, it wasn't possible. Dave could never have afforded diamond earrings on their tight family budget.

Emily should have asked immediately . . . and hadn't. She'd been afraid of ruining their special evening with her suspicions. But almost at once, other details had begun to add up in her mind. She could no longer ignore the fact that Dave so often worked late, especially since the private hour they'd shared after dinner had gone by the wayside. It might've been her imagination but he seemed to take extra long with his grooming, too.

Her suspicions doubled and tripled. She held them close to her heart, examining them over and over, trying to make sense of her husband's behavior. Whenever she asked where he'd been, Dave's answers were vague. Another warning sign . . .

"Mommy, when's Daddy coming home?" Mark, the younger of her two sons, asked as he looked up from his plate. He was eight and his dark brown eyes were identical to his father's.

Emily had the same question. "Soon," she said as reassuringly as she could. Two or three times a week, Dave didn't get home until well after dinner. At first she'd made excuses for him to their boys. Now she didn't know what to tell them.

"Dad hardly ever eats with us," Matthew complained, sitting down next to his younger brother.

Dave's lateness had started gradually. He used to make a point of being there for the evening meal. As she stared into space, Emily couldn't help wondering if he was having dinner with some other woman . . . some other family. She chased away the thought with a determination that stiffened her spine.

For the sake of her children, Emily dragged out her standard excuse. "Your father's been busy at the church."

"Every night?"

Her sons echoed Emily's own dissatisfaction. "It seems so," she returned lightly, pretending all was well as she joined them at the dinner table. They automatically clasped hands and bowed their heads while Emily recited grace. Silently she added a prayer for herself, asking for courage to face whatever the future might hold for her marriage.

"Shouldn't we wait for him at least one night?" Mark said as he reluctantly picked up his fork.

"You two have homework, don't you?" she asked, ignoring his question.

"But Dad —"

"Your father will eat later."

"Will he get home before we go to bed?" Matthew, her sensitive son, asked.

"I don't know," she said, swallowing hard.

She made a pretense of eating. Her appetite had disappeared the minute she'd found those diamond earrings. That was the start — the wake-up call she'd ignored for months. Naturally, she'd told herself, there could be any number of explanations for those earrings. She'd intended to ask him about it the very next day . . . and hadn't.

Emily knew what held her back. She didn't want to hear the truth; she simply wasn't ready for it. She dreaded the consequences once she did finally confront him.

She'd questioned her husband, more than once, about his late nights. But Dave brushed aside her concern and offered ambiguous excuses, mentioning people she'd never met and meetings she didn't know about. He almost seemed to resent her asking, so after a while she'd stopped.

She supposed she had her answer. Since the discovery of the diamond earrings, she had a perfectly clear picture of what was happening — what had already happened. Sadly, pastors were as susceptible to temptation as anyone else. Like all sinners, they, too, could be lured into affairs. They, too, could make irreparable mistakes.

If Emily had hoped this was just a misunderstanding, that she'd allowed it to grow out of all proportion in her mind, those hopes had been destroyed. Earlier in the week, she'd run into Bob and Peggy Beldon at the grocery store. They owned the local bed-and-breakfast, Thyme and Tide. As the three of them stood in the middle of the aisle exchanging pleasantries, Bob casually said that he missed playing golf with Dave.

As long as the weather permitted, the two of them had played weekly for the past three years. In a matter of minutes, she'd ferreted out the information she'd been afraid to learn. Dave had given up golfing more than a year ago. A year! Yet every week last summer, he'd loaded up his golf clubs on Monday afternoons and driven off, supposedly to meet Bob. Obviously he'd been meeting someone else.

Emily sighed. She couldn't continue to let

her mind wander down this well-traveled path of doubt and suspicion. Half the time she acted the role of the quiet, unassuming wife; the rest of the time it was all she could do to refrain from *demanding* an explanation. She wanted the truth no matter how painful it might be — and yet she didn't. What wife ever did?

So far she'd remained silent. She was astonished by how good she'd become at pretending everything was fine. None of her friends suspected. What bothered her almost as much as her suspicions was the fact that Dave didn't seem to have any idea that she'd caught on. She wondered if he'd broach the subject. Maybe if he knew she'd figured out what was going on . . . Perhaps that was what she'd been waiting for. She wanted *him* to ask *her*.

But Dave never asked. If she managed to put on a marvelous performance, then so did her husband. Last Sunday he'd actually spoken from the pulpit about the importance of marriage, of loving one's spouse.

Emily felt like the most unloved woman in the world. She could barely stop herself from breaking into heart-wrenching sobs right there in front of the entire congregation. Naturally everyone must have assumed she'd been overcome with emotion, since Dave's sermon, by implication, had honored her. She wanted to tell them that, beautiful though his words were, that was *all* they were. Words.

It was hard to believe this could be happening to them. Emily had always been so sure they had a solid marriage, and that Dave was her best friend. Apparently she was wrong.

The door leading to the garage opened and to her surprise he walked into the house.

"Dad!" Mark slid out of his chair, running toward his father as if he hadn't seen him in a year.

"Hey there, little man, how's it going?" Dave reached down and swung their son into his arms. Mark was too big to be picked up like a child, but he craved the attention from his father.

Dave kissed Emily on the cheek, then ruffled Matthew's hair before he sat down. "I'm glad I made it home in time for dinner tonight."

"Me, too," Mark said, his eyes glowing.

Despite everything, her own happiness sprang to life again, and Emily got up and brought a fourth place setting to the table.

When she passed him the enchilada casserole she'd made, he took a heaping serving, then grinned over at her. "You fixed one of my favorites," he said. "Thank you."

"You're welcome." She met his look, letting him know with her eyes how much she loved him. Maybe, regardless of the evidence, all her unhappy suspicions were wrong.

"Can you help me with my homework after dinner, Dad?" Mark asked.

Their younger son was the top student in his class, far ahead of the other second-graders. He didn't need any assistance. What he really wanted was time with his father.

"You promised to throw me the football, remember?" Matthew said. Never mind that it was late November and already dark outside,

He, too, wanted time with Dave. The children weren't the only ones; Emily needed all the reassurance he had to offer. Hard as she tried to cast aside these doubts, they refused to die. She didn't want to lose her husband. She loved Dave no matter what and was determined to keep her marriage together — or at least make every possible effort.

"Hold on, hold on." Dave laughingly raised both hands. "Give me a minute to catch my breath, would you?"

Both boys stared expectantly at their father. Emily couldn't bear to look at their eager faces. Seeing the love for him in their eyes made her feel like weeping.

"Let your dad eat his dinner," she said.

"After that, I'll help you both, but I'd like a few minutes alone with your mother first," Dave said, glancing at Emily.

A chill raced down her spine, and she was afraid to meet his eyes.

"Aw, Dad," Mark whined.

"It won't take long," he promised. "Eat your green beans."

"Okay."

Emily handed Dave the bowl of buttered beans with sliced almonds. He took a small portion. Green beans weren't his favorite vegetable, either, and this was her way of suggesting he set a good example.

Following dinner, the boys cleared the table, then went to their room for study hour. This had been Dave's idea. Whether they had homework or not, Matthew and Mark were to spend one hour every night reading, writing or reviewing their school-work. The television wasn't allowed to be on, nor were video games permitted.

As the boys trudged to their room, Emily made a pot of coffee, keeping her back to Dave as she worked. Asking to speak to her like that was unusual for him. If there was something on his mind, he generally discussed it with her after the boys had gone to bed.

Even before she could finish pouring their coffee, Dave asked her, "Are you happy?" His voice was urgent. Intense. The need to know seemed to burn inside him.

Dozens of possible questions had occurred to her, but this was one she hadn't expected.

"Happy?" she repeated, facing him. Still not meeting his gaze, she carried two steaming mugs of coffee to the table and set them down. "Am I happy?" She shoved her hands in the back pockets of her faded jeans as she contemplated her response.

"I didn't think it would take you this long to answer," Dave said. His dark eyes studied her and he seemed disappointed in her hesitation.

"Is there a reason I shouldn't be happy?" she asked, turning the question back on him. "I live in a beautiful house and I'm able to stay home with the boys the way we both wanted. My husband is madly in love with me, right?" she added, remembering his sermon from the Sunday before — and hoping she didn't sound even slightly sarcastic. Without giving him the opportunity to answer, perhaps because she feared what he might say, she asked, "What about you, Dave? Are *you* happy?"

"Of course I am." His reply was immediate

and impassioned.

"Then I am, too." Rather than join him at the table she started to load the dishwasher.

"Sit down," he said. "Please."

Reluctantly she did.

"You haven't been sleeping well."

So he'd noticed. She fell asleep easily enough, but an hour or two later she'd be wide awake. Then for the rest of the night she'd toss and turn, sleeping fitfully if at all. The scenarios that played out in her mind wouldn't allow her to rest. *Her husband might be in love with someone else. He might even be cheating on her.*

Emily considered herself an emotionally strong woman, one who remained calm in a crisis. A woman others counted on for guidance and support. Yet when it came to confronting her husband with her suspicions, she was a coward.

"If there's something bothering you, maybe I can help," he said. She recognized his tone, that caring, concerned voice he so often used with others. Only she wasn't just one of his parishioners, she was his wife!

"What could possibly be bothering me?" she asked airily. She didn't expect him to answer.

"I don't know. That's why I'm asking. Are the ladies from the missionary society making too many demands?"

"No." The cookbook committee had wanted her to organize the entire project and she'd told them she simply didn't have the time, which was true. Apparently there'd been more than a few ruffled feathers. The church family seemed to think that because Emily didn't work outside the home, she should be at their beck and call, just like Dave. Emily had no intention of becoming an unpaid employee of the church and had made that clear when they accepted the assignment in Cedar Cove. Her role was to support Dave and mother their young sons.

"You'd tell me if you were upset, wouldn't you?"

"Of course," she said, hoping the act of sipping coffee would hide her lie.

Mark stuck his head inside the kitchen. "Are you finished talking to Mom yet?" he asked his father. "I need help with my math."

Dave looked at her.

"I'm fine," she said emphatically.

He seemed to doubt her. She wasn't expert at lying and hated the fact that she was afraid to voice her concerns. Dave took a sip of his coffee and stood. "All right, Mark, show me what's giving you trouble."

Emily watched her husband and son walk

out of the kitchen and swallowed painfully. She'd been waiting for him to ask her a question like that. *Are you happy?* It was the perfect opportunity to address her suspicions — but she'd been too frightened to say anything.

The problem, she told herself, was that she wasn't prepared. For her own protection, she needed facts and details before she confronted him. He needed to realize she wasn't as naive as he obviously thought.

By nine that evening both boys were in bed and asleep. When Dave was home, getting her sons ready for the night was invariably a smooth, easy process. But anytime she was alone with them — which was most nights lately — they came up with a multitude of excuses to delay going to bed.

Half an hour later, she was in her sewing room, working on a quilt for Matthew. She ironed the fabric squares, pleased with her bargain. Always conscious of cost, she'd bought the material, a bright cotton print, on sale at The Quilted Giraffe. As she turned off the iron she heard Dave come in. He wrapped his arms around her waist from behind. "Alone at last," he whispered, kissing the side of her neck, his lips lingering there.

Emily smiled; she couldn't resist. This was how they used to be, spontaneously affectionate and teasing, until . . . She wasn't sure when things had begun to change. Earlier this year? "Oh, Dave, honestly." She gave a small laugh.

"I love my wife," he murmured.

She placed her hands on his, her fingers squeezing hard. "Do you, Dave?" She winced at the pleading quality that crept into her voice.

"With all my heart." He dropped one final kiss on her neck, then walked to the door.

"Where are you going?" she asked.

"I thought I'd work on Sunday's sermon."

"Oh." He used to write his sermons at the church office. Emily waited until he'd left the sewing room before she turned from the ironing board and stood in the doorway. She watched Dave go down the hallway to his small den; without looking in her direction, he closed the door.

Until recently his door had always remained open. To the best of her knowledge he'd never done this before. Slowly, she returned to her quilting, but she could no longer concentrate. She wanted to know why her husband suddenly found it necessary to shut the door.

He must have a reason. Of course — he was probably making a phone call. One he didn't want her to overhear. She waited an hour to be sure he was off the phone, then made an excuse to step into his office by bringing him a fresh cup of coffee.

She knocked on the door and walked inside before he could respond. As she'd expected, he sat at his desk with his Bible open and a yellow legal pad in front of him, making notes.

"I brought you coffee," she said.

"How thoughtful. Thank you, sweetheart."

"You're welcome." Setting it on the coaster, a ceramic tile Matthew had painted in first grade, Emily slipped out of the room. She closed the door quietly behind her.

Inhaling a deep breath, she went to the kitchen phone and hit the redial button. It rang three times before a woman with a soft, husky, thoroughly sexy voice answered.

"Is that you again, Davey?"

Davey?

"Oops, sorry," Emily said gruffly and replaced the receiver.

So she'd had him pegged, after all. Dave had placed a phone call to another woman. In their own home! He'd boldly contacted the woman who threatened to tear Emily's marriage apart. Her trembling hand still clutched the receiver. Knowing she was right didn't bring her any satisfaction — not that she'd thought it would.

TWO

"Hi, Daddy." A smiling Megan opened the front door and kissed Sheriff Troy Davis on the cheek.

"Hi, baby, how're you feeling?" Troy followed his daughter into the kitchen, hoping his question didn't sound too anxious. He couldn't help it, though. Megan had recently been tested for multiple sclerosis, the same disease that had claimed his wife, Sandy, several months before. Their small family was close, and the mere thought that his daughter, Troy's only child, would suffer the same debilitating disease as her mother terrified him. Megan had miscarried her first pregnancy a few months ago, and that loss, on top of her mother's death, had devastated her. And now this constant threat . . .

"Would you stop," Megan chided as she walked over to the stove and turned down the burner. Something smelled good — the aroma of a home-cooked meal tantalized him and he wondered what he'd make for his own dinner. Chili out of a can, probably. If he still had any. "The tests showed nothing conclusive," she was saying, "so there's no reason to worry."

Yet, Troy added to himself.

He didn't want to smother her with unwanted concern and unwarranted fears, but he needed to know that she was successfully dealing with the possibility of MS, that she could cope with everything it meant. The medical world was divided as to whether or not multiple sclerosis was hereditary. So far, there was evidence supporting both beliefs.

To complicate matters, an absolute diagnosis was often difficult. In Megan's case the results had been inconclusive just as she'd said. In one sense that felt like a reprieve; in another, it seemed as if they were still waiting for what appeared to be inevitable. He reminded himself not to borrow trouble. That expression echoed with a hint of foreboding, since it had been a favorite of Sandy's.

Troy was proud of Megan's newfound serenity, the way she calmly accepted the uncertainty of her situation. That was a hard-won acceptance, he knew, and he attributed a lot of it to her husband.

Thankfully, she'd chosen her life partner

well. Craig was a quiet, good-humored man who loved Troy's daughter and was completely devoted to her, the same way Troy had been to Sandy.

"I came over to ask what I can bring for Thanksgiving dinner," Troy said. That was a convenient excuse to stop by without being too obvious about checking up on Megan — although Craig and Megan no doubt saw through him quickly enough.

"Hey, Troy." Craig stepped into the kitchen, holding *The Cedar Cove Chronicle* in one hand. "Hard to believe Thanksgiving's this week, isn't it?" He shook his head. "Look at this — more ads than news."

Megan chuckled and waved them both out of the kitchen. "Quit whining, you two! Next thing I know, you'll be complaining about how commercial Christmas is."

"Christmas!" Craig groaned and winked at Troy.

Like her mother, Megan loved everything about Christmas. The leftovers from Thanksgiving dinner would hardly be put away before Megan would start decorating for the holidays. That involved Craig and Troy hanging strands of Christmas bulbs around the outside of the house and arranging the lighted deer in the front yard.

"Let me set a place for you," Megan said,

moving toward the cupboard. "We're having porcupine meatballs and a green salad."

Troy was tempted. The recipe — meatballs filled with rice and then cooked in tomato soup and served over mashed potatoes — was a family favorite from the time Megan had been a little girl. The salad he could take or leave.

"Thanks but no thanks, honey." Despite the enticing smells, Troy had no intention of intruding on his daughter and her husband. "Like I said, I just came by to ask what I can contribute to Thursday's dinner."

Megan paused as though mentally reviewing the menu. "I think I've got everything under control," she told him. "We're having turkey, of course, and I'm using Mom's rice-and-sausage recipe for the stuffing. Then I'm making a couple of salads and that sweet potato-and-dried-apricot recipe I tried last year that everyone liked so well."

Last year.

Just twelve months earlier Sandy had been alive; she'd spent Thanksgiving with them. It seemed impossible that she was really gone. They'd brought her from the chronic care facility, setting her wheelchair at the table, helping her eat.

One year, and so much had changed. Troy had buried Sandy and then, a short while

31

later, reconnected with Faith Beckwith. The thought of his high school girlfriend brought with it a rush of sadness. They'd become a couple again earlier that summer, he and Faith, and everything had looked promising — until Megan's miscarriage.

When his daughter had learned Troy was dating someone, she'd been shocked. More than shocked. Hurt and angry. She knew nothing about Faith, not even her name, but in her emotionally volatile state, she couldn't tolerate the idea of her father seeing another woman. Troy loved his daughter and couldn't risk alienating her. The night she'd lost the baby, he'd been with Faith. Not wanting a call from Megan to interfere with his evening, he'd turned off his cell phone, an act he'd lived to regret again and again.

With the possibility that Megan might have MS, Troy had made the painful decision to sever his relationship with Faith. He missed her, missed their long telephone conversations, missed spending time with her. There was no alternative, though. Painful as it was to accept, Faith was out of his life.

Ironically, in a recent conversation Megan had implied that it was time he moved on with his life. Troy wished he could believe she meant it, but he was afraid to put too much credence in her words. Yes, she'd attained a new maturity and had reconciled herself to — maybe — living with MS. But her reaction when she'd found out he was seeing someone indicated all too clearly that his daughter was nowhere near ready for him to begin a new relationship. A woman in his life, a woman other than Sandy, seemed a betrayal of her mother's memory. So, even though Megan was now saying what he wanted to hear, he'd reluctantly decided he couldn't act on it.

However, whether she truly approved of the idea or not, Megan wasn't the only one who'd mentioned that he should start dating. A deputy friend of his had suggested setting him up with his mother-in-law — Sally Something. Troy had absolutely no interest in a blind date. The only woman he wanted to see was Faith, and he'd ruined any chance of that.

"Last year," Megan repeated slowly, breaking into his thoughts. "Mom was here . . ." The realization that Sandy had been with them for Thanksgiving had obviously just struck her. "Mom always loved the holidays, didn't she?"

Troy nodded. Despite her physical limitations, Sandy had cherished family traditions and done her utmost to be part of them. He found comfort in the fact that his daughter was continuing where her mother had left off.

"You're serving mashed potatoes and gravy, too, aren't you?" He used the question as a diversionary tactic to turn their thoughts from Sandy.

"Of course!"

"What about pies?"

"Pumpkin and pecan. Oh, and I have a small surprise to go with dinner."

"Are you going to tell me what it is?"

Megan's eyes sparkled with delight. "I have one jar of the sweet pickles Mom and I made the summer before last. I was saving them for a special occasion."

Sandy hadn't been able to do any of the work, but Megan had brought her mother from the care facility to Troy's house. Together, they'd spent the day canning cucumbers, Sandy giving directions and advice, the two of them laughing often. That afternoon had been one of the best of the entire year for his wife. Sandy had treasured the time with Megan and loved being back in her own home, albeit briefly.

"Your mother will be with us, whether or not we have those sweet pickles," Troy said.

"I know." Megan shrugged helplessly. "It's just that . . ."

Rather than watch his daughter get emotional, he said, "How about if I bring the dinner rolls on Thursday? And a bottle of wine."

Megan seemed to struggle with her composure for a moment, then smiled. "Perfect."

Troy left a few minutes later. The evening stretched before him, long and empty. Instead of going home immediately, he drove to the local Safeway store, still wearing his uniform. He needed a few groceries and since he was already there, he might as well pick up the wine and dinner rolls he'd promised Megan.

Troy reached for a cart and wheeled it toward the vegetable aisle, starting in the same part of the store Sandy always had. He wasn't sure why he bothered to purchase anything fresh, because all it did was rot in his refrigerator. He was checking out the bananas when he saw her.

Faith.

He stopped abruptly and stared at her. It'd been two weeks since they'd spoken. That conversation had been among the most uncomfortable of his life. When she'd answered the phone, she'd been so excited to hear his voice. She'd told him her Seattle house had sold; before he could say anything else, she'd announced that she was moving to Cedar Cove. She'd said this with such joy and enthusiasm, expecting him to be just as pleased. And then he'd told her he wouldn't be seeing her again.

Even now he could clearly recall her pain. It haunted his sleep. He remembered how calmly Faith had listened as he haltingly explained about Megan. She hadn't raised her voice or argued. In the end, she'd wished him well.

At that moment, Faith glanced up and saw him standing not more than two feet away. Her reaction was the same as his — she went completely still as their eyes met over the large pile of bananas.

Troy was good at reading faces. Her initial reaction was shock, followed by a flicker of undiluted misery. Both emotions were quickly gone as she visibly took a breath and schooled her expression.

"Hello, Troy," she said pleasantly.

"Faith." He inclined his head slightly and wondered if she heard the regret in his voice.

Looking at her cart, he was surprised to see it filled with essential items — flour, sugar, coffee, milk, some fruit and vegetables. That suggested she was already living in Cedar Cove. He knew she'd sold her home, but he'd assumed it would be months before he'd see her again — months during which he could prepare for her presence in his town. He certainly wasn't mentally or emotionally ready for a face-to-face encounter so soon after their break-up.

"You've left Seattle?" he asked.

"I told you my house sold."

"Yes, you did, but . . ." He couldn't make his tongue cooperate. He was about to argue, to tell her this wasn't fair. However, when it came to being fair, he didn't have a lot of ground to stand on. He'd treated her badly.

His reaction apparently made her want to explain. "One of the stipulations was that the closing would be before the end of November, preferably before Thanksgiving."

"You mean you're living in town now?"

"I . . . yes." She seemed as uncomfortable as he was. "I just never thought I'd run into you so soon — my very first day. I'd hoped . . ." She let the rest fade.

Troy knew exactly what she meant. He'd hoped, too. Hoped they wouldn't see each other for a long time, because the pain of losing her, the disappointment of it, would be hard to conceal. Especially since he'd brought it on himself.

They had a history; they'd been high school sweethearts and then Troy had gone into the service after graduation to avoid being drafted for Vietnam. He'd planned to propose to Faith once he'd completed his basic training. Unbeknownst to them, Faith's mother had thwarted the relationship by withholding Troy's letters. Mrs. Carroll had decided they were too young to be so seriously involved.

Troy had gone on to meet Sandy later that summer, and Faith had left for college and met her future husband. Nearly forty years had passed before they reconnected — only to be separated by circumstances once again. Except that this time it wasn't Faith's mother but Megan who'd come between them.

"I saw Grace Sherman," Faith murmured, breaking eye contact.

"It's Harding now."

Faith nodded. "That's right. She's remarried. And I met Cliff. They've both been a great help. I simply haven't had time to look for a place to buy, and I didn't want to make a hasty decision I'd later regret."

"Of course." He wasn't sure if that was an oblique comment on their relationship.

Speaking quickly, she said, "I was visiting my son and his family last week. Scottie read the classifieds in the paper, and he mentioned the rental house on Rosewood Lane." She took a deep breath. "A day or so after that, I ran into Grace. I'd taken my grandchildren to the movies, and Grace and Olivia were just coming out. When I told them I was moving to Cedar Cove, Grace said her rental house had recently become vacant. It turned out to be the same place."

Despite the awkwardness of the situation, Troy grinned.

Faith frowned, obviously puzzled by the fact that he was smiling.

Troy felt obliged to tell her why. "Grace had bad renters, deadbeats who trashed the place, and it looked like it might take months to get them out legally."

"I didn't know that. So . . . what happened?"

"Cliff and Olivia's husband, Jack Griffin, used a . . . rather inventive means of convincing them to move — that same night."

"So that's why the walls have all been freshly painted," she said. He saw her fingers tighten around the cart handle and suspected she was about to leave.

Regardless of his own discomfort, Troy didn't want her to go. He'd missed her even more than he dared to admit. Seeing her unexpectedly was simultaneously agonizing and exhilarating, like warming frostbitten fingers before a fire.

"You're shopping for Thanksgiving?" he asked, gesturing at the contents of her cart, which included sweet potatoes and a bag of fresh cranberries.

She picked up a small bunch of bananas and added them to her groceries. "No. I'm buying a few things to stock my cupboards and my fridge. My daughter and daughter-in-law are at the house now, unpacking. I didn't intend to be gone long."

He should let her go, he realized, nodding mutely.

"Nice seeing you," she said, but she was obviously just being polite.

She took a few steps, nudging her cart, then hesitated. "Listen, Troy, I don't want you to worry."

"Worry?" Was she talking about Megan? He'd made a point of not bringing up the subject of his daughter and was grateful that Faith hadn't asked.

"I don't plan to make a habit of running into you. I'm sure you feel the same way."

"This was purely coincidental." It wasn't like he'd followed her into the store.

"I know. But I'll do my shopping when you're at work, and I doubt we'll frequent the same places." She threw back her shoulders as if that was her last word on the subject.

He managed a faint smile. "Good to see you again, Faith."

"You, too, Troy." Her steps were purposeful as she moved past him with her cart.

Troy watched her go, trying not to stare, forcing himself not to rush after her.

With a determined effort, he continued down the produce aisle and hurried through the rest of the store, collecting what he needed. Bananas. Paper towels. Cans of soup and chili, a couple of frozen entrées. Dinner rolls and wine for Thursday. When he'd finished, he pushed his cart over to the checkout.

As luck would have it, Faith was at the counter beside his, waiting her turn. He felt guilty glancing in her direction but caught her looking at him, too.

Finally he couldn't stand it anymore. He stepped away from his cart and toward her. "Listen, Faith, let's talk."

Her eyes widened.

"Let's go for coffee, all right? If now isn't convenient, then perhaps tomorrow. If you prefer to do it after Thanksgiving, that would be fine, too." He hadn't figured out what he'd say to her, but he'd come up with something. At least he could sit there and *look* at her.

He could tell immediately that Faith didn't share his enthusiasm. "Thank you, but I don't think that's a good idea."

She was right, of course. In retrospect it was perfectly idiotic. He was asking her to see him on the sly, and that must have seemed contemptible to her. But much as he wanted to spend time with Faith, Megan could never know. His motives were entirely selfish.

His suggestion might not have been very honorable, and yet if he wanted to see her, there was no other option.

He loved Faith. He was convinced she loved him, too. However, she wasn't going to let him into her life a third time when he'd already broken her heart twice.

Troy couldn't blame her.

"Have a nice holiday, Faith."

"You, too," she whispered with a catch in her voice.

Troy paid for his purchases and carried the bags out to his vehicle. If it hadn't been completely clear before, it was now — he'd lost any chance he'd ever had with Faith.

THREE

Tannith Bliss didn't want to attend the Thanksgiving bonfire at the high school on Wednesday evening. She hated school. The only reason she'd agreed to go was to get her mother off her back. Anything was better than staying home and pretending their lives were normal.

Nothing would ever be normal again. Sometimes her mother acted like her dad hadn't died, like he might walk through the door any second, and that upset Tanni. A lot. She didn't understand why her mother was working so hard to make this stupid Thanksgiving dinner. It was senseless to bother with turkey and dressing and all that stuff when it would only be the three of them.

Thanksgiving was just the start of it. Soon it would be Christmas and that was another nightmare in the making. Their first Christmas without Dad.

She was late, so the school parking lot was

already full. Tanni didn't know why she was even looking for a space. Wishful thinking, she supposed. The only place left was on the street and she was fortunate to find that. With her hands deep in the pockets of her full-length black coat, she hunched her shoulders against the bitter wind and trudged up the hill toward the football field.

As she neared the fence she could hear the laughter and the shouting. This was going to be even worse than she'd thought.

"Tanni, over here!" Kara Nobles called when Tanni reached the field.

She acted as if she hadn't heard. Kara was one of those bright, bouncy girls Tanni found annoying. Keeping her head lowered, she weaved through the crowd and walked to the opposite side of the field, as far away from anyone who might recognize her as she could get. No one else acknowledged her, which suited her just fine.

A goth group stood close by. Tanni wasn't one of them. She dressed in black most of the time simply because she liked black. It matched her mood and her disposition. She was in mourning, after all. Her mother might want to pretend but Tanni didn't. Her father was dead. He wasn't going to come home the way he used to at the end of a flight, hug them all and bring her small gifts.

Everyone else in their family might want to forget Dad, but not her.

Standing by herself, Tanni stared into the fire. The flames were mesmerizing as they crackled and sizzled, thrusting orange-and-yellow tongues toward the night sky.

One of the guys from the goth crowd separated from the group and walked in her direction. She didn't want to look at him for fear that would encourage conversation. Still, she gave him a brief surreptitious glance but didn't recognize him. That didn't mean much, since Tanni tried to remain as inconspicuous as possible. She didn't want or need anyone's attention. If she could've found a way to get out of school altogether, she would gladly have taken it. All she wanted was to be left alone.

The boy didn't say anything. If he'd spoken a single word, she would've told him to go away.

Instead he just stood there, silent as a rock.

She glared at him.

He ignored her.

"Hey, Shaw, you gotta see this," one of the other goths shouted.

This was Shaw Wilson? Tanni had heard plenty about him. He wasn't a student at Cedar Cove High anymore. Rumor had it that he'd never graduated. He hung around town and drove a blue Ford station wagon that everyone seemed to think was cool. The little Tanni knew about Shaw she liked.

The whole school had taken sides when Anson Butler was accused of starting the fire at The Lighthouse Restaurant two years ago, when Tanni was a freshman. The arson had been the main topic of conversation for months.

Shaw was Anson's best friend; he'd defended him no matter what anyone said. Allison Cox had, too, since she was Anson's girlfriend.

Later, when it turned out that Anson *was* innocent and some crooked builder had been responsible for the fire, most of the kids said they'd believed Anson from the get-go. Yeah, right. The same people who were ready to hang Anson out to dry were now claiming to be his close personal friends.

Other than Allison, the only person who'd been loyal from the very beginning was Shaw. He'd been the one real friend Anson had, and if no one else remembered that, Tanni did. She valued that kind of loyalty and hoped Anson appreciated everything Shaw had endured on his behalf.

"You're Shaw?" she asked, looking directly at him.

"Yeah. You're Tanni, right? Tanni Bliss."

She nodded. Trying not to be obvious, she stepped closer to Shaw.

"I've seen you around," he said. Like her, he kept his hands buried in his coat pockets.

"I've seen you around" was another way of saying he'd noticed her. Despite everything, Tanni felt pleased. If she had to be noticed, she wanted it to be by someone like this.

"Why aren't you with your friends?" he asked.

She shrugged rather than explain that she didn't really have friends. Okay, she had a few sort-of friends, Kara for one, but she didn't consider any of them *good* friends. Her old pals had drifted away after her father died in a motorcycle accident. Well, actually she'd *pushed* them out of her life because most of them seemed to think there was a prescribed amount of time to grieve and then she was supposed to snap out of it. It hadn't even been a year. But apparently Tanni was taking longer than they deemed necessary.

One so-called friend had said she should just "get over it." The thing was, Tanni didn't *want* to get over losing her father. She wanted to cling to every precious memory, remember every detail she could.

"I saw your pencil drawing," Shaw said, breaking into her thoughts. "You're good."

47

"Thanks." His words flustered her. The graveyard sketch had been a project her art teacher had praised. Without Tanni's knowing it, Mrs. White had entered the sketch in a local competition. Then, at some art fair sponsored by the community, Tanni had been awarded top prize. She didn't really care. The attention embarrassed her. Besides, her mother was a fabric artist who sold her stuff at the local art gallery, and Tanni was afraid that some friend of hers might have been a judge and given her the prize out of pity. She didn't need pity. What she needed was her father.

Not only that, Tanni preferred to avoid being identified with her mother. They'd never gotten along well, and it was worse now than ever. The last thing she wanted was any comparison between her art and that of the great Shirley Bliss.

"I draw, too," Shaw said. He must have regretted saying anything, because he added, "My drawings aren't nearly as good as yours, though."

Tanni didn't comment. Drawing came easily to her; it always had. Some people were smart at algebra and others struggled with it. Drawing happened to be her particular skill — and her escape.

She could sit in class, any class, and act as

if she was taking copious notes when in reality she was making little sketches. Doodles — geometric and circular designs — and tiny portraits of the people around her. Trees and flowers and horses and dogs. She'd filled notebook after notebook with these drawings. No one had ever seen them, not even her mother. Especially not her mother. If her dad was alive, she might've shown him, but no one else. Shortly after her father died, she'd destroyed a bunch of those notebooks in an act of grief and rage.

"Hey, Shaw, you comin' or not?"

Shaw glanced over his shoulder and then at her. "See you, Tanni."

"Sure." As he started to leave, Tanni realized she didn't want him to go. "How's Anson?" she asked quickly.

Shaw hesitated, then turned back with a shrug. "He's okay."

"I heard he's working with Army Intelligence."

"Yeah."

"That's impressive. What about Allison?"

"She'll be around this week. You know she's going to the University of Washington, don't you? In Seattle."

"Yeah." Tanni's brother was coming home from college, too, and their mother was making a big fuss about that. Still, Tanni would be glad to see Nick. He was supposed to arrive this evening, driving over from Washington State University in Pullman. By the time Tanni got back to the house, Nick would probably be there.

She missed her brother, although she'd never expected to. They used to fight constantly, but after the accident they'd established a fragile peace while they dealt with the upheaval in all their lives. Nick was the one person she talked to about her dad, the only person who felt the way she did.

Shaw took one step toward her. "I was thinking, you know, if you want, I could show you some of my drawings."

"Yeah, sure."

"Cool."

"When?" she asked.

"You doing anything after the bonfire?"

It wasn't like she had to check her social calendar. "Not really."

"I could meet you at Mocha Mama's in an hour."

Tanni looked at her watch. Mocha Mama's was new in town. She hadn't been inside yet but she knew where it was. "Okay."

He smiled at her and she smiled back. Despite the cold wind, she felt a rush of warmth that didn't come from the blazing fire.

After a few minutes, Shaw and his goth

friends took off. Tanni watched the bonfire for another twenty minutes. Her mood had improved since she'd talked to Shaw, so she walked over to where Kara stood with a group of friends.

Tanni wasn't sure why she hung out with Kara at all. Kara and the others were cheerleader types, although none of them was likely to make it onto any squad. They weren't really part of the popular crowd. But then, neither was Tanni.

Half an hour later, she parked in front of Mocha Mama's on Harbor Street. She entered the café, looking around with interest. The decor was typical coffeehouse, with lots of dark wood and old-fashioned lamps. There were only a few other customers — a couple engrossed in their conversation, heads close together, and two older men. Shaw sat at one of the half-dozen tables positioned near the window, nursing a cup of coffee. He'd dyed his hair black but his blond roots were showing. He used to wear it spiked, but he didn't anymore. While attending Cedar Cove High he'd sometimes worn dark, garish makeup; he didn't do that anymore, either.

He raised his head as she approached the table. "Want anything?" he asked.

She did if he was buying. "Coffee, I guess."

He stood and walked over to the counter and brought her back a steaming mug. "It's on the house."

"Thanks." She wrinkled her nose at him. "Why? Do you work here?"

"Yeah. If you ever want a frappachino or anything, let me know."

Shaw didn't look like the barista type. "How long have you worked here?" she asked. The coffee he'd brought her was black, like his, but she decided not to add sugar or cream.

"Since it opened. My aunt and uncle own the place. I manage it for them."

"Cool."

Shaw pulled a sketchbook out of his backpack, which rested on the floor next to the window. "My work's pretty amateurish compared with yours."

Tanni hated it when people said that. They demeaned their own efforts because *she* was supposedly so talented.

Tanni sipped her coffee as she started flipping through the pages of his sketchbook. The first bitter taste warmed her instantly. She studied each page. Shaw had talent, although the first few sketches, done in charcoal, were dark and weird. Buildings that had collapsed, blighted landscapes, a battlefield.

Suddenly Tanni turned a page and came across a field of blooming yellow tulips against the backdrop of a blue spring sky. The piece was done in pastels, so she was careful not to smudge it. She was surprised by the abrupt change in subject matter.

"I was up in the Skagit Valley," he said.

Tanni felt his scrutiny. He seemed to be waiting for her to comment.

"Well?" he pressed. "What do you think?"

"What do *you* think?" she asked him.

"Me?"

"It's your work. Do you like it or not?"

He didn't seem to know what to say.

"This," she said, shoving the sketchbook across the table. "The one you did after seeing the Skagit Valley. What did you feel while you were working on it?"

"Peace," he said after a moment.

"This?" She flipped the page back to the previous one, done in charcoal, a picture of the cratered devastation after an earthquake.

Shaw raised his shoulders. "I don't know."

"Yes, you do." She wasn't going to let him sidestep the question. "You wouldn't have drawn it if you weren't feeling something."

"Anger, all right?" he said with barely controlled emotion. "My mother told me she didn't want me drawing those kinds of pictures in the house. That made me mad. I hate being censored, as if I'm only allowed to have the thoughts and emotions *she* thinks are okay."

"I feel it," she murmured, studying the picture again.

"You feel what?"

She raised her head, meeting his gaze. "Your anger."

He frowned.

"That's the true sign of an artist. If I can feel what you did while you were creating this sketch, then it's good. Don't let anyone tell you otherwise. You've got to believe in yourself, Shaw. No one else will if you don't." It was as simple to Tanni as that. She and her father had often discussed art, even though he wasn't the artist; her mother was. He'd told her that craft and technique were important but they were a means to an end, which was the expression of emotion. It could be a reaction to something outside the artist, but it had to express what the artist *felt* about the scene or person or situation.

"Did you feel the peace?" he asked eagerly, turning the page back to the yellow tulips.

She stared at the tulip picture a long time and then answered truthfully. "Not really."

It obviously wasn't the response he'd expected. For a few seconds, it looked as if he was going to grab the sketchbook and shove it in his backpack. A moment later, he asked, "Why not?"

"You didn't have any real feelings when you painted that."

"I did so!"

"No, you were too concerned about color and shadowing to recognize your feelings about what you were seeing."

His eyes narrowed. "I didn't know I'd have to get all touchy-feely to be an artist."

"Art *is* feelings," Tanni said. "That's what it is to me, at any rate." Her sketches in the past year were the outpouring of her emotions after losing her dad. Her classroom scribblings were about her thoughts and feelings. Wasn't that the point? As her dad had said, any great piece of art made you *feel.* It used to annoy her when he used her mother's quilts and fabric collages as an example, but okay. She knew what he meant.

Shortly after her father's funeral, her mother had escaped into her workroom and hadn't come out for days. Tanni knew her mother must have slept some and eaten, too, but she never saw her do either. When Shirley finally emerged, she'd constructed a huge fabric fire-breathing dragon that Tanni had to admit was an incredible piece of art. No one needed to explain to her that the dragon was death. After her creative frenzy, her mother was better — more herself, less frantic. The dragon still hung in her work-room. Few people saw it and Tanni sus-pected the new owner of the Harbor Street Gallery would love to have it on display if her mother would agree. She wouldn't — at least, not yet.

"The emotion is what makes *your* art so good then," Shaw commented.

"I guess."

"Do you ever draw people?"

"Sometimes."

"It's hard, you know."

She did. "Is that what you want to draw?"

Shaw leaned back in his chair. "I think so." That sounded bogus to her. "You *think* so? You mean, you're not sure?"

"Okay, yes. I want to draw people." He made it seem like a big confession.

"You didn't show me any of those pic-tures."

"No, I —"

"Why not?" Although she asked the ques-tion, she already knew. Shaw was afraid her criticism would rob him of the joy he derived from his portrait work. "Show me one," she said.

He straightened. "I didn't bring any."

"Yes, you did, otherwise you wouldn't have mentioned it." He blinked as if he couldn't believe she'd read him so easily.

"Let me see." Tanni wasn't taking no for an answer.

Shaw stared down at the table. "It's no good. I did it fast and —"

"I don't care. I want to see it. Besides, you asked me to look at your art. That's why I'm here, remember?"

His hand hovered protectively over his backpack.

"Did you feel anything while the pencil was in your hand?"

A hint of what could've been a smile flickered in his eyes. "Yeah, I felt something."

"That's great." She waited and when he continued to sit there in silence, she said, "So, are you going to show it to me or not?" She was getting impatient. Either he showed her his real work or she was out of there.

Slowly, reluctantly, Shaw reached inside his bag and withdrew a second sketchbook. He hesitated before he slid it across the table.

Tanni opened it. When her eyes fell on the picture, her breath froze in her lungs.

"It's me."

"Yeah . . . I know." He spoke in a low, halting voice.

"Tonight, while I was at the bonfire."

"Yeah."

In a few quick lines Shaw had captured her

defiance and isolation, her anger and pain. Her long straight hair was flung about her face by the wind, half-covering her mouth and her chin. Her posture revealed a combativeness, a sense of lonely struggle. In those simple, economical lines Shaw had revealed *her.* He'd drawn the essence of her, Tanni Bliss, as she was right now.

Her throat thickened with tears.

"It's bad, isn't it?"

She couldn't answer him.

"I told you it was no good."

"Wrong," she whispered, despite the lump in her throat. "It's some of the best portrait work I've seen."

Shaw stared at her intently. "You aren't just saying that, are you?"

She shook her head, regaining her composure. "Nothing I ever did was this good. Besides, I'd never tell you something was good if it wasn't."

She could see that pleased him. "Maybe we could get together again," he suggested.

Tanni nodded. "I'd like that."

"When?"

"Anytime," she said softly.

"Tomorrow? Oh, forget that, it's Thanksgiving and you're probably tied up with family and stuff."

"What time?" She didn't care what day it

was; she wanted to be with Shaw.

"You can get away?"

She nodded again.

"Five?"

"I'll meet you here at five," she promised.

Shaw stretched his hand across the table and clasped hers. He held on tightly, intertwining her fingers with his own. Perhaps, Tanni thought, she'd found a friend, after all.

FOUR

Early Thanksgiving morning, Emily Flemming tiptoed into the kitchen, moving as quietly as possible. She didn't want to disturb her sleeping husband or the boys. As was their tradition, her parents had driven over from Spokane to spend the holiday with her family. She could hear her father snoring in the back bedroom, the sound comforting as she made a pot of coffee.

Soon the house would be bustling with activity. Dave and her father would be watching the Macy's Thanksgiving Day parade on television, while the boys raced around the house and Emily and her mother worked in the kitchen, preparing the twenty-two-pound turkey for the oven. Most likely these few moments of peace were all she'd get. If she was going to pull off today's dinner without her mother suspecting anything was awry, then Emily would need this time.

She'd always been close to her mother, and

it wouldn't be easy to fool Barbara Lewis. Emily sat at the kitchen table, taking deep calming breaths, trying to control her emotions. Her unopened Bible rested in front of her. She'd begun reading it every morning, seeking and finding solace in Psalms.

The coffeepot gave one last sizzling refrain. She got up and had just reached inside the cupboard for a mug when her mother strolled into the kitchen.

Barbara tied her long housecoat at the waist and covered a yawn. "I thought I heard you up and about. My goodness, what time is it, anyway?"

"It's early, Mom."

Barbara frowned at the oven clock. "It isn't even five!"

"I know." As it was, Emily had awakened before three, tossing and turning before giving up any hope of going back to sleep.

Her mother sat down. "The coffee smells great. Is it ready?"

"It is." Emily poured a second mug, added cream to both, and brought them to the table, joining her mother.

After a few sips, Barbara looked directly at Emily, who tried to meet her eyes but couldn't.

"Something on your mind, Em?" her mother said, eyebrows raised.

Hoping to distract Barbara, she murmured, "I was reviewing our menu. I was thinking we should make a double batch of stuffing this year. Everyone loves leftovers."

"We could."

"I made the cranberry salad yesterday before you arrived." The salad, which was more of a dessert, was a longtime family favorite and served only at Thanksgiving and Christmas. Cranberries, gelatin and whipped topping were stirred together and placed in the freezer.

Seeing that her mother was about to speak, Emily interjected. "Instead of Brussels sprouts this year, I thought I'd make a broccoli casserole. I found a recipe on the Internet that looks absolutely delicious."

"Em . . ."

"By my calculations, we should get the turkey in the oven around eight if we want to have dinner on the table by four this afternoon." Emily knew she was rambling, but she couldn't stop herself.

"Are you going to tell me what's bothering you or are you going to make me guess?" her mother asked.

Emily closed her eyes, then abandoned the pretense and buried her face in her hands. She wasn't someone who easily gave way to emotion. If she had been, the tears would've flowed nonstop.

Her mother rested her hand on Emily's forearm. "There's nothing you can't tell me. You know that, don't you?"

"Of course," she whispered brokenly.

"I knew the minute I walked into the house that things weren't right. Is it to do with the boys?"

Emily shook her head. "No, they're fine." She thanked God for that.

"Dave?" Her mother sounded hesitant, as if she didn't really believe there could possibly be a problem. Everyone knew Dave Flemming was a good man. He was everything Emily had ever dreamed of finding in a husband — loving, responsible, caring, gentle and so much more. She'd fallen in love with him while they were in college, and her love had grown and matured in the years since. Not once had she even considered looking at another man. She'd been so sure he loved her just as much until recent events gave her cause to wonder.

"He's working too hard, isn't he?" Barbara asked.

Emily swallowed. She couldn't deny that, although not for the reasons her mother assumed. "He's gone a lot, yes."

"It's all those committee meetings, isn't it?" Barbara pursed her lips. "Church duties can steal away family time if he lets them. He needs to take a stand."

Emily straightened. "I don't think that's it. I . . ." She could barely utter the words. "I believe . . . I have reason to think that Dave —" she paused, hardly able to continue "— that he might be involved with another woman."

Her mother's eyes widened in shock before she categorically denied the possibility. "Not Dave, Em. He's simply not the type. I'm sure you're mistaken."

"I used to assume that, too," Emily said flatly. "Do you honestly think this is something I *want* to believe?"

"Well . . . no." Her mother was suddenly speechless, and for Barbara Lewis, that was unusual indeed.

"The evidence had to practically hit me over the head before I recognized it for what it was," she whispered.

"Who?"

Emily shrugged helplessly. "I don't know and I don't want to know." She'd racked her mind in a futile effort to figure out who it could be. The only person she could remember him spending a lot of time with in the past year was Martha Evans. She was the elderly widow who'd died in September. Dave had gone to visit her every week. Visiting the sick and bedridden was one of his pastoral duties, of course, but he'd told her Martha was a friend, that they'd grown especially close.

Now that she thought about it, perhaps he *hadn't* been with Martha all those times. Visiting Martha might've been a convenient excuse Dave had given her and others. Maybe he'd spent those afternoons — not to mention all the evenings he'd come home late — with someone else.

"The truth is I have no idea who it might be," Emily confessed miserably, remembering the woman's voice on the phone Monday night.

"Wait." Her mother raised one hand, her expression thoughtful. "I'm getting ahead of myself. In the first place, what makes you think Dave's involved with anyone?"

"He lied to me," she whispered, keeping her voice low for fear another early riser might overhear.

"Out and out lied?" her mother asked.

Emily considered this. "I suppose it was more a sin of omission." She explained about her chance meeting with the Beldons, when she'd learned that Dave was no longer meeting Bob for their regular golf game. "There's plenty of other evidence, too," she added sadly.

"Such as?"

"We don't . . . we haven't . . ." It was more than a little embarrassing to discuss her sex life with her mother. "We — you know . . . haven't . . . in over a month." Prior to this point, they'd enjoyed a satisfying sexual relationship. Emily missed her husband in every way. On the few nights he was home early, Dave was often asleep by the time she got into bed. The nights she went to bed first, he crept silently into the room and slid between the sheets, doing his best not to wake her. Only Emily wasn't asleep. It troubled her to realize that if he *had* reached for her, she didn't know how she would've responded.

"He isn't as interested in you physically as he once was. Is that what you're trying to say?"

With her cheeks warming, she nodded.

"Have you checked credit card receipts?" her mother suggested.

"No!" First of all, it hadn't occurred to Emily, and secondly, she might have ended up with information she didn't want, information she wasn't ready to face.

"Em, it seems to me that you've blown a few minor details out of proportion," Barbara continued. "That's what happens when you keep your doubts buried. Ask him. Dave is your husband. He'll probably be shocked when he finds out you think he's got a woman on the side."

"He'll say it isn't true, of course. What good would it do to ask?"

"It'll clear the air. And his reaction will tell you if you actually have reason to worry."

Emily had given the subject a great deal of thought. She wouldn't, couldn't, confront Dave. If she was right, he'd only deny it — and if she was wrong, her husband would be deeply hurt that she'd accused him of such a fundamental betrayal. As far as she was concerned, it was a lose-lose proposition.

"My guess is that you've allowed your suspicions to build up," Barbara said. "A few unrelated events don't necessarily equal an affair."

"But, Mom —"

"I *know* Dave. It just isn't in him to do this."

Emily so badly wanted to believe that, and yet . . .

"Dave is a terrible liar," her mother went on. "If something's going on, I'm sure I'll pick up on it."

Emily grinned. True enough, her mother had a nose for anything suspicious. Emily and her brother had gotten away with very little while living under their mother's watchful eye. "I certainly never managed to hide anything from you."

"Darn right." Barbara smiled back. "Now put this out of your mind — at least for today."

"I'll try," Emily promised.

"You have a lot for which to be grateful," her mother said. "This is your first Thanksgiving in your beautiful new home, and you have every reason to feel loved and cherished by your family. Don't allow your suspicions to ruin Thanksgiving."

Emily had to agree. Still . . . "You'll tell me if you think something's wrong with Dave?" she pressed.

"Of course, but I'm positive you're imagining it. A week from now, you'll be phoning me, embarrassed you'd ever suspected Dave of anything so out-of-character."

For the rest of the day, Emily did as her mother had suggested and tried to put the doubts and fears completely out of her mind.

Just after two, Barbara helped her set the table. The formal dining room was one of Emily's favorite things about this new house. She'd always wanted one. For the first time since she'd been cooking the family's Thanksgiving dinner, they'd be able to eat someplace besides the kitchen.

She'd worked hard to make the dining

room as festive as she could. The mahogany table, chairs and matching hutch came from a second-hand store and had been a real bargain. Emily had loved the dining set the moment she saw it. She'd shown it to Dave, although even secondhand, the price was well out of their range. Later — to her surprise and delight — it had been delivered to the house. Dave told her he'd talked to the dealer, who'd agreed to sell it to them at almost half the asking price.

Looking at it now, she still felt thrilled. She'd used a dark green linen tablecloth and spread an array of colorful maple leaves all around it. Then she'd created a cornucopia for a centerpiece, filling it with yellow, green and orange gourds, as well as miniature pumpkins. Lighted pale green candles provided the final touch.

The table hit exactly the right festive note, she thought. It could've appeared in one of those glossy home magazines — and she should know because they were one of the few extravagances she allowed herself. The china had been a wedding gift and was only used once or twice a year, so arranging it on a real dining room table was a special treat.

As she stood back to examine her handiwork, Dave stepped up behind her and placed his hands on her shoulders. "You did a beautiful job," he said, kissing her affectionately.

Her mother smiled at her and then, as Dave turned away, she mouthed, "I told you so."

Emily rolled her eyes.

Once all the serving dishes were on the table and Dave had carved the turkey, it was nearly four. Everyone was hungry, since lunch had consisted of crackers and cheese.

"I get the wishbone this year," Matthew called out.

"No, I do," Mark insisted. Scowling, he protested, "Matthew got it last year."

"Boys, don't squabble." Dave looked sternly in their direction. They both instantly went quiet.

"Shall we say grace?" Dave said.

They all joined hands around the table and bowed their heads as Dave offered up a simple, yet heartfelt prayer of gratitude. When he'd finished, everyone at the table murmured, "Amen."

"Pass the stuffing," Matthew said before Emily had even opened her eyes.

"Matthew, the dish will come to you soon enough," Emily reminded her oldest son. "And it's *please* pass the stuffing."

"The stuffing's my favorite," he muttered.

"Mine, too," Mark said. "I like it with lots

of gravy."

Soon the platter and bowls circled the table and everyone's plate was heaped with turkey, dressing, two different potato dishes, special salads and more.

When they'd had dessert — the two pies, with whipped cream or ice cream — the family lingered at the table and chatted amicably, teasing one another, joking and sharing stories. This was Emily's favorite part of the holiday.

"The boys and I will load the dishwasher," Dave announced as he stood up half an hour later.

Matthew wore a horrified look. "Dad!" he burst out. "Don't *volunteer.*"

"Dad!" Even Mark seemed appalled. "There must be a hundred thousand dishes."

"Then I suggest we get started."

Both boys groaned.

"Your mother and grandmother spent all day cooking this wonderful meal. It wouldn't be right to expect them to wash the dishes, too."

"What about Grandpa?" Mark asked.

"I'll help," her father said with a chuckle.

"No, you won't, Al," Dave insisted. "You sit back and relax. The boys and I can manage."

"Dad, you can't turn down help," Mark

told his father urgently.

"All right, Al, if you're game, then by all means join us in the kitchen."

Emily and her mother put away the leftovers, then relaxed in the living room, drinking tea while the men handled the cleaning up.

"Well," Emily said, looking at her mother. "What do you think?" She didn't need to elaborate.

Barbara frowned thoughtfully. After a moment she bit her lower lip. "He's doing a good job of it."

"Of what?"

"Pretending," her mother said. "I don't know what's going on with Dave, but I feel he's definitely hiding *something.*"

The joy Emily had struggled so hard to maintain all that day immediately evaporated. "So you think —"

"No," her mother said, cutting her off. "I can't believe it's another woman. Nevertheless, I'm fairly certain Dave's keeping some kind of secret from you."

FIVE

Christie Levitt sat by herself at the bar in The Pink Poodle, her regular watering hole, and took a sip of her beer. She wasn't good company tonight. The Friday after Thanksgiving was the biggest shopping day of the year. The retailers called it Black Friday; she did, too, but for different reasons.

Christie had been at her job at the Cedar Cove Wal-Mart before six that morning. It was now 7:00 p.m. She'd spent a long day standing at that cash register and she was tired, not to mention cranky. Larry, the bartender and owner, plus everyone around her, correctly gauged her mood and gave her a wide berth. Fine, she'd rather avoid everyone, including her sister, who was probably mad at her. Christie was a no-show at the big Thanksgiving feast Teri had made yesterday.

Generally Christie was the life of any party. Tonight, however, she had other things on her mind. Although it wasn't a *thing* so much as a person.

James Wilbur.

Christie wasn't sure why this man, with his refined and formal ways, intrigued her. But he did. Her heart seemed to speed up whenever she thought of him, which was far more often than she should.

The two of them had nothing in common. *Nothing.* James drove the limo for Christie's sister and brother-in-law. Teri had sent James to pick her up any number of times, and they'd often chatted during the drive. Initially, their conversations had been stilted and, on her part, even hostile. That had begun to change. Then, one night, she'd found a red rose on the seat. Only later did she discover the rose was from James and not her sister.

Men didn't give her flowers. She wasn't that kind of woman and she hardly knew how to react when a man did something nice for her. James's interest terrified her; Teri said it was because Christie didn't know how to respond to a decent, hardworking man. She was more accustomed to losers, men who stole from her and smacked her around.

Even now she had no idea what had caused this brain malfunction when it came to men. Her genetic makeup must've gotten all messed up; it was the only reason Christie could figure. Either that, or a lifetime of bad examples — although Teri had broken the pattern when she met Bobby Polgar. In any event, Christie would meet a man, generally unemployed and down on his luck, which was all too frequently a permanent condition. Substance abuse, whether drugs, alcohol or both, always seemed to be involved as well. These guys would tell her their tales of woe: The world was against them, they'd been cheated by bosses and partners, cheated *on* by wives and girlfriends — an endless series of sad complaints that, somehow, all sounded the same.

Nonetheless, her heart would ache for them and before she knew how or why, Christie would end up taking responsibility and trying to make everything better. In no time, she'd be head over heels in love.

Talk about stupid, and yet she did it again and again. She wished she could meet someone like Bobby, someone who'd love and respect her the way Bobby loved and respected Teri.

Now Bobby's driver was interested in Christie. In contrast to all the previous men in her life, James Wilbur was the perfect gentleman. In fact, his politeness was downright excessive. And calling her Miss Christie, as if she was — oh, she didn't know what. Special? Hardly. It was just one of his affectations, she told herself grumpily. He irritated her so much that she'd insisted she didn't want him driving her anymore. She had her own means of transportation, such as it was, but despite the bald tires and faulty transmission, she did not require a chauffeur.

Teri might be used to such exalted treatment, but Christie didn't like it. Besides, James showing up at her apartment complex in that fancy car caused too much speculation among her neighbors. It embarrassed her.

James made her feel self-conscious, opening the door for her, helping her in and out of the limousine. She didn't need assistance to get into a car or out of one, either. That was so ridiculous it was laughable.

And yet, she had to admit his intentions were good. There was a kindness about him . . . . Christie closed her eyes. She couldn't bear to think of him in pain. He'd been hurt recently, beaten by a couple of thugs who'd attempted to kidnap her sister, only they got her friend Rachel Pendergast instead. And they got James.

It all had to do with a chess tournament and a rival player who'd wanted Bobby to throw the match. He hadn't; he'd won through some complicated maneuver and in the end the other player had been arrested.

Christie hadn't expected to like Bobby Polgar. And she hadn't gotten along with her sister for years. They'd simply avoided each other. It was just better that way.

Then all of a sudden they were back to being friends . . . being sisters. Christie wasn't sure who'd done the maturing — probably both of them. And she suspected Bobby's influence had made Teri more confident, more tolerant and forgiving. Bobby had been a good friend to James, too — not that she knew much about their history.

She reached for her beer and sipped it, wishing she could stop thinking about James. He lingered in her mind and she couldn't make him disappear, which flustered her. She'd demanded he leave her alone, and he had, which flustered her even more. No one had ever done what she'd asked before.

When she learned he was hurt, she'd hurried to him, but James no longer wanted anything to do with her. He'd made it plain that he didn't want her company. Christie got the message. She left him a rose, the way he'd left her one, and slipped out of his living quarters, feeling lower than dirt.

"You need another beer?" Larry asked, filling a couple of glasses from the tap.

Christie shook her head. "No, thanks." She quickly changed her mind. "On second thought, maybe I will."

Larry nodded approvingly, then leaned against the bar and whispered, "You feeling down about something?"

She shrugged. "You could say that."

Larry set a glass of cold beer on the counter. "If you want to talk about it, just say the word."

Christie shook her head again. Her feelings for James confused her; she wouldn't know what to tell Larry or anyone else. The person she needed to talk to was her sister. Maybe Teri would help her understand what was happening.

"Hey, look!" Kyle, a plumber and a regular at The Pink Poodle, called out. "That limousine's parked here again."

Christie instantly felt heat invade her face. James was parked outside, waiting for her.

A couple of men walked over to stare out the window.

"What's a limousine doing here?" Bill asked. He worked at the shipyard and was another regular. Both men were divorced and preferred spending time at the Poodle to sitting alone in front of the TV. Christie understood that desire for a social outlet; it was one of the reasons she was a regular herself.

"I saw that car before," Kyle commented.

"Who in here would ever need a fancy vehicle like that?" Bill asked, turning to look at Larry.

"We never found out." Larry headed to the beer taps with two clean glasses. "The car just seems to show up now and then. No big deal."

"Are you going to let him use your parking lot like that?" Christie asked, fearing the other regulars might connect her with the limousine. She'd never hear the end of it if they did.

"Sure, why not?" Kyle was the one who responded. "It brings a bit of class to the place, don't you think?" He directed the question to the bartender.

Larry was too busy filling glasses to respond.

Christie finished her second beer. She usually drank three, but after two she'd begun to feel light-headed. A third, which normally didn't faze her, might be too much. Time to call it quits. Besides, she was tired.

"You goin' home?" Larry asked when she paid her bill.

"Yeah."

"You need me to call you a cab?"

"No. I'm fine, thanks."

"See ya," he said.

Christie waved goodbye, pulled on her short wool jacket, then wrapped the scarf around her neck and set out to brave the elements. The wind had begun to rise, picking up the last few scattered leaves and sending them hither and yon. Christie noticed that the smell of snow hung in the air and while the schoolkids would love a snowfall, she could do without it.

Outside The Pink Poodle, she heaved a sigh of relief that James had apparently given up and left. He'd come here to talk to her. When she didn't immediately appear, he'd gotten the message that she wasn't interested, and that was okay with her. Moreover, she didn't want anyone seeing the two of them together.

In spite of all that, she felt disappointed. She was still worried about him and hoped his condition had improved. But ever since the kidnapping he'd acted as if he didn't want her around. Fine. She, too, could take a hint.

A hundred thoughts swirled frantically, like the autumn leaves at her feet, as she struggled against the wind and around to the side of the building, where she'd parked her car.

"Christie."

She'd recognize his voice anywhere. Peering into the darkness, she saw him. The limousine stood beside her dilapidated Ford and James was waiting for her there, out of sight of those inside the tavern.

"What are you doing here?" she demanded in a none-too-friendly voice. Her lack of welcome was part shock, part feigned anger.

"I came to check on you."

"I don't need a babysitter," she protested. "Did Teri and Bobby send you?" That would be just like her sister.

"No."

"I don't believe it." Christie knew that Teri and Bobby wouldn't have missed her yesterday; they'd invited plenty of friends to their Thanksgiving dinner party. Having to be at work so early this morning was a convenient excuse. Not that she'd given anyone the opportunity to question her about it. She'd stayed home all day and hadn't answered her phone, although it must have rung a dozen times.

"You didn't come to dinner."

"So? I didn't realize you were keeping tabs." She kept the derision in her voice so he wouldn't think she cared about his opinion of her. An opinion he would no doubt divulge any second now.

There it was. "You were rude to let your sister down."

"So now I'm rude," she muttered. "And

81

you're an expert on polite behavior?" Actually, he was, and he rightly ignored her question.

"Miss Teri held off serving dinner while she tried to reach you," he said.

Christie felt bad about that, although she wouldn't let James know. "What's it got to do with you?" she asked flippantly.

"You aren't usually a rude person, Christie."

"Apparently I proved you wrong."

"You stayed away because of me, didn't you?"

"Don't flatter yourself," she responded, although of course he was right. She'd skipped Teri's Thanksgiving event for fear of another rejection from James. Instead of feasting on turkey dinner at her sister's, she'd eaten a microwave pizza and watched reruns of *Seinfeld* for three hours straight.

"Is that why you're here? To criticize me? If so, message received. Can I go now?" she asked as though she'd grown bored with the conversation. Her ears were getting cold, even if her heart was pounding unmercifully fast.

"I'd like to apologize," James said.

"For what? Embarrassing me in front of my friends just now?"

"No." He paused. "For the other night."

"What other night?" she asked, pretending that his hurtful words had no impact on her, that she'd forgotten whatever he'd said. In reality, it was something she'd never forget.

"Last month. You came to me —"

"Oh, that," she returned breezily. "Hey, don't worry about it. You didn't want me around. I understand. It's not a problem — at least not for me."

He frowned, shaking his head. "I didn't want your sympathy. Or anyone's," he added in a lower voice.

"Do I *look* like the sympathetic sort?" she asked, making a joke of it. "Like I said, it doesn't matter." She forced a laugh and with it came a loud hiccup, which mortified her.

"You've been drinking?"

"No." She did an exaggerated double-take. "You think I sat in The Pink Poodle and *drank?*"

"I'll drive you home."

"Absolutely not." She'd had two beers over the course of as many hours. She was perfectly capable of driving herself home.

"Christie . . ."

"I said no." She wasn't going to put up with any more of his disapproval. "Just leave me alone. You don't want to see me and that's fine, because I don't want to see you, either. Do I need to make it any clearer than that?"

He turned away, then seemed to change his mind. "You don't mean that."

"Yes, I do," she said, wrenching open her car door, which to her intense embarrassment made a loud groaning noise. She should've taken it to the repair shop, but hadn't — because of the inconvenience and, more than that, the bill. A squeaking door was the least of her problems with this vehicle. It was on its last legs — or tires.

Rather than stand in the cold arguing with James, Christie climbed inside her car and started the engine. Thankfully it didn't die right then and there, as she'd half expected. That would've made her humiliation complete.

Without looking behind her, she backed out of the parking place and pulled into the street.

One glance in her rearview mirror told her that James had pulled in directly behind her. He followed her all the way to the apartment complex and waited there until she'd parked. Even then he didn't leave.

Christie was tempted to march over and demand he stop following her. Otherwise, she'd threaten to call the authorities and get a restraining order. It wouldn't be the first time she'd filed one against a man.

But she decided not to let on that she'd noticed him. She hurried into her apartment and slammed the door, breathing hard. Several minutes passed before she regained her composure. The first thing she saw in the dark room was the light blinking on her answering machine.

Five calls, all of them from Teri. Her sister was determined to leave messages until she phoned back. Still, Christie resisted. Teri was bound to lecture her for not coming to Thanksgiving dinner.

After ten minutes she couldn't stand it anymore and grabbed the phone. Teri answered after two rings.

"Okay, go ahead and be mad," Christie greeted her sister. "Yell at me and get it over with."

"Mad? Why would I be mad?" Teri asked.

"Because I didn't show up yesterday."

Teri sighed. "And we both know the reason for that."

"I had to be to work at six this morning."

"Bzzz." Teri imitated an annoying buzzer sound. "Wrong answer. You didn't show up because you were afraid to face James."

No use trying to fool her sister.

"He came looking for me tonight," Christie confessed.

"I know. How'd it go?"

85

Christie closed her eyes, debating how much to tell her. "Not good."

"What happened?"

She settled for the plain, unvarnished truth; Teri was going to find out, anyway. "He . . . tried to apologize but . . . I wouldn't let him."

"Christie," her sister said, "I thought you *liked* James."

Like was such a mild word for the way she felt about him. "I do," she whispered, wondering why she went to such lengths to prove the opposite.

"Then why did you — Oh, never mind, I know why. I did the same thing with Bobby. When he first showed interest in me, I did everything I could to chase him off. I thank God every day that he didn't listen. What's wrong with us, little sister, that we don't recognize love when it comes knocking at our door?"

"James doesn't love me —"

"Stop right this minute," Teri said. "He cares about you — a lot."

"If that's the case, then why did he send me away when he was hurt?" she cried, unable to disguise her pain. "I wanted to be with him."

"He was embarrassed, Christie. Surely you can understand. He didn't want you to see him in that condition. He'd been beaten up!

Give him a chance, will you?"

Christie was afraid to. She'd experienced so many disappointments — and this one would be the worst. "It won't work."

"You don't know that," Teri argued. "Look at Bobby and me. Who'd ever think the two of us would fall in love?"

"Listen, it might've worked out for you and Bobby, but that doesn't mean it will for me. Let me deal with this my own way, all right?"

Something in her voice must have alerted her sister to the fact that Christie was serious. "All right," Teri agreed with obvious reluctance, "if you're sure . . ."

"I am," Christie said firmly. "Promise me you'll stay out of it."

Teri sighed. "Okay then, if that's how you want it."

But Christie didn't. Not really.

Six

"What's for dinner?" Roy McAfee asked. His stomach growling, he glanced up from the Saturday edition of *The Cedar Cove Chronicle* and waited for his wife's answer. It seemed to him that Corrie had been in the kitchen longer than usual.

"Leftovers."

Again? Corrie was an excellent cook but it was the same every Thanksgiving. She chose the largest fresh turkey the store had available and then they ate bird for weeks on end. Really, how much turkey could four people consume? And how many versions of turkey did one man have to eat? Not that Roy was complaining — not really. He'd enjoyed Thanksgiving, and having two of his three children with Corrie and him was special enough.

"I'm making turkey pot pie," she called from the kitchen. "It'll be out of the oven in a few minutes."

"Okay."

"Mack will be joining us for dinner."

"Good." Lately Roy and his son had come to an understanding. He'd had high expectations of his only son. Then, as a teenager, Mack had rebelled and they'd been at odds ever since. All those years Roy was furious that Mack had refused to take his advice. Instead of finishing college and pursuing a solid career he'd dabbled in all kinds of things, often doing what Roy considered menial work, not worthy of his talents. They couldn't spend an hour together without arguing. Everything had changed around the time Gloria entered their lives.

Gloria was the daughter he'd fathered with Corrie back in college. When he broke off the relationship he hadn't realized she was pregnant. Not until much later did he learn that she'd borne their child and given Gloria up for adoption. For Corrie, pregnant and alone, it had been the right decision at the time. Still, their marriage had been haunted by the loss of the child they'd never known.

But life had, in a way, come full circle, bringing their child back to them. Gloria had searched for her birth parents, craving a relationship. And she'd found them. Roy had tried to steer his son into police work but it was Gloria who'd gone into law enforcement. She'd recently left the Bremerton police department to work for Troy Davis at the local sheriff's office. Roy was proud to see her in uniform, serving the community he and Corrie — and now Gloria herself — called home.

Corrie stuck her head out of the kitchen. "I forgot to tell you Linnette phoned this afternoon while you were at the office." As a private investigator, he often went in to work on weekends, especially if he had a backlog of cases.

Roy set the newspaper aside. Linnette was living in North Dakota, working as a waitress, and claimed to be loving it. Or perhaps it was more accurate to say that what she loved was the town of Buffalo Valley. He'd sided with his daughter when she'd announced she was leaving Cedar Cove, although personally he hadn't been in favor of it. However, as he'd told Corrie, it was Linnette's life and Linnette's decision. After the failure of her relationship with Cal Washburn, she'd been heartbroken and humiliated. She wanted out; Roy didn't blame her. He hurt for her.

"She told me Thanksgiving with Pete and his family was very nice," Corrie said, coming all the way into the living room now.

His wife's face was flushed from the

kitchen's warmth and her hair was disheveled from running floury hands through it. Corrie had put on a few pounds over the years — but then who hadn't? To him, she was more beautiful at fifty-six than she'd ever been.

"Roy McAfee, why are you looking at me like that?" Corrie demanded.

"I was just thinking I'm married to a gorgeous woman."

"Oh, honestly!" She rolled her eyes. "Don't you want to hear about Linnette?"

"Anything new with her?" He couldn't imagine there would be. They'd talked a couple of days before Thanksgiving, as well as on Thanksgiving itself. Linnette had spent the day with Pete Somebody, a farmer she'd met. From the sound of it, he was a decent, hardworking young man. It was a bit soon for anything serious between them, but he trusted Linnette's judgment and wanted her to be happy. He just wished she'd found that happiness a little closer to home.

"She's been working with Hassie Knight."

"The old woman who owns the pharmacy in Buffalo Valley?" he asked. It was hard to keep them straight, all the people Linnette mentioned in her phone calls. Generally, she spoke to Corrie and then his wife relayed the information to him.

"That's the one."

"Working on what?"

"Getting a medical clinic up and running," Corrie said excitedly.

This *was* news, and Roy couldn't believe she was just telling him now. He'd been home for a couple of hours. "Hey! That's great."

"Buffalo Valley is growing and they need a clinic. Hassie claims it's divine providence that brought Linnette to their town."

He nodded, pleased that Linnette would be using her education. She'd worked hard to become a physician assistant and it'd be a shame to see all that effort go to waste. Roy had said she'd eventually go back to medicine, and he'd called it right.

"She's thrilled about this opportunity. You might give her a call later."

"I might," he agreed, although it was always Corrie who did the phoning.

Roy had never been comfortable expressing emotion or, for that matter, being on the receiving end. Nevertheless, he loved his wife and his children, all three of them. They made him proud. Even Mack . . .

There was a knock at the door, but before Corrie could open it, their son stepped into the house. A blast of cold air came in with him.

"Whatever you're cooking smells great," he said appreciatively, rubbing his bare hands.

Corrie cradled his face and kissed him loudly on the cheek.

"That was the right thing to say," Roy told him with a grin. "Not that it isn't true," he added swiftly.

Mack guffawed. "Good save, Dad."

Roy lifted his hand in acknowledgment but didn't get up. He'd injured his back years before and as a result had taken early retirement from his job with the Seattle police. His back still caused him pain, which he did his best to ignore. Some days he succeeded at that better than others. This was one of his less successful days.

Mack pulled out the ottoman and sat down near his father. "I stopped by the Cedar Cove fire station this afternoon."

Roy straightened. This was what he'd been waiting to hear. He wanted to ask if Mack had been chosen for the position, but was patient enough to let him make his own announcement.

"Good grief, Mack," Corrie cried. "Don't keep us in suspense!"

"The captain said there's a letter waiting for me in Seattle."

"Oh."

Corrie's obvious disappointment echoed

Roy's. He'd hoped a job in Cedar Cove would bring him and Mack closer. They'd come a long way in the last two years but, as Roy was the first to admit, they still had a long way to go.

"Why the sad looks?" Mack asked. "My application's been accepted! Effective December fifteenth, I'll be working for the Cedar Cove Fire Department."

Corrie covered her mouth with both hands and shrieked with delight.

"Congratulations, son," Roy said. Leaning forward, he slapped Mack on the shoulder. Despite his more temperate response, he was no less elated than his wife.

Corrie's eyes gleamed. "Of course you'll stay with us until you find a place to rent."

"Actually, no."

"No?" Corrie frowned. "But . . . we're your family. Where else would you live?"

"The thing is, I've found a place."

"So soon?"

"Yes, and it works out great. Would you believe I'll be living in Linnette's old apartment? Will Jefferson's subletting it, and I'm assuming his lease."

"You?"

"Where's Will going?" Roy asked. "He's barely moved in. You mean to say he's moving out already?"

"He purchased the Harbor Street Art Gallery."

That was old news. Big news when it happened, because it had looked as if the gallery was about to close its doors for good. No one wanted that. The entire community had breathed a collective sigh of relief when Will Jefferson decided to buy it.

"Yes, we know about Will taking over the gallery," Corrie said. "He's not leaving town, is he? After all this, it would be a shame if he turned over the management to someone else."

"Nothing like that," Mack explained. "Apparently the gallery has a small apartment that's been used for storage during the past few years. Will couldn't see any reason to pay rent when he already has a place he could live."

"I didn't know the gallery had an apartment."

"Me, neither," Roy said. "It's got a second story, though, so it doesn't really surprise me."

"Up until now it's been crammed full of junk. Will's been working all weekend to get it cleared out. At last count he'd made three trips to the garbage dump. He's having painters come in on Monday."

"The place could probably use updating,

don't you think?" Corrie asked.

"I'll help him whenever I can," Mack said.

From habit Roy nearly spoiled everything by making some disparaging comment about Mack's carpentry skills. Thankfully, he stopped himself in time. His son was a capable carpenter; not only that, he'd worked as a painter and part-time post-office employee. He'd done a dozen other jobs since he'd dropped out of school.

"Will said he'll eventually buy his own place, but at this point, he's content to fix up the apartment."

"Sounds like a plan," Roy murmured. "Makes sense to stay on the premises."

"That's the cop in you talking, Dad," Mack said with a laugh.

Corrie laughed, too. "So when are you moving into Linnette's old apartment?" she asked.

"As soon as I can make the arrangements. The lease is up in a few months and that'll give me time to decide what I want to do — buy or continue renting."

"Good idea, son."

Mack met his eyes and they exchanged a smile. This was progress, real progress, for both of them.

The oven timer went off, and Corrie returned to the kitchen.

"Let me set the table," Mack offered, following his mother.

Roy reached for the paper but he didn't see the words in front of him. Instead he pondered the state of his children's lives. Gloria was doing well. Linnette was going to start a medical clinic in Buffalo Valley, North Dakota. And now Mack was taking on a responsible job with the Cedar Cove Fire Department.

Roy didn't think life could get much sweeter than this.

Seven

"She's going to be fine," Cliff Harding said, standing behind Grace as she prepared their morning pot of coffee. He placed his big hands on her shoulders in a comforting gesture of love and concern.

Grace pressed her hands over his and wished she felt as confident as he seemed to be. Olivia, her best friend, her life friend, had cancer. The word struck terror in her heart. This wasn't the first time a friend, someone she cared about, had been diagnosed with breast cancer. But this was *Olivia,* who was as close to Grace as a sister. They'd been best friends from the moment they'd met in first grade.

They'd seen each other through every life crisis — from Grace's teenage pregnancy to her first husband's suicide. From the death of Olivia's son Jordan to her divorce. They'd been through so much together, nearly every loss a woman could experience. Olivia knew

Grace better than anyone. And Grace knew Olivia.

But cancer . . . Grace wanted to scream, to howl, to weep. She felt helpless, impotent, with no idea what to say or how to support her friend. Her fears for Olivia overwhelmed her.

Cancer was so unfair. It didn't make sense. This shouldn't be happening to a woman as conscientious and positive and kindhearted as Olivia. She was the one who watched her diet religiously. She took her vitamins every morning without fail. She exercised and looked after herself emotionally and spiritually. What more could she possibly have done?

"You going to the hospital?" Cliff asked, although he already knew the answer.

"I told Jack I'd sit with him while . . . while they do the surgery." She turned around and slid her arms around Cliff's waist and hid her face in his chest. A shiver went through her.

"Hey, hey, relax," Cliff whispered soothingly, stroking her hair. "Everything's going to be okay."

"I won't be able to relax until we know for sure the cancer hasn't metastasized." So far, the tests were encouraging, but until the surgery was done, they wouldn't know whether the cancer was localized and her lymph nodes were clear. Grace wanted reassurance and she wouldn't rest until she heard the physician say the words.

Even when things were at their worst, Olivia had always seemed to be in control. From the time they were in grade school, Grace had admired her. Young as she was, Olivia had been so well put-together, so smart and organized. She wore crisp dresses with Mary Jane shoes and perfect pigtails. In high school she'd been elected a class officer every year. She was popular, intelligent, capable and her peers recognized it and sought her out.

But that lifelong sense of control had abandoned Olivia now.

When the coffee finished brewing, it was Cliff who got two mugs and filled them both. He handed the first one to Grace. "Would you like me to go with you?"

Grace's immediate reaction was that she would've liked nothing better. Then she remembered that Cliff had a meeting with a horse breeder he'd been looking forward to seeing for weeks. His willingness to reschedule the appointment touched her deeply.

"Thanks, but I'll be fine — and so will Olivia." She forced a smile, sipped some more of her coffee and then walked back to their bedroom to change out of her night-clothes. As she sorted through her wardrobe, she wondered what one wore to an event like this. Her normal attire at the library was a cotton turtleneck pullover with a jumper. She had quite a few jumpers, some of which she'd sewn herself. In the end, she opted for tan khaki slacks and a rust-colored V-neck sweater over a white polo shirt.

Grace couldn't imagine why her outfit seemed so important, yet somehow it was. She wondered if this could be a way of distracting herself from Olivia's surgery. Or perhaps it was a more complex psychological phenomenon, like . . . like suiting up for battle. Because this *was* battle, even if she was going to be standing on the sidelines.

When she arrived at the hospital, she discovered that Olivia had already been checked in and given a sedative before the surgery.

As Grace entered her hospital room, Olivia raised her head and glanced at the door. Grace hesitated. Seeing her dearest friend so vulnerable nearly brought her to tears. But the last thing Olivia needed was for Grace to turn into an emotional wreck. Swallowing the giant lump that blocked her throat, she managed to grin. "Hello, there," she said with a heartiness she was far from feeling.

"Grace," Olivia whispered. "I told you it wasn't necessary to come. I should've known you'd never listen."

"I wouldn't dream of being anywhere else," Grace said. "I need to be here — if not for your sake, then my own."

Olivia's eyes were serious and she nodded slightly. "Thank you."

Grace reached for her friend's hand and they held on to each other the way they had countless times through the years.

"Where's Jack?" Grace asked after a moment, wondering why Olivia's husband wasn't with her.

"He went to get coffee," Olivia explained. Their eyes met and Olivia bit her lip. "The coffee's just an excuse. He's not dealing with this well."

"Hey, in case you haven't noticed, I'm not exactly a pillar of strength myself."

Olivia smiled.

"This is crazy, you know?"

"The cancer?" Olivia asked.

"Well, that, too. But I was talking about something else." Grace paused to take a long breath, trying not to cry. "You're the one with cancer. Jack and I love you and so do Will and Charlotte and your kids. We're all willing to do whatever we can to help you through this. Unfortunately, we're falling apart, at least Jack and I are." She laughed, but it sounded more like a sob. "The crazy part is that *you're* the one who's comforting *us.*"

Olivia dismissed her words. "Nonsense."

"Look at me, Liv," Grace said, dashing tears from her face. "I'm a mess. I want this to go away."

"You think I don't?" Olivia teased. "I never thought it would happen to me. There's no history of breast cancer in my family. I eat right, exercise, get my yearly checkup and yet here I am. This isn't fair, is it?"

"Cancer usually isn't."

They continued to hold hands, still clinging to each other when Jack walked in holding a foam coffee cup. He looked as if he hadn't slept all night and was as pale as Olivia.

An orderly stepped into the room directly behind him. "We're ready for you now, Ms. Griffin."

"I'm ready for you, too," Olivia murmured. Her gaze moved from Jack to Grace and she gave them both a reassuring smile. "I don't want either of you to worry."

"Right," Grace lied.

"It is what it is," Olivia said.

That sounded too much like resignation to Grace. This wasn't the time for acceptance;

it was a time to fight.

Jack walked by Olivia's side, holding her hand, with Grace trailing behind. "I love you," he whispered.

"I know," Olivia whispered back.

The orderly rolled the entire bed out of the room and down the hall to the surgery center.

"Everything's going to be just fine," Grace reiterated aloud because she needed someone to say it, even if that someone was her.

"Yes," Jack said.

By unspoken agreement they moved toward the surgical waiting area. Jack sat in one of the upholstered chairs, which were clustered into groups of four and six. He drank his coffee as he stared into the distance. Right now they were the only people there and had chosen the chairs closest to the door.

"Did Olivia wonder why I took so long getting the coffee?" he asked, looking in her direction for the first time.

"If so, she didn't say anything to me," Grace assured him, although it wasn't the complete truth.

A sigh rumbled through his chest. "I decided to go to the hospital chapel," he said, his voice low. "I've done a lot of things I'm not especially proud of through the years. I wasn't sure I had the right to ask God for anything."

"I know what you mean." Grace had plenty of lapses herself, plenty of misgivings about her own right to ask.

"I took my chances and asked God to be with Olivia," Jack said. He leaned forward and splayed his fingers through his hair. "I want to do every single thing I can for her."

"You already are." Falling in love with Jack Griffin, marrying him, had changed Olivia's life, bringing her more happiness than she'd ever expected. This man had stood by her and always would.

Grace glanced at her watch, astonished to realize it'd been less than ten minutes since the orderly had come for Olivia. Time seemed to creep by; Grace felt conscious of every second. When another five minutes had slowly passed, Olivia's daughter, Justine, and her mother, Charlotte, walked into the waiting area. Charlotte, as usual, toted an enormous knitting bag.

"Is Mom in surgery?" Justine asked.

Grace nodded.

Charlotte sat down next to Jack and automatically pulled out her knitting. "It calms my nerves," she announced to no one in particular. Her fingers worked at an impressive speed, and Grace tried to guess what the multicolored yarn would become.

"I wish I could've seen her before the surgery," Justine said, pacing restlessly.

"It's all right, dear," Charlotte said calmly. "Your mother knows how much you love her. She knows you would've been here if you could."

Justine continued pacing. "I used to think I didn't really need my mother." She sounded close to tears. "I was so confident that I knew what I was doing." She gave a little shake of her head. "Mom never liked me dating Warren Saget. She didn't trust him. I think in some ways I went on seeing him out of spite, just so I could prove how wrong she was."

"Justine," Charlotte said quietly, setting her knitting down in her lap. "All daughters go through that with their mothers. Olivia did with me, as well. It isn't until we're mothers ourselves that we understand."

Justine folded her arms. "She was right, you know — about Warren, about me loving Seth and . . . and everything else. I need her in my life. Leif needs his grandma and so does our new baby." She flattened her palm against her stomach.

Grace had recently learned that Justine was pregnant with her second child and knew Olivia was ecstatic.

They all grew quiet for several minutes. In the distance Grace saw workers setting up Christmas trees and hanging decorations. She'd forgotten that this was the first of December.

Charlotte was knitting steadily, her fingers slowing to a more relaxed pace. "I told Ben this morning that we should cancel the cruise. I want to be with my daughter."

"Grandma, Mom would be furious if you did that," Justine said. "You and Ben have been planning this vacation for months."

"Yes, I know, but . . ."

"Go, Charlotte," Jack told her. "Justine's right. Olivia would be upset with you for staying home."

"I realize that. Still . . ."

Charlotte didn't finish what she was about to say. Her eyes brightened and she smiled as Pastor Dave Flemming joined them in the waiting area.

"Oh, Pastor," Charlotte murmured in relief. "I'm so pleased you were able to make it."

"I'm glad to do it," Dave said, sitting next to Charlotte.

"Olivia's in surgery now," Jack explained. "Everything depends on whether the cancer has spread. We won't know exactly what we're dealing with until we know that."

"Whatever happens, I wanted to tell you I'm available anytime. All you need to do is call."

"Thank you," Justine said.

"Would you like me to pray with you now?"

"Please." It was Charlotte who answered. She set aside her knitting needles and bowed her head.

Justine sat beside Grace and closed her eyes. Seeing how shaken she was, Grace took the younger woman's hand in her own. Justine held on tightly.

Pastor Flemming's prayer was brief, but it brought Grace a sense of peace. She didn't know what the outcome would be, but for the first time she was ready to leave that with God.

When Pastor Flemming finished, the small group whispered, "Amen."

The prayer affected them all. Jack looked more composed and so did Justine. Charlotte picked up her knitting needles. Grace found herself breathing normally again.

They chatted amicably with Pastor Flemming for a few minutes until he said, "I've got a meeting, so I'd better leave now." He got to his feet.

Jack stood, too. "I can't thank you enough for stopping by."

The pastor nodded and patted Jack's shoulder affectionately. "We can't always know what the future holds, but we know Who holds the future."

"That we do," Charlotte concurred, her fingers busy.

"Remember," Pastor Flemming said, "if there's *anything* you need, day or night, call me."

"Thank you again," Grace told him, grasping his hand as they exchanged goodbyes. "Please pray for her."

"Of course," he promised. "Olivia is in my prayers, as she is in yours."

He left soon afterward and the small gathering continued their visit, newly energized or so it seemed to Grace. As they talked, Jack reached sheepishly inside his pocket for a hand-held gadget.

"What's that?" Justine asked, looking over his shoulder.

"Video poker," Jack mumbled. "Bob Beldon bought it for me. He said it'd help distract me while Olivia's in surgery."

Justine planted her hands on her hips and glared at him. "You mean to say my mother's fighting for her life in there and you're going to sit here playing *video games?*"

"Uh . . ." Jack hesitated, then nodded decisively. "That's exactly what I'm going to do."

"Oh." Justine paused. "Do you think they have those in the hospital gift shop?" she asked, breaking the tension.

Grace burst into laugher, and so did Justine and Jack. Charlotte looked up, but didn't seem to understand the joke. They were still chiding one another when the surgeon entered the waiting room.

Simultaneously they all stood, their laughter instantly cut short. Every eye was on Dr. McBride.

The silence seemed to pulse through the room.

"We were fortunate to have detected the tumor when we did," he began.

"Do you mean it hasn't metastasized?" Grace asked in a hushed voice.

"No, it doesn't look like it. The margins seem to be clear. We'll have to wait for the final diagnosis to be sure, but we sent tissue down to the lab during surgery, and according to the pathologist, there appears to be no lymph node involvement."

"Thank God," Jack whispered. And then, as if his knees had given out on him, he sank back into his chair.

Tears formed in Grace's eyes and she hugged Justine. Sniffling, Justine hugged her back.

"I knew it all along," Charlotte said righteously. She, too, sat down and once again her knitting needles started clicking. "I told you, didn't I?"

"Olivia's oncologist has scheduled a regimen of chemotherapy and radiation treatments for her," the surgeon said.

Grace hardly heard a word after that.

Her friend had always been a survivor. Cancer was just one more obstacle Olivia would surmount with her unyielding grit and determination.

EIGHT

Dave Flemming left the Bremerton Hospital and drove directly back to Cedar Cove for his meeting with Allan Harris. The attorney had asked to see him before Thanksgiving, but with his busy schedule and the holidays pressing in on him, this was the first opportunity Dave had found.

Harris's office was off Harbor Street. Dave parked as close as he could, which happened to be two blocks away. At some point over the weekend, Christmas decorations had begun to appear. Evergreen boughs stretched across Harbor from one lamppost to another, strung with twinkling white lights. Every year the holiday season seemed to sneak up on him. He didn't have time to consider what this added expense would do to the family's already tight budget. Frankly, he preferred not to think about it.

The wind off the cove was cold and Dave hunched his shoulders against it as he walked up the steep hill to the office. When he stepped inside, Geoff Duncan, Allan's legal assistant, glanced up.

"Hello, Geoff," Dave said, holding out his hand. He knew the young man casually. They'd talked once or twice after Martha Evans's death. Allan Harris had been in charge of Martha's legal affairs; he was a man the older woman had trusted.

"Pastor." Geoff got up, his own hand outstretched. A moment later, Dave turned to a row of pegs and hung up his coat.

Geoff was a likeable young man with a firm handshake. He dressed professionally in a suit and tie, and his demeanor was low-key, unthreatening. A good attribute for someone in a small-town legal practice, Dave thought.

"Unfortunately, Mr. Harris phoned a few minutes ago and is tied up in a meeting," Geoff said. "He didn't think he'd be more than fifteen minutes. Would it be possible for you to wait?"

"Sure, no problem."

"Wonderful." Geoff rubbed his palms together. "Can I get you anything? Coffee, tea, water?"

"No, no, I'm fine. Thanks, anyway." Dave strode over to the small waiting area and sat down. No one else was in the office. He rested his ankle on the opposite knee and reached for a three-month-old issue of *Sports Illustrated.*

"Actually," Geoff said, following him. "I was hoping for a chance to talk to you."

"Sure." Dave closed the magazine. "How can I help you?"

"I don't know if Allan mentioned it or not, but I've recently become engaged." The young man's lips tilted in a pleased smile.

"Congratulations!"

"Thank you." Geoff's smile grew wider. "I feel like the luckiest man alive because Lori Bellamy's agreed to marry me."

The Bellamys were major landowners on Bainbridge Island. Dave had heard the name any number of times through the years because of the family's many philanthropic projects. If he remembered correctly, the Bellamys owned a theater and various prime pieces of waterfront in the downtown area of Winslow.

"When's the wedding?"

"June," Geoff said.

"Perfect month for a wedding."

"Yes." Geoff lowered himself into the chair next to Dave. "Lori said something about premarital classes. What's your feeling about those?"

"I highly recommend them."

"I don't know." Geoff didn't sound convinced. "She seems to think they're important, but . . ."

Dave tried to reassure the young man. "They help alleviate problems later on, Geoff," he went on to explain. "It's crucial for a young couple to establish the lines of communication *before* they say their vows."

Geoff shifted a bit and looked away. "Are these classes expensive?"

That was a tricky question. Dave didn't charge anyone in his congregation for counseling, whether individual or in a class; however, he couldn't speak for other churches. "I don't believe they are."

"Lori's family are willing to pay for them — along with everything else." This last part was said with some bitterness. "I don't mind them picking up the cost of the wedding — that's traditional — but for the rest, I believe Lori and I should pay."

Dave approved of his attitude. He speculated that while Geoff made a decent wage as a legal assistant, he couldn't handle an extravagant lifestyle. But Dave liked the young man's sense of honor, his determination to pay his own expenses.

"If you want, I could set you up with a couple of sessions," he offered. "You and Lori can meet with me and we'll see how it goes."

"What would that cost?"

"Nothing." Dave shook his head. "You can make a donation to the church later if you decide it was worth your time."

Geoff looked shocked. "Really?"

"Of course. I want you to start your marriage on the right foot." He paused, thinking a moment. "It'll probably be more convenient for you to do the sessions in Cedar Cove, anyway, rather than on Bainbridge Island, since you're working here. What about Lori? Does she work in the area?"

"She has a part-time job at a dress shop in Silverdale. This should be good for both of us," Geoff said. "I'll talk to Lori and get back to you."

"You do that."

Geoff returned to his desk, and Dave picked up the magazine again. He hadn't read more than a few paragraphs of an article about steroid use in professional sports before the front door opened and Allan Harris exploded into the room. He was a burly, energetic man.

"Dave, Dave," he muttered, "sorry to keep you waiting."

Dave placed the magazine on the nearby table and stood. "No problem."

Allan shrugged out of his wool overcoat and hung it on the peg next to Dave's. "Did

Geoff offer you coffee?"

"Yes. I'm full up, thanks."

Allan lifted the glass coffeepot, which sat in an alcove next to his office, and poured himself a cup. "It's colder outside than a witch's —" He stopped abruptly. "Beg your pardon, Pastor."

Dave didn't bother hiding his amusement. People seemed to assume he'd never heard or uttered a swear-word in his life, when in fact, he was as fallible and as prone to weakness as anyone else.

Perhaps even more so, he mused, cringing at the thought. He hated what was happening between him and Emily but seemed unable to tell her the truth. After Christmas, he'd fess up. That was a promise he fully intended to keep.

Carefully holding his mug, Allan led the way into his office. He motioned to the visitor's chair across from his desk, then claimed his own.

"I appreciate that you're willing to meet with me," Allan said, setting his mug on a coaster amid the clutter of papers and books.

"I'll admit I'm curious as to why." Dave guessed this had something to do with Martha Evans. The elderly woman had died in September. During her last year, Dave had made a point of visiting her as often as

117

he could. In many ways, she reminded him of his own grandmother with her indomitable spirit and sharp wit. She kept a Bible close at hand and had memorized large sections of Scripture.

"I've been talking to the heirs," Allan said.

"Yes?" Dave couldn't help noticing that the attorney suddenly seemed agitated, rolling a pen between his open hands.

Allan stared hard at him. "Several pieces of Martha's jewelry are missing."

"I know." But Dave didn't understand what that had to do with him. He'd already spoken to Sheriff Davis and told him everything he knew about the missing jewelry, which was next to nothing.

"Would you mind going over the details of the morning you discovered her body?"

"Of course not." Dave hesitated. He'd described it to the sheriff more than once, and had the creeping sensation that Allan was viewing him as a suspect. That unnerved him. "I stopped by two or three times a week to visit," he began.

Allan nodded, encouraging him to continue.

"That particular day was a Saturday."

"It was," Allan concurred.

"She didn't respond to the doorbell. Martha no longer left the house for anything other than doctors' appointments. When she didn't answer, I was afraid something might be wrong."

Allan dropped the pen and leaned forward. "Did you phone 911?"

The question surprised him. "Not right away. I didn't want to do that until I was sure . . ."

"So you went directly into the house?"

"Well, yes. I knew where Martha hid the spare key, so I unlocked the front door and let myself in." He paused. "I'd done this before," he added, "since Martha always kept the door locked. It saved her the effort of getting up."

"She was dead when you went in?"

"Yes. According to the coroner's report, she died peacefully sometime during the night. When I first saw her, I actually thought she was still asleep." Although he should've been emotionally prepared, Dave had felt a deep sense of loss at the old woman's death. She'd become his friend, and his confidante.

"How long after you discovered her body did you contact the authorities?" Allan asked next.

This was beginning to sound as if Allan was writing a police report. Dave had answered these same questions the day Martha died, when Sheriff Davis interviewed him, and again later.

"I walked into the bedroom, checked for a pulse and got out my cell."

"You didn't use her phone?"

"No . . ."

"I see." Allan made a notation on his pad. "Is there a problem?"

"No, not at all," Allan assured him. "How long before the paramedics arrived?"

Dave needed to think about that. "Not long. Between five and ten minutes."

Allan Harris nodded. "Where did you wait for them? Inside the house or outside?"

"Inside." Actually, he'd knelt at Martha's bedside and prayed. He met the attorney's gaze. "Is there a specific reason you're asking me these questions?"

"Like I explained —" Allan cleared his throat "— Martha's daughters came by to tell me that several pieces of their mother's jewelry are missing. They've already spoken to the sheriff and are pretty upset. Apparently Martha kept a number of valuable pieces in the house."

"You don't seriously think I'd steal from Martha, do you?" Anger rose to the surface and he struggled to disguise how insulted he was by such an accusation. Getting upset might imply guilt, however, so he held on to his temper.

"No one's saying anything."

"I didn't even know Martha had a lot of expensive jewelry." It wasn't as if he'd searched the old woman's cupboards or dresser drawers.

"I believe you," Allan said, "but the family insists everything was there on Friday evening, when they visited her."

"If they were so concerned about the jewelry, why didn't they put it in a safer place?"

Allan shrugged. "I asked them the same question. I gather they weren't comfortable suggesting it to their mother."

Dave could understand that. Once Martha made a decision she wouldn't budge. If she felt her jewelry was perfectly safe at the house, then little would persuade her otherwise.

"None of it was locked up?" Dave asked. He knew Martha kept at least some of her jewels hidden in the freezer; she'd told him so. But he'd certainly never looked.

"Apparently not," Allan said. "She liked things done her own way."

Dave was well aware of that, too. "I'm sorry I can't help you any more. Now, if you'll excuse me . . ." He refused to answer anything else. He didn't like Allan's implications or the tone of his questions.

Geoff was in the hallway outside the office when Dave opened the door. He seemed startled to see Dave and moved quickly out of his way.

"I'll call you soon," Geoff told him. "About those marriage counseling sessions," he added.

Dave responded with a nod, happy to be about his business. Because he was irritated and needed to calm down, he pulled out his cell and called home. Emily answered almost right away.

"How's your Monday going?" he asked.

"Okay." She sounded depressed.

"Just okay?"

"Yeah. What about you?"

"It's Monday, all right."

"How about lunch?" she said. "We could meet at the Pot Belly Deli or the Wok and Roll."

Both were favorites of his but Dave automatically declined. "Not today."

"Fine." Her voice was reluctant; she wasn't pleased and let him know it.

Dave hated disappointing her. "Maybe later in the week."

She hesitated, then asked, "Where've you been all morning? You left the house with barely a word."

"Sorry, sweetheart, I had to get to the hospital. Olivia Griffin was going in for cancer surgery. Her family's pretty shaken up, and I felt I should stop by. The morning got away from me because I had to meet with Allan Harris right afterward."

"Allan Harris?"

"Martha's attorney. I thought —" He paused, feeling stupid now and annoyed with himself. "I thought she might've left something to the church in her will and that was the reason Allan wanted to chat."

"She didn't?"

"No . . . not that I'm aware. Of course, I would never have suggested it to her, but I had the idea in the back of my mind." His presumption embarrassed him, and he felt guilty for having entertained the notion.

"So what did he want?"

Dave debated how much to tell his wife. He didn't want her to worry about any of this. "He had a few questions for me."

"Such as?"

"It was nothing important," he said dismissively, unwilling to lie.

"You're sure?" she pressed.

"Absolutely." Rather than launch into a lengthy discussion, Dave made an excuse and got off the phone. He had somewhere else he needed to be — a place he didn't want Emily to know about.

NINE

Moving back to Cedar Cove was a mixed blessing, Faith Beckwith decided as she prepared for her first day of work. The Cedar Cove medical clinic had advertised for a part-time nurse and she'd been hired right away. Her entire life had changed in the blink of an eye — or so it felt. It'd all begun with the sale of her home in south Seattle.

A widow for three years, Faith had rattled around the big house in the Seattle neighborhood where she and Carl had raised their family. It really was time to downsize, but she'd assumed that because of market conditions the sale would take months. Instead, the first family who'd stepped over the threshold had made a full-price offer with the stipulation that she be completely out of the house by Thanksgiving. If not for the help of her two children, Scott and Jay Lynn, Faith would never have been able to make the transition to Cedar Cove so quickly.

Thinking about the last few weeks — and the way her whole life had changed — gave her a breathless feeling.

Faith would've preferred to start her new job after January first, but it became apparent that if she didn't accept the position now, the clinic would hire someone else. Faith chose to start work.

With her children's assistance, she'd unpacked nearly forty years of her life in a rental house on Rosewood Lane, one that belonged to her high school friend, Grace Sherman. Except, as Troy had reminded her, it was Grace Harding now.

While Faith enjoyed living near her grandchildren, it also meant she was in close proximity to Sheriff Troy Davis. Her encounter with him Thanksgiving week had upset her. Living in a town the size of Cedar Cove made such meetings inevitable, she supposed. Still, she didn't expect to see Troy very often — especially if she was careful and Faith fully intended to be. She hoped to avoid any and all contact with Sheriff Davis.

The man had broken her heart, not once but twice. Okay, to be fair, her mother was responsible for the circumstances that had led to their breakup the first time. They'd been young; nevertheless, she still felt shocked that Troy could ever have believed she'd casually dump him for someone else after he went into the service. In retrospect, she wondered if he'd been so willing to accept her mother's lie because he was looking for an excuse to break off their relationship. Her mother had made it easy.

The second time she'd mailed him a sympathy card after hearing about the death of his wife, and they'd reconnected. Just when she'd made a commitment to him, to their relationship, he'd ended it. Well, enough was enough.

None of that made any difference now, she reasoned, annoyed that she was thinking about Troy at all.

Faith parked in the clinic lot, collected her purse and her lunch and walked inside, feeling excited — and a little nervous — about her first day. She was assigned to Dr. Chad Timmons, whom she'd liked on sight. He was certainly attractive, and she imagined he'd broken more than one heart.

Thinking about broken hearts brought her right back to the sheriff. Faith had to forcefully stomp on *that* thought. It might take some doing, but she was going to put him completely out of her life.

The morning went smoothly, and Faith discovered that she fit in well with the rest of the staff. Tuesdays and Wednesdays were apparently the least busy at the clinic, which was why she was scheduled for those two days this month. After the first of the year, she'd be working Monday, Thursday and Friday.

Her morning consisted of routine cases, innoculations and paperwork. She had one last patient to see before lunch — a twenty-nine-year-old woman by the name of Megan Bloomquist. Apparently Megan was distraught because she thought she might be pregnant. It seemed to be a case more appropriate for Pregnancy Crisis than the medical clinic.

"Hello," Faith said, opening the exam room door. "I'm Faith Beckwith."

"Hello." The young woman sat in the chair with her ankles crossed. Her red-rimmed eyes were fearful. "You're not the doctor, are you?"

"I'm Dr. Timmons's nurse."

The young woman nodded, clenching and unclenching her hands.

"I'm here to take your blood pressure and your temperature and find out how Dr. Timmons can help you," Faith explained. She pressed the thermometer lightly against Megan's forehead. Her temperature registered and Faith noted it on the medical chart — normal.

Megan sniffled. "I think I'm pregnant and I . . . don't know what to do."

Faith noticed the wedding ring on her finger. "You don't want the baby?"

"I do . . ." She covered her face with both hands and started to sob. After a moment she regained some control of her emotions. "Craig and I want children, but . . . but I had a miscarriage three months ago. I've only had one period since then." She took out a small day planner to check the dates.

Faith felt a sinking feeling in the pit of her stomach as she noted the details of Megan's last period. Troy's daughter was named Megan and she'd recently miscarried. Could it be? How was it that her very first day on the job, Faith would run into Troy's daughter? She struggled to hide her dismay.

"I took a home pregnancy test and it was positive." Slowly Megan straightened. "But I just need to be sure, and my own doctor's booked solid."

Faith didn't bother to point out that home tests were pretty reliable these days. She could understand Megan's uncertainty after having a miscarriage.

She was startled to hear Megan say, "Craig and I decided that it might not be a good idea for me to get pregnant again."

"Ever?" That seemed a rather drastic decision.

"Well, certainly not this soon," Megan told her. "We . . . we were hoping for some definitive word on my health."

"In what way?"

Megan lowered her head. "I might have MS. It's in the family and because there might be a genetic link . . ."

This could only be Troy's daughter. Looking away, Faith reached for the blood pressure cuff. "There are tests you can have that will reassure you," she said briskly.

"Oh, I've had those tests."

Faith waited.

Megan's shoulders drooped. "The MRI was inconclusive. You see, my mother was diagnosed with it when I was young, and it was after she'd miscarried several times. When I lost my pregnancy it occurred to me that it might be for the same reason."

Faith checked Megan's blood pressure and wrote it down. Again, normal. After Troy had used his daughter as an excuse to end the relationship, Faith had done a bit of research on MS, looking at reputable Internet sites and talking to a few doctors she knew.

"It's funny you should mention MS, because I recently read an article about the latest findings and heredity as a potential cause." Faith did her best to sound professional.

"You did?" Megan's eyes widened with interest.

"The article's about a University of Washington study. It states that the children of people with MS have a one percent chance of inheriting it."

"Only one percent?"

"The Mayo Clinic site says the chances are four to five percent. Either way, those odds are in your favor."

The young woman stared at her intently.

"I don't think you should be this concerned, Megan. Your mother would want you to live your life without this worry hanging over your head." She gave the girl's arm a squeeze.

Fresh tears welled in Megan's eyes. "That's really wonderful news."

"There could be any number of reasons you miscarried your first pregnancy. It doesn't mean it'll happen again."

"Craig and I were devastated." She blinked back tears. "My father, too . . ."

"It's never easy to lose a child," Faith said gently. "I had a miscarriage myself. That was many years ago, of course. Both my children are grown and married with children of their own. Yet even now I sometimes wonder about that lost baby."

"Losing the pregnancy came so soon after my mother's death," Megan whispered brokenly.

"I'm sorry." Faith took hold of Megan's hand, and the young woman gripped her fingers painfully hard.

Apparently unable to speak, Megan hiccupped a laugh. "That pregnancy wasn't planned, either. You'd think Craig and I would know how babies are made. I swear we do . . . It's just that . . . well, we didn't use the protection we should have."

"Let's wait and make absolutely sure you *are* pregnant, okay?"

"Okay. I guess I have to believe that whatever happens, God doesn't make mistakes."

"Dr. Timmons will be able to tell if you're pregnant, and we'll go from there."

"Okay." Megan's voice was a little stronger now.

"What you need," Faith said next, "is something to help you relax." She grinned. "And I don't mean drugs. Do you have any hobbies?"

"I do some scrapbooking, but I've been meaning to take up knitting. It's so popular now and if I really am pregnant, I'd like to knit a blanket for the baby — if I can hold on to this pregnancy."

"Think positive."

"I'm trying."

"Knitting isn't hard to learn," Faith said encouragingly.

"A friend showed me the basic stitches last year. I'm sure I won't have any problem picking it up again, but I don't remember how to cast on."

"There's nothing to it."

"Do you knit?"

Faith nodded. Her last project had been socks for Troy Davis. "I'll leave you now," she said, lightly touching Megan's arm. "Dr. Timmons will be in to see you shortly."

"Thank you. You've been very kind."

Faith managed a smile before she left the room, a smile that slipped as soon as she'd closed the door. What were the odds of this happening? Faith would never have thought that eliminating Troy Davis from her heart and her life would be this difficult.

Her lunch break was an hour long. Faith had brought a sandwich from home and an apple. When she'd eaten, she still had ample time to run a few errands, so she headed for The Quilted Giraffe, the local fabric store. Her granddaughter wanted Faith to sew her a special dress for the Christmas Eve church service.

Faith had chosen her fabric — a green velvet Kaitlyn would love — when Megan Bloomquist approached her.

"Hello, again," the young woman said, looking far more peaceful now than she had earlier.

Faith knew from the notation Dr. Timmons had made in her chart that Megan was indeed pregnant. That should make Troy happy.

She was doing it again. This constant thinking about Troy had to stop!

"Hello, Megan," she said cordially, if a bit stiffly.

"It's all right that I talk to you, isn't it? I mean, I don't want to go against medical protocol."

"No, it's fine. Don't worry." Faith felt that her response might have been a bit cool.

"Did you hear that I'm definitely pregnant?"

"I did. Congratulations."

"Thank you." The young woman's happiness appeared genuine. "You were wonderful. Thank you for helping me gain some perspective on this."

"Megan, really, I didn't do anything."

"But you did," she insisted. "I was an emotional wreck when I walked into the clinic and after speaking to you I felt a thousand times better."

"I'm glad I could help." Faith pulled the bolt of fabric off the shelf and carried it to a clerk to be measured and cut.

"I'm taking your advice," Megan said, following her. "Look." She lifted a small wire basket draped over her arm. Inside were knitting needles, several skeins of a variegated yarn in pastel colors and a pattern book that included a selection of baby blankets.

"You'll find that nothing calms you the way knitting does. In fact, there are studies that prove it."

Megan smiled. "You like reading studies, don't you?"

Faith smiled back. "I guess I do."

"The lady at the counter said she'd teach me how to cast on," Megan said, "but she's been busy ever since so I've been waiting around until she's free."

"Here." Faith set her fabric on the cutting table. "I can show you."

"Oh, thank you!"

Faith removed the needles from their packaging and pulled the yarn free from one of the skeins. In a few minutes, Megan had caught on.

While the woman behind the counter measured and cut the green velvet, Faith reviewed the pattern instructions with Megan to be sure she understood how to get started.

"I can't thank you enough," Megan said when she'd finished.

With their purchases in hand, Faith and Megan walked to the front door together.

"I'd better get back to work," Faith told the younger woman.

"Me, too. I work at the frame shop on Harbor. If you ever need anything framed, please let me know."

"I will, thank you." Faith almost mentioned that her son, Scottie, had recently had something framed at that very shop. But it was best for her emotional health not to encourage a relationship with Troy's daughter, so she walked away after a simple goodbye.

TEN

Teri Polgar hadn't heard from her sister in well over a week. A year ago that wouldn't have been unusual. They rarely saw each other regularly until last summer, when things between them had started to improve. They'd had their share of differences; still did. But despite their difficult history, family was important to Teri. She and Johnny, her younger brother, were close. More and more, Teri found reasons to keep in touch with Christie, too.

A week without any form of communication from Christie wasn't typical these days. What bothered her more was that Christie hadn't returned any of her phone calls. Teri knew her sister wasn't shy about sharing her feelings. If Teri had done something to upset her, Christie would've let her know. All Teri could come up with was Christie's ongoing determination to avoid James.

"Bobby, I'm going shopping." She didn't

say for what. Bobby didn't concern himself with budgets. He had enough money for all their wants and needs; that was the only thing that mattered on the financial front. His life revolved around chess — and her. He was a master chess player, one of the world's best. He'd always watched over her with vigilance, and now that she was pregnant, Bobby doted on her even more than usual.

He barely glanced up from the computer screen. "I'll call James."

"Bobby, no. I can drive to Wal-Mart on my own."

The look he cast her was filled with doubt and worry.

She sighed. "Oh, all right." It was easier to acquiesce than to argue. Bobby was far too protective, but how could she complain when he loved her so much? Ridiculous though it was to have a driver when she'd been driving all by herself since she was sixteen years old, she knew it set Bobby's mind at rest.

Within five minutes James, who lived on the property, had the car parked in front of the house, waiting for Teri. He stood by the passenger door formally dressed in his black suit and billed cap.

When Teri was first married to Bobby, she

felt embarrassed to have a car and driver, especially in a town the size of Cedar Cove. However, she'd grown accustomed to it, and apparently so had everyone else. No one commented on it — not to her, anyway.

As she approached the vehicle, James held the passenger door open.

"Thank you, James," she said as he helped her inside.

He stepped around the vehicle and climbed into the driver's seat. "Where to, Miss Teri?"

No matter how many times she asked him to drop the *Miss,* which made her sound like a preschool teacher, James persisted. After all these months she'd finally given up.

"I'd like to go to Wal-Mart, James."

His back stiffened ever so slightly. "Wal-Mart, Miss?"

"You heard me." Teri couldn't quite restrain a smile.

James knew very well that Christie was currently employed as a cashier at the local Wal-Mart.

"Right away, miss."

Teri relaxed in the luxurious leather seat as she listened to the soothing music coming from the speakers. "What are you playing, James?" she asked.

"Vivaldi, miss. *The Four Seasons.*"

She nodded. "I like it."

James preferred classical and used his own CDs. Early on, she'd requested he find a country-western radio station instead, and to his credit, he'd done so. Only when she saw him insert cotton balls in his ears did she stop requesting anything other than the classical music he chose. She'd come to see beauty in it and not boredom.

She was fond of James, more than fond; she now considered him a friend, although she let him impose the limits on their friendship. She also felt he was perfect for her sister.

The problem was that Christie was so closemouthed about the relationship. James was even worse. The two of them were equally adept at keeping secrets.

When they pulled into the Wal-Mart lot, she saw dozens of cars circling, searching for a parking space. Christmas shoppers were out in full force, although it was a midweek afternoon and still early in the month.

"James, do you have plans for Christmas?" Teri asked curiously. She knew so little about him.

"Plans? No, Miss Teri."

"You won't be traveling anywhere to visit family or friends?"

"No, miss."

She forged ahead. "I hope you'll join Bobby and me, then."

He hesitated.

"No need for a response just yet," she assured him. "The invitation is open."

"Thank you, miss."

He parked by the front entrance, leaped out and came around to open her door.

"Give me an hour, James."

"Yes, Miss Teri."

She walked into the store, receiving curious looks and hearing a few veiled whispers. Okay, so maybe not everyone in town was accustomed to seeing her with a driver.

Checking the long row of cashiers, Teri saw Christie in Lane Ten. Without looking, she grabbed a handful of sale items, had a word with the manager and then stood in her sister's line.

She waited patiently for her turn, then set the Thanksgiving decorations she'd scooped up on the counter.

"Merry Christmas," Christie said automatically before she looked up and saw it was Teri. "What are you doing here?" she demanded in a fierce whisper.

"You didn't return any of my phone calls," Teri whispered back. "I didn't know if you were alive or dead."

"Alive. I've been working a lot of extra

hours. In case you hadn't noticed, this is the Christmas season."

"I noticed."

Christie's supervisor approached the register and placed a Closed sign behind Teri. "Lane Three is opening up," she told the other customers. "Christie, take your lunch break now."

"So soon?" Christie asked. "Shouldn't Cookie go first?"

"No, she shouldn't," Teri inserted. "I asked your supervisor to give you your break so you and I could talk."

"Teri!"

"What was I supposed to do?"

"Fine. I should've known you wouldn't leave well enough alone." Christie slapped the sales items in a white plastic bag and handed it to Teri, then collected payment. When she'd finished, Christie checked her watch. "This isn't going to take long, is it?"

"That depends on you," Teri responded.

They decided to eat at the fast-food place near the store. Once they'd ordered, they were fortunate enough to find a vacant table, although the place was busy. Christie opened her container of chicken nuggets and the small peel-away top on the dipping sauce. Teri watched her sister with a look of envy.

Teri was being careful about her weight because of the pregnancy, so she'd ordered a Caesar salad. Her weight gain at her last doctor's appointment had been substantial. Okay, her diet hadn't been ideal. She cheated a bit now and then. Nevertheless, she didn't deserve to gain seven pounds in a single month. She'd protested loudly, but her obstetrician had dismissed her cries that the scale had been tampered with. Reluctantly Teri tore open the low-fat dressing packet and poured it over the romaine lettuce.

"I guess this has to do with James," Christie said with the air of someone resigned to an unpleasant conversation.

"Well, actually . . ."

"He told you, didn't he?" Her sister bit savagely into a nugget.

Something had obviously happened between her sister and James, during their encounter last week, and Christie assumed Teri knew all about it. James, of course, hadn't said a word.

"Well . . ."

"First," Christie stated emphatically, leaning forward. "I *wasn't* drunk."

"Okay," Teri murmured, wondering how to ferret out information without letting on that she had no idea what Christie was talking about.

"He's got to stop doing this."

"I agree," Teri said firmly. "This can't continue."

Christie looked more than a little surprised to find Teri taking her side. "It's embarrassing, you know."

"Absolutely."

Christie leaned even closer and lowered her voice. "When James parks the limousine at The Pink Poodle, everyone stares out the window and asks questions. It's only a matter of time before someone figures out he's there because of me."

This was beginning to make sense. "You mean he never goes inside?"

"Never." As if her appetite had completely abandoned her, Christie pushed away the remaining chicken nuggets. "You wouldn't believe the way Larry and the others were gawking."

"I can imagine."

"Eventually James moved around to the side of the building where I'd parked my car."

The scene was taking shape in Teri's mind. "So, when you came out, he figured you'd had too much to drink."

"But he was wrong," Christie insisted. "Wrong, wrong, wrong."

Teri nodded sagely.

"Besides, I thought he'd left. One of the guys said he saw the car drive away. How was I supposed to know he'd only moved it?" Christie reached for her napkin and began to shred it. "If waiting for me wasn't bad enough, he followed me home."

"Did anyone from The Pink Poodle see?"

Christie shrugged. "I don't know. I hope not." She gazed at the strips of paper, then wadded them up. "Tell him something for me, will you?"

"Ah . . . I, uh . . ." Teri would rather not serve as a messenger between them, although she was certainly eager to keep track of what was going on.

Before she could argue, Christie raised her hand. "All you have to do is tell James I don't want to see him again."

"You're sure about that?"

Her sister's hesitation was brief. "Positive," she muttered. "I don't like him," she continued as though convincing herself. "He's a stuffed shirt . . . . All that formality drives me insane."

Teri frowned. That wasn't the impression *she* had.

"Don't look at me like that," Christie said.

"Look at you how?"

"Like . . . like you don't believe me."

She gestured vaguely. "I can't help remem-

144

bering how worried you were when we found out James had been kidnapped."

Christie swallowed and glanced away. When she did speak, her voice was almost a whisper. "He might be stuffy, but he's a real gentleman, you know?"

"Yes," Teri agreed softly. She remembered her own reaction to James at their first meeting. So tall and frightfully thin, so formal and reserved. In the beginning his manner had irritated her until she realized what a good friend he was to her husband. He cared for Bobby, looked after him and saw that her absentminded husband reached his appointments on time. Bobby needed James, relied on him. And James had been a friend to her, too. Not only that, his actions during the kidnapping were nothing short of heroic, as Rachel could attest.

"Just a minute," Teri said. "I want to make sure I understand what you're saying here. Because — as we've discussed before — you don't seem to like men who treat you with respect."

"I . . ." Christie leaned away from the table, apparently studying something on the floor. She'd taken Teri's napkin and begun to shred it, too. "I don't know how to relate to a man who doesn't abuse me in one way or another," she said bluntly.

"Listen, Christie . . ."

"Men have used me my entire life. You'd think I'd hate them all by now." For a moment she looked as if she might dissolve into tears. "I meet one of these losers and I immediately want to fix his life and make everything right. I always figure that once I do, he'll love me and cherish me forever." She gave Teri a watery smile. "How come I can see the pattern but I can't break it?"

"Guess what, Christie, we share more than the same genes."

"But you have Bobby and he loves you and —"

"Talk about déjà vu." Sighing, Teri placed both hands on her stomach. "I tried to send Bobby away. I felt the same things you do. I didn't want him to love me, and I did everything I could to keep him out of my life."

Christie shook her head. "You're just saying that because you think it'll make me feel better. You've always made good decisions. You have a career and friends and . . . now you have Bobby and a real family." Her gaze fell to Teri's stomach and her eyes softened with longing.

"And you're afraid you'll be stuck with losers for the rest of your life."

Her sister didn't respond.

"So you reject any decent guy who comes around."

Teri didn't mean to sound sarcastic. "Listen, Christie, you say you want to break the pattern. James is your chance to do it."

Christie still didn't speak.

"He's attracted to you."

Her sister shook her head again. "No, he isn't. Otherwise —"

"Otherwise he wouldn't have driven down to The Pink Poodle and waited outside for you," Teri said, cutting her off. "Why else would James do that?"

Christie gave an unenthusiastic shrug.

"He wants to talk to you," Teri explained as if speaking to a third-grader. "*That's* why he did it."

Gathering up the pieces of her second shredded napkin, Christie swallowed several times. "It's too late."

"I doubt that."

Her sister's eyes were suddenly hopeful.

"I can try to help," Teri said. "If you want, I'll arrange an opportunity for the two of you to meet."

"How?"

"Dinner," she suggested. "Bobby and I can invite you both to dinner."

Christie instantly dismissed the idea. "That would be awkward for everyone."

True, Teri thought, but that way she'd have a close-up view of the proceedings. However, discretion won out over curiosity. "Okay, then, see James on your own," she said mildly.

Christie seemed to be considering that. "You really think I should?" she finally asked.

"I do." Teri offered her a smile of encouragement. She wanted Christie to experience the same happiness she'd found with Bobby. "Will you do it?" she prodded.

Christie nodded, tentatively at first, then more vigorously. Teri was relieved to see the light of anticipation back in her sister's eyes.

ELEVEN

Olivia sipped her tea and enjoyed the sheer luxury of being home in the middle of a workweek. She'd taken a medical leave of absence from the courthouse, and this was the longest she'd been at home since the children were born. Under normal circumstances, she'd be presiding over her courtroom right now, hearing cases, making judgments that would affect the lives of people in her community. Olivia took her job as a family court judge seriously, which was probably the reason some of her decisions had been controversial.

Once she'd denied a divorce on a technicality when it was obvious to her, but seemingly to no one else, that the young couple standing before her was still in love. She'd followed her heart and her instincts. Same with a joint custody situation in which she'd ruled that the kids would stay in the house, with the parents moving back and forth.

Olivia returned her teacup to the saucer and stretched out her legs so they rested on the footstool. She admired her fuzzy new slippers, a gift from Grace. Her dressing gown was from Grace, as well. The sun shone warmly into the room and, childish as it sounded, she felt as if it were shining just for her.

"You need anything else?" Jack called from the kitchen. He was home on his lunch break in order to coax her to eat. Her appetite was practically nonexistent.

Olivia sipped a little more of her tea. "I'm good, thanks."

"How about some Christmas cookies?" The day before, Justine had brought over a batch of Charlotte's special Russian Tea Cookies. Her Christmas baking was a family tradition.

"No, thanks." The tea had been soothing, but the thought of food held no appeal. She knew this was only going to get worse once she started chemo in early January. Jack was worried about her lack of appetite and seemed determined to keep her from losing any more weight than she already had.

"I picked up those iced raisin cookies you like at the grocery store," he called back, obviously trying to tempt her.

"Not interested, but thanks." She wasn't

unappreciative, but she didn't know how she'd manage a lunch of soup, let alone adding cookies.

Jack stuck his head out of the kitchen. A smudge of powdered sugar ringed his lips as he frowned at her in consternation.

"Jack," she protested, struggling not to laugh. "Cookies aren't on your diet."

"Who told you I ate those cookies?" His gaze narrowed.

"Come here and I'll show you," she teased, motioning him forward.

He walked in and Olivia held her arms open, inviting him into her embrace. When he bent forward, she sat up and tapped his lips, murmuring "sugar," then kissed him.

When the kiss ended, Jack eased away. "Yes, I'm your sugar," he said and she laughed. With a deep sigh, he looked at her. "That was nice." He cleared his throat. "In fact, it was *very* nice . . ."

"I liked it too," she told him softly. "Do I have powdered sugar on my lips now?" she asked with a smile.

"No." He gave a guilty start. "I only ate one."

"One?" Olivia had tasted those cookies from the time she was a youngster and eating just one would've been impossible. Besides, her husband had a notorious sweet tooth.

"One," he said again, then glanced at his watch. "In the last ten minutes, I only had one."

Olivia smiled again. No point getting upset. After Jack's heart attack, she'd watched his diet religiously although she tried to resist nagging. Following her divorce it had taken her nearly twenty years to fall in love again and she was determined not to lose Jack any earlier than she had to.

"I'm being careful," he promised, almost as if he was reading her thoughts. "I exercised this morning, and I had oatmeal for breakfast."

"Good boy."

He rolled his eyes. "The person who needs to eat these sweets is you." He sat on the footstool and gazed at her, worry tightening his expression. Then he took both her hands in his own. "Will you try to eat something?"

She sighed.

"Please," he coaxed.

"I'll have soup." Because she loved him, Olivia was willing to make the effort, although even the thought of soup or cookies — or anything else — made her feel queasy.

"Tomato?"

"Vegetable beef."

"I'll stay until you're finished," Jack said.

"Honey . . ."

"Don't you mean *sugar?*" he asked, grinning. "Anyway, no objections allowed."

"Yes, oh, great and mighty one." It was important to him to prove that he was capable of handling this stress without turning to alcohol. Sobriety was hard-won for Jack. She knew he'd faltered when she was diagnosed with breast cancer. She'd been badly thrown herself. Now, on the other side of surgery, she was confident they'd both survive; she thanked God for that.

While Jack prepared her luncheon tray, Olivia closed her eyes, lulled by the warm sunshine. It seemed only seconds later that he returned, carrying a tray with a steaming bowl of soup, two cookies and a small vase with a single rose. He'd even taken the time to fold a linen napkin.

"Have you been watching the Home Decorating channel again?" she teased.

"I thought the rose would brighten your day." He reached for her hand, raised it to his lips and kissed her knuckles. "Now, eat."

"If you insist."

"I do." He sat next to her until she'd finished the entire bowl of soup and even nibbled at one of the cookies.

"Satisfied?" she asked. She simply couldn't eat another bite.

"Yes." He brought the tray to the kitchen and when he came back, he'd put on his long raincoat, although he seemed reluctant to leave her. "I'll get home as soon as I can."

"Jack, I'm fine."

"Grace is coming over?"

Olivia nodded. "She should be here in an hour or two. And Pastor Flemming said he'd drop by later this afternoon."

"Good."

Between Jack, her daughter, her mother, Grace and her brother, Will, she was hardly ever alone. Olivia didn't mind being by herself, but she understood that this was their way of showing how much they loved her.

A few minutes later, Jack left for the newspaper office, and Olivia settled down with a new women's fiction title Grace had recommended. The doorbell chimed. When she opened the front door, she was delighted to see Pastor Flemming.

"I hope I didn't come at a bad time," he said.

"Not at all," Olivia told him as they walked into the living room.

"I realize I told you I'd come around four when I talked to you on the phone yesterday, but I had a free hour and thought I'd visit now, if that's convenient."

"It's fine." Olivia had hoped to take a nap

before Grace arrived, but she could go without one. Napping in the middle of the day could easily become addictive, and she couldn't allow that. As she'd joked to her husband, it wouldn't look good if she started yawning in court.

"Please sit down." Olivia gestured toward the chair across from her own.

"How are you feeling?" Dave asked.

"Better, thanks."

"I'm glad to hear that." He reached for his Bible and Olivia saw his wristwatch fall to the carpet. Frowning, Pastor Flemming picked it up. "There's a problem with the clasp. I'll need to have this repaired."

"It's a lovely watch." Even to Olivia's untrained eye, this was an expensive one. It seemed well-worn and well-loved; perhaps it had come from his father or grandfather.

"Thank you." He appeared to be flustered by her compliment and quickly changed the subject. The visit lasted about thirty minutes, long enough to drink yet another cup of tea, and after a short prayer, Pastor Flemming left, first returning their cups to the kitchen.

Olivia did get some reading done before Grace arrived. Much as she looked forward to seeing her friend, she also enjoyed the hour or so of solitude, although more than once she'd almost drifted off as she read.

"Can I get you anything?" Grace asked the instant she stepped inside. Her eyes were somber with concern. "You look tired."

"I am."

"Then take a nap."

"I'd like to, but . . . what if it becomes a habit?"

Grace shook her head. "Olivia. Your body's telling you it needs rest. For heaven's sake, listen to your body!"

This was sensible advice. "I'll only sleep for an hour."

"Sleep until you're ready to wake up." Grace walked ahead of her into the bedroom to pull back the covers.

"I'll start dinner while you're resting," she said.

"You don't have to do that," Olivia told her as she got into bed.

"I know, but I want to."

Olivia didn't argue. Like Jack, Grace needed to feel useful. She settled the covers over Olivia and tucked them around her shoulders. Then she drew the curtains, and as quietly as possible, tiptoed out of the room.

Olivia nestled against the thick down pillows and closed her eyes, savoring the indulgence of sleeping in the middle of the day.

Tired as she was, she assumed she'd immediately fall asleep. Instead, her mind took a series of unexpected twists and turns. It struck her as odd that Pastor Flemming would show up unannounced instead of at the time he'd previously set. She'd never known him to do that before.

Although he'd been solicitous and caring, Olivia was left with the distinct impression that something was troubling him. He seemed unusually rushed and unfocused, eager to be about his business.

After fifteen minutes, Olivia realized trying to sleep was pointless. She folded back the blankets and climbed out of bed.

Grace met her in the hallway, hands propped on her hips. "What are you doing up so soon?" she scolded.

"I couldn't sleep."

"Why not? You were about to keel over from exhaustion when I got here."

Olivia wished she could put her concern about Dave Flemming into words. A visit from the pastor had been a gesture of kindness. It shouldn't matter that he'd arrived at a time other than the one he'd arranged earlier. Yet it was more than that. She wondered what he was so worried about that he'd actually lost track of the conversation twice.

"Why don't I make us some tea," Grace suggested.

"Please."

They sat in the kitchen, across the round oak table from each other. "Anything new?" Grace asked.

"Well, yes. The pathology report came back and it confirmed that the cancer didn't spread to my lymph nodes."

"Oh." Grace raised both hands to her mouth. "That's so *great!*"

Smiling, Olivia nodded. "It's an incredible relief. Now, what about you — anything new at the library?"

Grace launched into a description of a board meeting she'd attended, and her plans for a Christmas story program for kids. She also mentioned that her new tenant, Faith Beckwith, whom they'd both known in high school, although she'd been Faith Carroll then, had visited the library. Olivia remembered that Will had done the same thing some time ago — and it wasn't to check out books.

"My brother hasn't made any inappropriate appearances, has he?" As much as Olivia loved Will, if he tried to get between Grace and Cliff again, she'd never forgive him. Will had begun an Internet — what? dalliance? fling? certainly not a relationship

— with Grace. And he'd done it while he was still married, telling her he was divorcing his wife. The divorce came later, at his ex-wife's instigation.

"Will's too busy with the art gallery to worry about me." Looking thoughtful, Grace raised her teacup, elbows on the table. "I have to admit that's a relief."

Olivia agreed with her. "He needs that kind of goal," she said. "It should keep him out of trouble for a while."

Grace nodded. "Cliff came by the library this morning with some news," she murmured.

"Good news, I hope?"

Grace shrugged as if to suggest she wasn't sure. "You decide. Cliff told me Cal and Vicki are moving to Wyoming to work with a mustang rescue operation."

Olivia felt this was both good and bad. Cal had been seriously involved with Linnette McAfee and then broken off the relationship when he fell in love with one of the local vets. From a superficial perspective, it was difficult to understand why a handsome man like Cal Washburn would be attracted to a woman as plain and unassuming as Vicki Newman.

In retrospect, of course, it seemed completely logical. Cal and Vicki shared a passion for horses that had brought them together, a passion more intense than his feelings for Linnette.

"I can only imagine how Corrie's going to react," Grace said. "Remember how upset she was when she found out Linnette was leaving town?"

"I would've been upset, too." Olivia sympathized with Corrie.

"The reason Linnette left was so she wouldn't run into Cal. She didn't want to see him, especially with Vicki," Grace added.

"And now Cal leaves the area anyway. Vicki, too."

"It's hard to look people in the face when you've been humiliated," Grace said quietly. "I know that from experience."

Olivia shook her head. "So, when are they going?"

"Soon. It puts Cliff in a difficult position. He's going to be shorthanded until January, when he can hire someone else."

"Will he be able to manage?"

"I guess so." Grace shrugged and sipped her tea. "We'd already agreed to house the animals for the live Nativity scene, but Cliff doesn't seem worried about that. I told him I'd do what I could to help."

"So Cal's leaving before Christmas."

Grace nodded. "Apparently Vicki's sold

her share of the practice and they're ready to go."

"I suppose Cedar Cove will get a new vet."

"It seems that way," Grace said. "From what Cliff said, Cal and Vicki are going to California, where Vicki has family, and they'll be married there."

"I wish them the best," Olivia said. She also wished Linnette hadn't been hurt, but it was too late to avoid that now.

Corrie had told her Linnette was seeing someone in the small North Dakota town where she'd ended up. She seemed to be happy, according to her mother, and Olivia certainly hoped that was the case.

"What's that?" Grace asked suddenly, sitting up straighter and staring at the floor behind Olivia.

"What's what?" Olivia echoed, glancing over her shoulder.

Grace stood and walked over to the kitchen sink. There, lying on the mat, was a man's wristwatch. "This," she said, picking it up.

"Oh, Pastor Flemming's lost his watch." Olivia might not have recognized it if the same thing hadn't happened earlier.

"Pastor Flemming?" Grace frowned, studying the back of the watch. "That's not the name inscribed here. It says, 'Micah

Evans. June 23, 1977 for Thirty Years of Loyal Service.' "

"Micah Evans must be some relative," Olivia speculated. He'd been concerned about losing the watch when it fell off his wrist the first time. It obviously held some emotional significance for him.

Grace continued to frown. "Evans . . . Evans," she repeated slowly. "For some reason, that name sticks in my mind."

"It doesn't in mine," Olivia said. "I'd better call to tell him I have his watch, otherwise he'll wonder." He'd behaved oddly and seemed almost sorry that she'd seen it. "There appears to be something wrong with the clasp."

Olivia pulled the telephone directory from the kitchen drawer and set it on the counter, opening it to the *Fs*.

"Are you calling the church office?" Grace asked as Olivia scanned the listings.

"I thought I'd try his house first," Olivia said. "He said he'd be out all day. If I contact the church office, he won't get the message until tomorrow morning, if then. I'll get in touch with his wife. Let me see. *Flemming, D. 8 Sandpiper Way.*"

Olivia punched in the number, and Emily Flemming answered on the second ring.

"Dave's gold watch?" she said when Olivia

had identified herself and explained why she was calling.

"Yes, it fell off his wrist while he was here visiting."

"Oh." The pastor's wife sounded tearful.

"I just found it," Olivia said, "or I would've called before."

"Thank you for letting me know," Emily Flemming whispered. "Goodbye."

Olivia hung up the phone with the oddest sensation. "Something isn't right between Dave and Emily Flemming," she announced.

"What makes you say that?"

"I'm not sure. Intuition, I guess." She clapped the phone book shut. "But mark my words, that relationship is in trouble."

TWELVE

Emily Flemming hung up the phone after her conversation with Judge Griffin and for a long moment didn't move. She bit her lower lip hard enough to taste her own blood. The news about the lost watch bothered her, but that wasn't the most upsetting detail.

Fifteen minutes later, she still hadn't moved.

"Mom!" The front door opened and Matthew slammed into the house. "I'm home," he yelled. His backpack slid from his shoulders and fell unceremoniously to the kitchen floor.

The door opened again as Mark came rushing in. "What's for snack?" he demanded, following Matthew into the kitchen.

Generally Emily had something ready for her sons as soon as they got home. Heartsick, she'd forgotten.

She reached for two napkins and the large

164

plastic barrel of pretzels she'd bought earlier in the month at Costco.

"Pretzels," Mark whined. "Why can't we have cookies?"

"Because cookies aren't good for you, stupid," Matthew muttered.

When Emily didn't instantly protest, Mark did. "Mom! Matthew called me *stupid.*"

"Don't do it again," she said halfheartedly. She set the napkins on the table and poured a pile of pretzels onto each. The juice she gave them was a special treat; it came in small boxes complete with their own straws.

"What time will Dad be home?" Mark asked, then stuffed his mouth full of pretzels.

"I . . . I'm not sure."

"What's for dinner?" Matthew wanted to know.

Emily glanced over at the stove. When the phone rang she'd been assembling a large pan of lasagna. After speaking to Judge Griffin, she'd gotten sidetracked. The sauce had cooled on the stove as she'd stood by the phone, trying to understand what she'd learned. This *shouldn't* be happening, and yet it made a weird kind of sense. It wasn't as if Emily hadn't suspected Dave had been lying to her. She'd known all along.

"Mom?" Matthew asked her again. "What's for dinner?"

"Food, stupid," Mark said.

"Don't call your brother *stupid*," she returned automatically.

"He called me *stupid* first."

Emily would go slowly insane if she had to listen to this constant bickering. "Both of you, to your rooms." She pointed in the direction of the hallway. They had their own bedrooms since the move to Sandpiper Way, which had been one of the many attractions offered by this house.

"Mom!" Matthew shouted. "We just got home from school."

"Do your homework!"

"What about study hour?"

"You can do homework then, too."

"This sucks!" Mark dragged his feet and his backpack down the hallway. She didn't bother to reproach him for using a word she hated.

Emily waited until her sons were well out of earshot. With her mind in turmoil, she walked over to the telephone and called the church office.

Angel, the secretary, answered right away. "Cedar Cove Methodist," came her well-modulated voice. "Can I help you?"

"It's Emily," she said, trying to sound calm, despite the staccato beating of her heart. "Is Dave there?"

"Oh, hi, Em," Angel said. "Sorry, he's been out and about all afternoon. You might want to try his cell. He had it with him when he left the office."

"He either has it turned off or the battery's gone dead." Emily hoped God would forgive her for that lie.

"Can't reach him then?"

"Right."

Emily could hear Angel flipping pages of what she assumed must be Dave's appointment calendar. "It says here that he's supposed to visit Judge Griffin. She's home from the hospital now, but I guess you already know that."

"Is there a time?" she asked.

Angel made a small humming sound. "Four, according to his calendar."

"Four," Emily repeated dully. "Four this afternoon?" The secretary's words confirmed everything she suspected.

"Yup. That's what it says," Angel said cheerfully.

"Okay, thanks." Emily quickly got off the phone. At first she was too numb to think. Then, marching over to the sink, she looked down at the lasagna noodles she'd cooked. Lasagna was one of Dave's favorite meals. He'd asked her to make it again soon, and like a gullible, simple-minded wife eager to please her husband, she'd happily complied.

Four o'clock.

He'd written down that he'd be visiting Judge Griffin at four this afternoon.

Yet that very morning, Dave had made a point of telling her he'd be home late this evening. Late because he had an appointment with Olivia Lockhart Griffin at six o'clock. Not only that, he'd apparently gone to see her well *before* the scheduled time of four.

It wasn't difficult for Emily to surmise what he was doing during those unaccounted for hours.

He was with another woman. Someone he didn't want her or Angel or anyone in town to know about.

Why else would her husband, the minister, the pastor of their church, lie to his wife?

"Mom?" Matthew stood in the kitchen doorway. "Is everything okay?"

She forced a smile. "Of course. Why not?"

He frowned. "You've got a funny look on your face."

"I do?" She tried to relax. "How would you boys like to go out for dinner tonight?"

Mark joined his brother. "McDonald's?"

"Sure." She eyed the sauce cooling on the stove and the pile of grated mozzarella cheese.

"Mom?" Matthew asked when she started running water and turned on the garbage disposal. "What are you doing?"

"I . . . I ruined dinner," she said as she dumped the entire pan of sauce down the disposal. It made a disgusting gurgling noise as it ground up the meat, onions, tomatoes and herbs that had been simmering for hours. She followed that with the mozzarella, then painstakingly fed in the wide noodles.

"Mom," Mark said loudly. "I really *like* lasagna."

"I'll make it again soon," she promised, but just then it gave her a perverse kind of pleasure to discard the whole meal. Despite the waste — and she knew she'd feel guilty later — she needed the angry satisfaction of doing this. "The three of us are going out to McDonald's, remember?"

"What about Dad?" Matthew asked.

"He can fend for himself."

"But . . ."

"He's going to be late," she informed her sons.

"Again?" both boys chimed.

"Get your coats." Emily made an effort to sound excited. She grabbed a tissue to dab her eyes, which had begun to brim with tears.

This would never do. She squared her

shoulders and determined then and there that she wasn't going to cry. She would hold her head up and give the performance of her life. Her husband had lied. He might well be with another woman this very moment, but Emily would see to it that anyone looking at her, including her sons, would never guess. She refused to act devastated — or worse, humiliated.

"Hey, boys," she said, collecting her coat and purse. "What would you think of me as a blonde?"

"You mean your hair?" Matthew asked.

"Yes, my hair. I'm going to have it dyed blond."

"How come?" Mark studied her inquisitively.

"Because blondes have more fun."

The boys turned to each other and Matthew shrugged.

"I'm going down to the mall to see if Get Nailed can squeeze me in." On Thursdays the shop was open until eight. With luck one of the stylists had a cancellation.

"I'll get you each a roll of quarters and you can play at the video arcade while I'm in the beauty salon."

"Okay." Neither boy seemed enthusiastic, however.

"Would you rather stay with Mrs. Johnson?" she asked. The woman served as their babysitter on the rare occasions Dave and Emily left their sons for a night out. It'd been weeks since they'd last had a "date." No wonder, she thought bitterly. Dave was apparently *dating* someone else these days, while his wife sat home, cooking lasagna for him and ironing his shirts.

"I'd rather come with you," Mark said.

Emily looked at her oldest son. "What about you?" she asked.

Matthew shrugged again. "Me, too, I guess."

"You guess?" she said with a flippant air.

The boys silently followed her to the garage and slid into the backseat of the SUV. Christmas music was playing on the car radio but none of them sang along the way they usually did. The boys' mood seemed to reflect hers, and their skepticism was all too apparent. Impulsive spending wasn't normal behavior for Emily and they knew it. She wanted to reassure them but couldn't. She felt as if her entire marriage had been a sham.

"We'll check to see if I can get a hair appointment first," she told them.

"Okay," Mark murmured.

They stopped at Kitsap Bank for quarters, then drove to the mall. Everyone at Get

Nailed was busy and Emily had to wait at the counter for several minutes before the receptionist reappeared.

"I was wondering . . ." Suddenly she wasn't so certain anymore. Her anger, which had kept her determination alive, had begun to dissipate and she felt deflated.

"I realize it's last-minute and everything, but is there anyone available to color my hair this afternoon?"

The young woman checked the appointment book. "Rachel had a cancellation earlier. I can ask her."

"She did?" Emily took this as a sign. "Please check. It would be great if she could fit me in."

The receptionist returned a moment later. "She said that would work."

"Wonderful!"

Emily handed each of her sons a roll of quarters, with instructions to make the money last until her hair was done. They tore off for the video arcade across from the salon as the receptionist led her to Rachel's station. Fortunately Emily could keep an eye on them from her chair.

"I'm Rachel," a dark-haired woman introduced herself, draping a plastic cape around Emily's shoulders.

"Emily Flemming," she said. "We haven't

met before. Teri did my previous cut —" she frowned "— sometime this summer."

Rachel ran her fingers through Emily's hair. "So you want to be a blonde?"

"Yes. I hear they live life to the fullest and that's exactly what I intend to do." It was a flimsy reason, at best, and a silly one at worst, but at this point Emily didn't care.

Soon she was at the shampoo bowl and her hair was lathered and rinsed twice. While the water sprayed her hair, Emily closed her eyes, trying not to think but unable to stop the thoughts from tramping through her brain, one after the other.

It didn't hit her until the coloring process was underway that she'd forgotten a crucial part of the conversation with Judge Griffin.

Dave didn't own a gold watch.

At least not one that she knew about. Since it was unlikely he'd purchased it for himself, that left only one other option. Someone else had given it to him.

A woman.

Fine, she decided furiously. She'd ask him about it. She was through letting her husband ruin their lives. Through with pretending nothing was wrong. Through with turning the other cheek. The pride, the pretense of indifference, was for public consumption. But Dave — she was going to confront him with the truth. Demand answers. Then she'd figure out what to do next.

When Rachel was finished, Emily barely recognized herself. Her straight dark hair was gone, replaced with a shorter, more stylish do. She was blond, all right. *Very* blond.

"This is a good color for you," Rachel was saying. "I was a little concerned when you wanted to go this light, but I have to admit it looks really nice."

"Thank you." Emily swallowed hard. The style and color were certainly . . . different. Eventually she'd get accustomed to this new look and so would everyone else. And when it grew out, she could always revert to her natural color. Depending on how she felt at the time. . . .

She paid the bill, wincing at the cost. Well, one extravagance wasn't going to ruin them. Dave would just have to live with it. She suspected *he* didn't have any qualms about spending money, even if it wasn't on her or the boys. In fact, she planned to check his credit card statements at the first opportunity, an idea her mother had suggested and she'd initially rejected.

Matthew and Mark stood outside Get Nailed, waiting for her as she left the salon.

Neither said a word.

"Well?" she asked them, patting the side of her head. "What do you think?"

"It's, um, different," Matthew ventured.

"That's good, isn't it?" Emily turned to Mark for confirmation.

"You don't look like my mom anymore," her younger son declared.

"But I am your mom. Now let's go have dinner. I bet you're hungry."

Matthew and Mark wolfed down their hamburgers and fries and then chased each other around the play area. Emily couldn't eat. Her stomach was in knots. She'd ordered a burger but after a single bite set it aside.

When they returned to the house, she saw Dave's car in the garage. She wasn't ready to see him yet, but as soon as she'd pulled in beside his car, he opened the door from the kitchen and stepped out.

The boys leaped from the backseat and ran toward their father. Dave hugged each of his sons in turn.

"Where were you? You didn't —" He stopped abruptly and a shocked look came over him. His head reared back as he stared at her. "What on earth did you do to your hair?"

"Mom colored it," Mark said.

"But . . . why?" Dave asked.

"You don't know?" She kept her voice casual as she entered the house. "You asked me where I was and the answer should be obvious. I was at the hairdresser's."

"Mom took us to McDonald's for dinner."

"Go to your rooms now, boys," Dave said curtly. "It's time for your homework."

"Aw, Dad," Mark whined as Matthew groaned. "But we just got home!" One look from Dave quelled their protest.

Sensing that it was probably best to do as they'd been told, Matthew and Mark moved sluggishly toward their bedrooms. Emily walked to the far side of the kitchen with Dave on her heels.

"Why did you change your hair?" he asked again.

"Why did you lie?" she fired back. Leaning against the kitchen counter, she glared at him.

"Lie? About what?" he asked with an innocence she found a little too practiced.

She whirled around. "You told me you were visiting Judge Griffin, and you implied it was this evening."

"Yes . . ."

"You weren't there."

"How do you know?" He raised his voice in defiance.

"As it happens, Judge Griffin phoned the house. Apparently you left your *gold* watch there when you went to visit *early* this afternoon."

His reaction was immediate. She saw the alarm flash in his eyes. She didn't know why it surprised her.

"You have a gold watch? This is news to me. Exactly where did you get it?"

"Emily, it's not the way it sounds." He sat down at the table, rubbing his face.

"Are you going to tell me there's no other woman in your life, Dave? Because if you do, that'll just be another lie."

The expression on his face was one of horror. "How can you even suggest such a thing? There's never been anyone but you. Never!"

"I'm supposed to believe that?"

"Yes."

"I'm not as naive as you seem to think," she muttered.

He sighed. "Believe what you want, Emily, but there's no one else."

"Oh, I suppose that same *no one* is responsible for the gold watch you had on?"

His hand went to his left wrist. "Does Olivia have it?"

The concern in his voice cut her to the quick. "She does, so don't worry about it."

With that, she walked out of the kitchen and into their bedroom, closing the door with a resounding bang — a clear signal to her husband not to follow.

THIRTEEN

Rachel Pendergast's schedule at Get Nailed was booked for the entire month of December. It seemed that every woman in Cedar Cove — and some of the men — had decided to cut, restyle, perm or color their hair.

She got to work early each morning and often stayed late. Bruce, her fiancé, and his daughter, Jolene, both complained that they missed her, but for the time being that couldn't be helped. The extra money she earned would go toward their February wedding.

The buzzer on the dryer went, and Rachel folded a load of towels. When she'd put away the last one, she saw that it was already nine-fifteen. The mall had closed at nine. Earlier Bruce had phoned to say he'd take her to dinner, and while she appreciated the thought, all Rachel wanted to do was put her feet up and relax.

"I'm finished here," she told Jane on her

way out the door. Jane usually stayed the longest, since she and her husband owned Get Nailed.

With the mall closed, the hallway leading to the exit was semidark and deserted. The dim light wouldn't have bothered her as little as two months ago, but everything had changed the night she was kidnapped.

Being abducted by two thugs had been the most frightening experience of her life. The bizarre thing was that they'd gotten the wrong woman. The kidnappers assumed they had Teri Polgar because Rachel was in the limo driven by James Wilbur. Teri hadn't been ready to leave and had offered Rachel a ride. When the kidnappers discovered that, the terror level had escalated by several incalculable degrees.

For a short while Rachel had been convinced they were going to kill her and James and dump their bodies somewhere. They spoke in a language she didn't understand — Russian, she'd later learned — and frankly, she was grateful for her lack of comprehension. She was terrified enough.

Knowing she might be dead within a few hours, Rachel analyzed her life. Well, not analysis exactly; more like an instantaneous assessment. Oddly, she remembered thinking she hadn't made her bed that morning because she was running late. The one time she'd left her bed unmade! After her body was found, or her disappearance noticed, all those deputies would traipse through her bedroom and figure she was a slob.

With that rather trivial concern established, her mind had immediately shifted from the mundane to the momentous. All at once it came to her that she might never see Bruce Peyton or his twelve-year-old daughter, Jolene, again. That was when she knew with complete certainty that she loved Bruce. At the time she'd been practically engaged to Nate Olsen, a navy chief. Only it wasn't Nate who flashed into her mind. Suddenly it became crucial to stay alive. She needed to tell Bruce she loved him. She wanted to be Jolene's stepmother and have other children with him and spend the rest of their lives together.

Once they'd admitted their love, everything had fallen swiftly into place. When they'd discussed a wedding date, Jolene, with a young girl's sense of the romantic, had chosen Valentine's Day.

Rachel wasn't sure she could get everything organized by then and favored a spring wedding, but Bruce insisted they should be married and living as husband and wife before the end of the year.

So Jolene was campaigning for February, Bruce said December and Rachel wanted April. In a spirit of compromise Rachel and Bruce agreed on Valentine's Day. Jolene felt vindicated.

Lately, however, two and a half months seemed too far away. Rachel was ready to be Bruce's wife and Jolene's full-time mother. Now.

A shadow moved and Rachel automatically tensed. She quickly realized the movement came from a security guard rounding the corner. Exhaling sharply, she walked toward the exit at a faster pace.

Bruce stood waiting for her at the outside entrance, pacing back and forth. When he saw her approach, he smiled — a slow, easy smile that crinkled the corners of his blue eyes and heightened the appeal of his all-American good looks.

"You're later than you said you'd be," he told her when she stepped into the cold night air, the mall door swinging shut behind her. The lights in the parking lot shone with a steady, reassuring glow. "I was getting worried."

"I know. I'm sorry." Rachel hated the thought of him waiting in the cold. She'd told him she could make her own way home, but Bruce came for her as often as he could, intent on making sure she got to her car safely. The kidnapping had frightened him as much as it had her.

She'd suggested he come inside the mall to wait, but he declined, preferring to sit in his car and listen to the radio until Rachel finished work.

Rachel cupped her warm hands over his cold ears and reached up to kiss him.

"Mmm," he whispered. He brought her close and clung to her for a moment before reluctantly letting her go.

"I missed you," Rachel said.

"I missed you, too," he murmured, taking her hand. "How much longer are you going to be working these late nights?"

Rachel knew he'd rather she spent the evenings with him and Jolene, but this time of year was just too hectic.

"After Christmas everything slows down," she said. She assured him of this at least once a day.

Bruce tucked her arm in his and they walked to her car. It was silly for him to come at all, and yet she appreciated his vigilance. Eventually he would believe she was safe. Eventually she'd feel safe again, too. The trauma of the kidnapping would stay with them both, but the possibility of anything like that happening again was remote at best.

"Christmas." Bruce gave a disgruntled sigh.

"Don't bah-humbug me, Bruce Peyton. I love Christmas and Jolene does, too."

He shook his head. "I don't understand why women are so crazy about holidays. *Especially* Christmas."

"It isn't necessary that you understand."

He laughed. "You've had quite an influence on my daughter. She said almost the identical thing to me."

Jolene and Rachel had shared a special relationship for years. Because she'd grown up without a mother, too, Rachel recognized the girl's need for a close connection with an adult friend who could occasionally act as a maternal figure. She'd willingly stepped into that role when Jolene was in first grade, six years ago.

Rachel slipped her arm around Bruce's waist and leaned against him.

"Have you had anything to eat since lunch?" he asked.

At his question Rachel realized how hungry she was and her stomach growled in response. "No, I didn't."

"The Taco House is in business now," he said. The restaurant, formerly The Taco Shack, had reopened earlier that week, and long lines had been reported. Rachel was eager to try it, but not late on a Friday night when she'd been on her feet most of the day.

"No, thanks. I'm too tired. Maybe next week?" She'd read in the *Chronicle* that the new restaurant was owned by the same couple who'd run The Taco Shack, which had been one of their favorite places to eat. When it closed, Rachel had been extremely disappointed. It had seemed to echo the end of her relationship with Bruce, too.

"What do you want to do about dinner?"

"I've got a couple of chicken pot pies in my freezer. I'll pop them in the microwave," she replied. "That way I can relax."

"I can't stay long," Bruce said.

"Where's Jolene?"

"Roller skating with her friends. She has a ten-thirty curfew tonight, and Carrie's mom is driving her home."

"Okay, that gives us about an hour."

They grinned at each other.

Rachel got into her car and Bruce waited until she'd locked the door. Then he sprinted over to his own. He followed her home, arriving at almost the same time she did.

Opening her front door, Rachel collected the mail and the paper and set everything on the kitchen counter. She hung up her coat and Bruce's.

He turned on the television. As was his custom he made himself at home, slumping on her sofa with his legs stretched out. He flicked through channels with the remote control, stopping occasionally at a talk show or newscast.

Bruce wasn't romantic; he didn't shower her with words of love. But Rachel knew how deeply he loved her. She didn't doubt the sincerity of his feelings. Not for a minute. Not for even a second.

While the pies heated in the microwave, she sorted through the mail, which included a number of Christmas cards and, as always, bills. She hesitated when she saw the San Diego return address on a square red envelope. Even though there wasn't a name, the APO address instantly told her who the card was from.

Nate Olsen.

They'd dated for about three years. He was the navy man she'd met through the Dog and Bachelor Auction sponsored by the local humane society. For a while she thought she was in love with him, and he with her, until she discovered that Nate was more interested in how a relationship with her could advance his political career. He was from a wealthy, well-connected family, and marriage to an "ordinary" woman like her would heighten his appeal to the voters.

"What's wrong?" Bruce asked as he came into the kitchen.

She considered hiding the fact that Nate had contacted her, but decided against it. Their relationship had to be open and honest from the very beginning.

"It looks like Nate sent me a Christmas card."

Bruce's gaze held hers, although he didn't reveal his thoughts. "Are you going to open it?"

"Probably."

Bruce didn't comment.

"Would you rather I didn't?"

He shrugged as if it were of little concern. "Might as well read it," he said.

She narrowed her eyes. "A small display of jealousy wouldn't be amiss, you know."

Bruce sent her a lopsided grin. "You're wearing my engagement ring, aren't you?"

"Yes, but —"

"You love me," he said with unwavering confidence.

She couldn't disagree.

"You had your chance to marry Nate. As I recall, I actually encouraged you to accept his proposal. He certainly had more to offer you than I ever will."

"And as *you* recall, that infuriated me." It

still did. What Bruce had to offer her was a love as unconditional as another person's love could be.

His grin widened. "You love *me*," he said again, "and that's not going to change."

Playfully Rachel wagged her index finger at him. "Don't be so sure of yourself, Bruce Peyton. It's a woman's prerogative to change her mind."

Bruce got a soda cracker from the box on the counter behind her and bit into it. "You won't. Or you would've already done it."

"Really?" She carefully slit the red envelope. Sliding out the glittery Christmas card, she opened it so Bruce couldn't see what Nate had written. She lingered over each word.

"So?" he asked after a long moment.

Purposely she closed the card and set it aside.

"What did he say?" Bruce asked, following her to the microwave.

"Are you *sure* you want to know?" she asked.

"If you feel like telling me."

She took a deep breath. "Nate said he'll always love me and that losing me has been the turning point in his life. He *begged* me to reconsider."

Bruce put down the soda cracker and his

eyes darkened.

The timer buzzed; Rachel removed the pies. "You can read it for yourself if you want," she said as she retrieved two plates from the kitchen cupboard.

Bruce declined with a shake of his head. "He addressed it to you."

"I'm giving you permission to look at it."

Again, he declined.

"You're not so cocky now, are you?" she teased, bringing the plates to the small kitchen table.

"You're marrying me," he stated flatly, but he didn't sound as confident as he had earlier.

She derived a small degree of satisfaction from the way his arrogance had suddenly diminished. But she'd made her choice and, in her heart, she knew it was the right one. Her future was with Bruce and Jolene and whatever children they might have.

"Bruce," she said as they sat down. She purposely changed the subject. "I'd like to get pregnant soon."

He blinked hard. "How soon? Tonight? I'm certainly willing but you're the one who says —"

"*After* the wedding."

"Uh . . ." His gaze traveled back to the Christmas card, which still lay on the kitchen counter.

Rachel stood and handed the card to Bruce, who took it with some reluctance.

He opened it slowly, read the two short lines. When he finished he raised his eyes to hers. "All he says is *Merry Christmas, Nate.*" He frowned. "Where's all that garbage about him never loving another woman?"

"Did I say that?" she asked with a giggle.

"Maybe not in those precise words, but basically, yes."

"You have to read between the lines."

"All he said was Merry Christmas," Bruce pointed out.

"Well, yes, that's what he *wrote,* but you and I both know he meant a whole lot more than that. He misses me."

"Good."

"But . . ."

"He can miss you all he wants, but you and I are going to be married and that's the end of it."

"Bruce," she said sweetly, "you *are* jealous."

"No way," he insisted.

She didn't argue with him.

"All right, maybe a little," he admitted. After a moment, he asked, "Should I be?"

Her heart melted at the uncertainty in his eyes. She couldn't continue to tease him.

"Nate is out of my life. I'm madly, senselessly in love with you, Bruce."

He grinned sheepishly. "I know that."

"It's nice to hear it once in a while, though, isn't it?" she said, and about this she was serious. While her fiancé might not be a man of eloquent words, it wouldn't hurt if he expressed his feelings now and then.

"What if I tell you how much I love you every day for the rest of our lives?" he asked. "Would that be enough?"

Rachel smiled. "That would definitely be a good place to start."

"Now about starting something else — our family."

"Yes?" *This* was a subject Rachel could get excited about.

FOURTEEN

"You were right about the knitting."

The young female voice seemed to come out of nowhere. Startled, Faith Beckwith looked up from the pattern book she was studying. She sat at a table in The Quilted Giraffe, searching for a knitting project, only to find Troy's daughter, Megan, staring down at her.

"Megan." She hoped the shock didn't show in her eyes. It took her an instant to get past the fact that this was Troy's daughter. Despite her intentions, forgetting about him was a futile effort. "How are you feeling?"

"Really good," Megan said, then lowered her voice. "This pregnancy feels so different from my first one."

"I'm glad to hear it," Faith murmured, genuinely happy for Troy's daughter.

"I haven't told anyone about the baby. Except Craig. I *had* to tell my husband."

"Of course you did." Faith was relieved to

hear that. She hated the thought of Megan keeping this pregnancy to herself.

"My dad and my in-laws don't know yet." She hesitated. "It's hard not to tell my dad."

"Then why don't you?" Faith asked. Troy would make a wonderful grandfather.

"We're really close," Megan went on to say. "I don't want him to worry unnecessarily." She smiled slightly smile as she pulled out a chair and sat next to Faith. "I have a good feeling, though."

"You'll know when the time's right to tell your father and your in-laws," Faith said without meeting her gaze. It felt odd to speak about Troy in such an abstract way. She noticed, however, that Megan looked healthy. Color showed in her cheeks and her eyes were clear and bright.

"I was glad when I saw you here," Megan said as she set her gigantic purse on the table. "You were so helpful the day I went to the clinic."

"Actually, it was my first day on the job."

"You're kidding!"

Faith laughed softly.

"I felt like you were there just for me. I was feeling so emotional. You calmed me down, and after we talked, I felt . . . a real sense of hope."

Faith was grateful for those kind words.

"But it was more than that," Megan continued. "You said knitting would be good for me. You were right. Every time I feel anxious about the baby, I pick up my needles and I remember what you said. It's almost as if . . ." She hesitated again. "I don't want you to get the wrong impression or anything, but you said exactly what I would've wanted my mother to say."

"I'm sure your mother would have been just as reassuring if she was with you."

"I miss her every single day," Megan said. She sniffled loudly. Obviously embarrassed, she searched inside her purse for a tissue. "My hormones are so out of whack these days, I burst into tears at the drop of a hat." She tried to laugh and only half succeeded.

"I was like that when I was pregnant," Faith told her. "I can remember watching a rerun of the old Mary Tyler Moore show, the one where Chuckles the Clown dies. Even though it's a comedy, I was bawling my head off and then all of a sudden I was laughing and crying at the same time."

"You liked *The Mary Tyler Moore Show?*" Megan asked, her eyes wide. "My mother and I used to watch it at the care facility. I know exactly which episode you're talking about. That was Mom's very favorite show."

Then, as if she'd suddenly remembered

why she was at the fabric store, Megan reached inside her purse and brought out her knitting. "I came here hoping I could find someone to help me with this." She set her yarn and needles on the table.

Faith saw immediately that Megan had stopped knitting in the middle of a row, never a good idea.

"I'm afraid I dropped a stitch and I didn't know what to do next."

"I can help you with that," Faith murmured, looking at the half-completed baby blanket.

Retrieving a crochet hook from her own knitting bag, Faith captured the renegade stitch and wove it into place. Then she slipped it back on the needle. "There," she said calmly. "Now you can finish the row. You saw how I did that, didn't you?"

Megan nodded. "I should probably buy a crochet hook, shouldn't I?"

"It's an excellent tool to have."

"Okay, I'll do it today. Thank you so much."

"My pleasure." Faith glanced down at the pattern book and tried not to think about Troy and how much she missed him.

"Would you . . . I mean . . ." Megan looked uncertain. "I realize you're working at the clinic and you don't really know me . . ."

"Yes?" Faith prompted.

"Would it be all right if I came to see you sometime? Not as a patient, though."

"You mean as a friend?" Faith asked.

Megan nodded eagerly. "Like on your coffee break or maybe even for lunch."

Faith was in a quandary. If Troy learned about their friendship, he'd assume she'd somehow arranged this because of him. He'd assume she was trying to reconnect with him through his daughter and nothing could be further from the truth.

"Would it be improper?" Megan asked, frowning.

"Not . . . improper," Faith said.

"Perhaps we could meet outside the clinic," Megan suggested, as if she'd stumbled upon the perfect solution.

"We could meet here at the store, I suppose," Faith said. "I'd be happy to help you with your knitting. This blanket's an excellent project but I could also show you how to knit booties and a hat for the baby to wear home from the hospital."

"You could?"

"I . . . could," Faith told her. "I have a pattern I use whenever there's a new baby in the family. We could meet right here at the table they have for classes."

"That's great! Thank you, Faith." Megan

paused, a look of concern in her eyes. "Is it okay if I call you Faith?"

"Of course. Faith is just fine."

They set a date for the following week and Faith wondered — fearing for her own peace of mind — if this was such a smart idea. She hadn't meant to get involved with Troy's daughter. Yet, at the same time, Megan was emotionally needy, especially with this second pregnancy so soon after losing the first.

Still, Troy might think —

No. She would not allow Troy Davis into her mind. It was over. If she became friends with Megan, it would have nothing to do with Troy. Megan was her own woman. So was Faith.

When she returned home from the fabric store, Faith made a pot of tea, then sat down in her living room. She'd found a lovely natural-fiber yarn in earth tones and had decided to knit a sample afghan. Eager to start the project, she picked up her needles and the new yarn and was about to cast on stitches when the doorbell rang.

Although it was only a little past four in the afternoon, the day had already grown dark. Faith turned on her porch light and checked the peephole in the door.

And then she saw him.

Troy Davis.

No doubt he'd heard about Megan and Faith meeting and felt he needed to wade right in, making unwarranted assumptions and judgments. If that was the case, and it probably was, Faith didn't intend to listen. She didn't require *his* permission to see Megan.

With reluctance she unlocked the door and opened it. She'd hung an evergreen wreath on the outside, and the scent, with its memories of childhood Christmases, wafted into the room.

Still in uniform, Troy stood there, his hat in hand. "Hello, Faith."

"Troy." She nodded, keeping her voice level and cool.

"Can we talk for a few minutes?" he asked when she didn't immediately open the door.

Without smiling, she unlatched the screen door and he came inside.

She noticed that he'd lost a few pounds since she'd last seen him almost two weeks ago and wondered briefly if he'd been ill. Worried despite her own resolve, she watched him closely — as if she were starved for the very sight of him, she thought with disgust.

She didn't *want* to care about Troy Davis. Didn't want to feel even a flicker of emotion. Letting him back into her life would only bring more pain. He'd proved that.

Troy entered the living room. "Would it be all right if I sat down?" he asked.

Faith nodded. Her lack of welcome and warmth went against the grain, but she was protecting herself. She had no choice.

She sat down again in the overstuffed chair that was her favorite and Troy took the one across from her. He sat on the edge of the cushion, hat still in his hand.

He didn't speak for an interminable moment. "You're looking well," he finally said.

"Thank you," she returned stiffly. She had to bite her tongue to keep from bragging how well she really was and how nicely she'd gotten along without him.

He nodded. "I was thinking . . ."

Faith reached for her knitting needles, needing something to occupy her hands.

"I was thinking, actually I was hoping, you might be free for dinner tonight."

Faith set the needles in her lap and raised her eyebrows. "I beg your pardon? Did you just ask me to dinner?"

"Yes. Cedar Cove has several good restaurants and —"

"How *dare* you, Troy Davis."

He blanched.

"Did I hear you wrong two months ago, not to mention last week? Did I somehow misconstrue your words or intentions?"

Troy frowned uncertainly.

"As I recall, you said it would be best if we no longer saw each other. That's the way I remember it, so correct me if I misunderstood."

"I did say that," he agreed. "But at the time I didn't have any idea how difficult that would be. I love you, Faith."

"No, you don't," she said flatly, unwilling to fall under his spell yet again.

His head snapped back as if she'd struck him.

"If you loved me," she continued in a cold voice, "you wouldn't have been so quick to break my heart. You have a habit of doing that, Troy, and I'm through. This was the last time." She picked up her knitting again, avoiding his eyes. "As for your dinner invitation —"

He didn't allow her to finish. "I've missed you, Faith."

She'd missed him, too, more than she wanted to admit, but that didn't change what he'd said — that he could no longer see her. She recognized how concerned he was about his daughter, and she sympathized, especially now that she'd met Megan. She would've understood if he'd asked for her patience. Instead he'd cut her out of his life.

Just like that. If she hadn't pressured him, he wouldn't even have given her a reason. Oh, no. She was done with Troy Davis.

"Not a day passes that I don't think about you," he murmured.

She refused to look at him.

"Whenever I drive past your house, I call myself every kind of fool."

"I have a few other names I could add to your vocabulary."

She hadn't meant it as a joke, but he laughed.

"Yes, I suppose you could."

Her hands tightened around the knitting needles.

"It's taken me this long to find the courage to come to your door. It isn't dinner I'm asking for, Faith. What I really want . . . is a second chance."

She pinched her lips together. "Isn't it a *third* chance?"

"Third?"

"You broke my heart when I was a teenager."

"Oh, come on, Faith, not that again. You broke mine, too, and if you're blaming me for that, then you're way off base."

"I don't think so."

"Your mother lied to me," he reminded her.

"And you believed her! You didn't even talk to me. You took her at her word and went about your merry way and met Sandy."

"You met Carl and married *him* quickly enough." Anger flared in his eyes.

There was no point in arguing. They were at a standstill, neither of them willing to budge.

"That was years ago," Troy said after a tense moment. "As far as I'm concerned, it was unfortunate, but it happened. We both went on with our lives and found other people. You married a good man and I married a woman I loved. We both had families. Everything turned out the way it was meant to be."

He made it all sound so reasonable. Troy didn't know how many nights she'd cried herself to sleep back in college, wondering why he'd dumped her — why he'd been so cruel. Yes, she'd met and married Carl but getting over Troy hadn't been easy. She'd genuinely loved him then — and she genuinely loved him now.

"Fate brought us back together," he murmured.

"And then you blew it."

"I did, and I apologize," he said without hesitation.

At least he admitted that much.

"I assumed Megan wouldn't accept another woman in my life," he explained, "especially so soon after Sandy's death."

Faith was curious as to whether Megan had mentioned her. Since she'd kept her pregnancy a secret from her father and in-laws, Faith suspected she hadn't said anything about their recent friendship, either.

"Megan's my only child and I love her, but I have my own life." He paused, then added in a soft, coaxing voice, "Right now my life feels very empty without you."

Faith could feel herself weakening.

"Shall we try again?" Troy asked.

Despite her stubborn insistence that they were through, she wavered. He watched her, waiting, his expression hopeful. Faith forced herself to look away. "I need to think about it." She paused. "Are you *sure* this time, Troy?"

"I'm sure."

Faith wanted to trust him but was afraid to. She knew she couldn't tolerate another rejection, another betrayal. "I'm not ready to make that decision yet," she said.

For a fleeting moment Troy seemed disappointed. But his demeanor quickly changed, becoming more businesslike. "Fair enough." He stared down at his hat as if carefully considering his next statement. "I'll tell you what. Once you've made your decision, you let me know."

"Fine."

"I won't trouble you again, Faith." He stood, walking toward the front door. "No need to show me out."

Nevertheless she got up and accompanied him.

Troy's posture was stiff and straight. She knew he'd stand by his word; he wouldn't contact her again.

The next move, if there was one, would have to come from her.

FIFTEEN

Justine Gunderson could hardly wait to see her mother. She called Olivia once or twice a day, but hadn't been able to visit since Wednesday. She wanted to continue their ongoing conversation about her new restuarant, a conversation that brought great pleasure to them both. The Victorian Tea Room was now under construction and Olivia's suggestions had made all the difference.

Her mother seemed to be recovering from the surgery well, with her chemotherapy scheduled to begin in early January. "What a way to start the new year!" she'd joked and they'd both laughed. After all, there wasn't anything to do *but* laugh — laugh and endure.

Justine finished her Saturday-morning errands: the dry cleaners, then the library and finally the grocery store to buy powdered sugar for the gingerbread house she was making with Leif that afternoon. Throwing everything in the car, she hurried to her mother's place on Lighthouse Road.

She parked in front of the house and bounded up the porch steps. After knocking once, loudly, she opened the door. "Mom? Jack?"

"In here," her mother called from the bedroom.

Justine ventured down the hall. It was unusual for her mother to still be in bed on a Saturday morning. Justine knew the surgery and anesthetic had taken their toll on her energy, but despite that, she couldn't help feeling a little shocked. Olivia was a lifelong early riser, and this was just so . . . uncharacteristic.

As she entered the darkened room, she found her mother sitting on the side of the bed.

"Could you hand me my housecoat?" she asked groggily.

Justine did. "Shall I open the drapes for you, Mom?"

"Please."

As she let in the day's weak light, she asked, "Where's Jack?"

Olivia stared up at her. "Oh . . . He's writing a sports piece on youth soccer in Kitsap County," she explained. "This was the only time he could get the interview." Her mother stood and tied the sash to her housecoat. "I'm sure he'll be back any minute." Blinking, she asked, "What time is it, anyway?"

"Ten-fifteen."

Olivia rubbed her eyes. "I can't believe I slept this late."

"You obviously needed it. Shall I make us a pot of tea?"

Yawning, Olivia nodded. "Thank you, dear."

Justine loved this old house, especially the kitchen. She knew it as well as she did her own. She moved confidently from stove to cupboard, putting on water to boil, setting out her favorite white ceramic teapot, choosing peppermint tea bags. She figured it was better for both of them at this point than the strong Irish Breakfast they tended to prefer.

"Is Leif at home?" her mother asked, joining her ten minutes later.

"He's visiting his other grandparents with his daddy." Justine had already set two cups and saucers on the kitchen table. She poured the hot tea, breathing in the fresh, minty aroma, as Olivia settled in her chair. She was still in her flannel pajamas with their snowflake pattern and her red fleece housecoat, a get-well gift from Grace Harding.

"It's wonderful to see you, Justine," her mother said, smiling over at her.

"You, too, Mom. I meant to stop by yesterday afternoon, but —"

"No, no, I didn't mean to imply that you should've been here. We talk every day."

Her relationship with her mother was on solid ground. It hadn't always been, and Justine didn't want to do anything to impede the progress they'd made since she married Seth.

"You're feeling well?" her mother asked, looking pointedly at Justine's stomach.

"Fabulous. A hundred years ago, I probably would've been one of those women who gave birth every year or two. I'm perfectly healthy and I love being pregnant."

Her mother smiled. "I loved it, too. With you and your brother . . ." She hesitated as she sometimes did when referring to Jordan. Pain shadowed her eyes for a moment, but if she hadn't known her mother so well, Justine might have missed it. She felt that sense of loss, too. Loss for the twin brother who'd died the summer they were thirteen.

"Do you think I might have twins?" Justine asked. She and Seth had been wondering about it; she supposed the coming ultrasound would give them a definite answer.

"They do run in the family." Her mother smiled again, clearly pleased by the thought.

"Grandmother had twin brothers, right?"

Olivia nodded. Her two grand-uncles were both gone now, but Charlotte had an album full of pictures.

"Justine, do you *feel* as if you're carrying twins?"

"Oh, heavens, I don't know. I don't think so." She shrugged. "Anyway, Mom, I wanted to tell you what's happening at the Tea Room."

Her mother sat up straighter. "Okay, fill me in."

"Well, I've decided to paint the outside a lovely shade of pink."

"Pink," Olivia repeated. "Pink," she said again, frowning as though she hadn't heard correctly.

Justine grinned at her mother's expression. "Your reaction is the same as Seth's when I told him." He hadn't tried to dissuade her but she could tell he found her choice odd. Justine was very sure about the color, though. She'd gone over every detail at least a dozen times.

She was at the site every day, discussing the project with her builder. So many decisions had to be made daily that it was prudent and sensible to check in with the construction crew. After every visit she felt more excited about the new restaurant and what it would mean to the Cedar Cove community, especially the women. They'd adore going out to lunch. It would be a special place to meet that catered to them specifically.

"The Tea Room's going to be a destination restaurant," she said proudly.

"It'll be pink as a flamingo," her mother teased, "which should make it easy to find."

"No, pink as in dusty rose." Feeling almost giddy, Justine laughed and her mother joined in. It took Justine a moment to realize that her mother's laughter sounded forced.

She wanted to ask if anything was wrong, but didn't. If her mother and Jack had quarreled, Justine had no intention of prying. Anything Olivia meant to share, she'd tell Justine without prodding.

"I'm so tired," Olivia said weakly, sipping her tea.

"Do you want to go back to bed?"

"Maybe I should. In a few minutes." She finished her tea and reached for the white pot. It shook precariously in her hand.

"Here, Mom." Justine quickly took the teapot away from her. "Let me do that." Her mother's frail condition after the surgery worried her. She looked dreadful, something Justine hadn't wanted to admit earlier. Her skin was flushed and she shifted uncomfortably in her chair.

"Is your grandmother done with the

recipes?" Olivia asked, diverting Justine's interest.

"Almost. Oh, Mom, you won't believe what a fabulous job Grandma's doing."

Olivia nodded, smiling. "I knew she would."

"Grandma's been collecting recipes for weeks." All Justine had asked for was a few of Charlotte's special recipes, but her grandmother had gone far beyond her expectations.

"Grandma's determined to finish organizing everything before she and Ben leave on their Christmas cruise in two weeks."

"She has quite a few, then?" Her mother's hand trembled as she lifted her cup.

"I'd say a couple of hundred. Mom, you've just got to see it. Ben typed everything into the computer for her. Then Grandma read over each of the recipes and added special touches and little anecdotes. She made me my very own family cookbook. She even included recipes from friends like Grace and Corrie McAfee and Peggy Beldon. All her holiday dishes are there, too. But the best part is the little notes."

"Give me an example," Olivia said.

"Well, for instance, on her recipe for cinnamon rolls, she says that if she's baking them for Jack to leave out the raisins."

Her mother nodded.

"Grandma thought it was funny that Jack would hate raisins since he likes grapes."

Her mother's eyes softened. "He likes plums, too, but not prunes, you know."

Justine thought they should avoid any further comment on Jack's dislike of dried fruit. "Anyway," she went on, "Grandma has all kinds of hints, plus she explains where she got some of the recipes. Remember all those wakes she attended over the years?" Justine and Olivia shared a complicit grin. "Mom, the cookbook's a real treasure."

"That's your grandmother," Olivia murmured. "When she sets her mind on something, there's no holding her back."

"It's the most wonderful gift she could've given me."

"Your brother's favorite cookies were gingerbread." Her mother seemed lost in thought.

"James?"

"Jordan. Only he didn't want me to bake them in the shape of little men. He was far too *cool* for that. So I made them round like every other cookie."

Justine didn't remember that.

"He asked me to bake them for him."

They seldom talked about Jordan's youth. Even now, after more than twenty years, it was simply too painful. The fact that her mother was talking about his favorite cookies was decidedly odd.

"Jordan wanted you to bake cookies? When?" He'd died in August and it was unlikely that their mother would've been baking cookies on one of the hottest days of the summer.

Olivia threw Justine a puzzled look. "This morning."

Justine froze. When she spoke, she kept her voice soft. "You couldn't have talked to Jordan this morning, Mom."

Olivia stared at her blankly and then, seemingly embarrassed, shook her head. "Of course it wasn't this morning. I don't know what I was thinking. Jordan can't ask me to bake cookies, can he?"

"No, Mom, he can't." Alarmed, Justine studied her mother carefully. Her eyes were far too bright, and they glittered with fever.

"I'm so thirsty," Olivia said. She picked up her cup and this time her hand shook uncontrollably. Tea splashed over the sides before the cup fell from her fingers and crashed to the table, spilling tea on the Christmas-themed place mats.

Leaping to her feet, Justine dashed to her mother's side.

"What have I done?" Olivia cried. "Look at

this mess!"

"Don't worry about that. I'm getting you back to bed."

Olivia regarded Justine with a confused expression, as if unsure where she was.

Supporting her mother, Justine managed to get her out of the kitchen and down the long hallway to the master bedroom. With one arm around her waist, she half carried, half dragged her to the bed.

Once Olivia was covered by the sheet, Justine felt her mother's face and nearly gasped aloud at how hot she was to the touch. She located a temperature strip in the bathroom, then pressed it against Olivia's forehead.

The reading nearly sent her into a panic. No one needed to tell her that with a temperature of a hundred and five degrees her mother was in a life-threatening situation.

"I'll be fine, Justine," Olivia insisted in a slurred voice. "Jack will be home soon."

"I'm calling him right this minute!"

"No . . . don't do that. No need. I'll go back to sleep and . . . be fine."

Rather than argue, Justine left her mother and rushed into the kitchen. She ignored the spilled tea as she scrambled to find Jack's cell number. Ever organized, her mother had written it neatly in the telephone directory under *Jack*.

He didn't answer for three rings.

It felt more like three years. When he did pick up, Justine burst out, "Something's wrong with Mom. Her temperature's a hundred and five . . . she's talking to Jordan. . . . Jack, what should I do?"

To his credit, Jack didn't ask any questions. "I'm on my way," he said urgently. "I'll get in touch with her oncologist right now. I'm close . . . I'll be there in under ten minutes."

Justine went back to check on her mother, only to find that Olivia appeared to be having entire conversations with Jordan now. She chuckled at something and murmured, "Oh, Jordan, you always made me laugh."

"Mom, Mom." Justine sat on the edge of the bed and took her mother's hand. Her heart raced and she struggled to hold back the tears.

The sound of a speeding car reached her. Justine ran into the living room, praying frantically that it was Jack. Instead it was a teenage boy, driving recklessly in a souped-up vehicle without a muffler. She scanned the road for any sign of Jack.

In another five minutes, he was there. He banged the door open and dashed into the house, shouting for her.

"In here," Justine cried.

Jack tore into the bedroom. Olivia gazed

up at him as though she'd never seen him before.

"She's out of her mind with fever," Justine said, not even trying to hide her fear. "It's high, Jack. Way too high."

"Dr. Franklin said we're to get her to the hospital." He scooped Olivia into his arms, blankets and all, and started for the front door. By this point Olivia was too weak to protest.

Justine hurried along at his side, gathering up the dragging blanket. They got Olivia into the backseat of his car and drove straight to the hospital in Bremerton. Justine rode with her mother.

"He never grew up," Olivia said, turning to Justine.

"Do you mean Jordan, Mom?"

She smiled and laid her head against the seat. "When he asked about the gingerbread cookies, he was thirteen. He still is . . ."

Justine clutched her mother's hand, working hard to keep the emotion at bay. Jack went over the speed limit when he could, with the windows open so the cold December air blew into the car. It was his desperate attempt to bring down her fever. Olivia closed her eyes as the icy breeze touched her heated face. Justine shivered. She hadn't bothered to grab her jacket or purse, and her teeth were beginning to chatter.

Once they arrived at the hospital, everything happened quickly. Her mother's physician had phoned ahead and the hospital staff was waiting for them.

Justine and Jack sat in silence until Dr. Franklin, the oncologist, appeared. His face was grim. "I'm afraid Olivia has a massive infection at the site of her incision," he said.

"How could this be?" Jack demanded. "We were so careful. We followed all the instructions to the letter."

"We probably won't ever know the exact cause. Our biggest concern at the moment is to get her temperature down. We'll be starting her on antibiotics intravenously."

He left them, saying he'd be back as soon as Olivia had been admitted.

Jack was pale, the look on his face anguished. He seemed to blame himself. "I should never have gone out," he said over and over. "Thank God you were there."

The Christmas music playing in the background seemed incongruous, but it reminded her that she and Seth had planned to put up their tree this afternoon. Now the prospect of preparing for the holidays was the farthest thing from her mind.

"Mom's going to be all right," she said because she needed to hear it. Needed to say it.

"Yes," Jack confirmed, but he didn't sound confident.

While they waited for news, Justine phoned Seth to explain where she was. He assured her that he could easily keep Leif occupied and sent Olivia his best wishes.

When Dr. Franklin returned, his voice was grave. "Olivia is stable. As I told you, I've started her on a high dose of antibiotics. Her temperature is down a couple of degrees. We have her lying on an ice blanket, which has helped quite a bit."

"Thank God," Jack whispered again.

"Although she's in stable condition, I don't want to discount the seriousness of this infection. Another four or five hours, and we might not have been able to save her."

Justine's hand flew to her mouth.

"We're going to fight this to the best of our ability. The problem, of course, is that Olivia's immune system is already compromised. This isn't something we can deal with overnight. She'll probably be here for several days."

Jack nodded. "I'd like to stay with her if I could."

Dr. Franklin nodded.

When he'd gone, Jack turned to Justine and handed her the keys to his car. She stared at them, not understanding his intent.

"Take the car home," he said. "When you come back, bring me a set of clothes."

"But, Jack —"

"I'm not leaving Olivia again," he insisted. "I'm never leaving her alone again."

SIXTEEN

Shirley Bliss glanced out the front window. The streetlights had come on more than an hour ago. Tanni was late for dinner again, which wasn't an unusual occurrence since she'd taken up with Shaw, the boy who seemed to have only one name. Shirley had met him once, briefly. Tanni was none too eager for her to talk to this young man, for reasons Shirley didn't understand. It was times like this that she missed Jim the most.

Her husband had been close to Tanni, and their daughter had never recovered from his death.

Shirley would never recover, either.

It was almost a year now. A very difficult year.

As long as she lived, Shirley would remember that January afternoon, when the young officer from the Washington State Patrol rang her doorbell. She'd been in her art room in the basement, working on a new quilt, and the interruption had annoyed her. Jim, a pilot for Alaska Airlines, had left for the airport two hours earlier. He usually flew the Seattle-Anchorage route. As he often did, he'd taken his Harley-Davidson motorcycle rather than his car.

At first Shirley couldn't figure out why there was a patrolman at her door. She had trouble taking in his words — that there'd been an accident and her husband had not survived.

Even then Shirley hadn't understood. There must be a mistake, she'd said. Two hours ago Jim had kissed her on the cheek, not wanting to disturb her work, and set out for the airport. Two hours earlier, the man she'd spent twenty years of her life with had told her he'd see her the following night.

Now he was dead? It couldn't be. It wasn't possible.

The officer, apparently accustomed to this sort of reaction, had asked if there was someone he could contact on her behalf, a family member, a pastor or perhaps a friend.

Closing her eyes, Shirley tried to force her thoughts away from that horrible afternoon, a time that had forever changed her life and the lives of her children.

Of the three of them, Nick seemed to have adjusted the most successfully to the loss of his father. He was protective of both Shirley and his younger sister. He'd stepped into that role in a way that astonished her. Jim would've been so proud of their son. Over Christmas, when Nick was home from school for a couple of weeks, Shirley planned to talk with him about Tanni.

Tanni wasn't the same after Jim's death. Unlike her brother, she'd withdrawn from her friends and family, especially Shirley. In fact, Tanni seemed to blame Shirley for the accident; she'd said as much. If Shirley had made more of a fuss, perhaps Jim wouldn't have bought that stupid motorcycle. Shirley should've insisted he take the car that afternoon. She should've known, should've stopped him, should've done *something*. On and on. That was pretty well the extent of any conversation with Tanni.

Shirley had stopped trying to defend herself. There was no point. These days, their daughter was immersed in her art, spending hours alone in her room. She talked to Shirley as little as possible and refused to show her anything she'd drawn.

In the beginning, Tanni's relationship with Shaw had encouraged Shirley. For the first time since her father's death, Tanni had shown some enthusiasm for life. She had a friend, someone who was important to her.

They'd met around Thanksgiving and been practically inseparable ever since.

Shaw always picked her up in front of the house and dropped her off there. Whenever he pulled up she shot out the door with barely a word and didn't return for hours. That left next to no opportunity for questions. When Tanni did get home, she hated what she called "the inquisition" and ignored her mother completely.

"Just leave me alone." That seemed to be her daughter's mantra.

But Shirley couldn't do that. Her fear was that in her vulnerable emotional state, Tanni would become physically involved with Shaw. Her imagination ran wild with distressing scenarios, from teen pregnancy to disease to substance abuse. Tanni was too young for such an intense relationship. Too trusting, too naive, too *hurt.*

Shirley felt helpless. Every time she tried to talk to her daughter, Tanni shut her out.

The phone rang, and it caught Shirley off guard. She reacted with a physical jerk, then reached for the receiver.

"Hello?" She hoped she'd hear her daughter, calling with a reason for being late. Or, better yet, a promise to get home soon.

"Is this Shirley Bliss?" It was a male voice, one she didn't recognize.

"Yes," she said anxiously. Her pulse raced. Worried as she was about Tanni, she was terrified that this stranger had bad news. After all, if it had happened once, it could happen again.

"Hello, Shirley. I'm Will Jefferson."

The name seemed familiar, but she couldn't immediately recall where she'd heard it before. Then it came to her.

"I hope you don't mind my contacting you like this."

She thought the new gallery owner sounded a little too smooth and polished. "What can I do for you, Mr. Jefferson?" She spoke in a businesslike tone.

"Please, it's Will."

Shirley rolled her eyes. "You called because . . ."

"I recently purchased the Harbor Street Gallery."

"Yes, I know." She was grateful the gallery had found a new owner and that there'd be an outlet for her work. Many of the local artists depended on the income generated there.

"I was told you'd be a good person to talk to," Will explained. "I'm interested in showing your work, of course, but I also have some ideas for renovating the gallery. I hoped we might have a chance to chat. I'd appreciate your feedback."

"Yes, well . . ."

"I realize this is Saturday afternoon and it's a very busy time of year, but I was hoping we could get together early in the week. Would that work for you?"

"I suppose." Shirley raised her head as she heard a car door closing in the distance.

"How about Tuesday?"

"Ah, sure." At this point she just wanted to get off the phone.

Will suggested they meet at the gallery and she noted the date and time on her calendar.

"I look forward to seeing you again," Will said, as they ended the conversation.

She frowned. "Again?"

"Yes, we met briefly a couple of weeks ago when you picked up the check for the sail-boat piece — the fabric collage."

Oh, yes — they *had* met. Shirley remembered exactly what he looked like now. Will Jefferson was strikingly attractive — and his reputation had preceded him. Apparently he'd been born and raised in Cedar Cove and was a known ladies' man, although he'd been back in town for only a few weeks. But she didn't generally pay much attention to gossip; she preferred to form her own opinions.

The front door opened.

"I'll see you later, then," she said quickly.

"Great. Thanks, Shirley." There was a significant pause. "I have the feeling we're going to become great friends. See you Tuesday."

"Goodbye."

Shirley stared down at the phone as she hung up. Their conversation, however short, had left her with the impression that he had an elevated view of himself and his charms.

Tanni went directly to her room and closed the door.

Shirley followed and knocked politely.

"What?" her daughter demanded.

Rather than ask questions that would only be resented, Shirley took another approach. "Dinner's ready."

"I already ate," Tanni said without opening the door.

"If you don't mind, I'd like some company. Eating by myself every night is boring."

Silence.

She waited several minutes and then, dismayed, walked back to the kitchen. Earlier that afternoon, Shirley had made a soup that had been one of Jim's favorite's — cauliflower, potato and cheese. It was the perfect meal for a cold winter night.

She ladled a scoop into her bowl, then sat down at the kitchen table. As was her practice, she bowed her head for a brief prayer, adding a request for help in reaching her daughter.

When Shirley raised her head, Tanni was entering the kitchen. Rather than reveal any satisfaction, she shook out her linen napkin and placed it on her lap.

"What's that?" Tanni asked, gesturing at the Crock-Pot.

"Soup."

"Well, duh, I can see *that*. What kind?"

At another time, Shirley would have reacted to Tanni's rudeness; for now she'd disregard it. She knew its source, and knew it was more important to leave herself open and available. So she answered mildly, "The cauliflower recipe."

Tanni's eyes showed the first sign of pleasure Shirley had seen in weeks.

"Want to join me?" she asked, then instantly wished she could cancel the invitation. Anytime she showed any desire for her daughter's company, Tanni withdrew.

"I said I already ate."

"Sorry, I forgot."

Her daughter lingered in the kitchen, which encouraged her. Shirley dipped her spoon into the soup, afraid to say anything more.

She couldn't resist for long. "Did you and

Shaw have a good time?" The question was a risk but Shirley hoped it was benign enough not to offend her daughter. She took another spoonful of soup — and did her best to ignore the hickey on Tanni's neck.

Tanni shrugged. "I guess."

She wanted to ask where they'd gone, but decided not to jeopardize this opportunity for communication.

"I was on the phone when you came in," Shirley said pleasantly. "The man who bought the Harbor Street Gallery wants to meet with me next week."

"I heard the gallery sold," Tanni murmured. "What does he want to talk to you about?"

"The renovation he's got planned. Apparently he's interested in my ideas."

"Oh." Tanni pulled out a chair and sat down across from her.

Shirley tried to conceal her surprise — and relief. Then it dawned on her that if Tanni was willing to talk, it was probably because she wanted something.

"Do we have plans for Christmas?" she asked.

"Yes." Shirley didn't elaborate.

"Like what?" The question sounded more like an accusation than a request for information.

"Your brother will be home and —"

"Big deal."

"And," Shirley added pointedly, "we're going over to see your grandparents." Jim's parents lived in Seattle, and Shirley felt it was important for their sakes, as well as Nick and Tanni's, that they keep in touch.

"I can see them anytime," Tanni protested.

"True, but unless you set a date, it doesn't happen. They're really looking forward to our coming."

Frowning, Tanni glanced down at her hands; she seemed to be struggling, caught between duty and desire.

"Did you have someplace you'd rather go?" Shirley asked without censure.

Her daughter shrugged. "Shaw and I . . ." She didn't complete the thought.

"Would you like to invite him to join us?"

Tanni raised her head. She seemed to seriously consider the question. "I might."

"He's welcome."

"He's talented, Mom."

Shirley didn't want to appear dense, but she had no idea how this supposed talent manifested itself. "In what way?"

"Art." She sighed as if it should've been obvious.

That explained a great deal. Tanni was gifted, too, although she hadn't let Shirley see her work in ages. No one was more surprised than Shirley when she learned that her daughter had won a local art competition. Tanni's teacher had entered the drawing and hadn't told her. Tanni had been upset, insisting the whole thing was "meaningless."

"Would you like me to look at his work?" she offered casually.

Again her daughter mulled over the question. "He's not ready yet, but I think he will be soon."

"That's fine, then. Whenever he's ready."

"The thing is . . ." Tanni paused.

"Yes?"

"The stuff he draws might bother you."

"I can look beyond the subject matter," she assured her daughter.

"Could you . . ." Tanni seemed uneasy about whatever she wanted to ask.

"Could I what?" Shirley pressed.

"If you think his work is good — and I do, Mom, I really do — could you talk to Mr. Jefferson about Shaw?"

Shirley needed a moment to make the connection. "You want me to find out if he'd be willing to display Shaw's art?"

Tanni's eyes met hers and she nodded.

"Well, if he's as good as you say, I wouldn't have a problem with that."

Tanni smiled at her, something she hadn't done in months. Granted, it was more of a quirk of her lips than a real smile. But it would do.

"So . . . you think he's got talent."

Tanni nodded.

"More than you?"

Her daughter hesitated and then responded without vanity. "No, but then he doesn't have a mother who's an artist or a dad who was really interested in art, so he hasn't got that advantage."

Her heart warmed at the acknowledgment — and at Tanni's reference to her dad. She hardly ever spoke of him, let alone in such a natural, easy way.

"I'm teaching him everything I learned from you guys," she was saying.

In the early years, before Shirley had begun to work with fabric, her daughter would play at her feet while Shirley drew. She gave Tanni her first sketchbook when she was four and the girl had been drawing from that point on. Shirley was devastated when she'd learned that Tanni had destroyed those early sketchbooks after Jim's funeral.

"I'm happy you're teaching Shaw."

"The relationship isn't as one-sided as that makes it sound," Tanni said, smiling again. Her fingers crept up to cover the hickey on the side of her neck. "Shaw's teaching me quite a bit, too."

That was exactly what she was afraid of.

SEVENTEEN

The tension between Dave and Emily had escalated until he found it almost intolerable. Whenever he tried to talk to her, she acted as if he were invisible. As soon as he made an attempt, she simply walked into another room.

Although they were civil in front of the children, Emily avoided him as much as possible. She didn't speak to him unless it was to answer a question, and then, only if others were present. Moreover, she'd answer it with the minimum number of words. Her blond hair taunted him. Still, Dave was reluctant to tell her the truth, fearing what that would do to their marriage.

Sunday morning's sermon was the most difficult Dave had preached in all the years of his ministry. Afterward he knew, deep inside himself, that he'd let down his congregation, his family and, most important, his God.

By the time the church emptied, Emily had already taken the two boys home. Dave stayed behind, sitting in the front pew, feeling like a complete failure. He'd lied to his wife, misled his staff and tried to hold everything together on his own. He'd failed every person in his life.

The only thing to do now was admit to his shortcomings. This situation couldn't go on.

Dave accepted *what* he had to do, but wasn't sure how to do it. For a full thirty minutes, he sat there in church, pondering the conversation with Emily. Who would've guessed he'd have such a problem telling the truth?

He bowed his head and prayed, asking God to forgive him. When he finished, he left the church to seek forgiveness from his wife.

As he walked into the parking lot, he felt as if someone had poured lead into his shoes. He would've welcomed some kind of interruption, anything that allowed him a few minutes' reprieve while he tried to overcome his qualms, his feelings of inadequacy. He'd never meant for things to go this far. If he could have turned back the clock, made better choices, he would've done so. Instead he had to confess his pride and where it had led him. Now he had to confess to his wife that he'd fallen into the trap that very pride had set.

When he arrived at the house on Sandpiper Way, he sat in his car for several minutes. Emily loved this house. She'd wanted it so badly and because he loved her and tried to please her, he'd done everything possible to make it happen. He hadn't predicted all the grief this house would bring him. Yet he had no one to blame but himself.

The boys, who sat at the kitchen table, looked up when Dave came in.

"Hey, Dad, Mom made macaroni and cheese."

Dave ruffled his youngest son's hair. "Yum."

"What took you so long?" Matthew asked. "Mom said we shouldn't wait lunch for you."

"Where's your mother?" Dave asked, instead of answering his son's question. He'd do his best to make it up to his sons, compensate for all the time he'd cheated them out of. He hoped to make it up to Emily, too.

"In your room, I guess," Mark responded. His face was concerned. "Mom's not feeling good. She made lunch and then went to bed."

"Yeah," Matthew said. "She was crying, too."

The boy seemed to look straight through

Dave, as if silently blaming him for his mother's tears. Dave's stomach tensed.

"I'll go check on your mother. Listen, you two, save some of that macaroni and cheese for me." He added this on a cheerful note, although it sounded forced even to his own ears.

Dave made his way down the hall to the master bedroom. He hesitated before opening the door and stepping inside. The drapes were closed. It took him a few seconds to adjust to the darkness. Once he did, he saw that Emily was in bed, either asleep or pretending to be.

Undecided, he hesitated once more, weighing his options. He was tempted to delay this, and yet he knew his confession wouldn't be any easier if he put it off.

Slowly he approached the bed. When he sat down, the mattress dipped slightly with his weight. Emily lay on her side, facing him. Even after four days, he wasn't used to seeing her as a blonde. The new color and style had received plenty of attention at church that morning. Of course, that was what she wanted. Attention. Love. Recognition. All of which Dave had failed to give her.

Her eyes remained closed. If she was awake, she certainly succeeded at pretending otherwise. But then, she'd become an expert at ignoring him.

"I think it's time for us to resolve this, once and for all," he said. His voice was tight and controlled.

In response Emily rolled over, now facing the opposite wall. Apparently she wasn't interested in clearing the air. He understood her anger; nevertheless, he forged ahead.

"You think I'm having an affair, don't you?" He realized almost immediately that he shouldn't come at her with questions. What his wife needed was reassurance. "Don't answer that," he said quickly. "It's not important."

"Not important?" Emily startled him when she bolted upright and glared at him.

Once again Dave saw his mistake. "I didn't mean it like *that.*"

"Oh, but I think you do." She folded her arms across her chest, her body language unambiguous.

"Emily, on my life, I swear I've always been faithful to you and I always will be." She deserved that assurance, that pledge. Everything else could wait. It was crucial that she know he'd never betray her or the vows they shared.

Her face soured with skepticism and doubt. "Every husband who's cheating swears he's being faithful." She spoke with open sarcasm. "Shall I bring out the Bible so you can swear on it?"

"Emily, please . . ."

"You think I don't know the signs? Well, I've got them memorized and frankly, the evidence damns you."

She sounded so knowledgeable that her unwavering certainty struck him dumb.

"You think I'm naive and stupid, don't you?" she demanded, eyes narrowed. "I've read articles on the subject. All wives know. This kind of betrayal is too deep, too fundamental not to feel it, not to recognize it on a gut level. Some women choose to ignore the signs, but on a subconscious level each one knows."

"I . . ."

"They say the wife's the last to find out. Wrong. We're the first."

"Emily, if you'd listen —"

"No. It's *your* turn to listen to *me.* Do you honestly believe I didn't notice those two and three nights a week you were late? It got to be like clockwork. How stupid do you think I am?"

"It was three nights."

"So you're admitting an affair!"

"No." He had a hard time getting in even one-word responses. He decided just to let her vent. When she'd finished, he'd explain.

"I didn't think so. You're going to try and talk your way out of this. But I won't pretend any longer, Dave. If you want a divorce, you can have one. I'm through."

Nothing could have shocked him more. "I don't want a divorce! If you'd give me a chance, I could —"

She cut him off yet again. "Of course you don't want a divorce. It wouldn't look good on your pastoral résumé to say you're a divorced father of two, now, would it?"

"Emily, stop! This is crazy."

Tossing aside the covers, she rose onto her knees. "I'm not going to stop! There's a lot of anger stored up inside me. I'm ready to explode with it. How dare you embarrass me in front of my family and friends! Even my mother said she thought something wasn't right."

"You talked to your mother about this?" It was all he could do not to groan out loud.

"Does that surprise you?"

It did, and it humiliated him even further. "You shared your suspicions with your mother and not with me?" That hurt. It hurt more than the fact that she'd brought her doubts to his mother-in-law.

"At first, I didn't want to know," Emily said. "No wife cares to admit that her husband's involved with someone else. According to the articles I read, that's common."

"Emily," he began forcefully. "I'm saying it again, and it's the truth. I am *not* having an affair."

She rolled her eyes toward the ceiling, her arms still crossed, blocking him out. "Right," she muttered with more than a hint of sarcasm.

"I took a part-time job."

Her arms fell to her sides as she studied him, her eyes puzzled. Confused. Dave met her gaze full on, not flinching.

"A . . . job?" she asked after a moment.

"I'm working at First National Bank as a security guard after hours, three nights a week." He'd considered it the perfect solution. He was inside the building ninety-nine percent of the time, so no one saw him. Very occasionally, he filled in for someone else, like the afternoon he'd gone to Olivia's house. Normally, though, he did swing shift, from four to ten. Not much was asked of him, other than to watch a series of television monitors. It was a position created after a series of break-ins in the area. He didn't carry a gun, just a radio.

Emily's mouth sagged open as she weighed the viability of his explanation.

Dave could see her wondering whether to believe him, wondering whether this was another lie, like so many others.

"Why . . . why would you do that?" she asked in a quavering voice.

This was the most difficult part of his confession. Before he could explain, she came up with her own reasoning.

"Are you a gambler, Dave?"

Dave was beginning to get irritated. "How can you ask me something like that?" Despite his best efforts, he couldn't keep the anguish out of his voice. "Don't you know me at all, Em? Have I destroyed everything because I wanted you to have this house you love so much?"

In the blink of an eye, her expression went from suspicion to shock. "The . . . house?"

"It was a financial stretch when we signed the papers."

"But I thought . . . I assumed . . ."

"And I let you," Dave said, not allowing her to finish. He was the one to blame. Little did he realize at the time that he'd set them up for financial ruin. Emily had wanted the house and Dave wanted her to have it. He handled all the finances, paid the bills. Every month he gave Emily a budget and she did a masterful job of keeping their living expenses within it.

"Do you mean to say we can't *afford* this house?" she asked.

His heart in his throat, Dave lowered his head, unable to meet her eyes. "The mortgage broker managed to get the payments within reach, with the understanding that they'd increase every six months." As it was, their budget had been strained to the breaking point and then, six months out, the mortgage company had hit him with the first increase.

"You took on an extra job without talking to me . . . without telling me why?" Pain bled into each word.

"I didn't want you to worry that we might lose the house," he mumbled.

"You'd rather let me think you were with another woman?"

It hadn't actually dawned on him that she'd make such an assumption. "I didn't really think you'd notice. I thought you'd figure I was just working later than usual."

There were often committee meetings in the evenings, and he'd figured Emily would believe he'd skipped dinner and stayed late because of them.

"I did think that in the beginning," she murmured softly. "But I started to notice how distracted you'd become. It wasn't like you. Then . . ." She hesitated.

"Then what?" he prompted.

"It was a few weeks ago. You closed your

office door, and after a while I picked up the phone and hit Redial." She lowered her eyes. "A woman answered and asked if it was Davey."

Dave nearly groaned. "That's Maxine. She works as a guard, too. She needed to change schedules with me. She'd left a message on my cell and I called her back to arrange it. If you met her, you'd see that she's sixty years old — and a grandmother. I'm *not* involved with her."

"But . . . you were gone so often."

Dave had to agree the extra hours had drained his energy to the point that when he arrived home, he was exhausted and out of sorts.

"We'll sell the house," Emily said. "You can't continue like this."

With that part, Dave agreed. He'd grown tired and impatient with those around him. Even Angel, his assistant, had commented. He hated the changes he saw in himself and yet seemed powerless to overcome them.

"We can't sell." They were trapped. This was the worst of what he had to tell her.

"Of course we can."

"Emily, don't you suppose I've thought of that?" he said. "In this market, the house is no longer worth what we paid for it. I got us into a huge financial hole."

She sank down, sitting on her heels. "I'll get a job," she said, as if that would solve everything. "I've been volunteering at the school, and a position may be opening up there. I'll apply. . . ." She closed her eyes in concentration. "I can try The Quilted Giraffe, too. They all know me there."

"We decided when we married," Dave reminded her, "that you'd be a stay-at-home mother for our children."

"I will be," Emily said. "I'll make sure it's understood when I apply that my hours have to coincide with the boys' schedule."

Even then Dave didn't really like it. "I hate the thought of you having to get a job. I should be the one to provide for our family."

"Oh, honestly, Dave, get a grip. Join the twenty-first century. I appreciate that you'd like me to be at home and I enjoy it, but I want to make a financial contribution to our family. Besides, the boys are older now. And I *need* to help. In fact, I insist on it."

It went against his pride to acknowledge his relief. "You really think the school or the fabric shop would agree to those hours?" This was a solution, although not one he would've asked Emily to consider.

His wife nodded enthusiastically. "The job

at the school would be as a classroom aide. The principal already suggested I apply if they get permission to post it."

"You didn't say anything." If she'd mentioned it earlier, he didn't remember.

She grinned. "Well, no, because I was still thinking about it. I do have a few secrets of my own, you know."

Dave felt almost dizzy with relief. "I should've said something sooner. I should've told you what was going on."

"Yes, you should have."

A huge weight had lifted from his shoulders. He was a pastor, a man of God, and yet he'd ignored a basic creed found in the Bible. *The truth shall set you free.* And he *was* free for the first time in months.

Emily moved closer to him and Dave slipped his arms around her. For a long moment all they did was hold each other. Emily had her arms around his neck. When she whispered something in his ear, he stiffened.

"The watch?" he repeated.

"You'd better explain that to me as well."

Dave sagged onto the bed. He'd been sick with guilt over losing that watch. And yet its appearance at the judge's house embarrassed him all the more.

"Dave," Emily said. *"Where did you get a gold watch?"*

He sighed and then explained. "Before she died, Martha Evans gave it to me."

His wife frowned as if she didn't believe him. This was his biggest fear. "I know what you're thinking," he murmured. "That I should never have accepted a family heirloom, and you're right."

"That's not what I was thinking . . ." Emily withdrew her arms and stared at him with such intensity that Dave wanted to cry out in anger and frustration.

"Do you seriously believe I'd steal Martha's jewelry?" he asked. "What kind of man do you think I am?"

"I . . . I —"

"First you accuse me of having an affair and now you suspect I'm a thief." His wife's low opinion of him shocked Dave. Despite what she'd assumed was evidence, Emily was the one person he'd expected to stand by his side. Now it was clear his own wife doubted him. And if Emily did, so would everyone else. Thankfully he had proof of Martha Evans's intentions.

Emily was quick to apologize. "I know, and I'm sorry."

"A few days before she died, Martha told me she wanted me to have her husband's retirement watch."

"Dave —"

"I refused," he broke in. "I had no interest in accepting such a gift, but Martha said she'd talked to her attorney and everything had already been settled. She left that watch to me in her will."

Dave wasn't entirely innocent in the matter. He should've asked Allan for confirmation. He was uncomfortable with the fact that the attorney hadn't said anything about the watch. "As you might understand, when I heard that some of Martha's jewelry had turned up missing, I was afraid suspicion would fall on me because I had the watch in my possession."

"You didn't wear the watch until this week?" she asked, making his behavior sound suspect, just as he'd feared.

"You're right, I didn't wear it. Then I decided I didn't have anything to hide. She gave it to me, and that's noted in the will, which the family has read. So there wasn't any reason not to wear it. My own watch needs a new battery. What I didn't realize was that the clasp on the gold watch was loose."

"Oh."

"I'd never take anything that didn't belong to me." That was not only a fundamental tenet of his faith, it was a painful lesson Dave had learned in his youth. Even his wife didn't know about his criminal record as a teenager.

Emily remained silent.

"You believe me, don't you?"

Her hesitation was slight, but Dave noticed it nonetheless.

"Emily?"

"I believe you," she said and hugged him again.

"I'm sorry," he whispered. "I should've told you about our money problems, and about the watch, too."

"I need to be more aware of our finances, Dave."

He nodded. "You're right." In fact, he'd be more than happy to hand over the bill-paying to Emily so she'd appreciate the pressure he'd been under. Despite his part-time position, things hadn't really improved.

Every time he thought they were making headway, something would come up. Last month it was new tires for Emily's car. They couldn't afford them, but Dave refused to ignore the safety of his wife and children. He'd cut up all but one credit card and that was just for emergencies. He was maxed out on that card and only able to make minimum payments.

Dave wished he'd sold the gold watch. It

had been a foolish mistake to wear it and even more imprudent to lose it . . . especially at Judge Griffin's house.

EIGHTEEN

It was late afternoon. Grace Harding dozed fitfully in a chair in Olivia's hospital room, jerking awake every once in a while. Olivia was hooked up to an IV; antibiotics flowed through it, as did a saline drip to prevent dehydration. She was connected to various pieces of monitoring equipment via other tubes, as well. The fever was down, thank God, but the medical staff continued to watch her carefully.

The room was dark now, and Grace glanced at her watch. The daylight hours were dwindling as winter solstice approached. Signs of Christmas were everywhere, but rarely had Grace felt less like celebrating. Her dearest friend was seriously ill. And soon after Olivia had recovered from this, she'd be starting her chemotherapy. There was no way of knowing yet how bad that would be.

Straightening, Grace bent forward to get

the kinks out of her neck. Jack would be returning any minute, and the last thing he needed was to find her fearful and worried. He'd been at Olivia's side constantly. Grace and Cliff had come at noon, and Grace had finally convinced him to leave for a few hours — to let Cliff drive him back to the house to shower and change clothes. Even then, Jack had been reluctant.

The door slid open and Cliff stuck his head in. "Any change?" he asked.

"None that I can see." Olivia had been asleep the entire time. "Where's Jack?"

"He met Justine in the hallway. He's giving her an update."

Grace would be forever grateful that Justine had gone to her mother's house yesterday morning. It might well have meant the difference between life and death.

"Charlotte and Ben are here, too," Cliff said. Olivia's mother had spent the morning at the hospital, along with Ben. They'd gone home for a few hours but were obviously back.

The private room was small, and when Justine and Jack came inside a few minutes later, Grace decided to take a break. She needed a cup of coffee and some fresh air. Cliff sat with Charlotte and Ben in the waiting area, watching television.

"I'm going down to the cafeteria for a cup of coffee," she announced.

Charlotte, who was contentedly knitting, was the only one who seemed to hear. "Oh, you're up," she said. "I glanced in earlier but I didn't want to wake you."

Ben and Cliff were both concentrating on the last few minutes of the Seattle Seahawks football game.

"Does anyone need anything?" she asked.

Charlotte looked up from her knitting again. "I'm fine, Grace, thank you."

"Cliff? Ben?"

Her husband smiled briefly in her direction. "I'm good, thanks."

"Me, too," Ben returned without moving his eyes from the screen.

Cliff had told her that this game would determine the team's ranking in the playoffs later in the season. Grace liked football well enough, but at the moment it seemed irrelevant to her. She was too concerned about Olivia.

When she got to the cafeteria, she stood in line with a couple of male nurses and reached for a midsize cup. Someone came to stand behind her, but she didn't look over her shoulder.

"Hello, Grace."

She made an effort to disguise the effect

Will Jefferson's voice had on her. She shouldn't be surprised that he'd shown up at the hospital. Olivia was, after all, his sister, and he was as worried as anyone. Apparently he'd visited Olivia yesterday evening, but their paths hadn't crossed.

She turned. "Hello, Will." She spoke in a controlled, even voice. Their history made her wary of him. It wouldn't be out of character for Will to say or do something to make her uncomfortable.

"How's my sister?"

"There hasn't been any change since early this morning."

"She's out of danger, isn't she?"

She nodded. "Immediate danger, yes. She's still fighting the infection."

"Poor Liv," he murmured.

Grace reached the coffee machine and filled her cup. Will followed and filled his own. She noticed that his shoulders were wet.

"It's raining?" she asked, disappointed because that meant she couldn't go out for fresh air.

"Afraid so," Will said. "Actually, I was hoping for snow."

Grace smiled. "You and every school-age child in Cedar Cove."

Will grinned back at her. "Hey, I guess I'm

still a kid at heart."

"Apparently so." In more ways than one, she mused. She got to the cash register and was digging in her pocket for change when Will beat her to it.

"Both coffees," he instructed the cashier.

"Thank you, Will, but that isn't necessary."

He shrugged. "Consider it a peace offering." He gestured toward an empty table. "Do you have a few minutes?"

Grace hesitated.

"If Cliff objects, I'll understand."

Grace knew he was baiting her. Her husband wasn't an unreasonable man, nor was he particularly jealous, although Will had given him cause to doubt her.

"I just wanted to ask you a few questions about the gallery," he said.

She looked pointedly at her watch. "I don't suppose five minutes would hurt."

"Good." He led the way to a small table and sat down.

Grace joined him.

"I signed the final papers last week," he said proudly.

"Already? I didn't think you were taking over until January."

"I didn't, either, but the paperwork went smoothly and there was no reason to wait. The previous owners thought it would be to their advantage tax-wise to close early, so I agreed."

"Congratulations." She raised her cup in a gesture of celebration.

Will touched his own cup against hers. "If not for Olivia, I would never have known about the gallery."

"The community is grateful." Grace knew the art gallery had given many local artists their start. Jon Bowman, her son-in-law, was one of them. His photography was first displayed at the Harbor Street Gallery back in the days when Maryellen had managed it.

In fact, they'd met through the gallery. Jon's work was displayed in a large Seattle gallery these days, and he now had an agent. His photographs appeared in print ads, including a series of high-profile tourism ads for the state.

"I was astonished at the amount of artistic talent in this area," Will told her. "When's the last time you were in the gallery?"

Grace had to admit it had been some time. "I've only been by once or twice since Maryellen left." Her daughter had been instrumental in the success of the Harbor Street Gallery. When Maryellen was forced to give up her job due to a difficult pregnancy, the gallery's fortunes had steadily declined.

"That's the message I'm getting from everyone," Will said. "I'm talking to Maryellen, of course, but I'm also meeting with local artists and getting their suggestions on how to generate interest in the gallery again."

"That's a great idea," she said, and meant it.

"Thanks." He accepted her praise in an offhand manner. Staring down at his coffee, he asked, "Do you know Shirley Bliss?"

The name was vaguely familiar to Grace. "I think so . . . I seem to recall Maryellen being impressed with her work."

"She's a fabric artist. She quilts, but she also uses other techniques and she's very inventive about materials. Her work's really exciting."

The gallery had occasionally displayed fabric art, like Shirley's, but had tended to feature paintings and photography.

Will glanced up. "I'm hoping Shirley has some fresh ideas. We're meeting this week. I'd like to do more with fabric art." He added a little more sugar to his coffee and stirred. "Quilting and knitting are incredibly popular activities these days — as my mother has pointed out."

Grace nodded. "That's true."

"Mom thought I should have a special

quilt display," Will said. "They're usually seen as practical — you know, a traditional domestic craft — but they can be works of art."

Grace was pleased by Will's enthusiasm . . . and relieved that he'd found a focus for his time and energy. She finished her coffee, then said, "I really should get back."

"Right." Will held his cup with both hands. "Tell everyone I'll be there in a few minutes."

"Sure." Grace stood and turned to leave. "See you later."

When she entered the waiting area, the football game appeared to be over. Both Ben and Cliff spoke animatedly about the last-second win.

As Grace took the seat next to her husband, Cliff reached for her hand and intertwined their fingers.

"I met Will in the cafeteria," Grace told Charlotte casually.

"Oh, I'm glad," Charlotte murmured, pausing in the middle of counting stitches. "He said he was coming by."

"We talked for a few minutes." She mentioned this so it wouldn't come as a surprise, should Will bring it up in front of Cliff.

Her husband nodded, not questioning the comment, and she squeezed his fingers.

Justine came out of the hospital room and joined them, with Jack following a moment later.

"Shift change," he explained. Everyone was asked to leave when the next staff group came on duty and the nurses were updated on each patient's condition.

"How does Olivia look?" Charlotte asked anxiously.

"Not bad," Justine answered. "Mom's a trooper."

"She's awake now," Jack informed them. "You were right," he told Cliff and Grace, "she didn't know I'd been gone."

"Mom's going to be fine," Justine said with the certainty and optimism of the young.

Grace had every intention of believing those words. And if love, faith and prayers could make a difference, Olivia would indeed be fine.

"Hey, everyone."

Grace glanced up as Will stood in the entry to the waiting area.

"Hello, Will." Cliff got up and offered his hand.

They shook hands, then Will bent to kiss his mother's cheek and sat down next to Ben.

"Did you hear the Seahawks won?" Ben asked.

"I heard it from one of the physicians in the elevator." He leaned forward and rested his elbows on his knees. "So what's the latest on my sister?"

"She's improving," Jack told him. "Although she gave us all a fright."

Will nodded. "I'm glad she's doing better."

"We all are," Charlotte said with feeling. "But I'm still not sure Ben and I should be taking that cruise."

"Grandma." Justine shook her finger at Charlotte. "You're going. If Mom hears you're even thinking about not getting on that ship she'll have a fit."

"I did purchase travel insurance," Ben told everyone, "so we can cancel if we have to. I want Charlotte to have a good time, and she can't do that if she's worried about Olivia."

"Then there's only one thing to do," Jack said, looking at each person gathered there. "We'll all have to make sure Olivia recovers quickly."

Charlotte beamed. "I'm going home and making my chicken noodle soup. It worked when Olivia was a little girl and it's bound to work now."

"I love that soup," Will said, smiling at his mother. "I used to pretend I was sick just so Mom would make a batch."

"You sneak!" Charlotte burst out, and

everyone laughed.

"But like you always said, Mom, it cures whatever ails you."

Jack chuckled. "I wonder if those cancer specialists know about the medicinal qualities of Charlotte's soup."

"I'll tell them," Justine said.

Charlotte shoved her knitting in her bag. "Let's go, Ben. We'll be back with a thermos of chicken noodle soup." She stood up slowly, reaching for her husband.

Not for the first time, Grace noticed that Charlotte was showing her age. Ben, too, she thought as he rose awkwardly to his feet. They held each other, arms linked, and shuffled out.

Jack's gaze met hers, and it was plain that they shared the same concern. If Charlotte was going to make a batch of her chicken noodle soup, it might be a good idea if she and Ben had some, too.

A few minutes later, a nurse stepped into the waiting area.

"Olivia is now receiving guests," the woman said cheerfully. "She's doing well. I spoke with her physician, and Dr. Franklin thinks she should be able to go home in another day. Two at the most."

"That's great news!" Grace said, clasping her hands together.

"Yes, it is," Jack agreed. "And she hasn't even had her chicken soup yet."

Grace smiled. If Jack's sense of humor was back, things really were looking up.

NINETEEN

Christie was embarrassed to admit how nervous she felt about this dinner party her sister had arranged. When they'd met the previous week, Christie had agreed to contact James on her own. It'd sounded like a good idea at the time . . . .

And yet Christie couldn't make herself do it. The fear of rejection was just too strong. In exasperation Teri had intervened and asked both James and Christie to dinner. Christie knew James would be attending, but apparently he'd been left in the dark. She wasn't entirely comfortable with that — it didn't seem fair — but Teri insisted she knew what she was doing.

The two sisters had discussed their plan several times over the course of the day.

"What are you wearing?" Teri asked an hour before Christie was due to arrive.

So far she hadn't decided. She'd tried on almost every outfit she owned and discarded them all. "I . . . don't know yet. Do you have any suggestions?"

"Nothing too fancy," Teri cautioned. "The evening's supposed to be relaxed, low-key. Think casual."

Christie glanced at her reflection in the bedroom mirror and started to unfasten the sequined top. She hadn't liked the way it fit, anyway. "How about jeans and a sweater?" she asked next. Earlier that week, Wal-Mart had offered jeans on sale. Christie knew a bargain when she saw one and with her employee discount, the store had practically given her those Levi's.

"That's a little *too* casual. Do you have any black pants?"

Christie's gaze shot to her closet. "Yeah, I think so." Somewhere buried deep in the back there was probably a pair. She tended to stick to jeans; they fit well and were comfortable.

"Wear those and a sweater. Listen, I've got to scoot if I'm going to get dinner on the table."

Christie stopped her. "James still doesn't know I'm coming, right?"

Her sister hesitated. "Unfortunately he does. Bobby wasn't supposed to say anything but he forgot."

"Oh."

"He'll be here, don't worry."

"Okay."

"See you in an hour."

That hardly seemed long enough. Christie tore into her closet again. Clothes were scattered all over the floor and across her bed. Anyone looking at her room would assume she'd been the victim of a burglary. She'd worked today, so she hadn't bothered to make her bed, and between that and the clothes strewn everywhere, the room was a hopeless mess. Christie was pretty sure she knew what James would think if he were to see it.

Instantly the image of James naked and in her bed flashed into her mind. She couldn't begin to imagine what kind of lover he'd be. Polite to a fault, no doubt. She shook her head to dispel the image. Her heart raced, and she couldn't even figure out why she cared about this overpolite stuffed shirt, anyway.

But for reasons she didn't completely understand, she did care. She wanted him to like her; she wanted to be a better person for James.

She could still see the disappointment in his eyes when she'd come out of The Pink Poodle. Yes, she'd been drinking, but she wasn't drunk. Far from it. Besides, it wasn't any of his business where she was or who she was with or what she was doing. But . . . she couldn't forget that look in his eyes.

As Teri had said, James Wilbur was the first decent man who'd shown interest in her, and that left Christie feeling vulnerable and exposed. The man seemed to disapprove of Christie as much as he was attracted to her, which confused Christie. That confusion made her resentful, and her resentment made her . . . confused.

Tonight's date was a perfect example. It wasn't really even a date, just a "casual" dinner, and she should wear what she wanted. Yet here she was, worrying about every aspect of her appearance simply because James was going to be there.

Walking closer to the mirror, Christie studied her reflection. The woman who stared at her revealed none of the poise or elegance she'd worked so hard to create. Shaking back her hair, Christie wondered if this was just another instance of wanting what Teri had.

As a kid, Christie had followed her big sister around like a shadow. Teri had hated it and done everything she could to ditch her. In their teens and twenties, the animosity between them had nearly destroyed their relationship. If Teri had it, Christie wanted it. *It* included boys.

And later, men. She asked herself if what

Teri had this time was really so appealing. Well, yes.

First, her sister was married to a man who loved her, while Christie's marriage, brief though it was, had been a disaster from the start. The man who'd promised to cherish her had beaten her in a drunken rage instead. At the rate the violence had escalated, Christie figured she would've been dead within the year.

Her sister had security, too — financial *and* emotional. That was something neither of them had experienced in their youth. Teri wasn't the same person she'd been before marrying Bobby. Love had changed her. Christie envied her that.

Christie frowned at herself in the mirror. She didn't have time to stand here analyzing her feelings for James. They were just . . . there. Right now, she had an outfit to throw together, makeup to put on, hair to brush.

When she finally arrived at her sister's house, Christie was fifteen minutes late. She hadn't located a single pair of black slacks and had worn gray stretch pants and a long red sweater. The combination was festive. She chose a necklace made of silver bells that jingled whenever she moved. Her shoes were too tight but there was nothing she could do about that.

Teri opened the door, looking pregnant and just as radiant as a pregnant woman was supposed to.

"Christie, you're late," Teri hissed, grabbing her arm and dragging her into the house. It'd been a while since Christie had been inside and she was astounded at the transformation that had taken place. Every nook and cranny was decorated for Christmas.

"Wow," she said, gazing around. From where she stood in the entry she could see three Christmas trees — on the landing, in the living room and in a corner of the hall. She saw Nativity sets of different styles and sizes on various available surfaces.

"Bobby said I could decorate for Christmas however I wanted to."

"Why all the trees?" Christie asked, forgetting about James for the moment. "How many are there, anyway?"

"Five."

"*Five* decorated Christmas trees?"

"I love Christmas," Teri announced.

"No kidding," Christie muttered. She loved Christmas, too, but she could never have afforded anything like this — or had the space for it. "This must've cost a fortune."

Teri smiled sheepishly. "Bobby doesn't care, as long as I'm happy."

Christie scowled at her. "It would be easy to hate you."

Teri giggled. "None of this means anything without Bobby and the baby." She rested her hand on the gentle swelling under her green velvet tunic.

Christie glanced around again, half expecting to find James standing awkwardly in the corner. He wasn't. "Where's James?" she asked, lowering her voice.

"He isn't here yet."

"James is late?" That didn't sound like him.

"He isn't coming," Bobby said as he stepped into the room. "I'm sorry, Christie, I let the beans out of the bag."

"*Spilled* the beans, sweetheart," Teri corrected her husband. "Or let the cat out of the bag."

Bobby nodded solemnly. "When I told him you'd be at dinner, too, James said he couldn't make it."

Christie shrugged. "Hey, it's fine." She removed her coat and draped it over the back of a chair, then left her purse there, too.

"Dinner's almost ready," Teri said as she picked up Christie's coat and hung it in the closet. When they'd walked into the kitchen together, Teri hurried over to the oven and opened the door to peek inside. "This is one of Bobby's favorite dishes," she explained.

Christie peeked, too, and couldn't see anything special about the rice casserole. Her stomach had been upset most of the day and the truth was, she didn't have much of an appetite. It was just as well James wasn't coming or she wouldn't have been able to eat at all.

"I'm sorry to disappoint you," Teri said. "I know you were looking forward to this evening."

Christie shrugged again. "Hey, I've scared off better men than James."

Teri said something Christie didn't catch. "I'm so upset with him I can't even tell you," she added.

"Don't worry about it. You suggested I approach James and when I couldn't, you arranged this party and now it's backfired. From my perspective this romance simply isn't going to happen. *C'est la vie.*"

Teri raised her eyebrows. "You speak French now?"

Christie slapped her sister's arm and they both giggled.

Dinner was pleasant enough, although Christie ate very little. She didn't want Teri or Bobby to know how depressed she was, so she kept up a steady stream of chatter. As soon as she could, she made her excuses and gathered up her coat and purse. Besides, Teri looked tired. She'd been decorating and cleaning all day. Twice during the meal, Christie caught her sister yawning.

Bobby said good-night and disappeared into his study, then Teri walked her to the door. They both glanced up at the large three-car garage with James's living quarters above. The lights were on, so he was obviously home.

"Talk to him," Teri urged in a whisper.

Christie shook her head. "Forget it." He didn't want anything to do with her and in retrospect that was probably for the best. She had enough to deal with in her life without this aggravation.

"I'll give you a call later. I've got a doctor's appointment on Wednesday. I'm getting my first ultrasound, and he said I could have a picture of the baby."

"Really?" Christie couldn't wait to see that. They hugged goodbye and she headed for her car. As she slipped inside, her gaze fastened on the light coming from James's apartment. Coward! As far as she was concerned, James Wilbur was a full-fledged coward. Fine. But she wasn't chasing after him.

Christie inserted her key in the ignition. Nothing.

It cranked and cranked and wouldn't start.

Great, just great. She was stuck. Bobby Polgar wouldn't be any help. All he knew was chess. Teri wouldn't know what to do, either. And Christie wasn't going to drag her pregnant sister out on a chilly night. There was no point in going in to phone the auto club, either, because she'd let her membership lapse years ago; she couldn't afford it.

Reluctantly, Christie looked at the upstairs apartment. Apparently she was going to see James, after all. She trudged up the outside staircase and knocked twice, then stepped back and waited.

James opened the door wearing a suit. Christie wondered if he even owned a pair of jeans.

"My car won't start," she said without preamble.

"What about Triple A?" he asked, still holding the door handle as if he thought he might have to close it quickly.

"Do you think I'd be here pestering you if I was a member?" she asked sharply. She modulated her voice. "I would very much appreciate a ride home."

"Of course. I'll be just a moment."

"Thank you." This was *so* embarrassing.

When he returned, he'd donned an overcoat, hat and gloves. "I'd like to see if I can get your vehicle started, if that's all right."

"Sure." She gestured toward her car. "Have at it."

James released the latch and raised the hood. He fiddled with the engine for a couple of minutes, then looked at her gravely.

"I believe you need a new alternator."

"Wonderful." She had no idea how expensive that would be, but it went without saying she couldn't afford it. With rent and debts to pay, she was barely subsisting as it was.

"I'll bring the car around," James told her.

She nodded, still numb at the news. Somehow or other, she'd have to get the car towed from Teri's to a repair shop. That wouldn't be cheap, either. This couldn't have happened at a worse time.

James slowly backed the limousine out of the garage. He stepped out and opened the passenger door for her.

"I can open my own door."

"Yes, miss," James said in the formal tone she hated.

"I told you before I don't want you to call me *miss.*"

"You did," he agreed.

"Then why do you insist on doing it? Do you *look* for ways to irritate me?" She was angry now. This entire evening had been a disaster and that was his fault. "Listen, I don't need a ride, after all, thank you very much. I prefer to walk." She slammed the car door, jerked her purse strap over her shoulder and started walking. The bells on her necklace jingled with every step. Her feet already hurt but it wasn't as if she could take her shoes off.

She hadn't gone more than a few yards when James silently joined her.

"Go away."

"I can't do that."

"Why not?" When he didn't respond, she added, "I don't want you walking with me."

"You're alone. It isn't safe."

"I've been alone practically my whole life. I don't need a bodyguard, understand?" She made her voice as hard and unwelcoming as she could.

"I know," he said gently.

"What do you know?" She turned to glare at him. "You don't know anything about me." Her voice cracked and she buried her hands deep in her pockets, shivering against the cold.

"Christie." His voice was soft, soothing, as if he were speaking to a child.

That irritated her even more. "Go away!" she shouted. "Just leave me alone. I don't want you walking with me," she said again. "Don't you get it?" They hadn't even reached the end of the long hilly driveway and already she was winded and her feet had begun to swell. Her apartment had to be a good five miles away.

He drew back slightly, but still he followed her.

"Everyone thinks you're this big hero," she muttered, trying to distract herself from the agony of walking. "You fought those two thugs and Teri says you might have saved Rachel's life." She stopped for a few seconds. "Only I know the *real* truth about you, James. You're a coward, aren't you?"

He said nothing.

Whirling around she confronted him face-to-face. "Did you hear me, coward?"

"Yes."

"Don't you have anything to say for yourself?"

"No."

The man infuriated her and she childishly stamped her foot — big mistake — before whirling back around and walking again. A blister had begun to form on her heel. She'd known the shoes, very cute ballet flats, were a size too small, but they'd been on sale and they went so nicely with her red sweater.

"Why are you limping?" he asked.

"I'm not. Go away."

"Christie, be reasonable."

"No!" she shouted back, struggling not to cry. "I hate my life, I hate myself and I hate you."

"No, you don't," he said calmly.

The man was impossible to fight with. She'd had it. Turning abruptly, she placed her hands on her hips.

"What's it going to take to get you to *leave me alone?*"

He didn't respond.

"Fine, if that's how you want it, walk behind me." She made it all the way to the end of the street before she just couldn't walk anymore. Her right shoe rubbed against raw, bloody flesh. Now she *had* to stop and remove it. She'd taken about five uneven steps when James came from behind her and casually swept her into his arms as if she weighed next to nothing.

"Put me down, you idiot!"

She wanted to kick and scream and argue with him. His jaw was tight, and from the angry set of his mouth she could see he wasn't going anywhere without her.

She sniffled.

"Are you in pain?" he asked.

She nodded and sniffled again. "Why do you hate me?" she asked plaintively, furious with herself for caring. She didn't *want* his gentleness or his kindness; they confused her.

"I don't hate you."

"You wouldn't come to dinner tonight because I was there."

He remained stubbornly silent.

After another minute, she demanded he put her down. "Please, please just leave me alone." She was an emotional wreck. Tears stung her eyes, but the last thing, the very last thing, she wanted was for James to see her cry.

He sighed audibly, but instead of releasing her, he held her closer. Christie rested her head against his shoulder and absorbed the warmth and comfort he offered.

"Allow me to drive you home?"

She nodded. She was in such pain, and she was finished being stupid. She'd been ridiculous to think she could actually walk that distance.

"Good." He carefully lowered her to the ground.

Holding hands, they walked side by side. Clutching her shoe in her other hand, Christie limped back down the driveway. Once they reached the car, James opened the passenger door for her. This time she didn't protest.

She was half in the vehicle and half out when he stopped her. Leaning forward, James pressed his mouth to hers. His hand was in her hair, his lips urging, questing, deepening the kiss until she trembled. When he lifted his head, she nearly fell the rest of the way into the car.

She wanted to ask why he'd done that, but found she couldn't speak. She didn't say a word during the drive. At her apartment complex, he parked and helped her out.

She couldn't meet his gaze. "Thank you."

He nodded formally.

She lingered, hoping he'd kiss her again.

James didn't disappoint her. He kissed her long and hard. While she was still reeling from his touch, he climbed into the car and drove away.

TWENTY

Troy's daughter had called her at work that morning, and Faith was actually looking forward to seeing her. Poor Megan had sounded hesitant about interrupting her at the clinic, but it was the only number she had, since Faith's home phone was unlisted.

In the intervening days since she'd seen Troy, Faith had thought almost constantly about his visit. Perhaps she'd been more unyielding than necessary. She also wondered — *had* to wonder — whether he'd used Megan as an excuse. Megan didn't seem unreasonable and she clearly loved her father. Faith couldn't believe she wouldn't want him to be happy. Perhaps Troy had misread his daughter's attitude. Or perhaps he was inconsistent about his own feelings for Faith.

"Could we get together?" Megan had asked. "I'm having some problems with the baby blanket. I'd really appreciate if you'd take a look at it for me. I'll buy your lunch," she'd added.

"Nonsense. You don't need to pay for my lunch and I'd be happy to look at the blanket." They arranged to meet at the deli Tuesday afternoon, during their lunch break.

Afterward Faith reviewed their brief telephone conversation. The two of them had developed a relationship, although Megan didn't know Faith had been involved with Troy. This lunch would be the perfect opportunity to tell her. Faith had no interest in the kind of secrecy Troy had tried to maintain. She'd noticed early on that he hadn't wanted his daughter to know they were seeing each other. In any event, it couldn't possibly matter now.

When she got to the restaurant, Megan was already there, having secured a table by the window. She waved, and Faith walked across the crowded room to join her.

"I came a bit early so I could grab us a table," Megan explained. She stood, quickly hugging Faith.

Megan looked healthy, Faith observed; her hair shone and her color was good. That cliché about pregnant women glowing was certainly true for her. Knowing how close Troy was to his daughter, she assumed he was thrilled with the news of this pregnancy. If Megan had told him . . . When the opportunity arose, she'd ask.

The waitress rushed over to their table, menus tucked under her arm and two water glasses in her hands. "The soup of the day is broccoli and cheese, and the special is a crab melt," she informed them.

Megan and Faith each ordered soup and decided to split the crab melt. They both wanted tea, so the waitress returned minutes later with a large blue teapot and two cups.

Megan brought out her knitting. "I made a mistake way back here," she said, her brow furrowed as she stared down at the blanket. The pattern was relatively simple but did involve a four-row pattern. Faith knew, at a glance, what Megan had done wrong. She'd repeated the third row twice.

"Does it bother you?" Faith asked, studying the half-completed blanket.

Megan nodded. "At first I didn't think it would, so I just kept knitting."

Faith had done that plenty of times herself. "But now, it seems glaring, doesn't it?"

"Sure does."

"Then go back and correct it," Faith advised.

"Really? You're saying I should tear all this out?" She sighed as if that was exactly what she'd been afraid of hearing.

"I do it quite a lot," Faith told her. "Sometimes I'll tear out a section three or four times before I get it right. If the mistake's really minor, I might leave it in. In those cases I'm usually the only one who knows it's there."

"This is a big mistake, though, isn't it?"

"That depends on how you see it," Faith said carefully.

"If something like that bothers you, you tear it out?"

"Well, I generally do. I feel better about the project, and it seems that whatever I reknit goes twice as fast."

"Then I'll rip away," Megan said, apparently satisfied with her decision. "By the way, I told my dad and Craig's parents about the baby."

"I imagine they were all excited."

"Especially my dad." Megan returned her attention to her knitting.

"If you'd like, I'll help you with that after lunch."

Their tea had steeped, and Megan put the knitting back in her bag, then filled their cups. "Thank you for meeting me like this," she said, engrossed in the task of pouring tea.

"It's my pleasure, Megan." She strongly suspected it wasn't merely — or primarily — the knitting question that had prompted

Megan's invitation. "Is there anything else I can do for you?" she asked.

Megan leaned back in her chair. "I guess you could see through me asking to meet you."

"Not really. If there's something on your mind, though, I'd like to help if I can."

"Oh, Faith, thank you," she said in a rush. "I needed to talk to someone, and I've been on pins and needles."

"I'm honored that you chose me."

"You're exactly the right person," Megan insisted. "I know you'll be honest with me and . . . and I trust your advice."

"Thank you," Faith murmured, although she did feel a little guilty.

"I told you how close I was to my mom when she was alive."

"Yes."

"I saw her every single day. By the end she couldn't speak all that well, but she always listened. Dad and I were with her when she died and it was . . . beautiful." Megan tried to blink away tears. "Death can be beautiful, can't it?"

"Yes, I believe it can." Faith reached across the table and squeezed Megan's hand.

"Mom was sick for a very long time."

"I know."

Megan struggled visibly with her emotions

and managed to control them. When she spoke again, her voice had gained strength and conviction. "Shortly after my mom died, my father implied there was someone he wanted to date. I can't even begin to tell you how horrified I was."

Faith's guilt quotient rose several degrees. Obviously Troy hadn't exaggerated his daughter's reaction, and she understood more clearly why he'd hidden their relationship.

Megan pursed her lips. "At first I thought he was joking. Good grief, Mom had only been gone a few months."

Faith hesitated, unsure what to do. Megan didn't have any idea that the woman Troy had been seeing was her. Mentioning it now would be awkward beyond belief.

"As you said, your mother had been ill for a long time," she said cautiously.

"I know, and I also realize how lonely my father must've been all those years. The thing is, he was completely dedicated to my mother."

The waitress approached with their order and a spare plate. They spent a few minutes dividing the crab melt, tasting their soup, commenting on the food. Faith welcomed the interruption. She needed to think. It was wrong to accept Megan's confidences without telling Megan about her involvement with Troy.

"Your father's Troy Davis, the sheriff, isn't he?" she asked. She had to introduce the topic somehow and this seemed a relatively safe way to start.

"You know him?" Megan's eyes widened.

"I do. Your father and I went to high school together." She held her breath waiting for Megan's response.

Megan clapped her hands delightedly. "Oh, my goodness, I would never have guessed. That's great!"

"Your father was a handsome young man."

"I know," Megan said, beaming with pride. "I looked through his high school yearbooks and he was just so cute."

Faith had thought so, too. She still did.

"So your father wants to date again?"

Megan nodded. "I told him not long ago that I think he should, but I'm not sure he believed me, especially after the fuss I made earlier . . . . I regret that now, but it was such a shock. It didn't occur to me that he'd be interested in anyone so soon after losing Mom." Megan lowered her gaze. "It was probably selfish of me, but I couldn't help feeling the way I did."

"Everyone's entitled to their feelings, Megan. Don't beat yourself up over it."

Megan swallowed a spoonful of soup before she responded. "Dad isn't that old. He doesn't want to spend the rest of his life alone and I don't blame him. I mean, it wouldn't be easy seeing my dad with someone other than Mom, but I don't want to be selfish, either."

"I think your feelings are only natural," Faith murmured. "The fact that you're talking to your father about your concerns is important."

Faith took a bite of her meal, then broached the subject. "This might come as a surprise, but your father and I dated in high school."

Megan stared at her. "You and my dad?"

Faith paused ever so slightly, then nodded. "As you said earlier, he was a popular guy."

Megan giggled. "That is so cool."

"I liked him a lot back then," Faith told her, using the past tense to keep the situation in perspective. Eventually, if there was an easy way to do so, she'd lead into the fact that they'd briefly reconnected following Sandy's death.

"I think I could accept it better if Dad was dating someone like you," Megan said, picking up her spoon.

It was on the tip of her tongue to explain that she *had* been seeing Troy, when

Megan continued.

"But I don't like this other woman at all."

"Other woman?" Faith blurted out, unable to stop herself.

Megan nodded. "Her name's Sally, and she's a widow."

The chills that ran down Faith's back had nothing to do with the December weather. Troy Davis was just as inconsistent as she'd suspected. Worse than that, he was fickle, swearing undying love one day and taking up with someone new the next.

"I got the feeling he didn't want me to know about her," Megan said with a frown.

Faith rested her spoon beside her plate. "No, I'm sure he didn't," she said tartly. Apparently keeping his romances a secret was quite a pattern of his.

"Craig says," Megan went on, "that some men need a woman in their lives. I would never have thought my father was one of them, but now I think he must be."

"Why's that?" Faith asked, a little fearful of the response.

"Well, because," Megan said. "There was that other woman earlier on and now there's Sally."

"It might be the same person," Faith suggested. How was she to know when Troy had started seeing this Sally? Her face burned with anger and mortification. It wouldn't surprise her to discover he'd been dating both of them at the same time.

Megan was quiet for a moment. "Now that you mention it," she said, "Sally might be the woman Dad alluded to after Mom died."

Faith was finding this rather difficult to take. Anger surged to the surface. How dare he treat her in such an underhanded way? He'd led her to believe she was the only woman he cared about. He'd even said he loved her!

"So you met . . . Sally," Faith said. Apparently the other woman was higher on the food chain than Faith, who'd never been introduced to Troy's daughter.

Megan took a sip of her tea. "Craig and I were out Christmas shopping and we ran into Dad and Sally at Wal-Mart."

"I . . . see." That was an interesting note, considering how Troy felt about shopping.

"I could see right away that Dad was embarrassed. He tried to pretend he didn't see me."

Faith nodded. She'd just bet he did. "What's Sally like?" she asked. If this other woman was young, tall and blond, Faith didn't know if she could be held responsible for her actions.

"Sally? Oh, she's okay, I guess. She's

287

around Dad's age and kind of . . . I don't know, dumpy-looking."

"Pretty, though, right?"

"Not really."

"What didn't you like about her?" Faith asked, disgusted with herself for encouraging Megan.

"First off, she's bossy," Megan said without hesitation.

"Bossy," Faith repeated.

"Yeah. She said she and Dad were going out for sushi later and I happen to know my father hates sushi."

"Uh-huh."

"He doesn't like shopping, either."

That, Faith knew. "So, your father must be quite impressed with . . . Sally." Faith could barely get the other woman's name out of her mouth. She felt her anger growing and knew she should leave.

She resolutely picked up her purse and set it on her lap. Only a few days ago Troy had been at her front door trying to talk her into giving him another chance. The man juggled women the way a clown juggled balls. Hmm. *Clown.* Not a bad word for Mr. Sheriff Troy Davis.

"What do you think I should do?" Megan asked, looking expectantly at Faith.

Caught up in her own emotions, Faith

didn't understand what she was asking.

Megan, apparently sensing her confusion, explained, "Should I say anything to Dad about Sally? I mean, I don't like her and if he does, well . . . I think it could be a problem. If she's that bossy with Dad, she will be with me, too."

"Ah . . ."

Megan sighed. "I suppose it really isn't any of my business. I should probably keep my nose out of it."

"Yes, well, I'm not . . . well, quite sure what to tell you. It's — it's just that . . ." In the course of a few minutes, Faith had turned into a stuttering fool.

"I don't understand why my dad doesn't realize Sally's all wrong for him." Megan shook her head as if she couldn't fathom what had gotten into her father.

"You have a point there."

"Men can be dense, can't they?"

"You're telling me," Faith muttered, faking a short laugh.

The restaurant was filling up and it was time for both of them to return to work. The waitress had dropped off the bill at their table, and Faith reached for it.

"I wish you'd let me pay for your lunch."

"Of course not," Faith insisted, opening her purse. Her hands shook as she withdrew the cash from a small zippered pouch. "That should cover my half plus tip," she said, placing twelve dollars on the table.

"I appreciate your coming on such short notice."

Faith did manage a genuine smile. "It was my pleasure. I don't know that I was much help, though." This lunch had been instructive and in that sense probably more of a help to her than Megan. Her eyes had been opened in regard to Troy Davis.

"But you were," Megan said. "Really, you were."

With a minimum of farewells, Faith was out the door. Because of the cold, she'd driven to the restaurant and parked on a side street. Slipping into her car, she started the engine and the heater, then sat there as the anger subsided and became sadness instead.

TWENTY-ONE

This was Emily Flemming's first day at her new job — which was also the first job she'd had since the early days of her marriage. The quilt shop was ideal for her. And it felt good to be part of the solution to their money woes. In fact, Emily felt good about a lot of things today, but mostly about Dave; her faith in him had been restored. Of course, there were still those diamond earrings to be explained, and she'd ask him, in time. Emily was confident that he'd have a logical explanation. She'd actually forgotten about the earrings when they'd spoken on Sunday. But she suspected Martha had given them to Dave, along with the watch, and he was waiting for Christmas to present them to her.

In retrospect, Emily knew she'd been foolish not to confront Dave with her suspicions earlier. If she had, she could've saved herself, and her husband, a lot of grief.

Of course, Dave had been at fault, too. He

should've told her about their financial problems sooner. Until he'd shown her the stack of unpaid bills, she'd had no idea how precarious their situation was. The fact that her husband had taken a second job in order to make ends meet had come as a total shock.

On Tuesday morning, after Emily got the boys off to school, she drove to The Quilted Giraffe, in the same mall as several other local businesses, among them Get Nailed. Roxanne York's store sold a large range of fabrics, yarn and quilting supplies. Not only that, she offered classes of various kinds, including one by well-known fabric artist Shirley Bliss, who'd taught a class there last year, before her husband's accident. Unfortunately Emily hadn't been able to attend because those sessions conflicted with a series of women's group meetings at the church. Emily would've preferred the quilt classes but she'd already committed herself and couldn't, in good conscience, back out.

Over the years Emily had frequented the store and become friends with the owner. On several occasions, Roxanne had asked Emily to work for her. She and Dave could hardly believe how easily everything had fallen into place. In minutes she had a job, with the hours she wanted.

When she announced that she'd taken the job, her boys had immediately objected. They hadn't like the idea of Emily working and barraged her with questions and complaints.

"What happens if I get sick and somebody has to pick me up at school?" Matthew had asked.

"Who'll bake cookies for after school?" was Mark's main concern.

"If you need me," she assured her oldest son, "all you have to do is phone and I'll be right there. It won't be any different than if I was at home."

Matthew wasn't mollified and sulked the rest of the morning.

"As for cookies, I'll still bake them," she told Mark.

"You promise?" he'd asked skeptically.

"I promise." She'd bought everything she needed for his favorite date bars. She usually baked them only during the Christmas season.

"Good morning, Roxanne," Emily said happily, entering the familiar store. Business was especially good at this time of year, and Roxanne was delighted with the extra help.

Her employer had a name badge for Emily, plus a special apron with half a dozen pockets. After putting her coat and purse in the back room, where she'd been given shelf space with her name on it, Emily proudly donned the apron and tag. She was ready for business. Roxanne had an errand to run at the bank, and within ten minutes of her arrival, Emily was alone in the store.

That didn't last long. All too soon, before she'd even finished reviewing the new inventory, she had her first customers.

"Emily, you're working here now?" Peggy Beldon asked, coming in with her friend Corrie McAfee. "Oh, I like your hair!" Whether or not that was true, it was nice of her to say so.

Peggy was an excellent quilter. Her eye for color had long been the envy of everyone in the quilters' guild. She and her husband, Bob, owned Thyme and Tide, a local bed-and-breakfast that had received a glowing review in a national travel magazine.

"It's my very first day," Emily said, smiling. She'd worked briefly at a large department store after she'd married Dave and before the boys were born, and she found herself grateful for that experience.

"Can I help you with anything?" she asked.

"Not yet," Corrie responded. Corrie was new to quilting but had taken to it with enthusiasm. She'd joined the quilters' guild, too. In Emily's opinion, Corrie couldn't possibly have a better mentor than Peggy Beldon.

The two women wandered along the rows of fabric.

Emily never liked it when a sales clerk hovered over her, so she remained at the cash register, waiting in case they required assistance. Roxanne would be back soon, if Peggy and Corrie had any questions Emily couldn't answer.

"Roy's in one of his moods," Corrie was saying as she smoothed her hand over a bolt of fabric.

Emily knew all about men and their moods. Dave hadn't been himself for months; thankfully she now understood why. Money problems were the worst.

"Something on his mind?" Peggy questioned.

"It has to do with Martha Evans's missing jewelry. Roy and the sheriff have been discussing it."

Emily came out from behind the register and moved closer to the two women. She occupied herself with a display of pattern books because she didn't want to look as if she was intentionally listening in on their conversation. In truth, however, she was curious to hear what they had to say.

"According to Troy, Martha's daughters

are terribly upset," Corrie said. "They've come to him several times. Their mother hadn't insured the jewelry properly and her policy has a low loss limit."

"I imagine those pieces have a sentimental value, too."

Emily swallowed, feeling guilty about eavesdropping on their private conversation . . . and yet, she felt she had no choice. She needed all the information she could get.

"Sorry to interrupt, but I couldn't help overhearing you. I've been praying the jewelry will turn up," Emily said. It was all rather embarrassing because Troy was well aware that Dave was the one who'd found Martha's body.

"I think everyone must be," Corrie commented. "The latest has to do with her husband's gold watch."

Emily's skin prickled.

"Martha's oldest daughter . . . I've forgotten her name. Roy said she was in to see the sheriff just yesterday. She says she'd forgotten all about it. She wanted to add it to the list of what's missing."

Emily returned to the front of the store. Her legs were shaky, like they might go out from under her. Dave claimed Martha had *given* him the gold watch. He'd actually been wearing it! No thief in his right mind would flaunt such a thing. There had to be some mistake.

Thinking over their conversation, Emily remembered Dave telling her that he'd been reluctant to accept such a valuable gift. He'd told Emily that Martha had the watch entered into her will so there'd be no question about it later.

"Mack's completely moved into his apartment," Corrie said, changing the subject.

"That's good news," Peggy murmured as she lifted a bolt of fabric from the rack. "I understand Will Jefferson's living above the gallery now."

"That's what Mack said, too."

"I'm so glad we still have an art gallery."

The rest of the conversation flew past Emily.

The two women each purchased several yards of fabric and then drifted out of the store, discussing where to have lunch.

Emily found herself reeling. The gold watch was said to be missing and now listed as one of the items that had been stolen? That had to be a misunderstanding. Well, it was one that could easily be resolved. Emily would see to it herself.

On her lunch break she drove to Allan Harris's office, which was empty except for a well-dressed young man at the front desk.

He looked up when Emily walked in.

"What can I do for you?" he asked.

"I'm Emily Flemming," she said.

"Hello." It was clear he hadn't made the connection between her and Dave.

"Pastor Flemming's my husband."

"Oh, yes, of course." Instantly Geoff was on his feet, extending his hand. "I'm Geoff Duncan."

"Hello, Geoff."

"When I spoke with Pastor Dave a little while ago, he agreed to give my fiancée and me premarital counseling."

Emily nodded, unsure how to bring up the subject of the missing gold watch. She was convinced this was all a mix-up and once she showed Sheriff Davis a copy of the will, everything would be sorted out.

"Dave enjoys working with couples," Emily said.

"Do you need an appointment?" Geoff asked. "Unfortunately, Mr. Harris is currently in court and isn't expected back until late this afternoon. I can schedule you in then, if you'd like."

"Not a real appointment." They were already in a financial bind, so Emily didn't want to complicate their problems by adding attorney's fees, especially for a matter as simple as this. "I just need some information."

"Then perhaps I can help," he offered.

"I . . . I need to see something." It seemed terribly bold and perhaps unethical to ask for a copy of someone else's last will and testament.

Geoff stared at her blankly.

"Something my husband mentioned," she added.

"And what would that be?" Geoff's questioning eyes searched hers.

Emily hadn't come this far to leave without answers. Taking a deep breath, she plunged ahead. "I need to see a copy of Martha Evans's will."

Geoff's eyes narrowed and he slowly shook his head.

"Is it wrong of me to ask for something like that?"

He clasped his hands in front of him. "I'm afraid I can't do that."

"Oh, drat," Emily said, feeling like a fool.

"Is it important?" Geoff asked.

"Yes!" she cried. He must know she'd never make a request like this if it wasn't. Emily considered it her responsibility to uphold her husband's good name in the community. Olivia Griffin had seen the watch; she wouldn't be shy about pointing the finger at Dave. And the earrings . . . Would they turn up on the list of stolen jewelry, too?

Geoff studied her for several seconds. "Can you tell me why it's so important?"

Emily wasn't sure how much she could explain without implicating her husband. "As you're probably aware, Dave found Martha's body."

"Yes, of course."

"I suppose . . . I suppose it's only natural that, since things are missing, suspicion might fall on him."

Geoff frowned. "Pastor Flemming wouldn't take anything that wasn't his."

Emily loved the way Geoff was so quick to defend her husband. "There's a problem, however."

"Yes?"

"Martha gave Dave a gold watch that had belonged to her husband."

"Okay," he said tentatively.

"I asked him about it when I found out he'd lost it. The clasp was broken and —"

"He lost the watch?" An alarmed look appeared on his face.

"Oh, don't worry, it was recovered."

"Thank goodness. A gold watch is expensive to replace."

There would be no replacing it on their budget, but Emily didn't feel it was necessary to explain that. "Thankfully, Judge Griffin found it following a visit Dave made after her surgery."

"That's a relief," Geoff commented.

"Yes, it is."

"So Dave's been wearing the watch?"

"Yes, of course. There wasn't any reason *not* to, seeing that it was a gift."

Geoff sat back in his chair. "It gets a bit sticky because of the missing jewelry, though, doesn't it?"

Geoff understood the situation perfectly. Emily didn't dare mention the earrings. She'd check into those, too, but so far, she was the only one who knew Dave had them.

"What does Mrs. Evans's will have to do with all this?" he asked.

"Everything," she said, leaning toward his desk. "Mrs. Evans told him she'd have the watch included in the will as a gift to my husband. I need to see if it's there as she intended."

"Ah."

"Now you know why I need a copy of the will."

Geoff tapped his ballpoint pen. "Oh, boy," he muttered under his breath. "I mentioned that Pastor Dave offered to counsel my fiancé and me, didn't I?"

"Yes." Emily nodded.

"As you might've guessed, I don't make a lot of money as a legal assistant."

Emily wouldn't know.

"Your husband is such a kind man, he's giving us the counseling sessions gratis."

That sounded just like Dave, always willing to help others.

Geoff sighed and glanced around the room, although no one else was present. Lowering his voice, he told her, "If anyone finds out I gave you a copy of that will I could lose my job."

"I would never ask that of you," Emily said immediately. "I'd *never* want you to take that risk."

Geoff raised his hand, stopping her. "If this clears your husband's name, then it'll be worth the risk."

"You said Mr. Harris is in court right now?"

"Yes."

"Then it might make more sense for me just to read the will. I'll make a copy of the pertinent page and if anyone — like Troy Davis — asks him about it, then Dave will have the proof."

Geoff stood. "That's an excellent suggestion," he said, walking toward a tall filing cabinet behind him.

Emily remained standing. "I can't thank you enough."

"Like I said, the pastor's doing me a favor,

and if I can help him, I'm happy to do it."

"This will be our little secret," Emily promised him. "No one ever needs to know. The only other person who'd see it is the sheriff."

"I have to be able to trust you." She could hear caution and concern in his voice.

"You have my word I won't tell anyone." Emily's fingers itched to grab the will and start flipping pages.

Geoff located the file and removed it from the cabinet. He took out the stapled will, which he handed to Emily. She sank onto the leather sofa in the waiting area and began to rapidly turn pages. While she might not have a law degree, she realized that anything aside from the standard clauses would be on a separate schedule. Sure enough, she came across those pages toward the end.

She scanned the items listed. Martha had an extensive jewelry collection. Dave had once mentioned that she liked to reminisce about the traveling she and her husband, an executive in a paper products company, had done through the years. He'd delighted in buying her beautiful jewelry, much of it antique, and each ring or pair of earrings had reminded her of a particular place. The schedule included two entire pages of itemized pieces, each with a designation of her chosen recipient.

Emily didn't see any notation having to do with the gold watch. She read the list a second time, more carefully now.

"Did you find it?" Geoff asked a bit anxiously.

Emily swallowed. "Is there another section of the will not included here?"

"Not that I know of."

"Would you mind checking the file?" she asked, making an effort to sound positive.

Geoff returned to the filing cabinet. "Oh, wait, there *is* something else here."

Instantly Emily relaxed. For a moment there, she'd started to panic.

"Oh." Geoff's voice lost some of its enthusiasm. "It's photographs."

"Of what?" Emily asked.

"The jewelry. Mrs. Evans had several pairs of diamond earrings and some emerald brooches. The pictures are to distinguish which piece of jewelry she meant." He hesitated. "I believe Mr. Harris had been urging her to do this for some time because she wasn't adequately insured."

"Can I see that?" Emily asked. She knew it was risky to delve into this any further and yet she couldn't stop herself. She reached for the document.

"Perhaps the gold watch is in here,"

Geoff suggested.

"I'm sure it is," Emily said with a confidence she didn't feel. Flipping through the pages, she glanced at each photograph until she saw the one she'd hoped not to find.

The diamond earrings.

The pair she'd accidentally discovered in Dave's suit pockets the afternoon of their wedding anniversary.

"Do you have what you need?" Geoff asked, his anxiety growing. If anyone were to step into the office and discover what he'd done, he could be in serious trouble.

"Here," Emily said and handed him back the will and the papers.

Geoff immediately filed them and closed the drawer. He studied Emily. "Is everything all right, Mrs. Flemming? You look pale."

"I'm fine," she lied.

"Well . . . I hope that answered all your questions."

"I appreciate your help," she said, evading the question.

"You can't tell anyone I let you see what was in Mrs. Evans's file," he told her.

"No one will ever know," she promised.

Only a few hours earlier, Emily had felt that her marriage was rejuvenated. Dave loved her. He was doing two jobs because of the increase in their house payments. Now, in an effort to do her share, Emily had started work, too.

They needed money if they were going to hold on to the house she loved.

All Emily could do was hope Dave hadn't found another way of paying their bills . . . a way that could land him in prison.

TWENTY-TWO

Teri Polgar was still reeling. The gynecologist's news had been a shock. An incredible, wonderful, joyous shock, but a shock nonetheless, and she wasn't sure Bobby was ready to hear it. She hadn't completely taken it in herself.

"James," she murmured from the backseat of the car. "Please drive me over to Get Nailed." She needed to talk to someone, and she couldn't think of anyone better than her best friend, Rachel.

"As you wish, Miss Teri," James responded. He rarely had a comment or a question.

"Thank you." Teri started chewing on her thumbnail, then jerked her hand out of her mouth as soon as she realized what she was doing. Nail-biting was a bad habit of hers, one she'd managed — for the most part — to break.

James pulled up in front of the Cedar Cove

mall. Without giving him a chance to come around and open her door, she leaped out.

He stood uncertainly by the driver's door. "Would you like me to wait?" he asked.

"Please," Teri said over her shoulder. The mall was busier than she could ever remember seeing it. A woman standing beside a huge red kettle rang a bell, reminding others of those less fortunate than themselves. Teri automatically stuck a twenty-dollar bill inside. As kids growing up with an alcoholic mother, she and Christie had a very limited experience of Christmas, which might explain why she went overboard now. The only gifts they received came from charities like this one. Any extra cash her mother had was spent on booze.

The warmth inside the mall chased away the chill that had come over her. She moved quickly, eager to get to the salon. When she arrived, she walked directly through the waiting area and into the main body of the shop.

"Hey, look who's here!" Jane called out. She wore a sprig of plastic holly in her hair as she worked on a customer's nails.

Teri was instantly surrounded by her friends.

"Merry Christmas!"

"Teri, it's so great to see you."

Her gaze flew instinctively to Rachel. Rachel would reassure her. Rachel would help her put everything in perspective. Rachel would calm her nerves.

Intuitive as always, Rachel recognized immediately that something was wrong.

"Can you talk?" Teri asked, grabbing her friend's hands.

Rachel nodded. "I just finished my perm. Mrs. Holman's coming in for a cut and style, but I can put her off for a few minutes. What's up?"

Teri released Rachel's hands and gestured weakly toward the break room. Her knees felt unsteady. "Let's talk privately."

"That bad?" Rachel's eyes turned soft with concern.

"No, not really. Just . . . overwhelming."

Rachel led her to the back of the shop and pulled out two chairs. Teri nearly collapsed into hers. "I had the ultrasound this morning," she said. "Bobby's so anxious about the baby. He had an important radio interview so he couldn't go with me. I didn't think it was a good idea for him to be there, anyway. He worries too much." She exhaled slowly.

Rachel frowned. "Your appointment was at nine, right?" She glanced at her watch. "It's nearly noon. Why'd it take so long?"

"Because about a dozen people had to take a gander. Let me tell you there's nothing like having your stomach exposed to the whole world."

"It could've been worse. It could've been your butt."

Leave it to Rachel to look at the bright side.

"Everything *is* all right, isn't it?" her friend asked, studying her closely.

"You tell me." With trembling hands, Teri opened her large purse and took out the photograph the technician had given her. She laid it gingerly on the table, watching Rachel's face as she did.

Her friend studied the photo. "Teri!" she cried a moment later. "You're having twins!"

"Look again," she said, her voice catching.

Rachel stared at the hazy picture and then gasped. Her hand went to her heart. Her eyes widened. She swallowed hard. "Triplets?"

Teri nodded. "Last week the doctor told me he thought he heard two heartbeats, which is why he scheduled the ultrasound." The shock had yet to fade. Twins she could've dealt with — once she got used to the idea — but triplets? Bobby was already a local celebrity and here she was, pregnant with *triplets.*

"You weren't using fertility drugs, were you?"

"Good heavens, no." That was one of the reasons the ultrasound had attracted so much attention. Natural triplets were exceedingly rare.

"This is why you've been feeling so drained and tired."

Since this was her first pregnancy, Teri hadn't known what to expect. "I've been really emotional, too."

"Well, no wonder."

"Originally, the doctor said I might've been farther along than we assumed. I never keep track of my periods, so I didn't think anything of it."

"That extra weight!"

"Yes, I made Dr. Joyce apologize about that. I told him I'd been eating properly and that I didn't deserve to gain so much weight."

Rachel grinned. "I can imagine you're pretty shaken, but Teri, this is wonderful news. You've told Bobby, haven't you?"

That was the problem. "I haven't said a word and I'm not sure I want to."

"You can't keep this from your husband."

"But maybe I should. He's worried about me giving birth to *one* baby and now you want me to casually announce I'm having three? Three babies. Rachel! I'm scared out of my wits."

Her friend dismissed her concerns a little too easily. "You're going to be a terrific mother. And don't worry, Bobby will take it in stride."

"I was thinking one baby," Teri moaned, "and now I learn I'm practically going to have my own hockey team."

"Give yourself a chance to adjust first, and then tell Bobby," Rachel advised.

Teri was lost in her thoughts. She didn't have much of a role model when it came to mothering. She'd already read six books on parenting. None of them had truly reassured her. Some of the information conflicted with other information. One theory clashed with the next.

"Three babies," Rachel said. "You'll do great — and you can afford to hire help if you need it."

"A nanny?" That hadn't occurred to Teri. A nanny could come in part-time and help her feed and bathe the babies.

"Can I see the picture again?" Rachel asked. "I was so surprised when I looked at it that I didn't notice if they're boys or girls."

"One of each and the third's turned in such a way that it's impossible to tell," Teri told her friend. She buried her head in her hands.

"I have news of my own," Rachel whispered. She checked over her shoulder as if she wanted to make sure no one else could hear.

Teri looked up.

"Bruce and I are getting married."

"That's not news. I've had Valentine's Day circled on my calendar for weeks." It was such a romantic date. Rachel wanted a nice, formal wedding and even though Teri would be almost six months pregnant, Rachel had asked her to serve as matron of honor.

"The *reception's* taking place in February," Rachel confided. "But . . . are you doing anything December twentieth?" she asked, keeping her head lowered.

Teri stared at her. "You're getting married early?"

Rachel nodded. "What's the point of waiting another two months? We both know what we want and the wait's driving us crazy."

"Move in with him now," Teri suggested. "People do it all the time."

"I know, but there's Jolene to consider. We're trying to do everything properly for her sake. But Bruce is getting impatient and frankly, so am I. I'm so much in love with him, I don't want to wait a minute longer than I have to."

Teri understood. Her own wedding had been a rushed affair. Bobby had insisted on marrying her rather than just living together. As Bobby had somehow known — and as Teri had discovered — it *wasn't* the same. Marriage was a promise. A promise that was often broken, but a promise nonetheless — of enduring love, of enjoying the good and coping with the bad together. A marriage was more than a living arrangement, according to Bobby.

For a girl who'd been around the block more times than the mailman, this told her everything she needed to know about Bobby. The memory of their wedding night brought quick tears to her eyes.

Rachel noticed right away. "Teri, are you still worrying about the babies?"

"No . . . I was just thinking about Bobby and how much I love him."

"Tell him soon," Rachel urged. "He's going to be thrilled. Yes, he'll be concerned. Who could blame him? He probably won't let you out of his sight until May."

"No, April. The doctor wants to schedule a C-section for the last week of April. He's afraid of complications, so the babies are now due April twenty-seventh."

"Oh, Teri, this is so exciting!"

"It certainly explains why I feel like Elsie

the Cow at three and a half months," she said wryly. "Can you picture me at eight?"

Teri didn't even want to think about it.

"While I've got you here," Rachel murmured. "Give me an update on what's happening with your sister and James."

Teri knew the abrupt change of subject was Rachel's way of distracting her from her worries. Teri had been keeping her friend updated on the romance, such as it was, between Bobby's driver and her younger sister.

"Where did I leave off?" Teri asked, leaning closer.

"Last I heard, you and Bobby had invited them both to dinner."

"Well, *that* totally backfired. James refused to come."

Rachel rolled her eyes. "Men are so stubborn."

"My thought exactly," Teri said. "Something must've happened afterward, though."

"What?"

"I'm not sure. The next morning, my sister's car was still in the driveway."

"Christie didn't leave? Do you mean to tell me she spent the night with James?"

Teri shrugged. "Well, she wasn't with us, so I assumed the same thing as you. But . . . I assumed wrong."

"Well, where was she if she wasn't

with him?"

"At home." Teri had been discouraged by the news. "Apparently her car wouldn't start."

"Oh." Rachel sounded disappointed, too. "So James gave her a ride home?"

"It appears that way. When I asked him about it, he was pretty closemouthed. I only know she was having car problems because James was out tinkering with her car."

"He fixed it?"

"I guess so. The next time I looked out, the car was gone and so was James." She sighed. "Unfortunately he wasn't away for long, which tells me he probably dropped off the car without saying a word to her."

"What is it with that man?" Rachel asked, groaning theatrically. Ever since the kidnapping incident, she'd taken great interest in the health and happiness of James Wilbur.

"The thing is, I know my sister. She's falling for James, but she's fighting it."

"James would certainly be an improvement over her ex," Rachel said.

"A serial killer would be an improvement over her ex," Teri joked. "Well, not really, but you know what I mean."

Rachel glanced out at the shop. Her client was waiting at her station; someone, most likely Jane, had already put a plastic cape around her shoulders and given her the current *Vogue.* "I need to get back to work."

"Thanks for listening, Rach."

They stood and hugged. "Keep December twentieth hush-hush, okay?" Rachel said.

"You bet."

"We haven't told anyone else yet, not even Jolene. Pastor Flemming offered to marry us in the church that afternoon. It'll be a private ceremony."

"But I'm invited, right?"

"Of course! I can't get married without my matron of honor, can I? Not to mention her husband."

Teri gently squeezed her friend's arm. "Bobby and I will be there," she promised. "Thank you."

"No, thank *you*," Rachel said. "Anyway, I should go. Some of us still work for a living." Her good-natured laugh told Teri there was no jealousy in her words. Rachel was merely teasing, exercising her privilege as best friend.

"Don't be afraid to tell Bobby about the babies," Rachel said as they left the break room. "And call me tonight. He's going to be *thrilled*," she insisted again.

Teri wished she felt as confident as Rachel. *She* was the one who'd wanted to get pregnant. Bobby had been afraid for her physical

317

safety and thought they should wait. The news that they were having a multiple birth was bound to send him into a panic.

As soon as Teri left the mall, James brought the limousine toward her. Before she could open the door, he was out of the car and opening it for her. Once she was tucked inside, he took his position behind the wheel.

"Is everything all right, Miss Teri?" he asked with a look of concern.

"Yes, I think so. Why do you ask?"

James started the engine. "Your doctor's appointment was exceptionally lengthy and you seemed upset. Then you asked me to take you directly to the salon — to Miss Rachel, I presume."

"Rachel's my closest friend. She's — Oh, sorry." Her cell phone interrupted her. She took it from her purse and saw at a glance that it was her sister.

"Hi, Christie," she said, flipping it open. She watched as James's shoulders tightened.

"Hi," Christie returned. "I called the house and Bobby said you weren't home from your appointment yet. Are you doing anything this afternoon?"

"Ah . . . not really."

"Would you mind giving me a haircut?"

"Sure. Can you come around four?" That should leave ample time to tell Bobby her news, with a few hours built in to let him adjust. She hoped.

"I'll be there at four." Her sister hesitated. "Do you think James will be around?"

Teri squelched a smile. "I imagine so."

"He fixed my car," Christie said, speaking quickly. "So I bought him a little gift as a thank-you. Could you give it to him for me?"

"You should do it yourself."

"I . . . don't know about that."

"Play it by ear, then," Teri said. "Let's see how things go."

"Okay."

They hung up soon after that and Teri stuck her cell phone back inside her purse. "My sister's stopping by later this afternoon," she said blandly.

"Is there still a problem with her vehicle?" he asked.

"If there is, she didn't mention it."

"Her car isn't going to last much longer, I'm afraid." James shook his head. "She needs new tires, too."

Teri was worried about Christie driving that old rattletrap. But she'd worry about it another day.

"My sister has something for you. A small token of appreciation for helping her with the car," Teri said, studying his reaction.

"There's no need."

"You have a good heart, James."

In the rearview mirror she saw his face redden at her praise.

"Thank you, Miss Teri."

By the time they arrived at the house on Seaside Avenue, Bobby was outside pacing. "What took so long?" he demanded, thrusting his head into the car as soon as James had opened her door.

"Everything's fine, Bobby," Teri said calmly. "But I do have news."

Bobby looked perplexed — and fearful. "News from the doctor? What kind of news?" He helped Teri out of the car, then took her hand as they walked into the house.

"You'd better sit down," Teri suggested.

His face went, if possible, even paler. He chose the sofa and Teri sat on his lap, looping her arms around his neck.

"What would you say if I told you we're having twins?" she asked, thinking she'd ease him into the idea of a multiple birth.

"Twins!" He nearly unseated her. "Twins," he repeated, as a slow grin slid into place. "Twins," he said again.

"Isn't that exciting?"

Bobby nodded. "A boy and a girl?"

Teri cleared her throat, which immediately told Bobby there was something else. He looked at her warily.

"Sweetheart, what's one more?"

He frowned as only Bobby could. "One more what?"

"Baby."

"You want another baby?" He seemed completely confused.

"No," she said, "there already *is* another baby."

It took him a moment to catch on. His eyes met hers. "Are . . . are you t-telling me we're having t-triplets?" he stammered.

Teri nodded.

"Triplets," he said again, and he started to laugh. Sober, serious Bobby Polgar laughed, a rich, joyous sound that seemed to come from deep inside him. Then he was hugging and kissing her, proving in every possible way how much he loved his wife.

And Teri loved Bobby right back.

TWENTY-THREE

Christie knocked politely at James's apartment door. Drawing in a deep breath, she stepped back and squared her shoulders. As she waited she raised her hand to her hair. Teri had cut it shorter than it'd been in years. Christie had been wearing it shoulder-length, but this new style suited her and was easy to care for.

James answered her knock.

For a moment all they did was stare at each other.

Then, remembering the reason for her visit, Christie thrust out a small wrapped package. "This is for you."

James glanced down at it, seemingly embarrassed.

"I . . . I wanted to thank you for fixing my car," she said quickly.

"I was able to get the alternator working. But you're going to need a new car. Soon." With that he accepted the gift, still looking uncomfortable.

"I can't afford a new car," she said. "I can't even afford to have this one fixed on what I make." Living alone, it was difficult enough to cover rent and pay off her ex-husband's debts, plus meet all her other expenses, so overtime during the Christmas shopping season was a real bonus.

"Thank you for the gift," James murmured, "but it wasn't necessary."

"It's nothing big." She hoped he liked Almond Roca candy, which was made locally. Wal-Mart had it on sale, and she'd bought some pretty silver wrap.

"This was nice of you."

She began to turn around and walk back down the stairs.

James stopped her. "You really shouldn't be driving that car anymore," he said.

She lifted her shoulders in a shrug. "I'm sure you're right." She was on borrowed time with this vehicle and she knew it. In the next little while, something else would go wrong. The car would die, and that would be that. Then she'd have to investigate public transportation, and in a town the size of Cedar Cove, there weren't a lot of options. In the meantime, James had made it possible for her to drive to work, at least for this week, and for that she was grateful.

He continued to hold the box of candy in both hands, as if he didn't know what to do with it.

"Could I ask you something?" Christie asked.

"You cut your hair," he said, apparently just noticing.

"Teri did. Do you like it?" Her hand went to the back of her neck.

"You look different."

His answer probably meant he didn't approve of the change. Every man she'd ever dated had wanted her to keep her hair long. Not that she was exactly *dating* James, but that wasn't the point. Christie didn't understand men's attitudes toward women's hair, although Teri no doubt had some opinions on *that* subject.

He'd evaded her question, but she wasn't going to let him sidetrack her. So she asked another one. "Why'd you kiss me Monday night?"

James's mouth was a stern line. "Do you want me to apologize?"

"No," she said. "I just want to know why." Naturally she hoped he'd admit he was attracted to her, that she'd driven him mad with longing. That was a bit melodramatic — perhaps, but it was nice to dream.

"You don't have to tell me if you'd rather

not," she said when it was obvious he didn't plan to answer her question. Maybe he didn't know how.

"I was relieved that you were willing to listen to reason that night," he finally told her. "You seemed so angry at first."

"I was."

"And irrational."

She had to agree. But she'd been desperate. He would've felt the same way if it'd been his car and he didn't have the money to fix it, especially if he needed to get to work at six the next morning.

"Okay, the first kiss was about you feeling relieved," she said. That had been gentle, almost a brushing against her lips. "What about the second kiss?" She'd felt his longing and his need, and it'd matched her own.

He blinked hard. "That was pure selfishness."

"Oh." Her hand reached for the stair railing.

"Did it shock you?" he asked.

"No." James apparently didn't know much about her past. One hungry kiss wasn't likely to offend her. There'd been a sweetness in it, an appreciation. She would hardly have called it "selfish."

When he didn't stop her, she started reluctantly down the stairs. With each step she prayed James would say something to delay her departure. There was nothing else she could come up with; as it was, she'd already asked every question she could think of. It was dark now, time to head home. The December sky was clear and bright with stars.

"Christie?"

At the sound of his voice, she whirled around with such speed she nearly slid off the step. "Yes?" she asked anxiously.

"Be careful driving, understand?"

Her disappointment was like a weight that made her shoulders droop and her feet drag. But she didn't know why she should care if James invited her into his apartment. Why did it matter whether or not he wanted to see her again? There were plenty of men who'd welcome her company. So what if he wasn't one of them.

"Your tires are nearly bald."

She pretended not to hear him. Her ego had endured as much of a battering as it could take. What did it matter, anyway? Besides, she didn't even like him with his fussy manners and his formal speech. Fine. She wouldn't go out of her way for him again.

Driving home, she went past The Pink Poodle and was tempted to stop in. Beer cost money, though; she might be in the mood to drown her sorrows, but there were more productive ways to while away an evening. Instead, she drove down to the waterfront park, which was gaily decorated for Christmas. There'd been a notice in the Wal-Mart employee lounge indicating that the high school band was giving a Christmas concert that evening. She could use a bit of holiday cheer.

She was fortunate to find a parking space. As she walked toward the gazebo and the public seating, she recognized several customers — people she'd seen in her cash register line. Sheriff Davis was there with a young couple, obviously his daughter, judging by the family resemblance, and his son-in-law.

Charlotte and Ben Rhodes were seated in the front row. Everyone in town knew them. Charlotte had gone shopping that afternoon, picking up supplies for her cruise. She'd been high-spirited, excited about the trip, and they'd chatted away as if they were old friends.

Next she saw Grace Harding from the library. She and her husband stood on the outskirts of the crowd. He'd slipped his arm around her waist, and her head rested against his shoulder. There was something touching about the pose, something that bespoke tenderness and trust. Beside Grace were two young women and their husbands and families. Each held a baby in her arms. Christie knew they were Grace's daughters, but she couldn't remember their names.

The high school band began to play Christmas music, starting with a lively "Jingle Bells," accompanied by actual sleigh bells. By the time they got to "O, Little Town of Bethlehem," Christie felt the overwhelming urge to cry. All these people around her had someone who cared about them. Someone to whom they were special. Everyone except her. She could vanish off the face of the earth and no one would notice. Well, Teri and maybe their brother, Johnny, but not for days or even weeks.

Tears stung her eyes and she dashed them away with her bare hand. Being alone at Christmas was the worst. Teri had invited her for Christmas dinner, but it was a pity invite. Johnny already had plans to spend the day with his new girlfriend's family, so there'd only be Christie. She hadn't given Teri an answer yet. She figured she'd just be in the way. Bobby and Teri didn't need her intruding on their home and their lives, especially now that Teri was pregnant with triplets. She didn't need the extra bother of guests at her Christmas celebration.

Feeling morose and sorry for herself,

Christie left the park and strolled along the waterfront. She could still hear the music as she paused in front of the marina and watched the sailboats. Many of them had Christmas lights strung on their masts, and a few had Christmas trees on their decks.

As she turned away, ready to go back to her car, she saw that the library had set up a huge barrel to collect new toys for disadvantaged children. Growing up, she'd been one of those children.

That was when she knew exactly how she wanted to spend Christmas. She'd volunteer to deliver food baskets and gifts. Instead of moping around, filled with self-pity, she'd do something positive. More than one person had generously reached out to her when she was a hurting little girl, and now it was her turn to help others.

Yes, that was what she'd do. And if she couldn't deliver gifts, perhaps she could serve dinner at a nursing home Christmas Day.

Feeling better, Christie hurried back to her car and drove home. When she got there, she was astonished to see James parked outside her apartment.

He climbed out of his car when she stepped out of hers.

Her heart pounded furiously as he came

toward her.

"I'm going to be a volunteer," she said excitedly, needing to tell someone about her momentous decision.

He blinked as though she'd spoken in a foreign language.

"If I can, I'm going to deliver charity baskets and gifts to underprivileged children on Christmas Eve." She laughed at his puzzled expression. "I was feeling sorry for myself, and then it occurred to me that what I need to do is reach out to someone else." All at once she realized that she didn't know why he was there.

She stopped and waited for him to tell her.

James never seemed to find it easy to explain himself.

When he didn't say anything, she asked, "Do you want to volunteer with me?"

He nodded. "Okay."

"Would you like . . ." She almost said a beer. "Tea," she offered instead.

"Yes, please," he said with a grin.

She led him into her apartment, which was clean for a change. It wasn't the Ritz, by any means, but at least it was comfortable. In a burst of holiday enthusiasm she'd strung a tinsel garland across her drapery rod and stuck a ceramic snowman in the middle of her coffee table.

James folded his coat neatly and laid it on the back of her sofa.

"Did you, um, have a reason for coming?" she asked as she filled her teakettle.

"Where did you go?" he asked, which seemed to be a habit of his — answering a question with a question.

"Down to the waterfront. The high school band's is putting on a Christmas concert. I listened to the music for a while and that's when I decided to be a volunteer."

"Why at Christmas, though?"

She didn't want to tell him she didn't have anywhere to go. It was too personal, too . . . embarrassing. Too sad. "Payback," she told him. "Someone was kind to me when I was a little girl without a gift at Christmas. Now I'm returning that kindness."

"It's a very thoughtful thing to do."

Rather than discuss the worthiness of her idea, she said, "You didn't answer my question. Why *are* you here?"

"I wanted to see you. I thought you'd go to The Pink Poodle."

She almost had. "You wanted to see me. That's sweet."

He nodded rather sheepishly.

"I like you, James."

There it was — without a lot of fancy words to dress it up — just the plain truth.

He could accept it or reject it and frankly, she wasn't sure which he'd do.

His gaze held hers for a moment, and then the most enchanting smile fell into place. "I like you, too."

That was as big an admission as he'd ever made in their decidedly odd relationship. Fearing he'd see the joy it gave her, she busied herself getting tea bags and sugar from the cupboard.

As soon as their tea was ready, she carried the two mugs to the small coffee table and set them on her Christmas coasters. There was only the one sofa, so she had no choice but to sit next to James.

He waited until she'd sipped from her tea before he picked up his own mug.

"I'm glad you came," she said, not looking at him.

"I am, too." He paused, then added, "I like your hair."

She'd almost forgotten she'd had it cut. "Thank you."

"You're very pretty."

Christie was accustomed to flattery. Most men seemed to know exactly what to say in order to get what they wanted from her. She listened to their lies because she so badly needed to believe they were true. James's three words meant more to her than any compliment she'd ever received.

For several minutes she couldn't respond. "Thank you," she murmured at last. "Do you want to kiss me again?" she asked, only half joking.

He took her seriously. "Yes, but not yet. Later."

She nearly laughed out loud. Later? Any other man would've had her in bed by now. They would've found more interesting ways of keeping warm than sipping tea.

"I don't know anything about you," she said.

"I realize that."

"You've been Bobby's driver for how many years?" She waited for him to answer. He didn't.

"Bobby and I are friends."

"You've been friends for a long time?"

"Yes."

The silence stretched between them. "You don't want me to know anything else, is that it?"

He shifted uneasily. "Maybe now," he said, leaning forward to set his mug on the coaster.

She frowned, not understanding. "*Maybe now* what?"

He smiled that sweet boyish smile of his and took her tea out of her hands. "It's time to kiss again." He moved closer and pressed his lips to hers.

Christie nearly gasped at the explosive desire that erupted inside her. "James," she whispered. "Oh, James." She locked her arms around his neck and kissed him back. But he wouldn't allow her to deepen the contact. He maintained his gentle pressure until she thought she'd melt at his feet if he didn't hurry up and kiss her properly.

Then his hands were in her newly short hair. He angled his mouth over hers and showed her that there was no need to hurry, after all. He was hers and she was his.

When he released her, Christie collapsed against the back of the sofa. Her eyes were still shut and she couldn't catch her breath for what seemed like minutes.

"Wow," she sighed.

"That was nice," he agreed. He, too, was breathing hard.

She leaned foreward and touched her forehead to his. "James, there are things you don't know about me," she said.

"It doesn't matter."

"It does to me." She wanted to tell him the truth so there'd be no surprises later on. "I've been married before . . . . It wasn't a good marriage." She gave him some of the details, just enough so he'd understand that her husband hadn't been her first lover nor had he been her last.

James listened quietly, then held and kissed her again. Occasionally he'd ask a question. When tears fell from her eyes, he kissed them away. Once she'd finished her confession, she buried her head in his shoulder.

James cradled her with comforting hands. "Thank you," he whispered.

She couldn't figure out why he'd say that and looked up. His eyes met hers. "Telling me all this couldn't have been easy."

"It wasn't."

"I'm important to you?"

She nodded. "Important enough that I want you to know the truth."

He kissed her temple. "The truth is a precious gift."

He continued to hold her. Then, reluctant to leave, he murmured against her hair, "I have to get back to the house." When he came to his feet, he seemed a bit unsteady. "Thank you, Christie," he said a second time.

She gestured weakly, not knowing what to say. A plea to see him again was on the tip of her tongue. She swallowed the question unasked. He would call her. She saw it in his eyes. She was important to him, too, otherwise he wouldn't have come. She'd poured out her heart to him, and he'd accepted what she had to say without censure. He knew everything about her now; she'd held nothing back. She hated that he had to go.

After one last kiss, James saw himself out, which was a good thing. Her legs didn't seem to work properly. He'd been gone for at least five minutes before she found the strength to stand.

She'd never done anything so bold as to lay out her sins for a man to examine. In a strange way she felt better. Telling James everything had unexpectedly freed her. At first she was afraid she'd chase him away, but nothing could be further from the truth. His touch had been gentle, his words kind and encouraging. He hadn't said he loved her, but he did. She knew it. She *felt* it. And Christie knew something else.

She loved him, too.

TWENTY-FOUR

"Mom, I know you're disappointed," Linnette said into her cell phone. She was just as disappointed, but she couldn't possibly return to Cedar Cove for Christmas. Not if she was going to accomplish everything that needed to be done for the Buffalo Valley medical clinic to open on schedule.

Linnette cast an apologetic glance at Pete Mason. He'd invited her to lunch and they sat in the Three of a Kind restaurant and bar, where Linnette had, until recently, worked as a waitress. They'd just been served their meal and Linnette had taken a couple of bites of her sandwich when her cell phone rang. She wished she hadn't answered it, but too late now.

"You told us over Thanksgiving you'd make it home for Christmas," her mother protested.

"I know I did, and I'm sorry." She already felt guilty, and hearing the frustration in her mother's voice wasn't helping.

Silence followed Linnette's announcement. Repressing a sigh, she wondered what else she could say to comfort Corrie — and herself. She missed her family and her friends in Cedar Cove. She'd like nothing better than to spend the holidays at her parents' home. But she was deeply involved with the medical clinic, which would be opening — she hoped — by February. Not only that, she didn't have the extra money to make such a trip. Airfares at this time of year were simply out of reach.

"Mack will be with you. And Gloria will, too. Right?"

"I'm not sure yet." Her mother didn't hide her distress. "They're both the most recent hires, so I'm afraid they'll end up working. It won't be Christmas without my children."

"I'm sorry," she said again. Changing the subject, she asked, "How's Mack?"

"Fine. He's settling into his job with the fire department. He seems to be enjoying it."

"I knew he would," Linnette murmured.

"I had a surprise for you, too," her mother lamented.

"A . . . surprise?" Linnette felt guilty enough.

"Yes. Bob Beldon got your father and your brother parts in the live Nativity scene at the church."

Linnette could hardly believe it. "You've got to be joking! Dad — and Mack, too?" She could imagine Mack enjoying such an event, but it must've taken some fast talking to get her father to agree.

"Mack's playing a shepherd and your father's one of the Wise Men."

Linnette giggled, thinking she'd love to see that. "How did Pastor Flemming and Mr. Beldon convince Dad to do this?"

"Don't ask me, but whatever they said worked." Her mother finally seemed to relax. "You should've seen Mack chasing sheep at the first practice," she said with a laugh.

"Real sheep?"

"Oh, yes. We've got a camel, too," Corrie bragged. "I have no idea how Pastor Dave managed it, but he found a camel for your father. Roy's going to lead him — or is it her? — around the stable where Jesus, Mary and Joseph are on display."

"Dad . . . and a camel?"

Pete's eyebrows shot up and Linnette sent him a smile.

"Camels can be nasty. I don't think anyone but your father could handle him."

"I hear they spit and bite," Linnette said, enjoying this.

"Oh, yes. You heard right." She paused. "Gloria and I laughed ourselves silly."

"Dad must've been seriously annoyed." The image of her father in robe and sandals struggling with a recalcitrant camel almost made her rethink the possibility of going home.

"We were going to surprise you," her mother was saying in that wistful tone.

"Promise me you'll take lots of pictures."

"I will. In fact, I bought myself an early Christmas gift — a digital camera. I can even take movies. Your dad's showing me how it works." Linnette knew that her father, as a private investigator, had used one for years.

"I'll e-mail you a movie of the Nativity scene. Or," she added dryly, "I'll get Roy to send it for me."

"Mom, please do. I want to see it all." Linnette suddenly felt more homesick than she had the entire time she'd been here. This would be her first Christmas away from her family.

"What'll you do about Christmas if you won't be home?" her mother asked.

Linnette turned to Pete and apologized that this conversation was taking so long. She gestured for him to continue eating his lunch, which he did. "I'm spending the day with Hassie Knight. We'll make a small dinner and play cards." Hassie owned Knight's Pharmacy and was the inspiration behind the medical clinic. She'd formed a committee that included Linnette and several local businesspeople; they were working with state agencies and applying for a grant.

"You won't be with Pete?"

"I doubt it, Mom. He has his own family."

"You've mentioned him quite a few times now. But I'm glad to see you're sensible enough not to get serious about this farmer."

"It's too soon." She didn't have to say any more than that; her mother knew what she meant. Linnette's relationship with Cal Washburn was over, and she didn't need a rebound romance. The last news she'd received was that Cal and Vicki were now married and had moved to Wyoming. She wished them every happiness — and she was sincere in that.

The funny thing was, she didn't feel any lingering pain over losing Cal. In retrospect, their break-up was probably for the best. She and Cal had been too different in both their interests and expectations. She'd loved him, and she'd been devastated when he ended the relationship, but as with most life experiences, Linnette had learned valuable lessons.

"Cal's in Wyoming," her mother said, as if

reading Linnette's thoughts.

"I know," she said without emotion. "How's Judge Griffin doing?" she asked, moving to another subject. During their previous conversation, her mother had told her that Olivia had suffered a medical setback.

"Much, much better. She's home from the hospital and the infection's under control."

"I'm so glad."

"It's been very hard for her husband," Corrie said. "Oh," she added, "speaking of Jack Griffin, he wrote a hilarious piece on the Nativity scene. There was a practice with the animals — they're being kept at Cliff Harding's place," she said quickly, and Linnette suspected she was worried about referring to Cliff's ranch, since Cal had lived and worked there, and Linnette would always associate it with him.

"Send me the article, okay, Mom?"

"I will." Her mother sighed again. "I do wish you could come for Christmas."

"Mom, please. Don't make me feel worse." Any more of this and she'd start to cry. "The airfare is outrageous and it isn't safe for me to be driving all that way by myself in winter." She looked out the window, her gaze falling on a two-foot-high bank of snow.

"Your father and I will pay for your ticket." The offer was tempting, but Linnette couldn't let them do that. "No, Mom, I'm an adult. I'll be home for a visit soon."

"A visit," her mother repeated slowly, her meaning clear. Corrie wanted Linnette to move back to Cedar Cove, especially now that Cal and Vicki were gone.

The truth was that Linnette hadn't once considered doing so. She'd found solace in this small Dakota town. When she'd graduated as a physician assistant, it had always been her goal to use her medical skills in an out-of-the-way area, some rural community where the need was greatest.

Her parents, particularly her mother, had been unhappy when she left her job at the medical clinic in Cedar Cove. But more than ever, Linnette realized it'd been the right thing to do.

"Tell me how *you're* spending Christmas Day," Linnette said.

"We're going to open gifts around ten. I suppose I can mail yours, although I don't know if they'll reach you in time."

"Mom, thank you, but I don't need anything."

"Do you have an apartment now?"

Linnette nearly laughed out loud. Never having seen Buffalo Valley, her mother couldn't begin to guess what this place was like. Until recently, she'd lived in a small room on the second floor of Three of a Kind. "There aren't any apartments here, Mom. At the moment I'm renting a room from Hassie."

"A room?"

"It works out well for both of us." If everything went as she hoped, Linnette would have living quarters at the medical clinic. The state needed to approve all this, of course. The house they planned to use, which had been vacant for several years, would require a lot of renovation. Once the funding approval came through, at least twenty men and women — even teenagers — were ready, willing and able to tackle the project.

"You left a lovely apartment here," Corrie said. "One with a great view."

"But Mack told me he's moving in! You must be pleased about that. And speaking of Mack, is there anyone special in his life these days?"

Her mother exhaled. "Not anyone he's mentioned, but then you know your brother — he's pretty tight-lipped about anything personal."

"True," Linnette said. She'd have to have a conversation with him soon, see what she could ferret out. "Listen, Mom, I'd better go."

Her mother tried one more time. "Are you

positive you won't let your father and me buy you an airline ticket home?"

"I'm positive. I'll call on Christmas Day, Mom."

"It won't be the same," Corrie muttered.

"I know."

They said goodbye and Linnette closed her cell phone, setting it on the table.

"Your mother's awfully disappointed, isn't she?" Pete asked, his blue eyes studying her. "And so are you."

Linnette shrugged, wanting to make light of her own disappointment. "It'll be fine. I'm a big girl. I don't have to rush home to my family for the holidays."

"But you'd like to be there, right?"

"Well, of course." She picked up her bacon, lettuce and tomato sandwich, but her appetite had vanished. Putting it back on her plate, she shoved it aside, leaving the bag of potato chips untouched.

Elbows on the table, Linnette surveyed the restaurant with its handful of customers. She knew it well; after all, Buffalo Bob Carr had hired her when she ended up in this town, low on cash and looking for a place to stay.

Now that she was here, however, she couldn't imagine living anywhere else. Not even Cedar Cove.

Bob came out from the kitchen, wearing a

stained white apron. "The cream of mushroom soup's ready, Pete, if you're still interested."

"Sure thing," Pete called back.

"You can finish my sandwich if you want," Linnette told him. Pete was six-three and had a hearty appetite.

"No, thanks. You should have it."

Bob carried out a large bowl of soup, which he deposited in front of Pete. He glanced at Linnette. "You okay?" he asked with a concerned frown.

"Of course . . . I'm just not hungry."

"It isn't your lack of appetite that worries me. It's the miserable look on your face," he said bluntly.

"I am not miserable," she said and then, to prove her point, she smiled up at him. "It's December. Christmas is around the corner. How can I possibly be blue?"

"You've heard of 'Blue Christmas,' haven't you?" Buffalo Bob asked. "Elvis sang that for a reason."

"You 'Have Yourself a Merry Little Christmas,' Bob," she bantered back.

"Yeah, you too," he said with a grin. "But seriously, Linnette —"

"I'm fine. Really."

Bob's physical appearance led strangers to assume he was a biker. He was a burly man who always wore jeans and a leather vest over a short-sleeved T-shirt. His thin hair was tied in a ponytail that hung nearly to the middle of his back. He might seem menacing, but as Linnette had immediately discovered, he had a huge heart. Watching him with his wife, Merrilee, and their three kids had told her exactly what kind of person he was.

Pete finished his sandwich and soup and reached for the bill. "My treat."

"Thank you," she said, feeling a little chagrined. She hadn't been good company, especially with her mother phoning in the middle of their lunch. She realized a lengthy conversation at a restaurant was rude, but she couldn't seem to do much about it. Pete, however, didn't take offense easily.

"I'd better get that part my brother needs and head back to the farm," he said.

He'd driven the hour into town to pick up a tractor part Dennis Urlacher had ordered for them. Linnette knew he jumped at any excuse to come to town — because of her. Frankly she enjoyed his visits. Pete had made his feelings plain and she felt comfortable with him. It was too soon to make a commitment, although she sensed he'd like that. They were still in the getting-to-know-you stage, and Linnette was in absolutely no rush to leap into another relationship as intense as the one she'd had with Cal.

"The movie's changing this weekend," Pete said. He pulled his wallet out of his hip pocket and placed twenty dollars on the table. "Are you interested? I'll buy you the biggest popcorn they have."

"You don't need to bribe me, Pete. I'd love to go to the movie." The theater only had one screen, unlike the multiplex in Cedar Cove, and the movies were often second-run, weeks if not months behind the major markets. When she'd first moved to town, Linnette had been amused to see the theater playing shows that were just a week or two from being released on DVD.

Pete's grin was as big as if she'd announced he'd won the state lottery. "I'll pick you up at Hassie's around six."

"Perfect." He took her long wool coat from the back of her chair and helped her into it. Linnette wrapped her scarf around her neck twice, then slipped on her hat and gloves. The winters in North Dakota were frigid; she needed a heavy coat, boots and all the other cold-weather paraphernalia, even if she was only walking from Three of a Kind to the pharmacy, a distance of less than one block.

Stepping outside, Linnette accompanied

Pete to his truck. This was a new model and although it was just a few months old, it already had several scratches and dents. She'd been upset when she saw the first minor dent, but Pete had said this was a working truck and a few "dings," as he described them, were to be expected.

He touched her face briefly. "I'll see you Saturday, then."

"Okay." She hunched her shoulders against the sharp wind.

"Call you later," Pete said.

She nodded.

He seemed reluctant to leave her. "You can spend Christmas with me, you know."

"Pete, stop it. Hassie and I will be fine. It's not that big a deal."

"I know." He sighed. Looking around to be sure no one was watching, he kissed her. Not a deep or lingering kiss, but a very nice one nonetheless.

Pete didn't normally display his affection publicly, and the gesture surprised her. She smiled up at him. Then, with a quick goodbye, she hurried down the street to the pharmacy.

Hassie was all smiles when Linnette got there. "I heard from the state. We got the funding for the clinic!"

Linnette clapped her gloved hands together. "That's fabulous!"

"I've already got the word out."

Her head was spinning. "I didn't have any idea it would happen this fast."

"That —" Hassie winked at her "— is because I know the right people in Bismarck."

"You certainly do."

An hour later, Linnette was over at the abandoned house that would become the new clinic. Men from town, including Buffalo Bob, had started to arrive, and before long an entire wall was down. The renovations had begun. When school ended for the day, a group of teenagers came by to sweep up and carry out debris. Several times, Linnette found herself in the way, more of a hindrance than a help.

As dusk fell, everyone else left. She parked the broom and dustpan in a corner, glancing around the large front room with satisfaction. An astonishing amount of progress had been made in just half a day. Her cell phone rang and she scrabbled for it in her coat pocket.

"Hello?"

"It's Pete."

"Oh, Pete, guess what?" The sound of the door opening made her turn, and Pete Mason walked in. She laughed, closing her phone. "You heard?"

He nodded. "Congratulations! But that's not the only news."

"Oh?"

Pete brought her close, his hands on her shoulders. "You're going home for Christmas."

"I'm what — I can't possibly leave, Pete, especially now."

"I'm driving you. Everyone's pulling together and all the supplies can be delivered by the weekend. We should have the renovations finished within ten days if we work weekends. Then as soon as everything's done, you and I are taking off."

"Taking off?"

"We'll drive straight through to Cedar Cove so you can surprise your parents."

Emotion welled up inside her. "Oh, Pete." She threw her arms around him and hugged him with all her might.

"Thank you," she whispered, "thank you, thank you, thank you."

His arms slid about her waist. "I'm looking forward to meeting your family," he said.

"I want you to."

"Gloria and Mack, as well as your parents," he said. "I've heard so much about all of them. Seeing that I hope to be part of this family one day, I feel it's time to meet them."

Linnette's eyes widened and she could feel

the wariness in her expression.

Pete must have read her stricken look because he was quick to add, "I don't intend to rush you. All I ask is that you let me know when you're ready. Until then, I'm willing to wait. Like I told you before, I'm a patient man."

TWENTY-FIVE

Just when it seemed Dave Flemming's life was back on an even keel, he noticed that something else was bothering his wife. Emily hadn't been herself for a few days. At first he'd assumed it was because of her new job, but that didn't appear to be the case. In fact, anytime she talked about the store, her face lit up.

Dave hadn't questioned her, hoping that whatever was wrong would take care of itself. He was busy doing two jobs, preparing for all the Christmas events at the church, including the live Nativity scene, plus his other pastoral duties. He didn't have the energy to deal with a moody wife.

Any other time of year he *would* have asked, but right now the demands on him were too consuming. He figured that sooner or later, Emily would approach him and they'd talk about her problem, whatever it was. If that hadn't happened by New Year's, he'd definitely ask her.

Thursday afternoon Emily arrived at the church just as he was about to leave.

"I need to talk to you," she announced. Entering his office, she closed the door behind her.

"I've got a meeting in ten minutes with the choir director and —"

His wife cut him off. "Then you're going to be late." Her authoritative tone shocked him.

"All right," he said in a resigned voice. He sat back down, hoping this wouldn't take long.

Emily sat across from his desk, clutching her purse with both hands. Her eyes darted every which way.

Dave waited patiently for several minutes. "Em?" he finally prodded.

A sigh shuddered through her. "I went to Allan Harris's office Tuesday morning," she said abruptly.

All kinds of crazy thoughts flew through his head. Was she in legal trouble? Did she want — God forbid — a divorce? Did she —

"I asked to see Martha Evans's last will and testament."

Dave stared at her. "Whatever for?" Besides, he knew very well that it would be unethical to reveal a document like that to anyone other than family. "Emily, they can't —"

"I know," she said, cutting him off again. "The nice young man was kind enough to allow me a peek. He could lose his job over this, so I'm asking you not to say anything."

"Of course not." At the mention of Allan Harris's assistant, Dave remembered that he needed to set up another marriage counseling session with the couple. Geoff had canceled the first one.

Tears filled his wife's eyes. "Emily, what is it?" he asked urgently. "What's wrong?"

"There's nothing in the will that says Martha wanted you to have her husband's gold watch."

Instantly Dave was on his feet. "There *has* to be."

"I'm telling you, Dave, there isn't. I read the will and I didn't see one single word about it."

He felt suddenly queasy. He couldn't believe his wife had checked up on him — or that Martha hadn't done what she'd said. But she had; he knew that without a doubt. "It *has* to be there. Martha showed it to me herself."

"The will?"

"No, the letter she wrote for Allan Harris. It said she'd voluntarily given me the watch that had belonged to her husband. Since she didn't have sons to pass it to, it was her wish that I wear it in good health."

"What about her sons-in-law?" Emily asked.

Dave shrugged uneasily. "The older daughter's divorced. And I gather Martha never saw eye to eye with her younger daughter's husband." He shook his head. "That watch meant a lot to her, and I was really honored that she gave it to me."

"She didn't have grandsons?"

"No." Dave couldn't understand why his wife was questioning him this way. Her obvious lack of trust offended him — and wounded him.

Emily continued to study him. "Don't you realize how bad this looks?"

The queasiness intensified. "You're right. I'll return the watch immediately." He should never have taken it, only Martha had been so insistent. And as he'd told Emily, he'd appreciated the old woman's gesture in presenting him with a gift that meant so much to her.

Dave stood up and started to pace the small office. This whole mess was a big misunderstanding. He'd call Harris and ask about the letter. He hadn't actually seen Martha hand it over, but she'd had an appointment with Allan that very day.

Dave's last conversation with the attorney had been awkward. Unpleasant. Allan had drilled him with questions about the day he'd found Martha's body. He'd been irritated by the man's tone; Harris had practically implied that Dave was responsible for the missing jewelry. Because of that, Dave had acted defensively. Otherwise, it would've occurred to him to have Allan check the will to make sure the matter of the watch was settled.

"I'd better talk to Allan soon," he mumbled, eager to clear the air.

Emily remained in her chair. "There's something else," she said in a low voice.

"What now?" he asked with a groan.

Emily opened her purse clasp and withdrew a clear plastic bag that she held out to him.

Dave stared at the diamond earrings, then back at her, utterly perplexed. "What's this?"

"You don't know?" She sounded astonished.

"No." He was beginning to feel angry. What was she up to?

"You don't recognize these earrings?"

"Should I?" He dropped them on his desk.

Reaching inside her purse for a tissue, Emily dabbed her eyes. "I found them in your suit coat pocket."

She might as well have hit him in the stomach with a baseball bat. Dave literally fell back in his chair. It took a moment for the information to sink in. When he spoke, his voice was hoarse. "When?"

"The night of our anniversary dinner. I picked up your coat and one of them fell out. I discovered the second one in the other pocket."

"And you thought . . ." He couldn't say the words.

"In the beginning I assumed you were involved with another woman. Then later, after I learned about the watch, I assumed Mrs. Evans had given you the earrings, too, and that . . . that you intended to give them to me for Christmas."

"The earrings belonged to Martha?"

Tears spilling down her pale cheeks, Emily nodded.

"How do you know that?"

"I . . . I saw a photograph of them in the file that came with her will."

No wonder Emily had been so moody. Dave shook his head helplessly. "Emily," he said, holding her gaze, "I swear to you on my life that I've never seen those earrings until this minute."

"How'd they get into your pocket then?" she demanded.

He didn't have an explanation nor could he guess how it had happened. "I don't have a clue."

Pressing her hands to her mouth, Emily doubled over and started to weep in earnest.

Dave felt like weeping himself. The news about the watch had horrified him, but that was minor compared to what he felt now. "It can't be," he murmured. "It just can't be."

"I saw a picture with my own eyes," she said through her tears. "Mrs. Evans had more than one pair of diamond earrings, so . . . so she had everything photographed."

Dave was too stunned to speak.

Emily had managed to control her sobbing, which had dwindled down to a series of indelicate sniffles. "I think you should talk to Troy Davis," she said, her eyes imploring him.

Had she lost all sense? "He'll arrest me if I do." The evidence pointed directly at him and Troy wouldn't have any choice but to hold Dave for questioning.

"You have to," Emily insisted. "Otherwise no one will ever believe you."

But Dave had nothing to offer the sheriff. Nothing to justify his possession of the watch, unless that letter came to light. And certainly nothing to explain the earrings. He wouldn't know what to say.

"*Please,* Dave."

"I can't." He had to get through Christmas first and then he'd deal with this situation. He simply couldn't do it now.

"Why not?" She watched him intently.

"Emily, think about it. We're less than two weeks from Christmas. I'm responsible for organizing all our Christmas events, which includes delivering the charity baskets. *And* I have my hours at the bank." His mind whirled with everything that needed to be done before and during the holidays. He had yet to write his sermon for the Christmas Eve service and frankly he'd prefer not to do it in jail.

"Dave, you can't put this off."

"I have no other option." A thought suddenly struck him. "Have you told anyone else about this?"

"No."

"Thank God." That, at least, was a relief.

"You've got to talk to Sheriff Davis! You can't have this hanging over your head. If the information somehow came out, it could ruin our lives."

"The only one who knows about it is you."

"But if Sheriff Davis finds out . . ." Her eyes pleaded with him. "Don't you remember you lost the watch at Olivia Griffin's?"

He dismissed her concern. He'd worried

about it earlier, but he doubted Olivia would place any significance on his having the watch. Dave had picked it up the next day. She'd probably forgotten the whole thing by now.

"It can wait," he said. He didn't think Emily fully understood the pressure he was under. "I'm innocent."

"Of course you are."

He noted the slight hesitation in her voice. "You don't believe that, do you?"

Quickly she looked away. "Of course I do. But I'd feel a lot more comfortable if you went to see Sheriff Davis. We could go together and talk to him. He's a reasonable man."

"I agree, but if we go to him now he might detain me and that can't happen. Not less than two weeks before Christmas. Don't you realize how many responsibilities I'm juggling?" Dave didn't need one more problem to complicate his already overloaded schedule. "It can wait for another two weeks."

"Can it really, Dave?"

"Trust me, Emily." He sounded — he *felt* — as though he was begging. "In all the years we've been married, have I ever given you cause to doubt my integrity?"

She hesitated again. "No."

"Well, then?"

"Until recently," she amended.

"I don't believe this!"

"Look at it from my perspective," Emily said. "A little while ago you admitted we're having financial difficulties, yet you didn't respect me enough to tell me that."

"I've apologized. And I took a part-time job to make ends meet," he blurted out. The choir director was waiting and this conversation was putting him on edge.

"You're out of sorts most of the time," she added, "and I don't know why."

"You would be, too," he snapped, "if you worked as many hours as I do. I've got people vying for my attention, tugging at me from every direction. Everyone wants something from me."

"I thought you loved being a pastor."

"I do. This is what God intended for me and I love my job, but there are times when the stress and the demands are more than any man should have to endure. And then factor in this second job . . ." He raised his shoulders in a shrug. "I love you, Emily, and I'm asking you to trust me."

She didn't respond.

"Is that so hard?"

"I wish you'd listen to reason," she said quietly.

"Reason?" he echoed. "As far as I'm concerned, *you're* the one who's being unreasonable."

"You're in denial," she asserted.

"Oh, stop it with the pop-psych nonsense. *Denial.*" He snorted.

"It's not nonsense. You think if you sit back and do nothing," she said, rushing her words, "you think if we keep our mouths shut, everything will blow over. The culprit will be uncovered and you'll be off the hook without ever having to explain yourself."

"That's not true," Dave argued. "What I want is to do my job. I want to tend my flock and deal with this ridiculous mess after Christmas."

"Oh, Dave."

"Emily, please bear with me. I can't talk to Sheriff Davis yet, but I will. I give you my word of honor."

There was a knock at the door. Dave closed his eyes and exhaled noisily. "Yes, Angel," he called out.

His assistant opened the door, glancing apologetically toward Dave and Emily. "I'm sorry to interrupt."

"It's fine," Dave assured her. "We were just finishing up."

Angel stepped into the office. "I thought I should tell you the truck with the animal feed is here."

"Here?" Dave groaned. "He's supposed to deliver it to Cliff Harding's place." He would be forever grateful that the Hardings had agreed to house the animals.

"I know," she said, "but the driver says he has to talk to you because the paperwork specifically states delivery's to be made to this address."

"Okay, I'll be there in a moment."

"And Mrs. Stevenson's in the sanctuary."

The choir director prided herself on her punctuality and disliked being kept waiting. "Please tell her I'll be with her in a moment," Dave said.

Angel nodded and shut the door.

Dave turned to his wife. "We can discuss this later if you want."

"What's the point? You've already decided." Emily snatched up the diamond earrings and dropped them back in her purse. Coming to her feet, she dashed to the door, but not before Dave saw the tears glistening in her eyes.

The problem was that Emily didn't understand what she was asking of him. It broke his heart to fight with his wife and to flout her advice. There had to be a way to give her the peace of mind she needed — and stay out of jail at the same time.

Dave didn't have a chance to talk to Emily

again until much later that night. It was almost ten-thirty when he finally got home. After sorting out the confusion with the feed delivery and meeting with Mrs. S., he'd had to forgo supper to get to the bank on time. Following his shift, he'd grabbed a muffin at Mocha Mama's. He walked silently into the house, first checking on his sons, who were both asleep. Emily didn't look up when he stepped inside her workroom.

He was weary in body and exhausted in spirit, but Dave knew he had to make this right with his wife.

"Emily." He spoke her name softly.

She sat at her sewing machine working on a quilt. The radio played Christmas music, but he doubted she was listening.

"Let's talk," he said, sitting on a chair next to her sewing desk. He reached out and stroked her knee.

"Have you changed your mind?" she asked. She slid aside to avoid his touch. "Are you willing to tell the sheriff what I found?"

"No." He couldn't cope with the consequences of such an action.

"Then we have nothing else to talk about."

"Please listen to me, Em," Dave pleaded. "I've been thinking over everything you said, and you have a valid point. If someone came across this information, it could be a problem."

She gave a humorless laugh. "That's putting it mildly."

"I agree with you — I should tell someone."

For the first time since he'd entered her room, she turned to look at him. "Who?"

"I thought I'd make an appointment with Roy McAfee."

"You'd be willing to do that?"

"Yes." Dave rubbed his tired eyes. "I trust Roy, and while he isn't an attorney, he knows the law. He can tell me my rights."

Emily nodded, accepting his suggestion.

"Then, after Christmas," he continued, "the two of us can go and talk to the sheriff together."

"Okay," she whispered, appeased. "Thank you."

It wasn't the perfect solution, but a workable one. As soon as Christmas was over, he'd settle this somehow, once and for all.

TWENTY-SIX

"Come on, Dad, don't be such a stick in the mud!" Megan stood, hands on her hips, in the driveway next to her car. "You've *got* to come with us."

Troy wasn't in the mood to go shopping for a Christmas tree. The last few years, he'd brought Sandy on this expedition, and the four of them had driven to a nearby tree farm. Once Sandy had gone into the care facility, Troy hadn't bothered with Christmas decorations, so Megan and Craig's tree became theirs, too.

He wanted to forget about the holidays this year; his Christmas spirit was nonexistent. He had better things to do on a Friday evening than tag along with his daughter and her husband. Better things like . . . watching reruns of *CSI,* for instance. He'd tried his best to get out of the excursion, but Megan wouldn't hear of it.

"Artificial trees are much safer," he

pointed out. "And they don't lose their needles."

"Dad," Megan moaned, "it'll be *fun.* We do this every year, remember? It's tradition."

And who was he to fight tradition? "Oh, all right," he said with ill grace.

"Come on!" she cried again and clapped her hands. "Show a little holiday spirit. We're going to pick out our tree and drink hot cocoa and get a free candy cane. Doesn't that make you happy?"

"Yeah, yeah, I'm happy," he muttered, but he wasn't. The week had seemed interminable. Yesterday Martha Evans's two daughters had stopped by his office and made a big fuss. They wanted to know what he'd done to find the culprit who'd walked off with their mother's jewelry, and more importantly, their inheritance. Never mind that he considered them grasping and unpleasant, they were entitled to answers, although he had none to give. He had his suspicions but nothing concrete. He was waiting and watching, but so far the person he suspected hadn't slipped up. Not yet, anyway. And reliable as a cop's hunch might be, at least in the mystery novels Sandy used to read, it wasn't enough to justify an arrest.

And all week long, he'd thought about Faith. He missed her. He wished now that he'd approached her with more finesse. He'd been unfair to her because he'd overreacted to Megan's fears.

Having lived with Sandy all those years, watching her decline little by little, had taken a toll on his psyche. He couldn't tolerate the prospect of Megan going through the same ordeal. In retrospect, he realized he'd discounted the difference thirty years had made in the treatment of MS. While he wouldn't wish the disease on Megan or anyone, it wasn't the death sentence it had once been.

But Megan had been his reason, his excuse, for breaking off the relationship with Faith. His daughter needed him, he'd told himself, and she did, without a doubt. Deep down, however, Troy had begun to wonder if he was afraid of finding new happiness. If he believed, maybe not even consciously, that he had no right to experience joy while his daughter was struggling.

"You're old enough that your father doesn't need to come with you," Troy complained, trying one last time to back out of this family trip.

Megan smiled that sweet innocent smile of hers. "That's true. But this is the first Christmas without Mom. Please, Dad?"

Troy couldn't refuse her. "All right," he

muttered again, no more graciously than before.

"Next year there'll be the baby," Megan reminded him. "We'll start a new tradition with your grandchild."

"Will it involve freezing my tail off stomping through acres of trees that all look alike?"

"Oh, Dad," she chided him. "What's with you this year?"

He shrugged. "I'm just not in the mood to celebrate Christmas, I guess."

"This evening will help," she promised gently.

Craig drove, and Troy sat with his son-in-law in the front seat while Megan sat in the back. Christmas songs, one after the other, blasted from the radio and they sang along. Well, Megan and Craig joined in; Troy bobbed his head now and then. He didn't much care about either Frosty or Rudolph at the moment.

When they arrived at the tree farm, it was packed. It seemed as if every family in Cedar Cove was there, which surprised Troy because this was a Friday night. Colored lights were strung around the area, brightening the trees. There was a big kettle of hot chocolate and one of warm apple cider, both of them, in his opinion, grossly overpriced.

"Why is it so busy tonight?" Troy wondered aloud as he ventured away from the car. They were fortunate to have secured a parking space.

"Rain's predicted for tomorrow," Craig told him.

That explained it. Darkness had fallen, but the sky was clear and stars were starting to show. Any families planning to put up their Christmas trees this weekend would have to purchase them tonight.

While Craig took the saw out of his trunk, Troy glanced around. He recognized several families.

He heard Megan behind him. "Dad! Oh, Dad, there's someone here I want you to say hello to."

He looked back at his daughter and abruptly went still. Standing next to Megan was Faith Beckwith.

"Do you remember the wonderful nurse I mentioned?" Megan was asking.

He didn't. All he could do was stare at Faith.

His mood instantly lifted. "Hello, Faith," he said. He couldn't have arranged this any better had he tried.

"You *do* remember her," Megan chirped. "She talked about you when we had lunch this week."

Now that got his attention. "You and Faith

had lunch? Together?" He glanced from one to the other, wondering how this had come about.

Megan nodded. "I had some questions about the baby blanket I'm making and I asked Faith to help me."

Vaguely Troy recalled that his daughter had taken up knitting.

"While we were at lunch, Faith said the two of you knew each other in high school."

"That was a long time ago," Faith murmured, studying the ground, which was littered with evergreen twigs and clumps of needles. When she did happen to meet his gaze, she gave him a look that could charitably be described as unfriendly. Given how they'd left things, he had no idea what that was all about.

Megan appeared oblivious to the tension between them. "I meant to tell you about seeing Faith earlier," she went on to say. "I think it's so cool that the two of you were friends in high school."

"We were hardly friends," she said, slipping her hands in her coat pockets.

"Are you getting your Christmas tree here, too?" Megan asked her.

"I'm with my son and his family," she said.

"I dragged my dad along, too. He could use some holiday cheer."

Faith glanced behind her. "Good to see you again, Megan," she said, nodding curtly in Troy's direction, "but I should get back to my family. Have a wonderful Christmas," she added as she turned away.

Something was definitely wrong. Faith had just given him the cold shoulder and he didn't know why.

"She is so nice," Megan said.

"Yes," Troy agreed, watching Faith hurry away.

"I think it's so cool that the two of you know each other," Megan said again.

Troy didn't respond.

"You should ask her out."

What? Frowning, Troy looked at his daughter. Only a few months ago, she'd been adamantly opposed to his seeing other women. "What do you mean?"

"A date, Dad," she said and laughed at his blank expression. "Faith is a warm, lovely woman. She's helped me in so many ways, and I don't just mean with my knitting. It was Faith who gave me those statistics about MS. She's been a real encouragement with the pregnancy, too." Megan slid her arm through his. "You know, Dad, she's a widow."

He made a noncommittal response.

"If you were going to date again, I think

Faith would be perfect." His daughter hesitated. "Craig told me not to say anything, but . . ."

Troy regarded his daughter. "About Faith?"

"Not that." She raised one shoulder in a shrug. "It's about that other woman I saw you with . . . I think her name's Sally." Megan pressed her lips tightly together. "I was pretty upset when Craig and I ran into the two of you, but Craig told me it was none of my business. You have your own life and if you want to start dating again, it's strictly up to you."

"I . . . I appreciate that."

"The thing is," Megan continued, "I thought Sally was kind of bossy."

"Frankly, so did I," Troy said with a grin.

"Are you going to see her again?"

He laughed. "Not on your life."

Megan laughed, too. "Gee, Dad, I see Faith over there. Why don't you go and discuss old times?"

He turned and saw that Megan was right. Faith was standing with her two grandchildren among the Christmas trees. She looked wonderful. Beautiful.

"Bring her a cup of cocoa," his daughter suggested.

In the interest of making some progress

with Faith, he was prepared to overlook the fact that the tree-farm people were gouging him. "I think I will."

Megan squeezed his arm. "Good luck, Dad."

"Thanks."

Troy purchased two cups of hot chocolate and carried them to where Faith stood, with her son and his family close by.

Scott Beckwith nodded at him. "How're you doing, Sheriff?"

"Fine, fine."

Faith was standing stiffly beside her grandchildren and seemed to make a point of ignoring him.

"I brought you some cocoa," he said and held it out to her.

Faith's hands remained buried deep inside her coat pockets. "No, thank you."

"I'll take it," her youngest grandchild said eagerly.

Troy handed it to the girl, who was about six or seven. "What's your name?" he asked.

"Angela."

"I'm Bradley," the older boy announced, staring pointedly at the second cup.

Troy willingly relinquished it.

Angela smiled up at him. "I have a loose tooth. Wanna see?"

"Angela. Bradley." Scott called his children

as he strode ahead. "Come help me cut down this tree."

The two kids scurried after their father, sloshing hot chocolate as they went.

Troy was grateful for these few minutes alone with Faith. "Megan says you've been a good friend to her."

She nodded and started to join her son.

Troy placed a hand on her arm, stopping her. "Are you angry about something?"

Her head reared back as if he'd shocked her. "*Angry?*" she asked. "What could I possibly have to be angry about?"

That was exactly his question. He gestured weakly and tried again. "You tell me."

She turned to face him then, her eyes flashing with fury. "You broke off our relationship."

"Can we forget about that, Faith? I'd like to go out again."

Her eyes narrowed. "Then I suggest you contact Sally."

Troy was stunned. One blind date — which had been a disaster — and it seemed the entire county had heard. Bad enough that he'd bumped into Megan and Craig that night, but now apparently Faith knew about it, too.

"She sounds like your type," Faith said in a withering voice.

"She isn't," Troy told her. "You are."

Her stance relaxed just a little, and for a moment Troy saw the pain in her eyes. "I used to think you were my type, too, but I was wrong."

"Come on, be fair." Troy was losing his patience. "So I went out with someone else — once. You're taking this too personally."

She considered his observation, then shrugged as if it was of no concern. "Perhaps I am. Let me assure you, you're welcome to date whomever you wish."

"I want to date *you,*" he insisted. He didn't understand why she was making this so difficult.

She shook her head. "I'm flattered but it won't work. I enjoyed our time together, but it's over."

"It's not over for me," he said.

She laughed softly. "I beg to differ. *You're* the one out there dating again. I wish you well, Troy, I really do, but I have a real problem with a man who says one thing and does another."

"What are you talking about?"

"You told me Megan couldn't accept the thought of you dating so soon after you lost your wife."

"Yes, but —"

"I guess that only applied to me. She

didn't appear to have a problem when you went out with Sally. Not that I care, mind you. As far as I'm concerned, this is an integrity issue."

Troy had heard enough. "You are way out of line here, Faith. I came to you and I tried to make amends — which you rejected because you were stuck in the past. What happened back then wasn't my fault, I might remind you."

Faith had the grace to blush.

"If you want to discuss integrity, then let's talk about you befriending my daughter behind my back." He had a few questions of his own. Faith wasn't blameless in all of this.

"Megan sought *me* out — but not because she knew about us."

"You certainly didn't discourage her, though, did you?"

"No, and why should I? She's a very sweet girl. Maybe that's why it took me a while to realize the two of you are related —" Faith paused long enough to shake her head. "Sorry," she muttered. "I shouldn't have said that. But I did tell her I knew you."

"Back in high school."

"True," she said. "I didn't feel it was necessary to go into our recent relationship . . . but perhaps I was wrong."

"Perhaps you were."

"Then I suggest that *perhaps* the best thing for us to do is agree to disagree."

"If that's the way you want it."

Her lower lip trembled slightly. "We gave it a good try. Twice. We both made mistakes. I apologize for my part and you've already apologized for yours."

"Can't we start over?" he asked.

"No," Faith said. "I don't think we should."

That seemed so final. "We tried and it didn't work out. I don't have the heart to make another stab at this. I guess I'm too old and set in my ways. I don't bounce back as quickly as I used to."

Troy had no alternative but to accept her decision. "Then I'd like us to part as friends."

"Oh, I agree." She removed her hand from her pocket and held it out to him.

Troy frowned at it. "I'd be more receptive to a hug."

Faith smiled, moving toward him.

Troy enveloped her in his arms and closed his eyes. He breathed in her familiar scent, holding her just a moment longer than he probably should have. When he dropped his arms, he stepped back.

"Since we live in the same town, I hope we

can be cordial to each other," Faith said, sounding like herself for the first time that evening.

"I'm hoping that, too." He shuffled his feet, still a bit uneasy. "As far as Megan's concerned, I appreciate that you took her under your wing. She obviously needed someone and I'm glad she chose you."

Faith's face grew red; he wondered if it was from the cold or something else.

"I'm sorry for getting so angry with you," she whispered. "I shouldn't have said anything about you and Sally."

Troy shrugged. "Sally was a blind date I got roped into. She's the mother-in-law of one of my deputies. She was visiting from New York. Bart had a social obligation that particular night, and his mother-in-law was going to be alone, so he asked me if I'd mind taking her to dinner."

"Oh."

"Although it's neither here nor there, it was only the one date."

"You were right, though. It wasn't any of my business. I must've sounded like a jealous shrew."

"You didn't," he assured her.

"Grandma, Grandma, come and look at our tree," Angela called out to Faith. Her brother trailed behind her.

"I'd better join my family."

Troy took another step back. "And I should go find Megan and Craig."

"I'm grateful we had this talk."

He nodded.

"Merry Christmas, Troy," Faith said softly.

"Merry Christmas."

Megan and Craig had already chosen and cut down their tree by the time Troy located them.

"So, what do you think, Dad?" she asked.

Troy studied the tree. "Good choice. Do you plan to decorate it this evening?"

"I'm not talking about the *tree*," Megan said. "I was asking about Faith."

"Oh, that," he murmured, unsure how to explain. "She's very nice but I don't think we have that much in common."

His daughter's mouth dropped open. "You've got to be kidding. Faith is perfect for you."

"Let it rest, honey," Craig said. "This is your father's decision, not yours."

It looked as if Megan wanted to argue but then she took her husband's advice.

Troy helped Craig tie the fresh Christmas tree to the roof of the car. As they pulled out of the parking lot, Troy caught sight of Faith. She stood apart from her family, watching him. When their eyes met, she raised her hand in a gesture of farewell.

This time it really was goodbye.

TWENTY-SEVEN

"Where *are* you?" Christie asked her sister, nearly shouting into her cell phone. Her heart pounded at an alarming rate. It was vital that she speak to Teri as soon as possible. She'd just finished her shift at Wal-Mart and had stopped by Teri and Bobby's house — a visit that was also a convenient excuse to see James again. Since the night he'd come to her apartment, she hadn't been able to stop thinking about him. Their time together had been so special — at least to Christie — and she needed to confirm that he felt the same way about her.

". . . shopping." Teri's voice faded in and out.

"I didn't ask what you were doing, I asked where you are. I need to talk to you, pronto."

"Seattle," Teri told her. "Bobby and I are shopping for cribs. We're driving to a mall."

"Oh." Christie's heart sank. "I went over to your house when I got off work . . . I thought you'd be here."

"Sorry . . . disappoint you, but . . ." Once again Teri's voice faded out.

"Are you with James?" Christie asked.

"Who? I didn't hear you."

"Never mind." Obviously she was.

"What's wrong?" Her sister must have detected the note of panic in her voice.

"Someone was here."

"Where?" Teri shouted back.

"At the house. By the gate."

A short pause followed, and Christie didn't know if it was due to the bad connection or her sister's worry.

"Who?"

"A reporter, and he wasn't interested in talking to Bobby."

"Then who . . ." Christie heard some static. "Me?"

"No, he wanted to talk to James."

"Really? What about?"

"Well, for starters, his name isn't James Wilbur."

"Then what is it?"

Her head was whirling with what she'd learned. "His name is James Gardner."

"That's . . . interesting." Since Teri was in the car with Bobby and James, the conversation was risky, but Christie had to chance it. Teri seemed to realize intuitively that she couldn't reveal what Christie was about to tell her. Still, there was a limit to how much she could say over the phone, especially with both men in earshot.

"What else did he tell you?" Teri wanted to know.

"The reporter thought I was one of the help, so I played along. I let him assume I was the housekeeper and said Bobby and you, plus James, were out of town for the next few days."

"Good idea." Teri's voice was louder now; wherever they were, cell phone reception had clearly improved.

"I need to talk to James. It's important, Teri. His cover is about to be blown."

"Cover?"

"I'll explain later. Ask Bobby. He knows everything — he's known all along."

"Okay," Teri said calmly.

Christie felt as though she might break into tears. "Haven't you ever wondered about James?"

Teri's voice fell. "To be honest, yes."

"James and Bobby go way back — back to when they were in their early teens."

Her announcement was followed by a short silence. "Bobby and I are staying in a hotel downtown, so you can —"

"I need to talk to James," Christie broke in.

"It's vital that he know what's going on."

"James is driving home to Cedar Cove. He should be there by six-thirty."

"Okay."

"Can you tell me any more?"

"It's too complicated." With a shaking hand, Christie brushed her hair away from her forehead. "I never guessed . . . Not in a million years would I have guessed."

"Christie, you can't keep me in suspense like this."

"I can't tell you right now, so don't ask me again. Only . . ."

"Only, what?"

"Tonight when you and Bobby are alone, you might ask him a few questions about James."

"You think I haven't already?"

"Just ask, and this time tell him the whole world's about to learn . . . everything."

Christie wanted to kick herself. She'd intended to keep her mouth shut and here she was, practically blurting it all out.

"What do you mean by 'everything'?" Teri demanded, and from her tone of voice, Christie knew her sister wasn't going to let this drop.

Teri was like a bloodhound tracking a scent. She was after details, and she wanted them now. Sighing heavily, Christie muttered part of what she'd found out. "Apparently James was born in a town called Wilbur — I think it's on the East Coast. That's where he got his surname."

"Who told you that?"

"The reporter . . . This is going to be big, Teri. Very big."

"You're positive this person is who you think it is?" she asked carefully.

"Yes." Christie didn't have a single doubt. "I saw the photos. It's James, all right. He's much younger in the pictures, but there's no mistaking him."

Her sister spoke in a whisper. "We're at the hotel. Give me ten minutes and I'll call you back."

"Okay, okay."

Sure enough, exactly nine minutes later, Teri phoned. "You want to talk to James, right?" she said without so much as a greeting. "Alone," she added. "In a private setting where you won't be disturbed."

"Yes . . . of course." Christie *had* to let him know, as soon as possible. "What do you mean, a private setting?" Teri had something in mind.

"Now listen," Teri continued, sounding authoritative. "James is driving back to Cedar Cove and I've asked him to bring some packages into the house."

387

"No, he can't do that!"

"Why not?"

"Because the reporter might still be around, looking for him." Once the article hit the newsstands, it would only be a matter of time before the Seattle stations were hounding James. Then would come CNN and Fox and the other networks, the Internet . . .

"I thought you told that reporter James was out of town."

"I did."

"Then you don't have anything to worry about." The reassurance in her voice calmed Christie. "No one can get into the house, so as soon as James arrives he'll be safe. The gate's electronically wired and we have the best security system money can buy. No one's getting in there without a whole lot of trouble, so don't concern yourself with that."

"You're sure?"

"Positive. Trust me on this. The safest place for you and James is the house."

"Okay."

"I want you there waiting for him, got it?"

It was just like Teri to start issuing orders. Except that in this case, Christie didn't object.

"When James gets there, you'll have

cooked a nice, romantic dinner, complete with soft music and lit candles."

"Why would I do that?" she asked. They were in the middle of an emergency, and her sister was planning a honeymoon retreat.

"I don't know what that reporter's about to expose, but don't hit James with it first thing. Let him relax and have a nice dinner and then tell him . . . gently."

"That's what you do with Bobby, isn't it?"

Her sister laughed. "I try, but it doesn't always work."

"So you have this all figured out, do you?"

"Yes, and I was pretty clever about it, if I do say so myself." Teri did seem excited. Weeks earlier she'd given Christie a key so she could house-sit. She and Bobby had spent a getaway weekend at the ocean, and Christie still had the key. She also had the code to the security alarm.

"There's a salmon fillet in the refrigerator and a really nice bottle of Sauvignon Blanc in the wine cooler. You're welcome to them both."

Christie was overwhelmed. "I doubt I'll be able to eat a single bite."

"You can and you will." Once more her sister sounded like a general barking orders to the troops. "Bobby's promised to tell me everything. Now, get going. You haven't got that long."

"Does James know anything?"

"No . . . I didn't tell him you're going to be at the house."

"You need to warn him!"

"No," Teri countered. "For the moment, the less he knows, the better."

Her sister was probably right.

Nervous though she was, Christie showered, washed her hair and borrowed Teri's makeup, which was of a much higher quality than the bargain brands she bought for herself. Then she followed her instructions to the letter. The salmon was just about finished baking and the wine was on ice when the security alarm beeped, indicating that someone had entered the house.

Christie panicked.

Teri hadn't given her one word of advice on what to say to James. Her impulse was to rush forward and blurt out what she'd learned — to protect him. But as Teri said, she needed to lead up to this carefully.

James must have sensed someone else was in the house, but when he stepped into the kitchen, he stopped cold. "Bobby didn't say you were here," he murmured. He didn't seem pleased to see her.

Christie remained standing in the middle of the kitchen. She fiddled nervously with the top button of her blouse, then hurriedly removed the apron.

"Hello."

James looked more than a little uncomfortable.

"Teri told me to prepare the salmon," she explained. "Would you like to have dinner with me?"

He didn't answer.

"I'm actually a fairly good cook."

Still silent, he glanced at the bottle of wine, nestled in a pewter wine cooler.

When he didn't answer right away, she decided to take action. Focusing her attention on the salad she was making, she said, "You could open that for us."

Instead James walked out of the room and Christie was convinced he wasn't coming back. To her relief, he returned a moment later — without his heavy winter coat.

"I know it must be a shock finding me here at the house but let me assure you there's a perfectly logical reason." The oven timer buzzed; using two pot holders, she opened the door and took out the salmon. The kitchen was instantly filled with the scent of fresh dill and lemon.

The wild rice mixture on the stove started to boil over, and they both moved toward it, bumping shoulders. James looked at her; she looked at him. Grinning, he calmly reached over and removed the pan from the burner.

"I'm glad you're here," he said.

His words almost made her cry. "I'm glad I'm here, too," she said, and to her acute embarrassment she blushed. It was harder than ever not to tell him everything.

He raised his hand to her face and slowly ran his finger from her temple down the side of her jaw to her chin. It was the most sensual thing any man had ever done to her. The only part of his body that touched her was his fingertip, yet Christie was ready to melt in his arms. She closed her eyes and struggled against her natural inclination to sway toward him. This wasn't the time. She swallowed and eased away.

When her eyes opened again, she found him studying her. She moistened her lips. "Are you planning to . . . kiss me?"

James nodded.

"Would you mind . . . could you do it later?"

He grinned again. "I think I do mind." With excruciating slowness, he lowered his mouth to hers. The kisses started out soft and easy, then gained intensity.

James was the one who took control. After several minutes, he broke the contact and simply held her. His breath was ragged.

Christie leaned against him. She couldn't believe she'd had the most sensual encounter of her life standing in her sister's kitchen — with all her clothes on.

"James, I . . . I have something very important to tell you," she said once she found her voice. Keeping this news inside suddenly became impossible.

His hands were in her hair and it seemed as if he hadn't heard her.

"Please," she murmured. "Let's sit down." Taking James by the hand, she led him to the family room and they sat on the sofa.

Christie angled her body so that their knees touched. She reached for his hands and held them in her own. For a long moment she contemplated how to begin. Finally she told him in the simplest, most direct manner she could. "I came by here earlier and there was a man at the gate looking for you."

"Me?" he asked with a frown.

"He seemed to think I was the housekeeper and I didn't set him straight. It turned out to be a good thing."

"Why?" His frown deepened.

"He asked me questions about you."

"What kind of questions?"

"About your past . . . How long you'd worked for Bobby, whether you ever played chess, whether you mentioned where you were from. Stuff like that."

James avoided eye contact.

"I know, James. I know everything now, and it doesn't matter. None of it."

His eyes widened and he tried to jerk his hands free of hers but she wouldn't let him. Scrambling up on the sofa, she knelt beside him. "I can't figure out how you and Bobby kept it a secret all these years."

Again James tried to get away, and this time she stopped him by sitting on his lap. "James," she whispered, pressing her hands against the sides of his face. She couldn't resist, so she kissed him.

Her kisses seemed to calm him. She could see the pulse in his neck pounding frantically. "Twenty years ago, *you* were the chess prodigy, not Bobby."

He looked away, refusing to meet her gaze. "I had a nervous breakdown."

"I know."

"I haven't played chess since I was thirteen."

She nodded. By dint of questioning and appearing to know more than she did, she'd persuaded the reporter to fill in what happened next. James and Bobby were rivals. James's parents drove him, expecting perfection, demanding that he beat Bobby each and every time. Then he'd lost the biggest chess match of his career and ended up in a mental hospital.

After James was released, he never played again. At least not publicly, according to the reporter, but Christie suspected that was the case in his private life, too. As far as the chess world was concerned, James Gardner had dropped off the face of the earth. He disappeared, and despite numerous and varied efforts to locate him over the next few years, he was never seen or heard from again.

Apparently he'd been forgotten. From the questions the reporter asked, she knew James's appearance had changed. He'd shown her a photograph of James at thirteen. The soft features of early adolescence had hardened, become defined. His hair had darkened. He'd shot up ten inches or more. He didn't look the same and yet she'd recognized him. She hadn't tried to hide that recognition from the reporter; there was no point. As the man, a stringer for one of the newspaper syndicates, had said, the information was out there, hidden in articles, public records, even photographs, if anyone cared to search for it.

"Bobby Polgar was my only friend back then," James murmured.

"Yes."

"He still is."

"You're wrong."

"What do you mean?"

Christie straightened. "*I'm* your friend, too."

"How did this reporter find me?"

"I don't think it was that difficult. He started with the kidnapping. He decided there was more to that story, so he dug up information about you *and* Bobby. He did the research, asked the questions and one thing led to another."

"When will it be published? His article."

"Soon."

His arms circled her waist and he held her as if he intended never to let her go.

His disappearance from the chess world, the reporter had said, seemed particularly puzzling because he hadn't *entirely* disappeared. He remained on the fringes, since he took Bobby to all his matches. That had begun when both men were in their early twenties. It must have felt risky at first, even staying in the background, but people hadn't really noticed him.

"Bobby was the only one who cared," James told her. "He came to see me in the hospital."

Christie had always been aware of Bobby's kindness and loyalty. When she met him, she'd been envious of Teri, unable to understand why her sister should have all the luck.

She'd even thought she could steal him away from Teri. Bobby, however, had quickly disabused her of that notion. He was a one-woman man, and he'd made sure Christie knew that.

"You never played chess again?" she asked, her head still on his shoulder. "At home? By yourself or with Bobby?"

"Never. I have the mind for it, but not the heart." His hand was warm on her back. "Bobby has both. He has the heart of a champion, far more than I ever did."

Christie sighed. Like her sister, she barely understood the rudiments of the game and didn't have the patience or the interest to learn.

"What do you do with your time?" she asked. He always seemed to be busy and she wondered if he'd tell her. She sensed that he didn't want anyone intruding on his life.

"This and that," he told her. "I read, especially history. But mostly I work on creating computer games. That's my creative outlet. I . . . I don't like being in front of the public."

Christie realized that James didn't need or want much interaction with others. He seemed happy with his own company, his own thoughts and routines.

"It keeps me busy when I'm not driving for Bobby," he added.

Christie could have stayed exactly as she was at that moment and found contentment. Was this love? She couldn't say; Christie wasn't sure she knew what it was to be in love. Lust, passion, desire — those feelings were familiar to her. But they never lasted. Every single time, what looked like a promising relationship had failed. The flames of attraction always died out, leaving nothing but bitterness and anger behind.

In the past she'd been quick to jump into bed, and the fact that she hadn't slept with James, that they'd only kissed on three occasions, would shock her previous lovers. They'd wonder if there was something wrong with her — or with James. The reality was that for the first time there was something *right.*

"You know my secrets, too," she said. "And mine are a lot more disreputable than yours." She wished he'd told her about his past earlier. She thought he might have continued to keep it to himself if the reporter hadn't shown up today. That hurt, but she tried not to dwell on it.

James kissed the top of her head.

"Do you and Bobby ever talk about when you were young?"

"No. It's in the past." His chest heaved. "I choose to live as I do. Bobby needs me and he was a friend when I needed one."

"What about your family?"

He shrugged. "I was their ticket to wealth and fame. They never forgave me. And they never spoke to me again."

"Oh, James. I'm so sorry."

"My parents are both dead. Bobby is all the family I have. Bobby and now Teri."

Christie longed to tell him that *she* loved him and wanted to be his family, too.

But she knew instinctively that it was too soon. James wasn't ready for that kind of intimacy. The habits of reserve and self-protection were too ingrained. Slowly, though, very slowly, he'd come to love her as much as she loved him.

She was counting on it.

TWENTY-EIGHT

As soon as the end-of-day bell rang, Tanni Bliss hurried out to the parking lot where Shaw was waiting for her. She climbed into the passenger seat of his old blue station wagon and leaned toward him. Shaw didn't hesitate to kiss her.

"How was school?" he asked as he checked his rearview mirror before pulling into the heavy flow of traffic.

"The usual." With only a week before the holiday break, no one was concentrating on schoolwork. Even the teachers seemed distracted and eager to escape.

"How was work?" she asked, already knowing how much Shaw disliked his job at the coffee shop. He was grateful to his aunt and uncle, grateful to be employed but it didn't help him advance toward what he really wanted, and that was a career in art.

Living at home allowed him to put away funds for art school. He'd applied for scholarships but had been turned down because of his lack of a high school diploma. His father, an attorney, had pressured him to follow in his footsteps. Shaw had rebelled, and the friction at home had become intolerable. It was because of his father and the constant battle of wills between them that Shaw had dropped out of high school just weeks before graduation. When the art school was unable to accept him, the registrar encouraged him to obtain his GED and apply again as a mature student. He was taking the test in January.

"All right, I guess."

He rarely said anything more about his job or what he did there.

"Did you do any work?" The question didn't refer to Mocha Mama's, but his current art project.

"Some."

"Are you going to show me?" Shaw generally didn't until he was satisfied his drawing or painting was the best he could make it.

He momentarily looked away from the traffic and grinned at her. "Maybe."

"Shaw!" she said. *"Please?"*

His grin broadened. "I might."

For a week or two now, he'd been working on something he wouldn't even tell her about. He usually did his sketches at the coffee shop, because doing them at the house seemed to infuriate his father.

"Do you want me to take you home?" Shaw asked.

Tanni had a surprise of her own. "Not yet."

"Where to, then?"

Tanni studied him, anticipating his reaction. "The Harbor Street Art Gallery."

His eyes left the road as he glanced in her direction. "Why?"

Holding back this particular surprise had been difficult; she'd nearly told him a hundred times. "I have a meeting with the new owner, Mr. Jefferson."

"You didn't mention that before, did you?" In other words, Shaw would have remembered.

"No."

"What's the meeting about?"

"You."

"Me?" he exploded in disbelief.

"Yes, you. Or rather, your portrait work. He's got the ones of Kurt Cobain, Jimi Hendrix and James Dean." Shaw had chosen people, public figures, who'd lived — and died — on the edge.

"Tanni . . ."

"I showed my mom a few of your other portraits, too, and she took them to Mr. Jefferson."

"Your mom did that for me?"

Tanni nodded. "Mr. Jefferson met with Mom and asked for ideas about the gallery." Her mother had come back, excited about the change in ownership and the new possibilities. "He asked her how to get the community involved, and one thing she recommended was showing the work of young artists."

"Cool."

Tanni smiled over at him, knowing he must be curious as to what Mr. Jefferson had said about his portraits. At the same time, he was probably afraid to ask.

"So . . . what did he think?" Shaw spoke casually as he turned onto Harbor Street.

"He wants to meet you," she breathed.

Shaw paled. "Tanni, I can't!"

"What do you mean, you can't?" She was dismayed by his response, which was the last thing she'd expected. "You're good, Shaw! You have real talent, and more than that, you have a vision."

"You go talk to him for me, all right?"

Shaw was serious. She was astonished by his lack of confidence, but she would do this for him without a qualm. After all, he'd helped her in ways she couldn't begin to calculate. For the first time since her father's death, she didn't feel like she wanted to die, too. Some days were better than others. She still grieved, still longed for him, but she could imagine a future now. A future without him. And that was largely thanks to Shaw. So if he needed her to do this, then she would. No questions asked.

"Okay," she said.

"You should've told me . . . you shouldn't have done this without letting me know." He frowned, as if her intervention displeased him, as if he thought she'd been presumptuous.

His lack of appreciation hurt her. "Why not? My mom and I wanted to *help* you."

"Tanni." Shaw whispered her name. He seemed to understand how badly he'd upset her. "I'm not ready . . . . I don't have the training or the talent . . . . Not like you."

"Yes, you do," she insisted. "You're every bit as talented as I am." It was true that he didn't have the formal training or encouragement she'd been blessed to receive, but he had the desire and his work revealed passion and honesty.

Shaw found a parking spot and pulled in. He turned off the engine but kept his hands on the steering wheel, holding so tightly that his knuckles went white.

"If you want, I'll go in with you," Tanni suggested, thinking all he really needed was her presence and support.

Shaw shook his head. "You go."

"But . . ."

"I'll wait here."

Reluctantly, she got out of the car.

Until they'd started seeing each other, Shaw had shown his work to very few. His friends knew he liked to draw but that was about it. The only people who really understood were Anson Butler and now Tanni.

The gallery was situated on the steepest part of the street, and she was almost out of breath when she reached the side entrance. Mr. Jefferson had asked Shaw to meet him there because of the renovations still in progress.

Looking back at Shaw, she gave him a small wave and then stepped into the gallery.

"Mr. Jefferson?" she called out, standing just inside the door. She heard the sound of hammering and the whining of an electric sander and called again, more loudly.

Will Jefferson came out, wearing a tool belt. He was tall and about the same age as her father had been when he died. Maybe older. He stared at her blankly. "I'm Tanni Bliss. My mom's Shirley Bliss," she told him. "Mom gave you a few pieces by my friend Shaw. And . . . and he asked me to stop by for him." She felt a little nervous, despite her unwavering faith in Shaw's talent.

Mr. Jefferson nodded, as if he'd suddenly made the connection. "Shirley's daughter. Right."

"Hi."

They shook hands, once he'd brushed the sawdust off his.

What if Will Jefferson didn't understand and appreciate her friend's talent the way she did? Tanni didn't know how she'd tell Shaw. A rejection like this could set him back, which was something she hadn't considered until now.

"So, you're here to talk about the projects your mother dropped off the other day."

She nodded.

Mr. Jefferson invited her over to a table, where sketches were carefully arranged in folders; paintings, both framed and unframed, leaned against the wall, covered with plastic dropcloths. "Your mother suggested it would be a good idea to involve young people in the gallery."

Tanni nodded again. She knew all about that.

"I had Maryellen Bowman and an artist friend of mine take a look at these pieces," Mr. Jefferson said. "I wanted some expert opinions."

Tanni held her breath, then released it as

she asked the question that pounded in her head. "What . . . what did they say?" Her heart felt as if it had stopped beating.

"Maryellen has an eye for what will sell in this area. She liked Shaw's work and recommended that I offer him a contract."

"And your friend — the artist?" she asked, her voice shaking just a bit.

"He had high praise for Shaw's work, too."

"High praise," Tanni repeated. What beautiful words! Relief, excitement, pure happiness spread through her.

"He felt that Shaw's talent is still pretty raw, but he definitely sees potential in these drawings. I'd like to have them on display."

"You would?"

"These portraits reveal maturity and sensitivity. And they have a vivid sense of energy."

"Yes, I agree," she said solemnly, trying to sound professional. She'd worked hard with Shaw to focus on the kind of art that suited his vision and his skills — and might also have some commercial appeal. Portraiture seemed the best choice.

"Is Shaw in art school?"

She wasn't sure how to respond. Tanni had the advantage of having attended art classes and camps through the years. In turn, she'd taught Shaw everything she'd learned, or as much as she could in the time they'd been together. If she said he was in art school, she was afraid Mr. Jefferson would discover she'd lied.

"Not yet."

Mr. Jefferson nodded. "I have an agreement here that I'll need Shaw to sign. Two copies, one for me, one for him. Once he agrees to my terms, which I think are fair to both of us, I'll be happy to display his work."

"What about the prices?" She didn't want Shaw to give his drawings away, but she didn't want them to be priced so high they wouldn't sell, either.

Mr. Jefferson named a price that felt exactly right. Apparently he'd taken the advice of Maryellen Bowman, who was obviously a good judge, not only of art but of the market.

"That sounds reasonable," she said, accepting the paperwork. "I'll be back later." She fairly danced out of the gallery.

Tanni ran to the car, breathless with joy and excitement. Shaw was pacing outside, his breath steaming in the cold air. He stopped abruptly when he saw her.

"What did he say?" he blurted out the instant she was within earshot.

"You have to sign these papers," she said and thrust them into his hand.

"Why?" He stared at her as he took the two

sets of pages from her.

Tanni broke into a wheezing laugh. "This is the agreement to sell your work."

"He likes my stuff?"

"Yes." She grinned widely. "A *lot*."

"You're not making this up, are you?" Shaw studied her skeptically.

"Did I make up those papers?"

Shaw clutched them so tightly, the edges had started to crumple.

"Read the agreement first," she said. "If you want, I can have my mother look it over. She's had contracts with this gallery before. Other galleries, too."

Shaw frowned uncertainly. "I'll do whatever you think is best."

She exhaled. "Then we'll ask my mother to read it."

"Okay."

Tanni slipped her arms around his waist and hugged him tight. "Are you excited?"

Shaw hugged her back, the papers still in his hand. "More than I thought possible. I can't believe you'd do this for me."

"I love you." She hadn't meant to tell him that, but it was too late. She'd said it.

Shaw's breathing became labored. And yet he didn't release his grasp on her.

"I shouldn't have said that." She was embarrassed now and wished she could take back the words.

"I love you, too."

"Oh, Shaw." She wanted to weep with joy. Her mother would say she was too young to be in love and maybe she was. All she knew was how she felt about Shaw. He was constantly in her thoughts. Their times together brought her happiness and peace — in sharp contrast to the intense grief of losing her father.

Her improved outlook was noticeable to those around her, particularly her friends at school, but her mother, too. Since Tanni had met Shaw, everything in her life had become a little better.

He continued to hold her. "I never understood why Anson would risk his freedom by calling Allison," he said close to her ear.

Tanni remembered how Anson had been unjustly accused of starting the fire that had destroyed The Lighthouse restaurant. Then he'd disappeared, and no one other than Shaw knew he'd enlisted in the army. The evidence was all circumstantial. No formal charges were filed against him, but Anson was considered a "person of interest," so if the police had learned of his whereabouts, he would've been taken in for questioning. And if there wasn't a more plausible suspect by then, he could actually have faced arrest.

Even with that risk hanging over his head, Anson had phoned Allison. Not once or twice but repeatedly.

"I told Anson he was an idiot," Shaw explained. "He could've ended up in jail. You know what he said?"

"What?"

"He said it didn't matter, he needed to hear the sound of Allison's voice. I couldn't imagine loving someone so much I'd take that kind of chance." He kissed her hair. "I understand it now, though."

"Oh, Shaw . . ."

Tanni noticed a couple of women coming down the street toward them and nudged Shaw. Reluctantly they broke away from each other.

"Can I ask you something?" he said.

"Of course."

"You're so talented, but you don't seem to care if anyone sees your work."

"I care," she said. "But a lot of what I draw right now is just for me." Her sketches were what had kept her sane — somewhat sane, anyway — after the accident. They were too private to share with anyone other than Shaw. Certainly not her mother, who'd probably get hysterical if she saw some of them.

Despite his lack of training and encouragement and everything she'd taken for granted,

Shaw was an artist. He would succeed.

Tanni knew it as clearly and precisely as if she could look into the future. A few drawings in a small-town gallery was just the beginning.

TWENTY-NINE

Dave Flemming folded his hands in his lap. He sat in Roy McAfee's office, across from the one man he trusted to help him.

"What can I do for you?" Roy asked. "I have to admit I was surprised to see you'd made an appointment with me."

Dave had never, ever thought he'd be in this position. He'd promised Emily, though, and he kept his promises. "I have a problem," Dave said. He didn't mince words; he felt the best way to clear himself of suspicion was to be as honest as possible.

He was busy, and he didn't have time to squander on speculation, worry and doubt. He wanted this resolved, preferably by Christmas Eve. If Roy could manage that, then Dave would thank him heartily.

"And you think I can help with this problem?" Roy asked.

"I don't know. I hope so." Dave still needed to visit a couple of ill parishioners, check with Cliff Harding about the Nativity scene animals and prepare an agenda for one of his committee meetings. The charity food baskets were being assembled that afternoon and he had to pick up some canned goods and get them to the church before the volunteers arrived at five. Then he'd head over to the bank for his shift.

"I take it this has to do with Martha Evans's missing jewelry?"

That question told Dave the rumor mill had been churning at full speed and his name had been bandied about town in connection with the theft. "It does."

Roy leaned back in his chair, crossing his arms, and his body language caused Dave a moment's chagrin. He wondered if his friend was attempting to distance himself from him and his problems.

"You don't want to talk to an attorney?" Roy asked.

Dave had considered this option and rejected it. "Do you think I should?"

Roy shrugged. "That depends. Are you guilty of anything?"

Of being foolish, perhaps. But the question stung his pride. "No." He didn't elaborate, didn't qualify his answer. He couldn't make it any plainer than that. He had absolutely *nothing* to do with Martha Evans's missing jewelry.

"What can I do for you, then?"

Enlisting Roy's assistance had seemed like a logical decision. Now he wasn't so sure. "I'd like you to hear my side of all this."

"Your side," Roy repeated, watching Dave, eyes narrowing slightly. "Is there something you want to tell me that you wouldn't want an attorney to know?" A frown drew his brows together, and he leaned even farther away. "Listen, Dave. Perhaps —"

"First," Dave said, interrupting his friend, or the man he'd assumed was his friend, "I need advice."

If Roy went any farther back in that chair, he was liable to topple right off.

"What kind of advice?"

Dave realized that the detective, along with Troy Davis and possibly Allan Harris, viewed him as a prime suspect. Painful and discouraging as it was to admit, if Dave had been given the same set of circumstances, he'd probably make the same assumption.

"Before I say anything else, I'd like you to return this gold watch to Martha Evans's heirs." He removed the watch from his wrist and handed it to the other man. He'd had the clasp repaired, so there was no chance of losing it again.

Roy accepted the watch. "You have it because . . ." He waited for Dave to explain.

"Martha wanted me to have it. Her husband retired as an executive, and Martha insisted I take the watch."

Roy didn't reveal whether or not he believed him. "Do you have any proof of that?"

Admitting he didn't mortified Dave. "Apparently not . . . I thought I did but I don't."

Roy frowned again. "Perhaps you better start at the beginning."

Dave wasn't sure where that was. "Martha attended the church for as long as I've been pastor."

Roy nodded for him to continue.

"She was an encouragement to me, and a strong supporter, generous in nature. I . . . I thought of her as a second mother."

"You told her this?" Roy prodded.

"No." He could almost read the other man's reaction. "But she was special to me and to anyone who knew her. When she became ill, I visited her as often as I could."

"How often was that?" Roy reached for a pen and pad, taking notes.

Dave couldn't tell if that was a good sign. "At least twice a week. She had a visiting nurse and I tried to stop by on days the nurse wasn't there."

Roy arched his brows and made another notation. "Any particular reason for that?"

"Well, yes . . . The way I figured it, someone should check up on Martha the days she was alone. Her daughters live in Seattle and they both work. I didn't have any nefarious motive, if that's what you're thinking."

Roy glanced up from his notepad. "I'm only asking you the questions Sheriff Davis will ask."

Will ask. Roy seemed to believe it was inevitable that he'd be questioned by the sheriff. Perhaps he was advising Dave to get his story straight, which made no sense because he'd never changed it.

"Go on," Roy urged, watching him closely.

"A few days before she died, Martha asked me to get the watch."

Roy glanced up again. "So you knew where she kept her valuables?"

Once again Dave felt as if he'd already been tried and convicted. "Yes, but I'd never —" He bit off the rest of what he'd intended to say. Verbal protestations weren't going to help.

"Where *did* she keep the watch?"

"The vegetable bin in her refrigerator."

Roy lifted one eyebrow. "With the broccoli?"

"Yes. And she kept some of her jewelry in an ice-cube tray in the freezer. She thought that was the last place a thief would look."

Roy shook his head. "That's as obvious as hiding your door key under a flowerpot," he muttered.

Dave merely nodded. "The watch would've been damaged in the freezer so she kept it in a temperature-controlled bin," he said.

"And she wanted you to have it?"

"She *insisted* I take it," Dave said, struggling not to sound defensive. He wanted to kick himself ten times over for accepting that watch. From the moment he'd slipped it on his wrist, it had felt like a mistake.

It seemed that every protestation of innocence fell on deaf ears. Even his wife doubted him. Dave went on to explain that Martha had written a letter saying he was to have the watch.

"You actually saw the letter?" Roy asked.

"Yes. Martha showed it to me. Her attorney was coming by later that afternoon and she said she'd give it to him."

"Did he?"

Dave hadn't followed up on that. "I . . . I don't know. I assume he didn't, because when Emily went to the attorney's office to check the file, the letter wasn't there."

That instigated another series of questions, which Dave did his best to answer. He told Roy that Emily had visited Allan Harris's office and been able to look at the file, thanks to Geoff Duncan, Allan's legal assistant. Dave stressed that Geoff's action had to remain confidential and that he'd done it as a favor.

"Emily was upset," Dave said. But not nearly as upset as *he* was when he'd learned that Martha's letter had never been received.

Roy tapped his pencil against the pad. "I can well imagine."

"I thought," Dave said, gazing down at the gold watch on Roy's desk, "that I was free to wear it."

Roy made another notation on his pad; Dave wished he could read upside down.

Roy looked up. "You want me to return the watch to Martha's family?"

"Yes." Dave met his eyes. "With my sincere apologies for the misunderstanding. I feel sick about this."

Roy didn't say anything for what seemed like hours but was probably only a few seconds. "I'm afraid this looks . . . incriminating."

Dave was all too aware of that.

"You were probably the last person to see Martha Evans alive," Roy reminded him.

"Yes."

"You're one of a handful of people who knew where she hid her valuables."

He swallowed uncomfortably. "That seems to be the case."

"You were seen wearing a valuable gold watch that belonged to Martha's husband."

Dave nodded slowly.

"Is there anything else?Anything you haven't told me?"

He might as well be speaking to the sheriff. Roy's questions and his own answers made him look — and feel — guilty. Only he wasn't.

"Dave?"

Unable to remain seated, Dave stood up and walked to the far side of the office. "Yes." His heart was hammering so wildly, it hurt to breathe. Turning around again, he reached into his pocket and removed the plastic bag that held the diamond earrings. He put it on the desk next to the watch.

Roy gestured at the earrings. "These were Martha's, too?"

"I believe so . . . Emily s-saw a picture of them in . . . in Martha's file." He couldn't keep the stammer out of his voice.

"You'd better explain."

Dave went on to tell him about Emily's discovery of the earrings. As hard as he tried to work out how they'd gotten into his pockets, he couldn't. Roy was very quiet when Dave finished describing what he knew.

"Do you want me to return these to the family, as well?" he asked.

Dave shrugged helplessly. "I . . . don't know what to do. The thing is, I don't want them in my possession. Anyone who saw them might assume . . . They'd believe I was guilty, and nothing I said would make a bit of difference."

Dave collapsed into the chair and covered his face with both hands. "That's not all."

"You mean there's *more?*" Roy asked, lowering his voice.

Dave lowered his hands. "It happened a long time ago."

Roy waited, and when Dave didn't immediately speak, he said, "Okay. Tell me what it is."

Dave felt his chest tighten with dread.

"Come on," Roy said, not unkindly. "Might as well spill it."

Dave would rather leave the past buried. But he no longer had a choice. He got to his feet and moved over to the window, turning his back on the detective. He closed his eyes.

"Dave," Roy said, "it'll come out sooner or later. You can tell me or not. Up to you. But I suspect that whatever it is, you can bet Sheriff Davis will find out."

Dave agreed. It would be pointless to even try to keep this a secret. "A month after my eighteenth birthday I was arrested."

"So you have a police record?"

This nightmare never seemed to end; it only got worse. "I'm . . . not sure. It was my first offense and I was given a light sentence — three months of community service." He turned around. "The judge said if I kept out of trouble, my record would be wiped clean."

"And was it?"

"I think so, but I can't say for sure." He obviously had a habit of making assumptions. He did his part and it seemed reasonable to take for granted that others had done theirs. All too often, it seemed, that turned out not to be true.

"You never checked?"

"No." He'd been too humiliated, too embarrassed. As much as possible, he'd wanted to put that part of his life behind him. "But I assume so because I work part-time at the bank, and they must've done a security check when they hired me."

Roy wrote down something else. Apparently this latest revelation wasn't welcome news.

"Other than my parents, no one knows about this," Dave said in a low voice.

"Not Emily?"

Dave shook his head. "I tried not to think

about it." Most people had at least one thing in their lives that they wished they could do over. Some mistake or error in judgment. Some act of selfishness or stupidity.

"You didn't mention what the crime was," Roy reminded him.

"You're right, I didn't."

"Any particular reason?"

Dave swallowed. "Theft."

Leaning back in his chair, Roy stared up at him. "What did you take?"

"It wasn't me." A protest rose automatically to his lips.

Dredging up these memories was painful, and he was a different person than he'd been all those years ago.

Roy didn't press him to continue. Dave started to pace, and after a few minutes, felt ready to explain. "I grew up a preacher's kid."

"So your father was a pastor, too?"

Dave ignored the question because the answer was obvious. "As is often the case, there's a lot of pressure on a minister's family. We kids were expected to set an example, to behave perfectly so not to embarrass our parents."

"That's a pretty high standard to live up to."

"It was for me. I tried to be the son my father wanted. Still, no matter what I did, my parents found fault."

"It's not all that different for a cop's kids," Roy told him.

Dave had never considered that the situation in other families might be the same, which was naive of him.

"When I reached my teens, I gave up trying to please my father," he said.

"In other words, you rebelled."

That was an understatement, to say the least. Dave had rejected all his father's values and principles. He'd skipped classes, hung around with a rough crowd, started drinking underage. Because he'd graduated from high school at seventeen he began his first year of college before his eighteenth birthday. That was when he connected with Tom Cummings and his friends.

Dave had never met anyone like Tom. He was a natural leader, and being part of his group had made Dave feel important, included. While it was true that Tom was a practical joker, a guy who always tested the limits, it was all in good fun. Or so Dave had thought. Until, one day, it ceased being fun.

Tom needed money. Dave couldn't remember why it was so critical that Tom have four hundred dollars. Of course none of them had that kind of money to spare. Although if he'd had the funds — or access to them — Dave would've blindly handed over whatever Tom demanded.

Someone came up with the idea. In the beginning Dave had been sure it was a joke. All too soon he discovered how real it was, and by then . . .

"What were the charges against you?"

"Theft and aggravated assault." The words sounded foreign to him, as if they were from a different language. One he didn't speak, didn't understand.

His admission hung in the air between them, like the dust that follows an explosion.

"What was the age of the victim?" Roy finally asked.

The tightness in his throat made it almost impossible to answer. "Seventy-three."

Roy set his pen aside and exhaled slowly.

"You don't need to tell me how bad this looks," Dave muttered.

If news of his youthful arrest went public, no one would ever believe that he hadn't stolen from Martha Evans. No one would ever believe him again, period. He'd lose all credibility.

He might as well give up now. The fact that the incident had happened almost twenty years ago didn't matter. Nor did all the years he'd served God and this community. People would remember only one thing about him

— what he'd done at eighteen.

Roy was suspiciously quiet.

"I suppose you're going to advise me to turn myself in," Dave said stiffly, his back straight and his voice hard.

"Did you steal Martha Evans's jewelry?"

"I already told you I didn't have anything to do with that!" he cried. "You don't believe me, do you?"

"On the contrary, I do."

"But everyone will think —"

"You know the truth," Roy said without emotion, "and since it is the truth, I don't feel you have anything to worry about."

Dave's relief was so great that for a moment he thought he might break down.

"You believe I'm telling the truth even though all the evidence seems to point directly at me?"

Roy shrugged. "Sheriff Davis would be the first to tell you that while circumstantial evidence *can* solve a crime, it can be misleading, too. The person responsible for the crime isn't always the most obvious. Everything you've told me amounts to circumstantial evidence. You claim you didn't have anything to do with those missing jewels. I've known you for a number of years and I've never seen you do anything underhanded or dishonest. So . . . I believe you."

It felt good to have at least one person on his side. "Why should you trust me? I mean, maybe I haven't really changed. Maybe I'm still a thief." He couldn't resist pushing Roy. He needed all the reassurance he could get.

"Why should I trust you?" Again Roy shrugged. "Because I do. First, you wouldn't wander around town flaunting that watch if you'd stolen it. For another thing, I feel I'm a good judge of character."

"Thank you."

"Last, and probably most important," Roy said, leaning forward and scribbling a note on his pad, "Sheriff Davis has a fairly good idea who might be responsible."

"He does?"

Roy met his gaze and nodded.

Dave continued to stare at him. "You aren't going to tell me who you think it might be?"

Roy grinned. Then he said, "That's not up to me. You've asked for my advice and I'll give it to you. Go see Sheriff Davis and tell him everything you've just told me."

THIRTY

Troy Davis decided this was destined to be the worst Christmas of his life. He could see it happening already. Everywhere he turned people were in good spirits. Even the crime rate was down. Folks around town had taken a kinder, gentler approach to life. Instead of lifting his own mood, however, that only irritated him. In a word, he was depressed.

The reason, and he was obliged to admit the fault was of his own making, could be attributed to a number of unpleasant factors. First and foremost, the woman he loved wanted nothing to do with him.

They'd parted on relatively friendly terms. But he wondered if it would've been better if they'd simply blown up at each other, if they'd stopped hiding the pain and the anger. But oh, no, that wasn't Faith's way. She'd wanted to end their relationship on a civilized note. For all the well-wishing between them, he told himself peevishly, you'd think they'd gotten engaged.

It didn't help his mood that Dave Flemming seemed to have involved the entire town in this ridiculous Nativity reenactment. The whole cast of characters, from Mary and Joseph right down to the drummer boy, was made up of volunteers. They were displaying the tableau nightly for two weeks, until December twenty-third. People who came to see it were asked to bring a nonperishable item to feed the hungry or throw a dollar or two into a donation box. Word had spread to the surrounding communities and there were whole caravans of cars and trucks making their way to Cedar Cove. So that meant traffic snarls and chaos on the road, which required him to add a rotation of deputies to deal with it.

Troy had no idea how Dave had managed to borrow a camel for the program. From some petting zoo, maybe? But camels weren't the friendliest or most tolerant of beasts, or so he'd heard. In addition, Dave had located a few head of sheep, a donkey and some cattle; all of them were required to stand in adoration for at least four hours every night. Nothing like this had ever taken place in Cedar Cove before and the event was an unqualified success. It was even more popular than the seagull calling contest, which was really saying something.

Successful as it was, though, the Nativity scene put a lot of pressure on Pastor Flemming. And things would only get worse because Troy was obliged to call him in for questioning. Martha Evans's relatives were on him like white on rice. Those two women wanted their mother's jewelry, and they weren't going to let up until Troy made an arrest. Circumstantially, everything pointed to Dave Flemming. But after all these years in police work, Troy knew he could rely on his instincts and he didn't believe for a minute that Dave was involved. Still, there were a few unanswered questions he needed to ask — not that Dave was the only "person of interest" here. Unfortunately the likely culprit had been cagey and Troy didn't have a legitimate reason to order a visit to the station — not yet, anyway.

The phone rang and he grabbed it, grateful for the interruption. "Sheriff Davis."

"Hi, Daddy." His daughter's sweet voice instantly made him feel better. "Merry Christmas."

"Same to you, sweetheart."

"I saw Faith this morning."

Troy gritted his teeth. Megan didn't realize she was rubbing salt in an open wound. "That's nice," was the best he could manage.

"She said to tell you hello."

Troy straightened. This might be a sign. Perhaps Faith was signaling that she'd be receptive to hearing from him. His mood lightened a little more. "Did she now?" Perhaps Faith had experienced a change of heart and was using his daughter as a messenger.

"I told you she's helping me with my knitting, didn't I?"

"I think you said something about it." He was afraid to reveal how desperate he was for every detail his daughter could give him.

"We're going to meet for lunch every week."

"That's nice." Again, he kept his voice even so as not to indicate any undue interest.

"It is. We talk about my pregnancy and she's been really helpful. She's a lot like Mom, you know. She listens and reassures me. I like her so much."

Troy let the comment slide, eager to hear anything Faith might have said, but not so eager that he'd ask his daughter outright.

"I asked her why the two of you didn't get together. You used to like each other, didn't you?"

"Yes, but that was eons ago."

Megan sighed. "That's what Faith said, too."

Troy knew she'd never say anything openly

critical of him, especially to Megan. He was astonished that the two of them had become friends without his knowing it. Who would've guessed? Now Megan was practically begging him to date the very woman she'd once feared would come between them.

"She had lots of nice things to say about you."

He resisted asking his daughter to list those things one by one.

"Something happened, didn't it?"

Before he could form a reply, Megan said, "Something you don't want to tell me because Faith doesn't want to talk about it, either."

Troy exhaled. "Sometimes it's best to leave the past in the past."

"Is there anything I can do, Daddy?"

"Do?"

"To make things right between you and Faith."

He considered the offer and could think of nothing. "No, but thanks for asking."

Troy glanced up and saw Roy McAfee in the doorway. "Let me call you back," he told his daughter.

"Do you have a visitor?"

"I do."

Megan sounded disappointed. "I wish it

was Faith."

So did Troy. If Santa was up to granting requests this year, Troy would ask for another chance with her. Unfortunately, all the evidence said there was no Santa.

"Bye, Daddy."

"Bye for now."

As soon as he'd replaced the receiver, Roy stepped into his office. Troy motioned for him to take a seat. "What can I do for you?" he asked. It went without saying that his friend wasn't making a social call. If Roy came to the office, it was on official business.

"Do you have any new leads on the Martha Evans case?" Roy began. He claimed the chair across from Troy, leaned back and ostentatiously made himself comfortable. It was an unspoken way of conveying that he had information to share.

"What makes you ask?" This was a routine they sometimes played out, dodging and feinting until the information was exchanged. Troy liked the private detective and trusted his judgment, but *he* was the lawman and he made sure Roy understood that.

"I had a visitor yesterday," Roy said.

"Was this in regard to the missing jewelry?"

A regal nod from Roy.

"Anyone I know?"

Roy hesitated, then inclined his head again.

"As it happens, I had a visitor myself regarding this matter. On Monday as well."

McAfee lifted his eyebrows. "Anyone I know?" he said, echoing Troy's own question.

But Troy could be as evasive as his friend. He inclined his head, too.

"*My* visitor was Dave Flemming," Roy told him.

"Geoff Duncan came to see *me*."

"Did he now?" McAfee went on to tell him everything Dave had said, which was quite a bit.

Troy then revealed that Dave had phoned and asked to speak to him but wanted to wait until after Christmas. After that, Troy was more convinced than ever that his theory was correct.

"Geoff came to tell me he was in a quandary," he said casually. "Apparently he's been wrestling with what to do and decided that even if he did lose his job, he couldn't keep quiet any longer."

"He told you about Emily Flemming's visit to the law office."

"Yes."

"I thought he might do that." Roy stood, reached inside his pants pocket and produced the gold watch and a pair of diamond earrings.

Troy immediately recognized both as part of the Evans estate. "You got those from Dave?"

Roy nodded. "He claims the watch was a gift from Martha."

"And the paperwork was supposed to be in the file, only it wasn't. Right?"

"Exactly," Roy said. Then he added, "Dave says he doesn't know where the diamond earrings came from. He told me he'd never laid eyes on them until his wife showed them to him. She found them in his suit jacket."

Troy said nothing.

McAfee studied him closely. "I believe him."

"I do, too." The sheriff relaxed in his chair and leaned back. "Want to tell me what you're thinking?"

"Sure thing, Sheriff — if you're willing to share your thoughts, too."

Troy chuckled. "I have a feeling we've reached the same conclusion."

"If I were a betting man, I'd lay odds on it."

"Cards on the table, then?"

"Cards on the table," Roy said.

THIRTY-ONE

Rachel carried a box of clothes into the living room and stacked it on top of the others. She couldn't believe she'd allowed Bruce to talk her into an early wedding at this time of year. Christmas!

It was insane.

It was wonderful.

She was eager to wake up in the morning with the man she loved by her side. She'd given notice on her small rental house but had until New Year's Eve to move everything out.

Jolene burst back into the house. "Anything else?" she asked.

"Take the box on top. It isn't heavy." Rachel bent to rearrange the dishes in one carton.

"Okay, got it." She grabbed it and headed outside to Bruce's truck.

Bruce, who was entering the house as Jolene went out, held the door for his daughter.

Rachel straightened and rubbed the small of her back. She was astonished by the amount of stuff she'd managed to accumulate during her seven years in this rental. Most of the furniture was second-hand and she intended to donate it to charity, but that still left a lot to pack.

"You're exhausted," Bruce said. "Maybe we should all take a break."

Rachel shook her head, despite the fact that she'd started work at eight that morning and been on her feet nine hours before rushing home to pack.

Walking over to her, Bruce drew her into the circle of his arms. "Thank you," he said.

"For what?"

"For loving me and Jolene. For agreeing to marry me now and not making me wait until February."

"Trust me, Bruce, I'm not complaining."

"Didn't I tell you we should have our wedding over the holidays?"

She smiled and ran her fingers through his hair. "I can see you're going to be the kind of husband who says 'I told you so.'"

"Was I right, or was I right?" he asked, leaning back enough to look her in the eyes, then kiss the tip of her nose.

The screen door slammed shut and Jolene bounded into the house. She came to an abrupt halt, sighing loudly. "Are you two going to get all kissy-face again?"

"Probably," Bruce said.

"Do you want me to leave?" It might have sounded like a joke but Rachel knew it wasn't.

"Not at all." She reluctantly broke away. Jolene wasn't comfortable with even the lightest of kisses between her father and Rachel. Bruce didn't seem to notice, but Rachel certainly had.

"I'm hungry," Jolene announced.

Bruce glanced at his watch. "Well, no wonder! It's after eight."

They'd started loading Bruce's truck as soon as Rachel got off work at six. She'd packed as much as she could the night before, but the salon was extra-busy so close to the holidays. Trying to adjust her schedule, pack and move in with Bruce and Jolene, get ready for Christmas *and* her wedding, all within a few days, plus get the rental house clean, was too much — and yet Rachel wouldn't have changed a thing.

"Let me drive this load to the house," Bruce suggested next. "On the way back I'll pick up something for dinner. What would you like?"

"Chicken!" Jolene shouted.

Bruce looked at Rachel. "Chicken sounds

good to me, too," she said.

"Should I come with you or stay with Rachel?" Jolene asked.

"I could use some more help packing up my bedroom," Rachel told her.

"Okay. Bye, Dad." Jolene hugged Bruce, then started to gather up empty cartons.

"Do I get a kiss goodbye?" Bruce asked, his eyes sparkling with mischief.

Remembering Jolene's response to the last kiss, Rachel said, "No."

Bruce pouted. "Don't tell me you're going to be stingy."

"I'm going to be sensible. We both have things to do."

"Anything we can do together?" he teased.

"Bruce," she murmured, glancing over her shoulder to confirm that Jolene had left the room. "As much as I'd like to spend the rest of the night cuddled up on that sofa with you, I can't."

He sighed, kissed her cheek, then sauntered out, closing the door behind him.

"Dad gone already?" Jolene asked, dragging a cardboard box into the living room.

"Yes, but he won't be long."

Jolene set down the box and threw herself on the sofa. "It's kind of weird."

"What is?"

Jolene shrugged. "You marrying my dad."

"You're happy about it, though, aren't you?"

"It's okay, I guess."

The lack of enthusiasm caught Rachel unawares. Dropping the tablecloth she was folding, she sat beside Jolene. "Maybe we should talk about this."

Jolene hung her head. "Okay."

"Are you worried things will change?"

"They will," she said, then added, "They already have."

Rachel had to admit she was right. Everything *had* changed — between her and Bruce, and between her and Jolene, too. Rachel was grateful for the girl's honesty.

"You and Dad will probably have a baby," Jolene muttered next.

Rachel and Bruce had discussed that very subject more than once. Because she was thirty-three, Rachel wanted to get pregnant within the first year. Bruce was in full agreement.

"I thought you *wanted* a brother or sister," Rachel commented.

"I do . . . sort of," Jolene said. "I used to think I did, but now that it might really happen, I know everyone will pay attention to the baby and —"

"And not you," Rachel finished for her. She placed her arm around Jolene's shoulders and brought her close. From the time Jolene was six, Rachel had been a constant in her life. She knew this child, loved her — couldn't imagine loving her more than she already did.

Jolene shrugged again.

"Your father loves you, Jolene."

"I know."

"Baby or no baby, that isn't going to change."

The girl sighed, staring down at her hands.

"It isn't going to change with me, either," Rachel told her.

After a short pause, Jolene asked, "Will I have to call you Mom?"

"What would you like to call me?"

Jolene looked at her uncertainly. "I think of you as Rachel."

"Then call me Rachel."

"I want you to be my mother!"

"Jolene, call me whatever makes you the most comfortable."

"But I *had* a mom," she cried suddenly, startling Rachel.

"Of course you did, and Stephanie will always be with you and part of you."

Jolene's face was anxious. "I don't want to forget her and I'm afraid I will."

The anguish in her voice was heart-breaking, and Rachel knew she had to respond carefully.

"Oh, Jolene, you aren't going to forget her. I can promise you that. Remember, I lost my mother, too."

When her own mother died, Rachel had gone to live with her aunt — her mother's older sister. Her father, unlike Bruce, didn't want a youngster underfoot. He was a busy man with a job that often took him out of town. He'd died of a heart attack when she was in her early twenties. She first came to live with her aunt at the age of ten and was supposed to stay in Cedar Cove just until school was over. Her father had intended to make other arrangements, which in retrospect probably meant a boarding school.

Her aunt was a levelheaded woman, strict and orderly, but not without affection. She'd never married. After the school year she'd suggested Rachel continue living with her. Her father was only too willing to agree.

"When you and Dad get married, will I have to take down my mother's picture?" Jolene asked.

"Of course not!" Jolene kept it on the dresser in her bedroom.

"I need it to remember."

"I know you do." Rachel smoothed the hair away from Jolene's brow. "This has all come at you pretty quickly, hasn't it? Your dad and

442

me getting married, I mean."

"I . . . I thought you were marrying Nate and moving away, and then all of a sudden Dad tells me *he* loves you and now you two are getting married. That was supposed to happen on Valentine's Day and now it's Christmas and you're moving in with us."

Hearing it from Jolene's perspective, it did seem rushed. "Would you rather we waited until February?" Rachel asked. If that was the case she'd delay the wedding.

"I . . . I'm not sure."

"We didn't give you time to adjust to the idea," Rachel murmured, feeling she'd failed Jolene.

"I want you to marry my dad. And I want you to move in with us . . . ."

"Just not yet."

"I . . . I don't know."

Rachel acknowledged the girl's indecision. "I understand you're feeling confused," she said. "Things really have changed too fast for you, haven't they?"

"Yeah," Jolene agreed, and Rachel sensed her relief.

How foolish she and Bruce had been. Without meaning to, they'd excluded his daughter. They'd been so focused on their own emotions, Jolene had taken second place.

"Shall we think about this for a minute?

What would you like to see happen?"

"I want you to be my friend again."

Rachel hadn't considered it that way. "I'll always be your friend, Jolene."

"I want you to be. Except . . ."

"Except what?" Rachel pressed.

"Except . . . I don't like it when you and Dad kiss and stuff. It's like I'm not even in the room, but I am and I see everything. It's *embarrassing.* None of my friends' parents kiss like that."

Rachel figured the newness of the attraction between her and Bruce would wear off in time. But in the meanwhile, Jolene's discomfort had to be taken into account. Rachel's heart sank as she thought about this. It was all more complicated than she'd realized.

Rachel spent the next fifteen or twenty minutes listening to Jolene, encouraging her to express her concerns, trying to reassure her. When the front door opened and Bruce strolled in carrying a large white bag containing their dinner, he seemed to sense that something was wrong.

"Hey, you two, what's up?"

Rachel looked at Jolene, whose eyes seemed to plead with her not to say anything.

"We're just talking," Rachel said.

Jolene squeezed her hand in thanks.

"Anyone hungry?" Bruce asked.

"I am," Rachel announced with feigned cheerfulness.

"Me, too," Jolene chimed in.

Bruce brought the takeout meal to the kitchen. The moment he'd left the living room, Rachel turned to Jolene again. "Let me talk to your father," she said.

"He'll be mad at me."

"No, he won't," Rachel told her. "Leave everything to me."

Jolene folded her arms, her expression downcast. "I shouldn't have said anything."

"About what?" Bruce stood in the doorway.

Rachel glanced at Jolene and then at Bruce. "Our lives are changing so quickly that Jolene's having a hard time keeping up."

"What do you mean?" he asked, frowning.

Rachel had hoped he'd understand. "I'm thinking she's probably right, and we may have let this whole marriage thing get ahead of us."

Bruce stepped into the room. "What are you saying? Don't forget, I'm a guy. You're going to have to spell it out for me."

"Well," Rachel said, reaching for Jolene's hand, "maybe we should wait until Valentine's Day. That was the original plan and now we're —"

"Delay the wedding?" he broke in. "No way!" Bruce shook his head vigorously. "I want us married, and the sooner the better."

"There's Jolene to consider," Rachel reminded him.

Bruce regarded his daughter for a moment and then knelt down in front of her. "Are you upset about Rachel and me getting married?" he asked.

Jolene refused to meet his gaze. "A little," she said in a small voice.

"I thought you liked Rachel."

"I do! A lot."

"So what's the problem?"

The girl shrugged, as if unable to voice her feelings.

"I love Rachel," Bruce told her gently. "And I love you, too."

Rachel was proud of him for being so sensitive to his daughter. Jolene needed to know that she was still as important to Bruce as ever. She and Bruce shared an unusually close bond because it had been just the two of them for more than six years; Rachel's constant presence in their lives would disrupt that, change it. And at twelve, a girl needed her father's approval, his pride in her. Rachel was very conscious of not having received that and she refused to let the same thing happen to Jolene.

The phone rang in the distance. Unwilling to answer it and risk breaking the mood, Rachel let the answering machine pick up.

"Ms. Pendergast, this is Cedar Cove Realty," a man's voice said. "Could you return this call at your earliest convenience? We have a renter for the house and need the exact date you plan to vacate."

Jolene stared at Rachel, eyes wide. "The house has already been rented?"

"Sounds like it," Bruce responded, looking far more pleased than he should.

"If Rachel doesn't marry you now, she won't have anyplace to live." Jolene's voice was horrified.

"That's not true —" Rachel started to say, before Bruce cut her off.

"Guess so."

"Bruce!" Rachel wanted to jab him in the ribs and would have if he'd been sitting beside her instead of Jolene. "I can stay with friends." She could bunk down in Teri's huge house for a couple of months. It would be an imposition, but Teri was the kind of friend who wouldn't have any objections — who'd insist on it, for that matter.

"Then . . . you and Rachel should get married this week," Jolene said after a moment.

"I say we wait," Rachel returned decisively.

She needed to let her soon-to-be stepdaughter know that she heard her concerns and took them seriously.

Bruce glared at her. "I want to marry you *now.* You want Rachel with us, too, right, Jolene?"

Jolene met Rachel's eyes. After a long pause she slowly nodded. "Right, Dad."

THIRTY-TWO

Olivia was gradually regaining her strength. She sat in the sunny kitchen and soaked in the warmth as she sipped a cup of green tea.

Justine was coming by later and Grace had just left. As little as two days ago she would've taken a nap but Olivia didn't feel she needed one now. That was encouraging. She really was recovering from the surgery and the infection. Her chemotherapy would start soon after the holidays, as originally scheduled. She'd joked that it was a late Christmas gift — the gift that kept on giving — and to her surprise Jack had looked at her with somber eyes. "Yes, Olivia, it is. It's giving me *you*. Your life, your health — to me that's the greatest gift." He usually joked and bantered his way through everything, so his emotional statement had moved her deeply.

She heard the sound of a car pulling into the driveway and immediately recognized it as Ben's. Ever the gentlemen, he parked, climbed out and came around to open her mother's door.

Charlotte seemed to sense that they were being watched and glanced up at the kitchen window. Seeing Olivia, she smiled and waved.

Olivia waved back. She stood up and went to the back door.

"We have company," she called out to Jack who was walking on the treadmill. He'd made a habit of exercising ever since his heart attack. Olivia enjoyed finding small ways to reward him for his diligence.

"Who . . . is . . . it?" Jack called back from the master bedroom, panting between each word.

"Mom and Ben."

"Give me . . . five . . . minutes."

Her mother and stepfather approached, and Olivia swung open the door. Charlotte carried a white wicker basket with a sprig of holly and a bright red bow attached.

Olivia bent to kiss her mother's cheek and then Ben's.

"My goodness, Olivia, you look wonderful! There's color in your cheeks and you're looking much more like yourself."

"I'm feeling better, Mom. Come and sit with me. Want some green tea?"

"Lovely." Charlotte set the basket on the

table. "I'll get the tea. You and Ben take a load off your feet."

"Mom," Olivia protested, "I can do it." Her mother refused to listen, and Olivia realized that ever since her diagnosis, Charlotte *needed* to wait on her. It was one of the few ways she could feel any sense of control — by taking care of her daughter. That typically involved food.

"What's in the basket?" Olivia asked.

"Dinner for you and Jack."

Everyone had been so kind and thoughtful. Grace had brought over a taco casserole the night before. She'd made it from scratch, using her homemade salsa and lots of cheese in hopes of tempting Olivia to eat. The fact was, Olivia had lost ten pounds in the last two months. Those were pounds she could ill afford to lose. Her clothes hung on her.

Jack, on the other hand, still struggled with his weight and all these delicious things around the house tormented him. He'd had two helpings of Grace's casserole while Olivia had barely managed a few bites. They'd frozen the leftovers.

"What's for dinner?" Olivia asked as she removed the layer of foil covering the basket.

"Soup," Charlotte answered. "Chicken noodle."

"Oh, Mom, that's perfect!"

"And fresh-baked bread."

"Any Christmas cookies or candy?" Jack wanted to know, stepping into the kitchen. He'd draped a towel around his neck and his face was red.

"Jack!"

"Hey, it's Christmas." He poked around inside the basket and triumphantly brought out a plate of decorated sugar cookies.

"My favorite!" he cried delightedly. "Sugar cookies."

"Every kind of cookie's his favorite," Olivia told Ben under her breath.

Ben chuckled and whispered back, "That's how I feel. Anything Charlotte bakes is instantly my favorite." He smiled at Olivia's mother as she puttered around the kitchen, making a fresh pot of green tea.

"Thanks, Charlotte," Jack said. He peeled back the plastic wrap and grabbed a cookie. On his way out of the kitchen, he kissed his mother-in-law's cheek.

Once the three of them were sitting around the table, Olivia asked, "So what's new with you?"

Ben glanced at Charlotte. "We leave for our cruise in the morning."

Olivia gasped. "Already?" With so much else happening, she'd completely forgotten about the cruise.

Charlotte placed her hands on the table. "I'm still not sure we should leave you."

"Mom, you're going."

"But —"

"Not only are you going on that cruise, I absolutely *demand* that you have the time of your lives."

"But . . ." Charlotte frowned. "You might need me. You'll be starting your treatment soon and —"

"I have Jack," she broke in.

Her mother sighed expressively. "Jack is a man. Don't get me wrong, I love him dearly, but no matter how much he loves you, he's not your mother. And when you're sick, that's who you need," she said.

That Charlotte and Ben would even consider not going at this late date nearly brought Olivia to tears. "I'm going to be fine, Mom. Before you know it, this will all be behind me."

Olivia clung to that belief. This was the longest stretch of time she'd spent away from the courthouse since she'd become a judge. She'd had no choice in the matter but she missed her work and her colleagues.

Her mother still seemed worried. "I just don't feel right about it."

"You're going, Mom, and you have to promise me you'll enjoy every minute."

Before Charlotte could argue anymore, Jack walked back into the kitchen and reached for another cookie. A bell-shaped one this time, with white frosting. He hesitated almost as if he expected Olivia to slap his hand.

"You aren't going to stop me?" he asked.

"Consider that cookie your reward for working out."

"My *only* reward?"

She raised her eyebrows and nodded.

Jack shook his head morosely and set the sugar cookie back on the plate. "In that case one cookie will do." He took the chair next to Olivia.

Olivia did her best to suppress a smile, but didn't succeed. With some effort she returned her attention to her mother. "Just think about lazing away your days in the Caribbean sunshine."

Charlotte reached across the table and entwined her fingers with Ben's. "Being in the sunshine over Christmas does sound wonderful," she said in a wistful voice.

"The warmth will do our aging bones good," Ben told her.

"Yes, I know . . . but the thought of leaving Olivia bothers me."

"Hey," Jack protested, "what am I? Chopped liver?"

"You're just a man." Olivia repeated what her mother had said, her mouth twitching.

"You've never complained about that before," Jack muttered.

Looking benignly at her mother, Olivia kicked him under the table.

Jack, being Jack, doubled over and grabbed his ankle, grimacing as if she'd injured him.

"Will you cut it out?" she said when he popped back up.

Ben laughed. "I think we can rest assured that Olivia is well on the road to recovery. Jack, now, might need intensive therapy for that ankle."

Charlotte rolled her eyes.

"A car's coming for us first thing in the morning," Ben told them. "Our flight for Fort Lauderdale takes off at eight and the cruise starts on December eighteenth. We'll be back home a week later on Christmas Day."

"Seven days never seemed so long," Charlotte murmured.

"Mom, a week in paradise and you're complaining?"

The lines between her mother's eyes relaxed and Charlotte smiled. "I sound like a silly old woman, don't I?"

Jack leaned back in his chair and crossed his arms. "Go. Your daughter's in my capable hands."

"That does it!" Charlotte burst out. "I'm not leaving."

"Mom!"

Ben laughed, and Charlotte's laughter joined his.

"I was just teasing," she told them.

"Will has a key to the house," Ben went on to say. "He said he'd check in every couple of days. And Justine will be coming by, as well, to look after Harry."

"What are you doing Christmas Day?" Charlotte asked.

"I'm taking care of dinner," Jack announced proudly.

This seemed to impress her mother and stepfather, and Olivia felt obliged to explain. "He's ordering in a meal."

"This isn't just any meal," Jack insisted. "Our dinner's being catered by D.D.'s on the Cove."

"Jack," Charlotte said, clasping her hands. "How romantic."

"Which is exactly what I want for you and Ben," Olivia told her mother. "I want you to fall in love all over again."

Ben's fingers tightened around Charlotte's. "We don't need a cruise for that."

"We don't, either," Olivia whispered, smiling at Jack.

Her mother and Ben stayed only a few minutes longer.

By the time they left, both seemed reassured and eager for their trip, promising to come back refreshed.

The sound of the car had yet to fade when Jack turned to her. "I believe you owe me."

"Owe you?"

"My reward, remember?"

"Oh, honestly, Jack."

"Yes, honestly."

Olivia laughed and held open her arms.

THIRTY-THREE

"Where are you taking me?" Tanni asked, standing at the edge of the highway some distance outside town. Cars streaked past her, kicking up rain water, splashing the backs of her pant legs.

"I want to show you something." Shaw had parked his car and already started walking into the woods. "Come on," he urged.

"Where?" she demanded a second time. Shaw had been acting so strange and secretive and that wasn't like him.

"Back here."

"In the *woods*?" She looked down at her new boots and sighed. The dense forest floor would be muddy and wet. If these got ruined, her mother wasn't likely to buy her another pair.

Instead of arguing with her, Shaw rushed back and grabbed her hand.

"Why all the secrecy?"

"You'll know why once you get there."

"This better be good," she muttered. Her feet made squishing sounds in the damp earth.

"I've only ever told one other person about this."

In other words, whatever *this* was, the fact that he was showing it to her was a sign of his trust. Her boots sank deeper into the mud but she refused to look at them. If Shaw was willing to share something he considered important, she didn't care how far she had to walk into the woods or how many pairs of boots she had to ruin.

"It's all the way back here?" she asked when they'd gone about a hundred feet. Tree limbs hung low, admitting very little light. Despite the darkness and the lack of a clear path, he seemed to know exactly where he was going.

"Not much farther," he assured her, his hand still clutching hers.

"Shaw!" she cried, grabbing his arm with her other hand when she nearly slipped on a fallen branch covered with moss.

He held her about the waist and kept her from falling. "Be careful," he said.

They continued at a slower pace. Tanni glanced over her shoulder and discovered that the road was completely out of sight. She couldn't even guess where he was leading her. Perhaps there was an abandoned cabin nearby or a —

"We're here," he said.

Tanni looked around and didn't see anything unusual or different. Thinking she might have missed something, she turned in a complete circle. "We're *where?*" she asked.

"I found this years ago when I was a kid," Shaw explained. He started to drag a heavy branch away. He removed three such branches, which he'd apparently arranged to hide the opening of a cave.

He stood back and grinned, making a sweeping motion with his arms. "Ta da!"

She'd lived in this area nearly her entire life and she'd never heard anything about caves. Her brother, Nick, would've loved exploring here. He'd never mentioned it, either. "Does anyone else know about it?"

"I doubt it," he said. "because it's state land. As far as I can tell, no one had been inside for years."

"How'd you find it?"

Shaw stared down at his feet. "When I was eight, I joined Cub Scouts. We were on a hike down here near Lighthouse Point and I got separated from the rest of the pack. Pretty soon I was lost."

"In other words, you don't have a good sense of direction."

He shook his head. "In other words, I wasn't paying attention. Nothing wrong with my sense of direction."

"That's when you found it?"

"Yup. It'd started to rain and I went inside and waited until I heard someone call my name. Then I ran out and met up with the others. I never told any of them, though."

"Why not?" She didn't understand his reason for keeping it a secret. This was an exciting discovery, and if *she'd* been the one to come across it she would've shared it with the world.

"The other kids were teasing me about getting lost and it made me mad so I didn't tell them what I'd found."

"But you said you told one other person. . . ."

He nodded. "The night Anson ran away, I brought him here," he began. "It took me a while to locate it again, but eventually I did. Anson stayed in the cave for two days until I could find a way to get him out of Cedar Cove."

"You did that for him," she breathed. Shaw would've been in real trouble if anyone had caught him with Anson. She knew Shaw had bought him a bus ticket in Seattle, then driven him there.

"He's a good friend, the best I ever had.

Until you."

His words nearly brought her to tears. Tanni had never had a friend like that, a friend who'd take risks for her. In her universe, friendship had meant exchanging insignificant secrets and chattering about boys.

"It was the only hiding place I could think of. He promised he'd never tell anyone about it and he hasn't."

"Not even Allison Cox?"

"I don't know what he told Allison, but I can guarantee you he didn't mention the cave."

"But . . . you're showing me."

"Yes . . . I came back here myself a little while ago." He reached for her hand and led her inside, warning her to duck at the entrance.

Within seconds, they were plunged into darkness. Shaw took out a small flashlight attached to his keychain and turned it on. The cave's ceiling was maybe ten feet high and they could stand up easily. Tanni saw that he'd cut arched slots into the hard clay. A large candle was positioned in each. He lit the first candle and the cave was dimly illuminated. Then he moved along the walls, lighting other candles. Each one added more light. The candles burned steadily, and she noticed the melted wax that had dripped down the sides, which told her someone had spent hours inside this cave.

"Anson made these candle holders," Shaw explained. "Two days is a long time when you don't have anything to do."

"The darkness must've freaked him out."

"Yeah. He asked for candles and I got them for him. It was his idea to set them in the walls of the cave." He shrugged. "Kind of primitive, but I got him a couple of flashlights, too."

She also saw a plastic-covered sleeping bag and a portable camp chair, obviously "furniture" he'd brought in for Anson.

"You said you came here recently. Why?"

Shaw took her hand again. "My dad and I got into it last weekend. He wants me to go to law school. He says he's worked his whole life to build up his firm so he could pass it on to me. If I want to piddle around drawing faces, that's a nice hobby, but it's no career."

"Oh, Shaw."

"We've argued before but this was the worst. He . . . he kicked me out of the house. He said either I go to college or I'm not welcome to live in his house."

This was the first time he'd mentioned the fight. Earlier in the week she'd realized something was bothering him, but when she'd asked, he'd brushed her questions aside and assured her nothing was wrong.

"So you came here?"

Shaw nodded. "I spent one night here and about froze to death."

Tanni covered her mouth with her hand.

"In the morning I called my mom and she said she'd talked to my father and I should come home. I did and I . . . I told my dad I'm taking my GED. That seemed to appease him for now. He gave me until the first of the year to make a decision about college."

"You can spend Christmas with me if you want," Tanni said. Her mother had already agreed.

"I . . . might. Let me see how things go at home, okay?"

"Sure." Tanni hated knowing he'd been alone in this cave for even one night.

As if reading her thoughts, Shaw said, "I didn't sleep much when I was here."

Tanni shivered. "I can imagine."

"I didn't mind it during the day — maybe because I knew it was still light outside."

"What'd you do that night?"

"I used my sleeping bag —" he pointed to it "— and I tried to start a fire near the entrance. I couldn't, though, because the wood was too damp. After a while, I got cold and bored, so I decided to explore."

"At night?" Not that there was much difference between day and night inside the cave.

"It was closer to morning. I had my flashlight and I found that this cave leads into another one and then another one. That's when I saw it."

"Saw what?" She had to admit her curiosity was piqued.

His hand closed more tightly around hers. "You'll see." He led her a few steps and stopped. "Just promise me you won't freak out."

"I won't." She wasn't the type to faint because she saw a spider or even a bat. She figured his big find was something along those lines, since she knew bat colonies lived in caves.

"Good." He kissed her and his lips were cold against hers.

When he broke away, he said, "Sometimes . . ." But he let the rest drop.

"Sometimes what, Shaw?"

He shook his head. "I'll tell you later."

"Tell me now," she urged, wrapping her arms around him.

He exhaled, closing his eyes and pressing his forehead against hers. "Sometimes when I'm drawing, I think about the two of us working together. Both of us artists . . ."

The image blossomed in Tanni's mind. At first being inside the cave had felt a bit frightening. It didn't when Shaw kissed her. "I'd like that," she said warmly.

He kissed her again.

This time Tanni broke it off. "You were going to show me something, remember?"

"Oh, yeah, I remember." He was breathing hard.

"First tell me — is it good or bad?"

He grimaced. "Bad."

"Bad," she repeated. "How bad? In what way?"

"You'll see." He paused. "I wasn't going to tell anyone. But I called Anson and he said I couldn't ignore it. I decided he's right."

Tanni was beginning to feel anxious; his tension was definitely communicating itself to her. Why was he being so mysterious?

"You ready?" he asked.

"Ready as I'll ever be," she said, with no idea what to expect.

"Don't be afraid, okay?"

"There's no one else here, is there?"

He hesitated before he answered. "No."

He pulled a flashlight out of a heavy plastic bag in the corner. Then he took her hand, fingers tight around hers, and led her deeper into the cave's interior. The light bounced against the sides, creating eerie shadows that seemed to loom over them.

As they moved forward, her feet made splashing sounds, and she began to tremble. If it was from the cold or from anxiety, she couldn't tell.

They ducked around a corner and into a smaller cave, and Tanni stopped.

"How're you doing?" Shaw asked.

"I . . . I don't know. How much farther is it?"

"Not very far."

A sense of foreboding filled her. Her heart started to race and despite the cold, sweat broke out across her forehead. They crept forward and suddenly Shaw came to a halt.

Then she saw it. For an instant she assumed it was a dead animal. Mere seconds later, she realized she was standing next to a human skeleton — probably that of a man. He sat propped up against the side of the cave, a baseball cap on his head. It had slipped to a jaunty angle, which looked grotesque — there was no other word — and she could see clumps of hair that clung to the skull. His clothes were in shreds and he wore a pair of tennis shoes.

She gasped and turned to Shaw.

"You okay?" he murmured.

"We have to tell the sheriff," she said, trying to quell the hysteria that wanted to rise.

"He's been here a long time."

"It doesn't *matter* how long he's been here — he was a human being, Shaw. He died in here alone and . . . afraid." She wasn't sure how she knew that but she did. "We've got to call the sheriff."

"Yeah." He nodded. "You're right. But I almost don't want to disturb him, you know?"

Frankly she didn't. This man had not died peacefully, and he deserved some kind of justice, a decent burial, some acknowledgment. "Come on," she said urgently. "Let's go. My cell's in the car."

An hour and a half later the road by the forest was lined with law enforcement vehicles, their red lights flashing. Tanni counted four different cars. The deputies had hauled out several large lights and carried them to the cave once Shaw had shown them the way.

Shaw and Tanni sat in Sheriff Davis's vehicle, holding hands. After a few minutes, the sheriff opened the door. He'd spoken to Shaw while a deputy questioned Tanni; apparently their stories aligned because he'd allowed them to stay together.

"How long have you known about the body?" Sheriff Davis directed his question to Shaw.

"Three days," Shaw said. It was the same

468

answer he'd given earlier.

"Let me ask you again — you didn't move the remains? You didn't touch anything?"

Shaw said he hadn't.

Sheriff Davis wrote that down on his pad.

"Who is it?" Shaw asked as two uniformed deputies carried out a body bag and brought it to the waiting ambulance.

The sheriff shook his head. "I can't say."

Tanni exchanged a look with Shaw. "Does that mean you've identified the body and can't tell us?" she asked. "Or that you don't know, period?"

The sheriff frowned. "Don't know, period."

"What about your missing persons file?" Tanni suggested. Surely there was some explanation.

The sheriff closed his pad and placed it inside his shirt pocket. "We'll find out what we need to know soon enough," he informed them. "There hasn't been an unsolved murder in this town since I became sheriff, and this one's not going to be the first."

THIRTY-FOUR

Christie knew something was wrong the instant she heard her sister's voice mail. She stood in the store lunchroom, her cell phone pressed against her ear to block out the other employees' chatter.

By the time she'd taken her break, Teri had left her three messages, each one more cheerful-sounding than the last. Something was definitely up. Christie wasn't that easily fooled.

"Can you stop by after work this evening?" Teri asked when Christie finally returned her call.

Christie exhaled slowly. "The article's out, isn't it?"

"I'll explain everything when you get here." Christie suspected all these frantic calls had to do with James and that reporter, but maybe not.

"The pregnancy?" she asked next, almost afraid to finish the thought.

"The babies are fine," Teri assured her. "All three. In fact, they're currently in the middle of a soccer match."

Despite her concerns, Christie smiled. "Whatever it is, you can't tell me now?"

"No. Just get here as soon as you're off work, all right?"

"Okay, I'll be there."

This was making her nervous. She was already a little depressed that she wouldn't be seeing James until Christmas. He'd phoned and left a message on her cell Tuesday afternoon, explaining that he'd be out of town for at least a week. That was just as well, since the article would hit the stands any day. Christie had tried to find out when, but the reporter either hadn't known or wouldn't tell her.

James hadn't given her much information or even told her where he was going, only that he'd get in touch. But Christie had listened to his message several times, closing her eyes and savoring the sound of his voice.

Their Saturday night had been magical. After a perfect dinner, they'd sat in front of the fireplace, her head on his shoulder, his arm around her. It'd been so . . . so beautiful. So intimate. She'd never experienced this kind of closeness with a man. She had a list of ex-lovers, a fairly long one, but none of them had made her feel like this.

Everything was different with James.

He could have made love to her ten times over and she would've let him. He wanted her. She felt it with every cell of her body, and she wanted him, too. And they *would* make love soon; she was sure of it. But their relationship was more than that. It was deeper. Truer. It wasn't just about her body or what she could do for him. He loved her. They loved each other.

In every previous relationship, Christie had felt insecure. Every time she was away from her lover of the moment, she'd wonder if he was with some other woman. Would he come back? And when — if — he did, she'd wonder if he still wanted her. Or was he thinking of someone else when they made love?

It wasn't like that with James. Although he'd left town, she wasn't worried that he'd stray or that he'd abandon her. He'd be back soon and they'd spend the holidays together. Maybe he'd help her deliver gift baskets on Christmas Eve. She'd already checked with the Salvation Army in downtown Seattle and arranged to serve meals to the homeless on Christmas Day. James would join her and afterward they'd have their own Christmas dinner at her place. She looked forward to cooking it herself. All week she'd occupied pleasant hours studying cookbooks and considering her menu. Christie was more domestic than anyone realized — even Teri.

As she drove through Cedar Cove to her sister's, Christie examined the decorations and the multicolored lights with new eyes. She usually felt sad over the holidays, but not this year. She hadn't been so excited about Christmas since early childhood. Of course back then it had always ended in tears.

Christie hoped that whatever was troubling Teri didn't have anything to do with the pregnancy. Despite Teri's reassurances, she couldn't help worrying. Triplets! Teri always seemed to do things in a big way.

By the time Christie drove through the gate and into the yard, her sister was standing at the front door, waiting for her. Christie parked and hurried to the house.

Teri's somber face frightened her. She reached for Christie's hand and pulled her inside.

"What's going on?" Christie asked.

"The article's out. You were right about that," she murmured, drawing her into the family room.

"Where's Bobby?" Christie asked.

"In the library. He's dealing with the phone calls. It seems as if every reporter in the world wants to talk to James. And since they can't reach him, they'll settle for Bobby." Her lips thinned in obvious disapproval. Clearly she felt that James should be fielding his own questions instead of leaving it all to Bobby.

Christie understood Teri's reaction, her desire to protect Bobby, but she didn't think it was entirely fair. James couldn't stay here now that a reporter had tracked him down, now that everyone knew who he was. Then it hit her. "Something's happened to him, hasn't it?" No wonder her sister hadn't been willing to tell her over the phone. "He's been in an accident?" Her heart slammed against her ribs.

"Christie . . ."

She grabbed her sister's arm. "How badly is he hurt? Tell me!"

"James wasn't in an accident," Teri said calmly.

Relief flooded through her and she sank into the nearest chair. "Thank God." On the heels of her relief came another realization. If he wasn't hurt, then something else was wrong.

"I made coffee," Teri said.

Standing, Christie followed her into the kitchen. "Just tell me."

Teri exhaled noisily. "He resigned."

"What do you mean, he resigned? Resigned from what?"

Teri met her gaze. "His job, Christie. James is no longer employed by Bobby."

It took her a moment to grasp Teri's words. As she stared at her sister, Teri poured a mug of coffee and handed it to her.

Christie accepted it automatically. "So he doesn't want to drive Bobby around anymore. That's not the end of the world, is it?" Okay, fine, the word was out that James had once been a chess prodigy, the same as Bobby. Big deal. It would be news for a couple of days, and then interest would fade and life would go back to normal. And if James decided he was finished with working for Bobby, it shouldn't be held against him.

Teri continued to watch her. "You haven't heard from him, have you?"

"No . . ." Christie hadn't worried about it, though — until now.

"What did he say the last time you spoke?"

Christie reviewed his brief voice mail. "Basically he told me he was going away for a little while." He hadn't said exactly when he planned to return. The assumption that he'd be back by Christmas was hers, and hers alone. She took the first sip of coffee and realized her sister had made it extra-strong. The bitter taste jolted her.

"Bobby's devastated," Teri told her. "What James did is a stab in the back."

"Isn't that a bit extreme?" Christie's hackles went up.

"No, it's not," Teri said in a sharp voice. "Bobby's been his friend all these years and then James turns tail and runs, and Bobby's stuck dealing with all the reporters. He doesn't deserve this."

Christie hadn't thought of it that way.

"To quit like that, too," Teri muttered angrily.

"Like what?"

"He didn't even speak to Bobby. He wrote a letter, in which he said his resignation was effective immediately. Then he walked away without a word to either of us. We don't even know where he is. Bobby's been worried sick. He's afraid James might've had another breakdown, but I doubt it. His actions are too calculated, too planned."

Christie straightened. Her inclination was to defend James — but her sister had a point. It occurred to her that James had purposely phoned when he knew she'd be at work. He hadn't wanted to talk to her — and now . . .

"James will be back," she said. The alternative was impossible. Unbearable.

"I don't think so," Teri murmured.

"Why would you say that?" Christie asked, finding it hard to hold on to her temper. James was hiding somewhere, until everything was quiet again. She refused to believe he'd simply walk out, just disappear from their lives. He wasn't like that. Other men were. Not James. He loved her. He loved Bobby and Teri, too. They were his family. He'd said as much.

Not only that, she'd bared her soul to him. She'd told him things she'd never told another human being. He'd shared a little of his own life, too. He'd told her about the trauma in his childhood, the pressure he'd endured from his parents and chess coach. The breakdown that had ended his career. Again and again he'd told her of his deep gratitude to Bobby.

"James would never leave Bobby," Christie declared.

Even if he could walk away from her, he wouldn't forsake his dearest friend. James was intensely loyal to both Bobby and Teri.

"I used to think that, too," Teri admitted hoarsely.

"He'll be back," Christie said again. "He might need a few days or weeks to sort everything out, but in the end he'll realize this is his home and we're his family." She included herself, unable to accept that he'd turn away from her like so many other men had. He wouldn't. He just wouldn't. Not after everything she'd told him. Because James wouldn't intentionally hurt her that way.

Teri didn't respond.

"You *don't* believe he'll be back?" Christie challenged.

"I wish I could."

"Listen, this might come as a shock, but I think I should tell you. James and I are in love."

"I know," Teri said without any enthusiasm.

"You know?"

"Good grief, Christie, I've known it for weeks, even before the kidnapping."

That was interesting, because Christie hadn't been aware of her own feelings until recently.

"It was so obvious," Teri went on.

Christie put her coffee on the counter. She wasn't really in the mood for it, anyway. When she turned back, she saw that Bobby had come into the kitchen.

"Hi, Bobby," she said, greeting him in a cheerful voice.

He blinked at her as if he couldn't quite place who she was.

"It's Christie," she said, bringing her hand

to her throat. "Teri's sister."

"Yes, I know." He seemed puzzled that she'd felt the need to identify herself.

"James will be back," she said once more, trying to inspire confidence in Teri and Bobby. "I don't understand why he resigned. That seems a bit drastic, but I'm sure he didn't mean it."

"He meant it," Bobby said dispassionately.

"This must be a knee-jerk reaction. It might even be a joke and he'll be home by morning." She couldn't imagine that, but felt she had to suggest it.

Bobby immediately discounted the possibility. "James doesn't know how to joke," he said. "James is like me."

"Oh." Christie couldn't figure out quite what to say to that. "Where would he go?" she asked instead.

Bobby shook his head.

"We've wondered the same thing," Teri told her. "Bobby's known him practically his entire life and James has never done anything like this."

"Why are you so sure he won't be back?" she asked.

Neither Teri nor Bobby seemed inclined to answer.

"See?" she cried with a sense of triumph. "You're not sure at all. I think we're overreacting here. James loves us. Give him a day or two, and once this has blown over, he'll be back in his apartment as if nothing happened."

Bobby stared at her. "He took everything with him."

"What . . . what do you mean, everything?"

Bobby and her sister exchanged a look.

"He's taken all his personal stuff — his computer, clothes, books," her sister explained. "He's gone, Christie, and we're guessing he'll never show his face in Cedar Cove again."

Gone. For good. Took everything. Won't be back.

Bobby knew James better than anyone, and if he thought James had left for good, he was probably right.

"Why would he do something like that?" Christie managed to croak out.

Bobby didn't answer.

Men never stayed in her life. She'd told herself he was different. Special. She'd trusted him, and at the first sign of trouble James had fled.

Gazing up at the ceiling Christie blinked back tears. "Why is it," she asked sarcastically, "that I have this ability to fall for all the wrong men?" At least this one hadn't beaten or robbed her or cheated with another woman. Nor had he drunk her out of house and home.

Oh, no, James "Wilbur" Gardner was special, all right. He hadn't done any of those things; instead, he'd broken her heart more thoroughly, more completely, than any other man ever had. An all-consuming pain rippled through her.

"Merry Christmas to you, too," she said and surged to her feet.

"I'm sorry," Teri murmured. "We didn't . . . I didn't want to ruin your Christmas."

"You didn't," she said flippantly. "In fact, the holidays are just getting started. Come to think of it, I've got a lot of celebrating to do." On a mission now, she grabbed her purse and headed for the front door. If she hurried, she'd make it to The Pink Poodle before the end of happy hour.

THIRTY-FIVE

This was exactly what Dave Flemming had feared. Sheriff Davis had asked him to "voluntarily" stop by his office for questioning, claiming this matter couldn't wait until after Christmas. He'd emphasized the word *voluntarily,* as if to suggest that if Dave didn't come of his own accord, he'd be obliged to send a deputy to escort him.

"You're going to go, aren't you?" Emily asked, standing next to him in the kitchen.

Dave still held the telephone receiver in his hand. "I don't think I have a choice."

His wife regarded him with wide, worried eyes. "Maybe we should have an attorney present."

Instinct told Dave that he should. "Attorneys cost money. We can't afford one."

"We can't afford *not* to have one," Emily insisted. "If there's any possibility that Sheriff Davis will arrest you, then . . ." She stopped abruptly.

"I didn't steal anything from Martha Evans," he said. He knew Emily believed him, but he couldn't resist defending himself. "The truth will set everything right."

"Don't you ever watch crime shows?" His wife flared. "The police don't care if you're innocent. They just want a conviction."

"Emily." That might be true in the land of television, but it wasn't the case in Cedar Cove. Sheriff Davis was an honorable man who cared far more about justice than his conviction record.

"I could sell something." Emily twisted her wedding band around her ring finger. "I could go to a pawnshop —"

"I refuse to even discuss it."

"What about Roy McAfee?" Emily suggested next, sounding panicky. "Since we're already paying him, maybe —"

"I offered to pay him but he wouldn't accept."

Emily wasn't taking no for an answer. "Dave, listen to reason, would you? If you go to jail —"

"That's not going to happen." He sounded confident but he had little to base that on. Just his own innocence and Roy McAfee's apparent belief that he hadn't stolen from Martha Evans's estate. Roy had mentioned another suspect but that was days ago, so

Dave assumed nothing had come of it. If the sheriff did decide to arrest him, then and only then would he have Emily hire an attorney.

His wife closed her eyes. "I wish you watched *Law & Order* more often. Then you'd know what I'm talking about."

He didn't have time for television. "You're overreacting. If I was in New York City, yes, I'd pay for legal representation, but this is Cedar Cover and the sheriff is a friend."

Emily considered that for a moment, then said, "I'm afraid Sheriff Davis won't be your friend once he looks at the accumulated evidence."

Dave sighed. From the outside, it looked as if he was indeed the guilty party. He couldn't even explain most of the so-called evidence stacked against him. He didn't have any idea how those diamond earrings had found their way into his suit pocket.

He couldn't explain why the letter he'd seen with his own eyes had never made it into Martha's last will and testament.

He decided to take Emily's advice.

"I'll call Roy," Dave said. He trusted Sheriff Davis, but it wouldn't hurt to have someone on his side. Dave hated the thought of having to defend himself. He was an honest man. But no one was above suspicion. Including a pastor.

Emily folded her hands prayerfully. "Thank God you're willing to have Roy there."

Dave tried to be optimistic. However, if he *was* arrested and charged, Emily would never be able to manage financially. Within a few weeks they'd be hopelessly behind on their bills. The house would go into foreclosure, and his wife and sons would have to move in with her parents. What a mess all their lives would be.

Dave couldn't allow his mind to wander down such dangerous paths. Still, it remained a possibility. He could very well be arrested.

He turned to the phone again and dialed Roy's number. Emily watched him closely. A minute later he hung up.

"Well?" his wife asked anxiously.

"I spoke with Corrie. She said Roy's already down at the sheriff's office and it would be a good idea if we left now."

Her face pale, Emily nodded. "I'll get my coat."

Suddenly uncertain, Dave wrung his hands. "I think I'd prefer to wait," he said.

"Wait?" Emily exploded. "For *what?* To be arrested?"

"I'd like to put this off until after Christmas."

"Dave, be realistic," she pleaded. "We can't

have this hanging over our heads through the holidays. You don't believe putting this off, even for an hour, is going to help, do you?"

"What about the Christmas Eve services at church?" Would Sheriff Davis let him out of jail to conduct a religious service? It didn't make sense, no matter how many promises he made to come back at midnight.

"Roy's with the sheriff. He'll protect you."

His wife held the private investigator in high regard. Dave knew that Roy would do what he could, but wouldn't stand in the way of the law. If Sheriff Davis felt he had no choice but to make an arrest, nothing Roy said was going to change his mind.

Then again, his wife had a point. The weight of all this had nearly buried him; he wasn't sleeping well, his appetite was gone and his nerves were stretched to the breaking point. He had to be willing to trust that God would see him through, regardless of the outcome. This was without a doubt the biggest leap of faith he'd made since accepting his call to the ministry.

"Let's go," he whispered, inhaling a deep, fortifying breath.

Neither of them spoke on the drive downtown. It seemed that everything had already been said. They were about to confront whatever needed to be confronted. Together.

Fifteen minutes later, Dave and Emily walked hand in hand into the sheriff's office. Phones rang, uniformed men and women scurried about, and there was an atmosphere that was both controlled and frenetic.

Dave introduced himself to the receptionist, who apparently recognized him.

"I'll tell Sheriff Davis you're here."

"Thank you," Emily said.

His wife's hand tightened around Dave's. "Geoff Duncan's here, too," she whispered.

They both knew why. He was there to explain that the letter Emily had asked to see wasn't in the file the way Dave had claimed it would be.

"He didn't show up for either of the counseling sessions I scheduled," Dave whispered back. The second cancellation had been a blessing in disguise. The stable for the live Nativity had to be rebuilt after the donkey had kicked the side wall and the entire structure collapsed.

Dave and several volunteers had spent a couple of hours repairing it. Later that afternoon, he'd been on the phone for a solid hour seeking a replacement donkey — one with a gentler nature. He couldn't have made the counseling session even if Geoff and his fiancée had shown up.

Allan Harris arrived, looking harried and

impatient. He frowned at Dave, then moved across the waiting area to his legal assistant. "Do you know what this is about?" he demanded.

Geoff seemed to be ignoring them and under the circumstances Dave couldn't complain.

"You were called here, too?" Emily asked.

Allan set his briefcase down and methodically removed his leather gloves, one finger at a time. "Yes. I've got appointments I've had to reschedule. And without Geoff to answer the phone, I had to close the office."

Dave was about to mention that this wasn't exactly convenient for him, either. He chose to keep the comment to himself and felt certain God would reward him.

Just as Allan seemed on the verge of saying something else, Sheriff Davis came out of his office. Roy McAfee was with him. The private detective's eyes went directly to Dave and Emily. He nodded once in recognition. Dave tried to read his look and couldn't.

"I'd like Allan, Dave, Emily and Geoff to step into my office," the sheriff said.

Chairs had been set up in advance, and they all took their places. Allan carefully laid his long tailored coat over his knees.

"This is a bit unconventional," the attorney muttered.

"Yes, I suspect it is," Sheriff Davis agreed. "However, I think my reasons will become quite clear." He glanced around the room. "Dave, would you mind if I asked you a few questions in front of the others?"

Dave turned to Roy, who gave him an almost imperceptible nod. "I don't have anything to hide."

"Good." Sheriff Davis claimed his own seat. The only one left standing was Roy McAfee.

"Dave, you were a friend of Martha Evans, am I correct?"

He answered forthrightly. "Martha was part of our church family."

"I understand," the sheriff murmured.

The attorney looked pointedly at his watch as if to say he didn't have time for this. Geoff Duncan, in the chair farthest from Dave and Emily, also seemed eager to get this over with. Dave felt the same way, but for his family's sake — and his own — he needed this settled.

"In the last days of her life you stopped by as often as two and three times a week."

"You have to realize that Martha was well into her eighties, but her mind was as sharp as the proverbial tack. Her body had started to fail but she wanted to stay in her home, which is why her family arranged for the visiting nurse."

Sheriff Davis inclined his head. "You say she gave you the gold watch."

"Yes. She'd written a letter to that effect. I saw it myself. She told me her attorney would be coming by later in the day and that she'd hand it to him."

The sheriff turned to Allan Harris. "Did you make a habit of visiting Martha Evans's home?" he asked.

Allan met the sheriff's gaze squarely. "She lived close to the courthouse and it certainly wasn't a problem. I'd known Martha for years. She was a good friend of my mother's. I was happy to do her a small favor."

"Did you ever send your legal assistant to her home instead?"

"Just once," Geoff inserted. "He asked me to drop some papers off on my way home from work one afternoon."

"Is that true?" The sheriff looked searchingly at the attorney.

Allan Harris concurred. "That's true. It was just the one time."

"Do you remember exactly when that was?"

Allan Harris reached for his briefcase. "I can tell you in a moment. It was the same day as the deposition for . . ." He let the rest fade as he checked the calendar on his Black-Berry. "I have it here. That would be September sixth."

"The sixth," Sheriff Davis repeated and wrote down the date. Then he glanced at Dave. "Do you recall when you discovered Martha's body?" he asked.

It wasn't something Dave was likely to forget. "Two days later," he said.

"The eighth." The sheriff nodded. "And she gave you the watch on which day?"

"The sixth."

"In other words, it was two days before her death. Is that correct?"

"Yes."

"And she had the letter at that time?"

"Yes."

"The same day Mr. Harris sent his assistant to Martha's home."

Geoff Duncan was on his feet. "Now, listen, if you're suggesting I had anything to do with this —"

"As a matter of fact I'm more than suggesting," Sheriff Davis said without missing a beat. "I've subpoenaed your bank statement." He opened a file and handed the sheet to Geoff Duncan. "I also have the statement of a Seattle pawnshop owner who's willing to testify that you pawned several diamond rings."

The room crackled with electrifying silence.

"Geoff Duncan?" Emily whispered, her eyes wide as she looked at Dave.

He squeezed her hand. He would never have suspected the younger man. It hadn't so much as occurred to him.

Geoff fell back into his chair and stared into the distance with a dazed expression. "I . . . I needed the money."

Dave briefly closed his eyes and recalled the conversation with Geoff a few weeks ago when he'd proudly told him about his fiancée. Lori Bellamy was from one of the most prominent families in the area, and apparently Geoff felt obliged to keep her in the style to which she was accustomed — even though he couldn't afford to do it.

"Geoff." Allan Harris said the other man's name in a hushed voice. He must've been feeling shock, incredulity and sadness, Dave thought. *"Why?"*

Geoff refused to answer. "I'm not saying another word until I speak with an attorney."

"*I'm* an attorney," Harris reminded him caustically.

"I want a criminal attorney, not one who specializes in probate." The other man's eyes sparked with indignation.

"Then by all means, find one."

Sheriff Davis opened his office door, and a deputy walked in. While handcuffing Geoff Duncan, he recited his rights.

"I know my rights," Geoff snapped. "This isn't necessary."

The deputy didn't listen and led him out of the office.

Dave sat there in stunned disbelief. "Martha gave him the letter."

"I'm sure he destroyed it," Roy McAfee said, speaking for the first time.

"How did he know where she kept her jewelry?"

Roy answered this. "As I told Dave, the freezer's not exactly an original place to hide your valuables."

"He probably took them that very day," Allan said. "Martha's hearing was bad and she wouldn't have heard him open the freezer door."

"But . . . why frame me?" Dave asked.

"You made a convenient target," Roy said. "You're the one who found her."

"When did he put the earrings in my suit coat?" Dave asked with a frown. "Oh — wait. I left my jacket at Martha's that day."

It had completely slipped his mind until now. The day had been warm and he'd taken off his coat, then returned the same afternoon — obviously after Geoff's visit — to pick it up. He'd hung it on the back of his office door, where it stayed . . . until Emily took it home.

"Geoff guessed, and rightly so, that you knew where she kept her jewelry. You had the gold watch and it was easy enough to destroy the letter and plant evidence on you."

Dave felt foolish. He hadn't even noticed that there was anything in the pockets; he'd carried it to the office and hung it up.

"How did you figure it out?" Allan Harris asked the sheriff.

Troy grinned. "Actually it was a simple matter of putting two and two together. Once I got hold of the pawnshop receipt and had Geoff's name, I was able to subpoena his bank records. There was no other way to explain those hefty deposits." He gestured at the private investigator. "Roy helped me out — he has contacts in the Seattle area who were able to steer me toward local pawnshops."

"Sheriff Davis gives me too much credit," Roy said. "We got lucky. Once we had a photo of Duncan and pictures of the missing jewelry, it was just a matter of doing a little legwork. So the sheriff sent a deputy to a few of the higher-end pawnshops — and everything fell into place."

Dave Flemming owed the sheriff and Roy

a debt of gratitude. He knew they'd say they were only doing their jobs, but they *could* have taken the evidence at face value. He would be eternally glad they hadn't.

"Are we free to go?" Emily asked.

Sheriff Davis nodded. "One question first."

"Sure."

"What do you want me to do with the gold watch?"

Dave didn't hesitate. "Return it to her family. Can we go now?"

The sheriff grinned. "You're taking up space in my office, Pastor Flemming. It seems to me you've got a Christmas program to prepare. Am I right?"

Dave looked from one man to the other. "I do. And . . . and," he stammered, "thank you. Thank you both."

"Thank you so much," Emily chimed in.

Dave and Emily left the police station and practically ran to their car. Dave unlocked the doors and once they'd scrambled inside they hugged each other fiercely. "It's over, it's over," he told Emily.

"Thank God," she said. "I'm sorry I ever doubted you. I'm sorry for everything."

"Given the same set of circumstances, I'm sure I wouldn't have behaved any differently."

"But I'm your wife!"

"Yes, you are," he said, gazing into her eyes. "My beautiful, beautiful wife." And then he kissed her.

Sheriff Troy Davis stood at his office window and watched Dave and Emily below. He smiled as he saw them hug and kiss. He was glad that, with a little help from his friend Roy McAfee, he'd been able to arrest the man responsible for the theft — and, in the process, clear Dave Flemming's name. So far his department had been able to track down all the missing jewelry except for a couple of pieces.

Troy had already contacted Martha's two daughters with the news and the recovered jewelry would be turned over to them. Although Troy believed that Martha had sincerely wanted Dave to have the watch, the pastor had insisted on returning it. He had nothing to prove to Martha's children that their mother had given it to him, and Dave wasn't comfortable with even the slightest doubt. Troy admired that.

Turning away from the window, he pinched the bridge of his nose. At least that case was satisfactorily resolved. The body discovered in the cave two days ago had yet to be identified, though. All he knew was that the skeletal remains appeared to be those of a male teenager, and that was an educated guess on the pathologist's part. An autopsy would be conducted in the new year. It was hardly a priority, as the doctor had rather acerbically pointed out. Troy suspected the boy was a runaway.

This case had the potential to stretch the limits of his department. County records didn't show anyone missing during the time period the pathologist had indicated. But *someone* must have seen him, talked to him, known him. A cold case was always difficult, but no matter how long it took, Troy was determined to find out who this young man was and what had led him to that cave.

If solving a twenty-year-old mystery wasn't enough, it also happened to be Christmas.

Christmas without Faith.

Three hours later, Sheriff Davis left the office. His day was finally over and he was going home. 92 Pacific Boulevard was a lonely place these days. Maybe he'd put up the Christmas wreath Megan had bought him and try to imagine what his evening would be like if he was spending it with Faith.

ABOUT THE AUTHOR

Debbie Macomber is the internationally acclaimed # 1 *New York Times* bestselling author of more than 125 novels. Several of Debbie's novels have achieved the number-one spot on Waldenbooks bestseller lists and earned prestigious berths on the *USA Today* bestseller list. A three-time winner of the B. Dalton Award, she is also the recipient of *Romantic Times' Magazine*'s distinguished Lifetime Achievement Award. She lives with her husband in Port Orchard, Washington. Their children are grown and she is now a proud grandmother.